Then, There Was Iron

By

Ellen Barton

http://www.Thentherewasiron.com

This book is a work of fiction. Places, events, and situations in this story are purely fictional. Any resemblance to actual persons, living or dead, is coincidental.

© 2002, 2004 by Ellen Barton. All rights reserved.

No part of this book may be reproduced, stored in a retrieval system, or transmitted by any means, electronic, mechanical, photocopying, recording, or otherwise, without written permission from the author.

ISBN: 1-4033-9118-1 (e-book)
ISBN: 1-4033-9119-X (Paperback)
ISBN: 1-4033-9120-3 (Dust Jacket)

Library of Congress Control Number: 2002095522

This book is printed on acid free paper.

Printed in the United States of America
Bloomington, IN

1stBooks - rev. 10/15/04

Then, There Was Iron

CHAPTER ONE

Dig a hole for her stomach. That's how it was told to Yuliss Crown by his mother, once she was informed that Matta, a prized slave was caught stealing bread from the kitchen. Yuliss was quite unprepared for such a reply, having saved Matta from his brothers William and James the original witnesses to the crime. Besides Matta, they also found their fathers supply of whiskey. Yuliss thinking that the whiskey was too much of an influence for whipping a female with child. Thought the matter best settled upon the return of his father. William, who was most excited about giving his first whipping, insisted they go to their mother for a solution.

What William did not know was that Mrs. Crown stopped allowing Matta her ration of food. Matta not being a field slave was fed in the house, given food rations daily, unlike the field hands who received weekly rations, given on Sunday nights. The problem with Mrs. Crown was as such. She knew the little thing in Matta's stomach was her husband's, and she wanted it dead. She figured 100 lashes to the back would help in this matter.

William and James were as happy as children on Christmas. This was the first time their father had left them in charge. The whiskey helped to provide a cruelty that would make him very proud. They proceeded to jump, laugh and dig a hole.

Matta was wailing. She feared for her life and the life of her unborn child. She had not eaten anything for three days and worried what damage this had already done to her child. Mrs. Crown's jealous rages were destined to kill her one-day. She had already given two sons to Mr. Crown who had sold them before their third year. Mrs. Crown could not stand the sight of them. Mr. Crown had promised that this one maybe she could keep. After five years of continual rape, master and slave were able to talk civil. Mrs. Crown hearing that this one may not be sold, and could be a girl, having not a daughter herself, waited for her chance. Now Matta was being forced to lie down.

The first lash felt as if a strip of skin was ripped from Matta's back. It only took 12 more lashes for Matta to arrive at the place where her grandmother held her hand. Matta was born and lived on a large cotton plantation until she was grown and sold to Mr. Crown.

Ellen Barton

She never knew her parents, both being sold when she was still crawling. But she did know her grandmother, who was probably the oldest person she had ever seen. Her name was Kate. The Massa from the cotton plantation had built her a cabin in the woods where she raised a little garden and waited for death. Kate's only joy was her granddaughter who would often come to visit. Kate had given birth to 27 babies in hell, as she liked to call America. Twenty of those babies by Satan's skinless servants, as she liked to call the white man. Matta was all she had left. Kate happily told little Matta of Africa, for she painfully remembered the life she could have had.

Kate talked of her girlhood, of falling in love, of being married, of celebrations in her village. Then she told the girl of the evils of being stolen from her country, along with her husband, six weeks after her marriage. About the big boats that brought them here; about the skinless ones forcing her to do things on the boat that made her want to die, about her husband one day seeing these things and attacking the skinless one, about the skinless one cutting off the head of her husband.

These stories scared little Matta, but so did the realization that she was a slave for life. Kate gave her the only comfort, the only love that Matta had ever known. As the blood poured from her back she tried to remember this love again. The pain was soul breaking. Between her cries she could hear Massa William counting the lashes. Did he say 39, three times? The pain was now being equally matched by a pain in her stomach. As the whip left dents in the skin, small pieces of flesh and blood flew around her. Matta used her last ounce of strength to push. She was now seeing her grandmother, who was opening her arms, telling Matta to come with her, she will keep her warm. Matta ran into the waiting arms of her grandmother. The last thing she heard was a baby cry.

Yuliss was watching this from the house. He saw his brothers beat Matta to death. He saw a baby fall into the dirt. His mother was running toward his brothers screaming "stomp on it!" He also ran to the scene. His brothers had just lost $400.00 and he was not about to explain another $100.00 to his father. He picked up the baby. Watching her escape the boots of his brothers, plus the way she entered the world he thought her to be a strong little one. He would call her Iron.

Then, There Was Iron

"I was in the field while Matta was meeting her freedom. I heard Massa Yuliss callin Pearl, Pearl and I came a runnin. What I saw, I will never forget. Most of Matta could of been cleaned up by throwing buckets of water. But I had no time to cry for my friend, for Massa Yuliss was shoving the baby in my arms telling me to take care of this. He said her name shall be Iron. I sure thought it fitting. Massa Crown returned after some time. I don't know all they told him about what happened to Matta. I do know that he wasn't home but a few days when he told me I was to be sold with Iron. Lord, chile, I done been sold 6 times in my life. It used to bring me terrors, this time, I was glad to be sold with the child of my friend. I had 4 babies sold away from my breast. This little girl was all of them to me. I wanted to keep her by my side, to protect her as long as I can. I know a slave woman can't keep no child from harm, but I wanted this chance to try. That's when we come over here to the Cumming's place. Chile, you ain't gonna like it here." Shelly sat listening to the older woman. Watching her wash bloody rags in a bucket. It was very late and they really should be sleeping, having to get up in a few hours for another long day in the field. Iron was sleeping on the floor in the corner. Shelly had just arrived on the Cumming's plantation. Brought from Maryland. All her young life (though she was older than Iron) she heard that slaves were worked to death on large plantations. She thought she was too young to die. She asked Pearl.

"How long you been here?"

"Bout 15 years. I try to keep up on Iron's age so many of us slaves don't know how old we are. I think Ise about 38 years old. Iron be 16 soon. That's about the time you start your woman business. She done good, her first day was today and she put about 18 hours in the field. The ovaseer only lashed her 3 times today. That's good. I've seen woman who had their business comin for years. They slow down so in the field the ovaseer be lashing them all day. I jes fraid that now her business has come, Massa be breedin her soon. You have babies?"

"I had two boys, they were sold right away. I don't know where they are. They looked so much like my Massa in Maryland that I don't care to know where they are."

Pearl looked at the new girl. She had never heard such talk. The mothers she knew mourned the loss of children not dead. Even if they were the children of the white man. Shelly must have had it extra hard. Pearl sure hoped Iron didn't go that way. Pearl hung up the rags and threw the water out the cabin door. They should be dry by morning for Iron's use. She then settled in the corner for sleep. Shelly did the same.

Seemed like only minutes before Pearl heard the first bell. The first bell tells you to get up and get your breakfast. The second bell tells you to be in the field. She got up first and wrapped up 6 of the 12 griddlecakes she made last night before doing Iron's washing. They were to be taken to the field for lunch. She woke Iron and Shelly. The three of them ate their breakfast in silence.

Pearl was wondering what they would do for supper, having to share their rations with Shelly would not last them the rest of the week. Shelly having come four days before Sunday wasn't given any weekly rations. Pearl was told that she will be sharing their cabin, and given no extra supplies. This was the time she felt that Iron needed more food, not less. If she felt she must, then she would go without food. It wouldn't be the first time.

Shelly was wondering what this new plantation would hold for her. Pearl had said that she would not like it here. Anything would be better than her old Massa's nightly visits, and daily whippings. Her last few whippings she hardly felt till the whipping was done, the skin on her back being so hard and dead. She did remember to cry and pray to God so that Massa thought he was doing a good job.

Iron was wondering about this woman's business. She didn't like it. She wasn't used to seeing blood without the sound of the lash. She also didn't like the stomach pains that went with it. Why did everything have to hurt? The next bell rang and the ladies hurried to the field with the others. Pearl was surprised to see Massa John himself ringing the bell.

"Come on you lazy niggers, get to work."

John Cummings had a large plantation with about 100 slaves. The plantation was given to him by his father, and so was about ¼ of the slaves. His father was a drunkard who drank himself to death. When John was about 18 years old his father informed him that he was dividing his property up equally between John, his brother Martin and his sister Clara. This was done for Thomas Cummings was deeply in debt. Being the dishonorable man he was, he gave his properties to his children before his creditors got to him. Thomas Cummings had a very large plantation with almost 300 slaves. He was the only child of William and Ruth Cummings, and was left a vast fortune. Thomas

Then, There Was Iron

was not the man his father was. William was a very smart businessman. He was one of the largest suppliers of cotton in South Carolina, plus he was good to his slaves. Meaning he fed them enough food, gave them just enough clothes, and only whipped them for what he felt to be legitimate reasons. His slaves were happy. Meaning they weren't hungry, and families were not sold apart. Thomas, not wanting to live in the shadow of his well-respected father grew tobacco instead of cotton and slowly destroyed the land, planting it year after year in the same fields. He also sold off families that William Cummings kept together for decades. When Thomas eventually divided his remaining slaves amongst his children, the slaves were grateful.

Clara received the smallest amount of property, and only 5 slaves. Unlike other women, she was not the sit around and wait to get married type. She built a modest home, bought some livestock, and planted a garden, enough to feed her and the slaves. She refused to hire an ovaseer, for her slaves were not forced to do back breaking field labor, and her slaves were never whipped. Clara spent her days sewing and gossiping with her two female slaves, making fancy dresses she sold at high prices, while her three male slaves tended to the livestock and the gardening. She looked at her two housemaids as her dearest friends. There was one especially, Adele, whom she couldn't imagine life without.

John and Martin received 50 slaves each, plus enough property to farm. Martin had just been married. John had begun courting his second cousin Mary. Martin, like his grandfather planted cotton. John continued with tobacco. The soil continued to die. His crops being worse every year made John a more miserable man. Refusing to admit defeat, he would not take his brother's advice and change his crop to cotton. He found himself relying more and on the breeding and selling of slaves. This was done to Mary's increasing discontent. Not long into the courtship, John and Mary had married. The young slaves her husband was selling had a very strong resemblance to him. She preferred crops to chattel. She found the nigger to be a very lazy animal. Lately the only time she found happiness was when one was tied up screaming while a pool of blood was flowing at it's feet and a whip was in her hand. Her whippings had become so horrific, the slaves would beg for a man to do it, and the overseer couldn't stand to watch, and he was a very proud "nigger breaker."

Ellen Barton

"Morning Pearl."

"Mornin' Massa."

Pearl knew there would be trouble now. Massa never said good morning to a slave. Pearl quickly said a prayer to God that she and Iron would not be separated. She watched the child grow for nearly 16 years giving her all the love that she had for her own babies. Pearl was sure she would just die if she lost Iron, but since Massa was acting so friendly, she asked about food.

"Massa, I was wonderin about Shelly's rations?"

"I'll be moving her into her own cabin tonight."

With that he rode his horse off into the field. Pearl now knew why Massa had spoken to her. He thought Shelly was listening. Pearl found of the Massa's, that couldn't get enough of the slave women, there were two types. The one that beat you and cursed you while doing the act, and the one that sometimes gave you a dime or a pretty ribbon, or a little extra food. Both of these beasts were able to sell a child away from its momma, beat a man to death and torture for their own amusement. But one did not want to show the monster he was, at least not right away.

Massa was planning to breed with Shelly. He already had 3 women with their own private cabins. The only slaves that lived alone were the ones he himself was breeding. Poor Shelly, thought Pearl. She ain't gonna want another white man's child. She quickly hurried to catch up to Iron.

"Massa said he be movin Shelly to her own cabin tonight."

Iron didn't know what to feel for the women, for they did not have to toil from sun up, to sun down in the field. They were also very rarely whipped. All they seemed to do was breed high yella babies, which Massa sold as quickly as he could. These girls were also kept far away from Miss Mary.

CHAPTER 2

The day in the field went fast. Shortly after the lunch break it started to rain very hard, so Massa called all the slaves from the field. It was the hoeing period, so the work to be done wasn't particularly immediate. Pearl could count on one hand the number of times they did not have to work in the rain. She truly thanked God for this one.

The slaves came back from the field singing even louder then they did on their way in, each thinking about what they would do with their little bit of time. The only time the slaves did not work was on Sunday's and the wee hours from about 9 or 10 at night, until 4 in the morning. This time was often used for food preparation, sleep, and household chores. Pearl had decided on sleep. Iron thought she would go out hunting with the men, maybe catch some possums or rabbits. The men had twice allowed Iron to accompany them. One time she caught herself three rabbits. They had good eating that day. As it looked, their rations were getting pretty low, and they may not make it till Sunday.

Shelly was thinking to have her wool combed out and plaited. She hadn't had a good combing out since an old woman did it for her in the slave pen. In the field today she met a woman named Patsy, who on Sunday's plaited the wool for most of the women on the plantation, for a few extra rations. All plans changed upon entering their cabin and seeing Massa standing in the middle of their one tiny room.

"Iron, collect your belongings, I'm moving you."

"Massa, you said that it be Shelly moving."

"Pearl, you know I don't take back talk from niggers, Iron's getting to be a big girl now and can use her own space. Shelly will stay here with you."

Iron quickly gathered her blanket, wooden bowl, cup and a few pieces of tattered clothing. She didn't say a word, just hugged Pearl and walked out the door with Massa. Pearl prayed that Massa would go easy on her. She thought that she should have known Massa would not breed a girl as dark as Shelly, all his breeding slaves were yella, like Iron. At least she wasn't being sold.

Iron walked silently behind Massa, the cabins were quite far away from slave row. The women up here hardly ever socialized with the other slaves. Iron wonders why.

They finally reached a cabin, quite off on it's own. From here Iron could not see slave row, the big house, or the three other cabins, but she could see one of the fields. Her new cabin had two rooms, one in the back for sleeping with a mattress. Iron had always slept on the ground. She was excited to try the new mattress, but she did not show her feelings to Massa. The front room had a fireplace, a table, and two chairs. There was also a bucket of water, a pan, and two big pots, one with a lid, one without, and curtains on the front and back windows. It was a luxury compared to the one room cabin she shared all her life with Pearl.

"Iron, settle in, I'll be back later tonight to check on you."

He did not wait for a reply, and he walked out the door.

Iron began putting her things away. She put her bowl and cup on the shelves in the kitchen. She was happy to see that the shelves already contained 2 bowls and 2 cups. She put her clothes in the backroom, noticing a small wooden little dresser holding a new skirt and blouse, both white. She tried them on and found that they fit her perfectly. Iron was happy. She danced around in her new clothes, singing a song she just created about not working in the fields, and being a woman now. She then rolled around on the mattress laughing. This seemed to be the happiest she had ever been.

Hearing someone enter the cabin, Iron quickly jumped up. It was Cynthia, one of the housemaids.

"Massa said for me to bring you this food."

"Thank ya."

"So, you be the new breeding wench."

"I used to work in the field."

"I seen ya. I don't know how you niggers do it. Working sun up to sun down I sure is glad to be a house nigger. The only thing worse than being a field nigger is a breeding wench."

When she left. Iron wondered why she had to say that. Those house niggers sure get uppity sometimes. She ate the chicken and cornbread Cynthia brought. Feeling tired, she lay down on her new mattress and fell asleep. Iron slept the rest of the day and most of the night. She would have slept the whole night if not for the loud noises she heard outside. It sounded like someone singing really badly. She

Then, There Was Iron

peeked out the window. It was Massa, and he was stumbling around. He was heading for her cabin. It also looked like he had been in his whiskey again. Oh Lord, thought Iron, please don't let him come in here. Then she heard the door open.

"Iron, Iron you black bitch, get out here!"

"Yes Massa, Ise comin."

"Hurry."

Iron quickly jumps out of bed and goes to the front room.

"Take off your clothes."

Iron did not know what she had done to deserve a whipping, but she was not going to cry. She had seen many whippings in her young life and it seemed that all the crying and begging of the slaves, did not make the whippings any easier. She began to undress. She didn't see a whip in his hands when he came in, she sure hoped he wouldn't use a log from the fireplace. She had seen slaves beaten with logs and handsaws. They never did walk the same. Iron removed her blouse exposing her bare back and bent over the table. John started pounding on the back of Iron with his fists.

"I said, take off your clothes, if your stupid, I'll do it for you!"

He began ripping off Iron's skirt. The bloody rag fell to the floor.

"I knew you be ready for breeding, but I ain't gonna take you tonight, not that way." He entered her. Iron thought she would die, the pain was extraordinary. This was not the way she had heard the other young slaves talk about. This was by the back and she didn't know anything could go in there. She didn't think anything should go in there. But she did not scream. He then bit her neck until blood ran out. But she did not scream. In her head she repeated the same small prayer over and over. Dear God, please let him hurry. She thanked God that he was listening. 15 minutes later Massa was walking out the door and she was passed out on the floor.

She did not know how long she had been lying there, but when she woke up, it was still nighttime. There was blood everywhere. She crawled to her mattress and went back to sleep. Iron awoke the next morning to the crowing of the roosters. She had overslept the bell for the field hands. She never did that before. Her linens were covered in blood. She had to get up, but the soreness was holding her down. She looked at the trail that led to where she lay and forced herself up. She got her bucket of water and washed all the blood off her body, plus the strange white sticky stuff. She washed the floor, dressed herself and took the linens off the bed. The soreness was beginning to subside, to her relief. She now began to understand Cynthia, for if this was the role of a breeding wench, than she would sure miss the field. She preferred the whip of her Massa to his touch and smell. She thought about running away, and then she thought about Pearl. She could not leave her. She went outside to wash her linens. Iron began walking to the creek, the one where the slaves washed their clothes on Sunday afternoons. There would be no one there at this time, for everyone was working. She began beating her linens against the rocks. Before she was finished, a beautiful mulatto girl arrived.

"What be your name?"

"Iron."

"Where you get a name like that? What are you, hard to bend?"

Iron smiled. She liked the woman who seemed to carry her head higher than any slave Iron had met before.

"What be your name?"

"Ise is Peaches. Looks like Massa visit you last night, by the looks of your linens. It be the first time you with a man? Is that so?"

"Yes'm."

"Girl, you sure is a lucky wench. I seen young girls forced to go with bucks more than 6 feet high. The white man is easier than them breeding bucks. The bucks take you all night long and they twice as long as a white man. Of course a buck won't beat you. But Ise always say is bes to start with a white man. Cuz if your first time was with a buck, ya wouldn't be up and moving around today."

"Ise sho don't feel very lucky."

"That's cuz you still a young girl, soon you know what I mean."

"Ya think Massa is gonna bring one of those breeding bucks to me?"

"Nah, Massa likes to breed us mulattos his self. I done have 4 babies for Massa. They bout as white as he is. They all been sold away. My babies being so white Ise think Massa would let them free. But he didn't. I feels they be free one day. I had 3 babies for one of dem bucks before I was sold here. Those babies probably never be free. I say a prayer for all my babies, wherever they are. It's the same prayer for the black babies and the white ones. Sometimes I dream that my white babies will own my black babies and not even know they have the same Mammy. But you shouldn't think too much on

Then, There Was Iron

your babies that sold away, it can make you go off in the head. I've seen it happen."

"What you mean bucks are twice as long as a white man?"

"You didn't see Massa naked?"

"No."

"One day you'll know what I mean."

Peaches laughed and walked off, leaving Iron to finish her linens.

Iron did not know what to do with the day. Not toiling in the field from sun up to sun down was something she was not used to. On her Sundays off she would usually rest or do the washing, or get her wool plaited by Patsy. Sometimes she would just sit on the porch of the slave row cabins and listen to the other slaves sing. But it not being Sunday, all the other slaves were working.

She decided to dig up earth next to her new little cabin, hoping to put a garden there. She never had a garden before. None of the field hands did, though a few of the house servants had one. She would share her extra food with Pearl. She thought to go to the big house for the supplies needed to start a garden. Miss Mary would surely give her a whipping for walking around doing nothing when she should be working somewhere. She didn't want to tell Miss Mary that Massa John took her out of the field to breed. She knew the slave wenches were not allowed to talk to the fathers of their babies, if he was a white man. She wondered if she was already with a baby inside her. She didn't want her child to be a slave, to work all it's life to be treated worse than a dog, then die. If her baby was white maybe one day it be free. But she knew the white man was evil and they all would surely go to hell. She didn't want her child to go to hell. She thought a black baby to be better even if it was sold away. Maybe it would get one of them good Massa's that she heard of but never met. She would wait and see. She decided every night she would make a prayer hoping not to have a white baby. Maybe tonight she would walk to slave row and talk to Pearl about it. She would go just before sundown and prepare Pearl's supper so that the woman did not have to spend time cooking after a long day in the field. If she could stand the pain Massa gave her last night, being a breeding wench might make Pearl's life a little easier. Iron thought that was worth all the pain she could take.

Iron arrived at her old cabin just before sundown. She had prepared fried herrings, corn bread, taters baked in ashes, and apple pie. She couldn't wait to share this feast with Pearl and Shelly. The only time she ate pie was on Christmas. Iron was shocked when a young slave boy arrived at her cabin leaving a huge bundle. Upon opening the bundle Iron found: herrings, taters, corn, flour, salt, pepper, turnips, cabbages and a whole apple pie. She could not believe the amount of food she was given. She had seen families of field hands sharing this amount of food for a month. She thought breeding wenches are sure fed well. She cooked the meal and ripped off a piece from the bottom of her skirt, wrapped it around her neck, and was off.

Pearl and Shelly weren't back from the fields as yet. Iron laid out the food so that they would see it as soon as they entered the cabin. Pearl entered first.

"Lord have mercy, Christmas done come already! Iron girl, where you get all this?"

"I get more rations now."

"Girl you don't know how long those rations spost to last, I don't never see those mulattos getting their rations with us on Sunday. You don't know when you be getting some mo."

"It's okay Mama Pearl, I be making my own garden soon and Ise going fishin tomorrow."

Shelly was already eating.

"Well it sure does this tired slave woman good to come home and have her supper waiting for her. Let's say a thank you to the Lord before we start. Shelly, you eating this feast with no thank you first to the Lord?"

"Pearl, I'm whispering a thanks with every swallow."

The three women laughed than Pearl gave a blessing and they all ate. Iron did not ask Pearl about the babies. She wasn't ready with Shelly there. They ate their meal and Shelly sang some songs she had learned on her old plantation. Iron thought Shelly had a beautiful voice. The songs were about freedom. Shelly's voice almost convinced Iron that one day they would be out of bondage. Other slaves also appeared at Pearl's cabin.

This was often done, slaves following music, patting their feet on time, often adding an "amen", or "tell it girl."

Iron was enjoying herself so much that she did not want to leave. Pearl reminded all the hands how early the bell rung in the morning. She told Iron to keep on praying everyday for freedom. The Lord will

Then, There Was Iron

hear their prayers. Iron agreed and went running back to her cabin. When she reached home she washed up a little than went to bed. She sure hoped Massa would not be visiting tonight.

"Iron, Iron."

Iron awoke to Peaches standing over the bed and tapping her on the cheek. She didn't like the cheek tapping, but Peaches was a nice sight in the morning.

"Yes'm, I'm awake."

"Now that you out of the field you coming to be one of those lazy niggers that sleep all day. Girl, you know there always be work to do. Now get up, I brought you some breakfast."

Iron got up, washed her face and began eating her breakfast.

"I brought you some things for your garden. Ise will help you with it."

"Thank ya Peaches. I planned to go fishin today."

"Girl, you don't need to worry about no fishin. Massa gonna bring you all the fish, beef and chickens you can eat. But he likes to see you workin your own garden, keep busy. Massa feed his wenches a lot better than other Massas. He put us out here and we don't work nearly as hard as those other niggers."

"Seem like you very dearing to Massa."

"I don't like no white person. I just know what he can do to us, and what he don't. A lot of those white men will take a woman in her cabin in front of her children. I done seen my mother took that way many of times. I seen my Massa on my mother so often, she couldn't look at me. She was glad when they sold me off, cuz she knew that soon he would be taking me in front of her. I thinks that be too much for her heart to take. Girl, you should be happy Massa don't cause you no barresment. Ain't nothing worse than seeing someone you love suffering. Girl you don't know yet the life of a slave woman. It's the hardest life there is. Ask anyone of us."

"I don't never see the other two women."

"They be Doll and Lizzie. See, Doll don't leave her cabin much. She got a pain in her, only a good tree could bring out. That girl could carve up a storm. Doll arrived here from Floridy. She was sold off with her husband and baby girl. Her husband was sold off to some big cotton plantation. When Doll step on the block she's hoping the cotton planter buy her too. But some nigger trader, who just deals in the breeding wenches, bought her and her baby girl. This time Massa have a mean ovaseer, him had the heart of the devil. Any such, Massa done send him out for some new niggers. He bought some wenches with their babies and some bucks. See when it's time to get on the ferry, too many babies crying. That devil man couldn't take the noise. He grabbed Doll's baby girl out of her arms and threw her against the ferry. Doll had seen the little girl hit the side of the boat and fall into the water. Ise reckon she ain't never been the same. Massa done breed 13 babies with her. He sole them all. He did buy her a fine knife, come all the way from Spain. With that she be carving all the wood she can find. I never seen no slave with a knife like that, and work it the way she work it, but she sure don't talk much."

"How long she been here?"

"Bout 15 summers."

"What about Lizzie?"

"Lizzie in love with some field hand on the next plantation. His name be Marcus. He sure is a kind-hearted man. Lizzie be spending all her time praying her babies will look like Massa. Let's get on that garden."

Then, There Was Iron

CHAPTER 3

Months had passed and Iron was now big with child. Massa had been visiting her about 2 times a week, each visit left Iron further and further away from the experience. She would close her eyes tight as she possibly could, and pretend that she was free. It now seemed that it wasn't her at all Massa was holding down, once he stopped beating her she even barely felt him. He began talking kind to her as if this was something she should enjoy. She did not like talking to him. She hoped that he would just do what he came for and leave. John Cummings thought he was a good man. Doing her a favor keeping her away from the hard work of the field and giving her extra food. Iron only wanted to dig his eyes out. The extra food she was receiving, she took to the field hands. Massa John did not think the field hands needed much food to live.

Before her belly became big, Iron spent most of her time hunting with Reuben the fiddler. He was another one of the slaves Massa felt he treated especially well. Reuben also did not have to work all day. He was left to do as he pleased. Only making money for Massa at what he called, "those damn white people balls." Reuben was the only slave that came to the cabins of the mulatto girls, making them laugh with his imitations of the dancing of the whites. Sometimes they would go to slave row and hold the "almighty white dance contest," where the worst dancer would win a prize. The prizes were usually something from the garden of Peaches or Iron. The field hands loved these nights, and often forgot what they were.

Now that Christmas season was coming upon them, Reuben was spending more time off the plantation, and Iron was missing him. Peaches told her that slaves shouldn't get into missing each other, because they could be sold at any time. She also made sure to ask if the baby is Massa's. If the baby looked like Reuben, she would surely be sold off. Iron informed her that she had never lain with Reuben; they only enjoyed each other's company. She didn't think Peaches believed her but that was all right. She knew Peaches cared for her.

It was Peaches that told her how to talk to Massa to get an extra blanket for Pearl when the cold weather started coming. It was Peaches that told her that she couldn't get a baby from the back, or right after you finish your woman business, and if she wanted another

Ellen Barton

man besides Massa, that is how she should do it. Iron thought one man sweating on her was more than enough. She listened to the advice of Peaches, though she did not think she would need it.

Peaches talked as if she liked what the men did to the women. Iron didn't think that she ever would like it, even if a black man did it. She couldn't understand the excitement the other women had when talking about men. She really didn't like the way she felt Peaches changed whenever she was around Benjamin, the driver for Miss Mary. Peaches admitted that she wanted to lay with him. This was the first time that Iron realized that women enjoyed what men did to them.

Peaches had said that she hated it with Massa, but would never let him know this or she might be sold, or made a field hand. She again said they were very lucky to be chosen by Massa to breed with. They were the best cared for slaves in all of South Carolina, all the other slaves knew this. Peaches told Iron to thank God Massa were breeding her. This Iron was still not able to do. Neither did she think she would ever be happy to lay with a man.

The only time she felt anything close to the "tingling," as Shelly called it, was the night Peaches came panting to her cabin. Peaches thought there was spirits on the roof of her own cabin and ran to Iron to spend the night with her.

Iron had a hard time sleeping that night. She lay there watching Peaches, trying not to touch her. She didn't know who to talk to about this, so she tried her best to forget it. She hoped as she got older her feelings would change, and she, like the others will get excited at the sight of a field hand paying her some notice. She wondered how long this would take. Maybe as soon as her baby is born. Maybe that's when it happened for everybody. She sure hoped so.

Christmas time came and went. Massa John gave the field hands one whole week from work. The field hands praised Massa John for being so generous. Massa John also gave each slave a present and plenty of corn whiskey for anyone over the age of 13. There were big celebrations on every plantation and the slaves visited each other freely. Some slaves on other plantations only had 3 days off. Again Iron was told that Massa John was a good man. Iron did not understand why the slaves thought so much of Massa John. When they were drunk with his whiskey, they seemed to forget that he starved them the rest of the year. That he allowed the young ones to run around in the snow with no shoes, or how he whipped them daily.

Iron found it hard to believe that Massa John was one of the good Massa's she had heard talk of when she was a young girl. She feared to meet a bad one. She asked Reuben how could Massa John be a good man, when he was now making plans to sell his own child? Reuben told her that no matter how good or bad a Massa is, black folks were all looked upon as animals.

"Reuben, if we be animals, how come we can talk?"

"Girl, we ain't animals, the white man just think we are."

"If they think we are animals, why does Massa visit me so often? Why don't he visit a horse, or a hog?"

"I don know what the white man be thinking all the time. Ise just play my fiddle and be a good nigger for Massa, cuz I sho don wan be sole."

"Pearl done tole me that the white man stole us all from Africa, and that he stole all this land from the Injuns. Yet, they whip us when one of us tries to steal enough food to live by. Those niggers on the Singleton plantation, where Marcus lives, that be Lizzie's man, they be starving all the time. Massa Singleton gives em a little bacon, and corn bread to last a week. It don't last but three days. Now if one of those niggers steal a chicken, Massa Singleton beat them nearly to death. How come no one whip the white man for stealing us?"

"Maybe the Lord will whip them come Judgment Day. Benjamin tell me that on one of his trips with Miss Mary, he hear talk about bolitionists. They be white people trying to free the slaves. So they won't all be whipped. Girl, there is some good white people."

"Good white people? I sure like to see them."

"They are out there."

"Well, how do you tell the good ones, from the bad ones?"

"Ise don't know."

On New Year's Day, Iron was again in Reuben's cabin. Most of the slaves were getting ready to go to dances on other plantations. Iron was not going for her belly was too big. Reuben had invited her to come over for rice and beans. He seemed to think if they ate rice and beans on New Year's Day, they would have a good year. Iron loved the company of Reuben but thought any year when she couldn't own her own body, couldn't be a good one. But she kept on eating and listening to his crazy talk of good white people. Everybody kept telling her how nice she had it. She thought maybe niggers were stupid if they thought that her life was good. Freedom, now that is a good life. They were happy with one more day off.

Massa John had all the slaves working in the morning. He said to start the year off right, but after lunch they could do what they please. Come tomorrow, things would go back to normal. Reuben would be playing at a dance tonight, but he wanted to spend some time with Iron before he left. He had come to look at her as the little sister who was sold away from him when he was a very young man. He felt sorry for Iron. She had too many questions for a slave girl. And worse, still she felt as if she deserved the answers to these questions. He sure hoped she was never sold to a really cruel master.

"How come you looking at me, like that?"

"Ise thinking on how some people are takin from ya, and how some are given to ya."

Reuben was about to tell Iron things he had told no one else, but he noticed that she was doubling over in a strange fashion.

"Iron, you alright?"

"Ise just got the strong stomach pain, it's gone now."

"Maybe you should lay down a spell."

"I be alright, aaahhh, it's coming back. Maybe you should call Mama Pearl."

Reuben runs out of the cabin to get Mama Pearl. He also got the old woman who birthed most of the slaves. That's when they were not unfortunate enough to have them in the fields. Pearl and Chaney rushed into Reuben's cabin, not allowing him to enter. Reuben waited at the door impatiently along with some other slaves that gathered around and listened to the screaming inside. He heard Iron's repeated calls to God, and thought of the many calls given cause of whippings or separations.

Reuben prayed for Iron and her child, than he prayed for his children. He didn't know where they were, or even how many he had, but he prayed. Then he prayed for all children and the mothers of all children. Then he prayed for all the bucks. Then he prayed for freedom. The freedom to know and teach your children. The freedom to keep your children. Before he began to pray for the abolitionists in the North, Pearl came out and said it's a boy, and Iron was doing fine, but resting.

Then, There Was Iron

Iron stayed in Reuben's cabin for three days. Her son was taken to Nell the slave that nursed the babies. Iron could have kept her son with her until time of sale, but she refused to look at the child, refused to hold, nurse, or name the child. She heard that Massa had called him David. Pearl kept saying, "Just turn your head girl, and look at your son". Iron knew that if she looked at him, she would want him. She was a breeding wench and she would surely have many more kids whose faces she'd have to remember, as she wondered where they were. She had seen women that had given birth to over 20 babies, and had none left with them. All these women ever talked about were the little faces of children they would know nothing of for the rest of their lives. Iron would not be haunted by any little face.

She could not explain this to the other mothers, they did not understand. They thought to have your children near and give them love, even for one day, was the greatest joy. Women who were separated from their children were now becoming angry at Iron, thinking she was wrong in the head. Iron knew that the slaves thought their actions and their words would persuade her to spend time with her child, or the next one, or the next one. In 7 years, Iron had given birth to 4 children, David, Janus, William and Henry. She had neither seen, nor held one. Iron was getting quite a bad reputation. There would be whisperings when she went to other plantations for hog killings, or corn shucking. Iron really did not care, for she was not haunted by little faces.

CHAPTER 4

Iron was now 23 and Massa's visits were now up to 4 times a week. She wondered when he had time to see his other 3 mulattos' or Miss Mary. She figured Massa John must of bred 100 babies. Miss Mary never had a child, and often claimed that it was a sin for her and her husband to go childless. No slave dared to inform her that Massa John was not childless at all. That with his mulatto wenches, he was producing babies just as white as she was.

Every slave in his heart believed Miss Mary knew of these happenings, and that contributed to her meanness, plus her taste for brandy all the day long. Miss Mary did have a fondness for the darker babes, treating them like kittens and claiming they were much more adorable than any of her own nieces or nephews, who often spent summers on the Cummings plantation. Her attraction to little slave babies never interfered in whipping their parents. It appeared that playing with a slave baby, and whipping a slave adult, almost brought her the same satisfaction.

Iron had once witnessed Miss Mary tie a young slave woman around a tree, having her hug it with both arms and legs. The girl about 17 had gone off to see a young man on another plantation without a pass. Miss Mary inflicted 200 lashes over the girls back, all the while screaming, "you damn savage, you will learn the rules!" The girl vomited and had a passing of the bowels. The latter extremely delighted Miss Mary. She laughed so hard that she had to stop whipping. She went back to the big house leaving the young girl tied to the tree.

Iron immediately ran to the cabin of Peaches, for she knew that if Massa John was not at home, she would find Benjamin there. The three of them took the girl down and carried her to the cabin of Chaney. She was wrapped in a sheet covered in lard, and laid down on her stomach. Two days later the girl was dead.

For nights Iron had dreamed of the beating. The glow in Miss Mary's eyes as she screamed, "savage!" at the poor girl. Iron figured that the slave was not savage at all, but the true savage was the one holding the whip. She now recognized the difference in the treatment she received, and that of other slaves.

Then, There Was Iron

Iron, or the three other mulattos never required a pass when visiting other plantations. They were known by all the patrollers as "Cumming's mulattas." She was never whipped and received the amount of rations equal to that of a family of field hands. Suggestions she made to Massa often came to pass. She had got Mama Pearl out of the field, and now performing a maid's duties in the big house. Massa John also demanded Miss Mary never whip Pearl, claiming she was a rabbit's foot, bringing him luck in business. Most house slaves had it easier than the field hands. On the Cumming's plantation this was not always so, for the house slaves were watched all day by Miss Mary, where the field hands could go days without seeing her. Pearl was happy to report that in the three years since coming out of the field, she had never felt the sting of the lash.

Iron could also convince Massa John to fire an overseer when the field hands complained to her, if one was particularly cruel. She found that if she talked softly directly after he rolled off her, she could get him to do almost anything, short of giving slaves their freedom. Iron learned this upon visiting the slaves of Miss Clara's farm. The sister of Massa John. All of Clara's slaves were fed such as she was. They were also never whipped. These slaves worked harder for Miss Clara than any other slaves that Iron knew. She did not understand why Massa's treated slaves so cruelly, starving and beating them. If a slave was fed properly, and dealt with not by the lash, he would more than likely work harder for his Massa. But they insisted on working their valuable property to death.

Iron thought maybe the white man wasn't as smart as he thought he was. Kindness seemed the most effective way of getting what you wanted. So she showed Massa John nothing but praise and sympathy. He granted her small favors, gave her money, fine garments, and increased his nightly visits. For this, all she had to do was give him children to sell, and give up the ability to love. She didn't know why slaves bothered to love anyway. It only caused more misery in their lives.

The fine dresses given to Iron by Massa often went to the female field hands. Iron found herself more comfortable in the garb of the males. She also found it more convenient for hunting and fishing. On the days when Massa was not visiting Iron could be found in a shirt and long pants. Unlike the other slave women, Iron was not interested in appearing her best at the few social gatherings the slaves attended.

She received more joy from giving a fine dress to a slave girl who was used to nothing but tattered rags. She also enjoyed admiring the strut of a woman who received her first beautiful garment ever.

The women of the Cummings plantation were probably the best-dressed slaves in South Carolina. This could be proven any Sunday when slaves from most neighboring plantations gathered in the woods for worship. Though all the clothes were supplied by Iron, she would be amongst the worst dressed. Although her beauty would never go unnoticed; Iron had grown to be very striking indeed. She was close to 5 feet and a half, with very dark brown eyes and a slender nose. Her color was very close to that of the white race except for the slightest hint of beige. It would have been very easy for Iron to pass for a white woman (though one as beautiful as her in all of South Carolina could not be found), except for the very thick head full of dark wool that she carried.

Iron was very proud of her wool. She felt without it, she would be close to having the look of a white woman. She often wished that she were blacker. When mentioning this once to Shelly, she was informed that Massa would not have treated her the way he did, if not for her complexion. She would be all day working in the field like Shelly was, and she should thank the good Lord, God made her as he did. Iron thanked the Lord for her health and for having Pearl in her life, but she couldn't thank him for giving her the blood of a race that held another in bondage. Iron was scared that went Judgment Day came, God would only look at her color, and not let her into heaven. She had asked Reuben about this.

"Girl, if God only looked at your color, he be just like the white man. Ise feels the Lord will take the good ones to heaven. He ain't gonna care what they look like."

"So ya thinks there be white people in heaven?"

"Yes."

"Will they be whipping everybody, and taking our children?"

"No. Just the good ones will make it."

"Won't be too many of em there."

"Iron, you can't hate the white man, cuz his blood runs in your body. You got to forgive him for what he does. That's what the bible says. Forgive your enemies. I know it's hard, I've seen the white man in his most evil form. I've seen white preachers praise the word of God and go home and beat a slave woman to death. Iron, you must

Then, There Was Iron

pray for them. Pray that they can understand God's word. They call us stupid, but they're the ones that don't understand. Pray they don't destroy themselves."

"I can pray they don't destroy us, but I can't pray for them."

"What about your children? They whiter than Miss Mary. You can't pray for your own children?"

This Iron could not answer. She thought that maybe the good white people Reuben keeps talking about were the ones with slave mammies and grand mammies that they didn't know of. It must be the blood of a slave inside that made them good, for she could not accept any white person of decency. They must have slave blood in them from far back. This also helped her to explain why some slaves told their white Massa's everything, such as plots to run away, or if something was stolen. These slaves she felt must have white blood in them, stronger than black.

"Reuben, the white preacher done tell us that the bible say the black man was made to serve the white. Well, with all his blood, lots of these slaves ain't barely black at all. Does the bible also say that you must sell your own children, or whip and starve them?"

"Girl, we all family and color has nothing to do with it. That's why you got to pray for the white man. Slavery is doing worse to him than it is to the black man."

"Reuben, now I know your off in the head. White's ain't the ones be dying and starving."

"They be dying inside and they don't even know it. White's are destroying their selves. They are bringing Satan's spirit from hell to walk amongst us. Blacks, we be saving our selves and making ourselves stronger. We be bringing God's spirit to walk amongst us."

"Reuben, Ise sure wish I done the travellin' you have, so I can understand your way of thinking."

"Please Iron, just pray for the white man."

"Youse pray for the white man, I be praying for freedom."

"Girl, a prayer for freedom, is a prayer for the white man."

"Reuben, Ise got to go."

Iron gets up to leave. She wasn't in the mood to hear Reuben's preaching today. She had heard it before from a Negro preacher who was traveling the South with his master. The preacher was claiming that everyone was a child of God. The only reason that people looked different was because they were born in the different parts of the world. We are only separated by weather and diet. Iron had never heard such talk. The preacher told her that he had learned these things from the white man he was now calling master. The man whose name was Wendall Smalls, lived in New York. He had traveled all over the world and had seen many colors of people. He felt slavery to be an evil abomination.

Meeting the preacher in New York whose name was Lewis, and was born a free man. They had together decided to journey to the South and spread the word. Iron couldn't believe that a free black man would trust a white man to bring him to the South. Lewis had told her that Mr. Smalls was one of the kindest men who had ever lived and he would trust him with his life. Lewis preached to the slaves, and Mr. Smalls preached to the slaveholders.

The more religious Negroes welcomed the words of Lewis, about all men being equal. He also talked about loving your enemies and that there were many races in the world. None of them being closer to God than the other. Iron did not like what she heard. Neither did the slaveholders, for after three days of Mr. Smalls and the preacher spreading the word, both were hanging from a tree.

Iron remembered seeing them swing in the wind. They were never taken down, but left to fall to pieces. She had often wondered about their families, if they knew what had happened to the two men. It was the first time Iron had saw a white man swinging from a tree. He fell apart, exactly as the black man.

CHAPTER 5

She sat staring at the strange markings with bewilderment. Iron had convinced Massa to get her a bible. John Cummings was not a religious man and whipped any one of his hands that were caught trying to read or write. Iron's plea that if she could share the words of the bible with the field hands, it would make them better and probably discourage the amount of stealing. She said that she would just hold the bible and tell them that their Massa always knew what was best for them. She had also asked for one with drawings, hoping also to make herself a better slave. She had hopes of living on the greatest plantation.

That night while rubbing the back of her Massa, Iron stated how hard it must be for a good man like Massa to put up with those ignorant field hands, who were stealing at an astonishing rate. The slaves needed minding that Massa was their only true master and they should never disobey his rules. John Cummings was happy that someone understood what he was going through, even if that someone was only three fifths of a person. Having said that she wanted a bible with drawings convinced him that she didn't want to learn to read. But in case it didn't, Iron asked him if it was true that they take smart slaves to the North and shoot them in the head. John said, "Yes," thinking blacks will believe anything. He again asked Iron if she truly thought that more religion would stop the stealing. She said yes, thinking that more food would stop the slaves from stealing, and whites will believe almost anything.

As she stared at the bible, she wondered how long it would take her to learn to read. She felt she must know for herself, what was being said in the book. Her talks with Reuben and listening to the various white preachers were leaving her confused. She was determined to know the word for herself. It seemed to her that the two sides could use the bible in the same fight. Secretly she believed that the white man was lying to the slaves about what was really written in there. She would learn to read and she would teach other slaves to read. For if the white man did not want the slave to read, it must be done.

Iron did not stare at the bible too long. For tonight there was a corn shucking at the Rhodes plantation. Iron was happy for the

Rhodes plantation were the nearest neighbors they had. The walk would only take about 2 hours. At other corn shuckings, Iron had found herself walking most of the night, though she did enjoy the singing the slaves did on the way. She wasn't as strong as the field hands. She would get tired and always fall behind.

The women on the Rhodes plantation were having a quilting at the same time as the shucking. Peaches and Iron preferred to stand at the back, while the men in two teams raced to shuck mountains of corn. Iron loved the singing the men did at these events. The atmosphere was similar to that of Christmas time. Though she did not enjoy walking great distances, she would walk 8 hours to a corn shucking, sing, dance, and then walk 8 hours back. Shelly entered the cabin.

"Girl, ain't you got no pretty dresses left?"

"Hello Shelly, how's Mama Pearl this evening?"

"She fine. She says she want to get some rest. Girl, how come you always trying to dress like Massa?"

"I ain't trying to dress like Massa. I dress like me."

"Well, you sho look a lot like Massa. Girl, you one but a few who has more than 2 pieces of rags to wear, and you be looking like Massa."

Iron had on a pair of long pants and an old shirt that Massa John gave her. She had her wool plaited back and left the collar of her shirt sticking up. She had taken soot from the chimney, mixed it up with some water and polished her shoes.

"Shelly, I be thinkin, Massa be trying to look like me."

The two women laughed and went on their way to meet Peaches and Benjamin. Peaches also wasn't impressed with Iron's attire, asking how come she don't ever wear no skirt. Iron ignored her, grabbed Benjamin by the arm and went walking down the road. Everyone in the area knew about the corn shucking, which meant there would not be many patrollers. The slaves did not need a pass, though Peaches and Iron never needed one. The slaves were more at ease without the fear of being stopped. Many of them were already on the road. You could hear the singing for miles.

Upon arriving at the plantation, they immediately went into the barn. The 2 teams for the shucking were already being chosen. Shelly raced to find the women participating in the quilting. Iron and Peaches moved to the back of the barn, not wanting to disturb the white people there, and not wanting to take part in the actual shucking

Then, There Was Iron

of the corn. A young woman begins to stare intensely at Iron. The woman released a smile. Iron returned it.

"Peaches, whose that?"

"That's Miss Bad Bell."

"Bad Bell?"

"See dat girl dere?" Peaches points to a stunning honey brown girl.

"Dat's Good Bell. She is a breeding wench on the Jackson plantation. Now Bad Bell was bought to breed also, but none of dem bucks could breed her. She was bought with a baby girl, but Massa Jackson done give the baby to his cousin. They say that Bad Bell can't be bred. When the bucks enter her cabin, she screamed so loud the plants died. Miss Bad Bell done make such a noise the bucks couldn't do it. Miss Jackson also never heard a sound like it and told Massa Jackson never to try and breed that girl again. See her hands?"

Iron looked at the woman's hands, if that is what they are to be called. She saw mangled pieces of flesh. Almost looking like a child's hands after being severely trampled.

"Lord, what happened to her?"

"When Miss Bad Bell was a little girl about 5 or 6, her missus drove a stake through her hands. Said Bad Bell was too mischievous, never stayed still. She left dat little girl nailed to the back step till the slaves came out of the field. Took till almost midnight to get that stake out of the little girl's hands. She near bled to death. They say she never talked again on that plantation. She did take the beatings though; they beat that little girl everyday for bout 10 summers. This was in Kentucky, Massa Jackson used to be a doctor there. One day he was called to Bell's plantation about a big buck that was very sick.

After checking on the buck he heard a strange moaning from another cabin in slave row. He found Bell with a new baby, beaten almost to death, and looking as if she gave birth all by herself. Massa Jackson said he never seen such a mess and bought Bell and the baby. He done have a Bell with two working hands. They started calling her Bad Bell, and the other Good Bell."

"What she do on the Jackson plantation?"

"She tend to the children, I think she did that on the other plantation too."

"Does she talk now?"

"I dunno, but she sure can sing. She been travellin bout the last 3 summers with Massa Jackson's sister. I dunno know where she's been. Massa Jackson's sister be havin her sing all over the country. But when she home, she tend the children."

Bad Bell stands on a big barrel. She slaps her hands, if that is what they are to be called, to her legs. Then she claps them together. Then she takes her right hand and hits her left shoulder, and then her left hand hits her right shoulder. She gets a good rhythm going. Some of the people, who haven't begun the actual shucking as yet, join in, including Peaches and Iron. Bad Bell begins to sing.

"All day long while in the field,
I've been thinkin bout a good meal,
I can't wait till I am told,
They shuckin corn down the road."

After she says one line, all the slaves repeat it. This was called call-and-sponse. Bad Bell was one of the best call-and-sponse slaves ever, which was usually done by men.

Peaches told Iron she knew maybe 20 great call-and-sponse men, but only 2 or 3 women. Bad Bell keeps it up for about an hour. Then she stops, allowing the captain of one of the teams to take over.

"Peaches, why she stop?" Iron had never heard a voice like Bad Bell's. It seemed to open up heaven. She had kept her eyes closed most of the time she was responding to Bad Bell's lines. Not looking at her surroundings, and listening to the beautiful music gave Iron a feeling like she had never had. She thought it might have been freedom. When Bad Bell stopped singing, she felt rudely waken from a beautiful dream.

"She might be saving her voice for the dance."

"I sho hope so."

Iron could not stop staring at the woman. Bad Bell was of a very dark complexion. She had a broad nose, small eyes, and very thick lips. Others would not have called her beautiful. Iron noticed when Bad Bell was not singing, she kept her head down and her shoulders slightly bent forward, as if she was trying to hide. When she was singing, she seemed taller; she seemed alive. It was like two completely different women. Iron wanted to run to the woman, put her arms around her and squeeze. She wanted to feel the beauty inside of Bad Bell that came out in her voice. She wanted to hold her till she kept her head up all the time. She decided the next dress Massa gave

Then, There Was Iron

her she would give to Bad Bell, and maybe a pretty scarf to wrap her hair. The one she had on, now looked really worn. Iron wanted Bad Bell to again smile at her. For the rest of the shucking, Bad Bell did not even look at Iron at all.

The shucking ended very late at night, than the feast was brought out. There was pies, corn, roasted potatoes, fried chicken, cabbages, turnips, lots of greens, and a whole pig was roasted. The women came in from the quilting and all including Massa Rhodes and his family ate together. Iron could not wait until the food was done, to begin the dance. Having more than a normal amount of slave rations, she unlike the field hands, did not get very excited about a large meal. It actually saddened her watching some of the slaves eat with such a ravenous hunger. She searched for Bad Bell who had placed herself in front of the fried chicken and didn't appear to have the desire to move. She watched as Bad Bell sat with her eyes glanced down and ate piece after piece of chicken. Iron wanted to go over to Bad Bell, but Peaches and Shelly, who were delighting in the barrel of whiskey Massa Rhodes had brought out, surrounded her. She also did not know what to say to Bad Bell, which was very strange to her. Finally the feasting was over and a young slave man brought out his fiddle. All began to dance except Iron, who was waiting for Bad Bell to sing. The family of Massa Rhodes began to dance with the slaves. The white's danced as if they were slaves, and the blacks were free. They seemed stuck within themselves. Iron thought maybe the whites kept the slaves in bondage because they were in bondage inside. They could not release the joy out of their bodies; they were contained. She had to turn her eyes away. Watching adult whites dance made her want to laugh, but watching their children always made her want to cry. Bad Bell began to sing again. Iron had never wanted to run away more than she did at this moment, and she wanted to take Bad Bell with her.

The walk home for the slaves was a lot different from the walk to the corn shucking.

Though there was still a lot of singing, it did not have the same energy level. Most of the slaves were feeling the after effects of too much whiskey, including Iron, who with the help of Peaches and Shelly, found herself getting carried away. Shelly was celebrating because it was now Sunday and she did not have to do a long day in the field. Her mulatto friends did not understand the blessing of free whiskey on a Saturday night, though they gave it their all in celebrating with her. The sun told them it was about noon, and Shelly was going to sleep till it was time to go to the field, sun up tomorrow. Peaches was going to curl up for a few hours with Benjamin. She knew that Massa would be visiting her this evening. Iron was going to sleep, until she felt like getting up.

Iron arrived home, undressed, washed up a little, and crawled under her sheet. It was nighttime when she awoke to find Bad Bell sitting on the floor, staring at her. Iron was completely naked, and did not know if she should hide herself. She didn't know if she should talk, she didn't know what day it was. She got off her mattress, and smiled. Bad Bell did not smile back at Iron. She sat on the floor, staring at the woman as she washed her face, hands and under her arms. She then slipped on a long incredibly clean white cotton dress. It looked like a white woman's bedclothes. She stared in astonishment at amount of oranges and apples Iron kept in a large wooden bowl on her table. Iron now understood 'baresment. Bad Bell must have known who she was to have found her cabin. She must know why she was so favored by Massa.

For a few seconds Iron wished she were a field hand, or a maid, or a cook. Anything, but a plaything for Massa. She than put all the oranges and apples into a sack and handed it to Bad Bell. The smile that Bad Bell gave her was worth 100 nights with Massa. Iron stopped feeling embarrassed. Bad Bell took the sack, and walked out the door. Iron stood staring at the door for a few minutes. Then she got out her bible. She lay back on her mattress and stared at the pages.

She knew the strange markings were called letters. When you put the letters together, you had words. She thought the first thing she needed to do was find out how many different letters there were, then she would worry about the sounds they made. Somehow she needed to get writing materials. She did not dare ask Massa John for any. She couldn't think of any white person she trusted enough to purchase it for her. Iron had $472.00 buried outside in her garden. This was given to her by Massa John over the last 6 years. He thought she was using the money to buy ribbons or other womanly things. She never spent a penny of the coins; he sometimes left by the bedside. She was planning to one day buy her freedom, and that of Mama Pearl's. She had heard that a good breeding wench could cost $800.00, and a maid

Then, There Was Iron

$500.00. She knew that Massa John would be doing a lot more visiting before she would have her freedom.

She thought of stealing the writing materials from the big house, but Miss Mary rarely left the plantation anymore. She decided to get a stick and practice on the dirt floor of her cabin. She would write down all the different letters that appeared in the bible. Then she would have to find a slave that could possibly tell her the names of these letters. It would take a long time, but she would do it. Iron fell back asleep. She woke up the next morning with a terrible feeling in her stomach. She immediately ran outside and vomited at the side of her cabin. Iron now knew what that meant, $200.00 more for Massa. She wondered how long before her belly got really big. She also wondered what Bad Bell would think of it. She wondered what Bad Bell thought of anything. Was she in the habit of entering other people's cabin, while they were sleeping? She also wondered when Bad Bell would be back.

Iron thought that she heard rustling in the trees, which led to the woods. Beautiful cypress and sycamore trees surrounded Iron's cabin. Of the 4 mulattos, John Cummings had tucked away, Iron seemed to have the best location. She was closest to the creek, and had the clearest path to slave row. Lizzie and Doll were deeper in the woods, than Peaches and Iron. Maybe that's why they alienated themselves from the other slaves. Peaches was the closest to the fields, and slave row. In the six years that Iron had joined their circle, Peaches now associated with the field hands almost daily, bringing them news, which she often received from Benjamin. Benjamin and Reuben were the only slaves that traveled. Most of the field hands had never been more than 12 hours away from their own plantation. This was only to go to a dance on another plantation, and not very often. Most slaves had no idea where they were.

Iron had learned that she was in South Carolina, and that it was a state. She also knew of Georgia, and Floridy. They were all slave states. She knew the slave states were South, and up North the blacks were free. The only state she knew up North, was New York. Iron did not know how many states there were free or slave. She would worry about that later. The four directions from her cabin ran; north was the way to slave row, a big well, and a giant tobacco field. West brought you into the woods, where you would find the cabins of the other 3 mulattos adequately spaced apart. If you kept walking west from

Iron's cabin through the woods, past Doll and Lizzie's cabins, there would be a large barn, another well, and a smokehouse, than a large vegetable garden. Directly off the road, turning right and walking through the vegetable garden, you would come to a long driveway that led to the big house. The driveway was between the vegetable garden and a small tobacco field. The field was small, for half of it was cut off for the graveyard. The graveyard was also directly off the road. Behind the graveyard was a row of very large trees that separated the tobacco field. Behind the tobacco field was a variety of small buildings. Iron knew that in these buildings they made the shoes and clothes for the slaves. There was also blacksmithing and carpentry but she rarely bothered to go where she had no business. There was also a whipping post in this area, and a few bigger cabins for the ovaseer and house servants. These cabins lined a little road that led to slave row. Slave row was between 2 fields, 1 being about 100 acres, the other about 35. The rest of the space being woods, where the mulattos were kept. South of Iron's cabin through the trees, there was a creek. East of her cabin was woods, and the woods got thicker the more you walked through them, for this was the end of John Cummings property. This is also where Iron felt she heard something. She walked closer.

"Friend, friend."

"Huh?"

"Is you a friend?"

Iron peeked through the shrubs to see a large black man in a horrid condition. The man looked as if there was not much life left in him. His clothes were completely tattered, looking more like strings than garments, and he was covered in blood, both fresh and dried.

"Is you a friend?"

"Yes. Yes, Ise a friend. Let me help you in the house."

Iron half dragged the man into her cabin. She left him lying on the floor in the front room, and then went out to brush the ground. The man was obviously a run away. Upon returning to the cabin, she found the man trying to drag himself to a pail for some water. His feet looked like a back after 300 lashes. She brought him a cup of water.

"Is you hungry?"

"Yes'm."

Iron begins to prepare a breakfast of ham and fried eggs. She offered him some corn bread while he was waiting for the food to

Then, There Was Iron

cook. Iron had never seen anyone eat as he did, and she had seen many a hungry slave. The man used two hands to put the food to his mouth, and left them there until all of the bread was consumed. He ate with his eyes closed while constantly moaning and praying.

"Ise don think Ise find ya, Miss friend."

"Find me, you were lookin for me?"

"Wese all wer."

"How many of you?"

"Dere wuz 6 of us, 2 'omens, 4 mens. Wese walkin 15 days fore the dogs get us, den wese all broke up. Ise don know where dey is. Ise keep on lookin for you."

Iron brings him his ham and eggs. He begins to eat while still lying on the floor.

"Ise Jasper. Ise comes from Georgia, youse was spectin us Miss friend?"

"My name is Iron. I was not expectin you."

"Youse say you is a friend."

"I is a friend, but I am not the friend that was expectin you. Who you lookin for?"

Jasper hesitates. Iron takes off her handkerchief from around her head.

"Youse a slave."

"Yes."

"Ise thinks youse a white lady."

"You lookin for a white lady?"

"Ise lookin for a friend."

"Well, Ise a friend. Let me go get more water to clean you up. Stay here and be quiet."

Iron returns to find Jasper asleep on her floor. She stares at the runaway. She can't let anyone see him. The punishment for keeping a runaway slave would surely change her life forever. She knew she would receive at least 500 lashes; she could also be sold, possibly taken further down South and worked to death in a cotton field.

Iron went outside to work in her garden in case someone came by, they would not have to enter the cabin. She thanked God Massa John never came to see her in the daytime. Jasper spent all of the day sleeping on the floor in Iron's cabin. She filled her washtub so that Jasper could bathe when he awoke. He didn't budge as she brought the big tub into the cabin, carried it into her bedroom, and made 13 trips to give him enough water for a good bathing. She had also killed a chicken, cut it up, covered it with flour and pepper, and began to fry it. She wanted him to have food to take with him. She was also going to give him fruit and greens. She had made some adjustments to her clothes, hoping they would fit him, but she doubted it. She thought of the way Peaches and Shelly always teased her for wearing men's clothes. This time it might be convenient. She had no shoes that would fit him, but had some cloth in which to wrap his feet. Jasper woke to the smell of fried chicken.

"You got to go before dark."

"Wher I go?"

"I dunno, but now you can go on in the back room and clean yourself up. There's some lard next to the washtub, for those cuts, and there's some fresh clothes. If you need any help, call me."

"Thank ya, Miss friend."

Iron was about to remind him of her name, than she thought, what if he got caught? There were things that the white man could do to you, that would make you admit to every rule you had ever broken, and who helped you along the way.

Jasper spent about an hour washing, and tending to his wounds, he did not ask for help. When he reentered the front room he looked like a different man. Iron placed some chicken, greens and potatoes on the table on front of him. The rest she wrapped up.

"Youse sho hav lots of eatins for a slave."

"You must eat fast and leave."

"Ise dunno wher to go."

"I hears you spose to follow the North Star."

"Yes'm, Ise been told bout the Nawth Sta. Ise headin fo New Yalk. Dere spose ta be friends to help us on the way."

"This white lady ya looking for, she helps slaves get to New York?"

"Youse neber say why youse hav so much good eatins. I sho do preciate it."

Iron could see that Jasper didn't really trust her. She obviously had a better life than any other slave he had seen. If she was him, and met a slave living such a high life, she herself would not tell them of whites helping blacks to freedom. Telling the wrong person could mean death to all. Though it shames her, Iron decides to be honest with Jasper.

Then, There Was Iron

"Ise is Massa's special breeding wench. That's why I gets so much food."

"Ise seen wenches Massa done lay with. They still don get as much eatins as you."

"They tell me my Massa is a good man."

"Sho look like it."

"Jasper, you ever see a good Massa?"

"I seen some Massa's dat don whip niggers so much. Seem to me the only good Massa, is a dead Massa. Dats why Ise is runnin. My Massa was de debil hisself. He sole off my wife and little daughta, Ise neber gon sees em."

Jasper begins to cry. He falls to the floor. Iron rushes to his side and puts her arms around him.

"Miss friend, Ise a man."

"Yes Jasper, you are a man."

"Ise work, Ise can make anything outa wood. Ise can work and feed my family. Miss friend, Ise loved her so much, so much."

Jasper is clinging on to Iron for dear life. She continues to hold him and stroke his head, though she was worrying about Massa. He usually came very late at night, or the early hours of the morning, but the risk was too great for Iron to relax.

"I'm sure she loved you also, very much."

"Nudder man hav her now. Youse got love?"

"No."

"Miss friend don love no slave man? Slave man can't be a man for ya. Slave man can be a hoss for ya, but not a man. Ise runnin to be a man."

"Jasper youse is always a man, white man want you to think you a hoss, but if you a hoss, than he is a snake. Jasper, keep runnin, I will pray for you, but you must leave now, for my Massa is comin."

"Yes'm Miss friend."

Jasper gets up and heads for the door. Iron runs to him and gives him a last hug.

"Jasper, we be free one day. God has a plan. Don't know what it is, but slavery days be over."

"Thank ya, Miss Friend. I be prayin for ya too."

Jasper walks out the door. Iron goes quickly to empty the tub and rid her cabin of anything that might look like she had a man there. She could not stop thinking about white friends that help slaves run away to the North. It seems like every day she was hearing something good about white people. Could Reuben be right? Something else bothered her. She kept thinking back to the preacher Wendall Smalls and the free man Lewis. She was amongst a handful of slaves that didn't agree with what they were saying. Like the white man, she did not want to hear it. She thought all whites were evil and the idea that blacks and whites were equal was an insult to her. The more she thought about this, the more she realized that the white man did not care to hear that blacks and whites were equal either. Maybe she was more like a white person, than she cared to be.

She needed to talk to Reuben about this. She wondered if he tired of all their talks being about blacks and whites. She sure was getting tired thinking about it. She thought if all the people were free, there wouldn't be so much talk about the good people and the evil people. Everybody could work and take care of their children. Not wasting precious time wondering who was better than the other. If she was free, and couldn't help hating white people then, she would just ignore them. Live her own life, work, cook, and tend to her garden. She would not waste her time hating others. If she was free, whenever she felt her detest of the white man growing, she thought maybe she would do something sweet. Like play with a child, or study her bible, anything so that the hate would not control her. She did not want to be a slave no more, a slave to anything, not of man, not of hate. She would try to be a servant of love and she would keep her eyes and ears open to these good white people. It couldn't be any harder than keeping her eyes and ears closed to the few evil black people.

It seemed that both groups had its good and evil. Iron's thoughts quickly change as Massa John enters her cabin. He was drunk and she thanked God. This meant the act was even quicker, and he wouldn't want her to talk, though he might slap her in the face. She actually preferred the slaps to the conversation. Massa John didn't say a word. He pushed her down, got on top of her. He kept his hand over her mouth as he penetrated. As hard as Iron tried to picture Jasper on top of her, she kept seeing Bad Bell.

This was only the second time in all of Massa's visits that Iron pretended he was someone else, usually she would just close her eyes and pray, or think about running. Not so much running away, but just running through fields. The first time Iron tried to pretend and enjoy it, was a few years after Massa John got a good price for his harvest.

Then, There Was Iron

That night he brought over a jug of whiskey, and insisted that Iron partake of it with him. Iron had drank way too many glasses and found herself thinking of a young girl Massa had just bought from an auction. Iron had given the girl a very fine red dress. The way the girl twirled around and smiled at Iron brought her a strange happiness. The effects of too much whiskey kept the vision of the girl in Iron's head. That night as Massa was taking her, Iron found herself pushing her hips up to meet Massa. Her body was moving as if it was searching for pleasure. She didn't find none for Massa was finished before she even felt the shame in what she was doing. She swore never to drink whiskey with Massa again. By his next visit, she was back to her motionless self.

This night Iron was not moving her body, but in her mind she felt an excitement. Jasper had left her feeling unfulfilled. She felt alive, alive and boiling over. She wanted to share this life, this heat with someone. She squeezes her eyes tight. There's Jasper pounding away on her, searching for freedom. He changes to Bad Bell, she can't pound. She touches her. She wants to touch her. She wants to be touched back. She has often wished that God made her a man. Especially, when admiring the beauty of a woman. She sometimes thought of this while lying in bed at night, tonight feeling the fear for Jasper, the hate for Massa, and the curiosity for Bad Bell. She thinks about touching Bad Bell as a woman, not as some male version of herself. She likes this thought and wonders if it can be done. She is awakened by a loud moan by Massa. He gets off her, adjusts himself, and walks out the door. Iron gets up and washes. She wonders if her thoughts of Bad Bell, would ever come to pass. She wonders if any women have ever thought of this before. She sure hoped it could happen before her stomach got too big.

CHAPTER 6

Well, her stomach got big. The baby came out and still her wishes of Bad Bell had not come to pass. The child, a boy, was called Quincey. The child stayed in Pearl's cabin for two months until John eventually traded him for two mules. Iron was a 25-year-old mother of 5. Like the other babies, she didn't look at, hold, or name Quincey. She refused to even look at the mules. If she walked by or even heard them, she got this feeling in her stomach as if it would come up in her mouth.

Iron had prayed more with this pregnancy than any of the others. She had a stronger feeling of sadness. Partially because she was a slave, and she was contributing to slavery by growing one inside her, and partially because Bad Bell was off on one of her singing trips with Massa Jackson's sister. She also used this time to study her bible. She had figured there were 26 different letters in the bible. She didn't know if there were more letters, maybe some not used. She didn't know their names, or the sounds they made. She didn't know in what order they appeared, or if there was any order at all. But she did know how to draw each one, and this was a good start.

What Iron really wanted was to be a friend. She wanted to rid slaves out of slavery. She wanted to end slavery. She wanted to do whatever she could to sabotage the system. Iron spent most of her time, sitting on a rocking chair outside of her cabin. The chair was made by a male field hand, in exchange for a month's supply of extra rations, for him and his family. That was 6 months ago, and Iron was still giving the extra food. Each night she could be found rocking and

listening. Listening for the word, "friend" to be whispered from the woods. This night she hears something. She runs closer to the woods.

"Friend, friend." She whispers.

"Sho hopin' so."

It's Bad Bell. Iron gives a joyful shout and runs to hug the woman. Bad Bell hugs her back. She notices that Iron is no longer pregnant, but doesn't say a word about it.

"How long you been back?"

"This mawnin."

Then, There Was Iron

"Let's go inside. Massa dropped a little jug of whiskey in my garden, I'll fetch it, you go in."

Iron runs to the garden. She thanks God that it is Saturday and Massa never visits on Saturday or Sunday nights.

"Ise got the jug. Youse hungry?"

"Naw, Missus Jackson made a feast for our return. I eats plenty."

"It's good to hear that. Sits down."

Iron gets two cups and fills them both with whiskey. She's surprised to see that the jug is full. It had sat in her garden the two weeks since Massa dropped it. She left a stick in it's place planning to return it to the exact spot, though she had figured John had completely forgotten of it. The two women take their cups and drink in silence.

"Massa's sister, she good to ya?"

"She done never whip me, never hit me once."

"Thank the Lord."

Bad Bell gets quiet. She didn't remember planning to visit Iron, or walking to her cabin; only being there. She was always paralyzed in Iron's company. She had only visited 3 times before, each time leaving with a sack full of goodies. She took a sip of her whiskey and looked up at Iron. She had never known anyone like Iron. Someone who made you not want to die in your sleep. How she wanted to rest her head on the space between Iron's chin and shoulder. Iron was smiling at her. She took another sip of whiskey.

Iron was trying not to stare at Bell's hands, if that is what they are to be called. It broke her heart that Bad Bell needed to use both to drink. A lot of slaves had deformities, given to them by perverted masters or over zealous poor white slave catchers. You learn not to stare. She couldn't think of what to say. Bad Bell was always very quiet around her. Maybe her greeting was a little too extreme. In the three visits Bad Bell had made to her cabin, she had only talked once. That was to say thank you, though her eyes and he smile spoke volumes.

Iron wonders why she doesn't talk. She seems happy just to sit with Iron. Maybe she has the same thoughts as her; the thought of touching. She doesn't know who touches first. Is there more talking involved? Do you just start touching without the talking? Are they courting? What if she touches her and Bad Bell was not thinking the same thing? Will she tell people? Will she be angry? She had to try yes, she'll do it. She'll do it now. Iron sits her cup down. She can't stop staring at Bad Bell holding the cup.

"Ever crawl underground with your heart and your mind? Ever see an old woman twisted up? From beatings given everyday, some parts can't bend, some parts can't straighten out. Ever had that twisted inside?"

Bad Bell's words shake Iron from her daze. If she didn't know what to say before, she is completely lost now. She turns and kneels in front of Bad Bell.

"I didn't feel right when you were gone."

Saying this, Iron takes Bad Bell's hands, if that is what they are to be called, into hers. Bad Bell slips from the chair and sits on the floor facing Iron. She is crying. Iron wipes the tears away with her hand. She then kisses the cheeks of Bad Bell as the tears fall. Bad Bell closes her eyes. She puts her arms around Iron. They bury their heads in each other's necks. Iron's hands begin to knead at the sides of Bad Bell. She moves them slowly lower. Shelly walks in. Both women jump up.

"Lord, wats happening in here?"

"Wat be happenin in my cabin, be my business. Ya know, some people be tapping on doors before they be walking in."

"Tapping on doors, Iron I do believe ya getting' newer everyday."

"Shelly, you know Miss Bell. Bell, this is Shelly."

"Miss Bad Bell. My, my. Ise seen ya sing up in Maryland many a time. Folks agree, ain't nothing sweeter than your voice. Is sho a pleasure. Iron, you did not tell me you knew such fine folks."

"There's lots you don't know about me Shelly. Youse wants a taste?"

"Girl, you know I don't say no to whiskey. Ise got to share a glass with Bad Bell, give me something to talk about."

"Nah, nah, you don't be talking my cabin business."

"Girl, it's Bad Bell. Every slave want to sing like Bad Bell, and she is the best singer God ever breathed life into. So let me do my bragging."

"Iron, I don't mind."

"Miss Bad Bell, would you sing a little song for me?"

Bad Bell was the most respected slave Shelly had ever seen. Even white folk called her "Miss." Whenever her name was mentioned, nothing but praise was said, and her name was mentioned often.

Then, There Was Iron

Slaves treated Bad Bell different than they treated each other. They kept their distance from her, only ever approaching with extreme caution. When she entered a new place, she constantly heard people whispering, "That's, Miss Bad Bell." She knew every slave she ever sung for, was proud of her. They were proud cuz she was one of them. Each knowing in their heart, that a white person could never make such a beautiful sound. She was famous all over the south for her voice. To spend any time in her presence was an honor.

"Now Shelly, Miss Bell just arrived back from months of singing all over, she needs some rest."

Bad Bell starts to drift off to the place she goes when she doesn't want to be seen. She wants Shelly to leave. She wants to be alone with Iron. She puts her head down and starts staring in her cup. Iron and Shelly stare at her. They are waiting for any sign of life. Bad Bell trembles a bit, then she starts singing, very low at first, a song that neither Iron or Shelly had heard before. The two women are spellbound. Iron really didn't understand the song, it seemed to be about love, lost flowers, and a hunger inside, but not for food.

"Miss Bad Bell, I ain't never heard that one before."

"Dats a new one, I done made it up on my last trip with Miss Jackson."

Iron notices that Bell is now sitting straighter and she seems more approachable. The certain sadness has left her eyes. She starts into another song. This one with a much happier feeling, about two slaves that cut up the body of their master and fed him to the dogs. Though the song had a lot of bloody detail, Iron and Shelly loved it.

Peaches and Benjamin enter the cabin. Benjamin has a jug of his own.

"Gal, I knew I heard Miss Bad Bell singing. Told ya Peaches."

"Benjamin, run and fetch Reuben."

Benjamin leaves, to get Reuben. Shelly is now singing back up for Bad Bell, adding "mmm uhms, yes girl, and I done tole ya," whenever she felt it necessary. Shelly had a magnificent voice, but nobody compared to Bad Bell. They sang 4 more songs before Benjamin returned with Reuben and his fiddle. Six more songs later Lizzie and Marcus arrived. Lizzie also had a jug of Massa's whiskey. Iron sat back and looked at the people in her cabin. They were all having a good time. Bell looked happier than Iron had ever seen her. Peaches and Benjamin were dancing like a couple in love. Lizzie was sitting while Marcus was doing some silly little dance in front of her. Reuben was honored to be accompanying Bad Bell. It showed in his face and you heard it through his fingers. Shelly was drunk. She had her eyes closed hugging one of the whiskey jugs and doing a little sway. Iron thought these are my people. Watching them gave her a joy inside. She thought this must be one of the reasons for life.

The party went on until the late hour of the night. Peaches and Benjamin left first. Peaches unsure if Massa would be visiting. Lizzie and Marcus were next. Then Reuben half carried and half dragged Shelly back to slave row.

"Ya want to stay here tonight with me? When Massa Jackson be needin you ya back?"

"I don't know nothing 'bout time."

Bad Bell is grateful for the invitation. She drank more whiskey that she was accustomed to and didn't want to make the long walk back to the Jackson plantation.

"My mattress is big enough for two."

Iron immediately regrets saying this. Bad Bell is undressing, her head is slightly spinning. She crawls into the mattress naked, and does not say a word. Iron does the same.

"Night Bell."

"Night Iron."

The two women fall asleep instantly.

Iron awoke to find Bad Bell washing in her big washtub in the middle of the room. Bell was completely naked and appeared more comfortable than Iron knew her to be. Iron got out of bed, put some of the baking soda she begged Massa for on her finger, and rubbed it on her teeth. Without word, she offered some to Bad Bell, who did the same. She steps into the tub. Bad Bell gives Iron a smile. Iron finds this smile to be somewhat sneaky in appearance. Iron's thinking that Bad Bell looks different this morning, somewhat bigger and stronger in appearance. Bad Bell takes the soap and starts washing Iron's body. Iron begins to speak but Bad Bell gently covers her mouth with her hands, if that is what they are to be called. Bad Bell kisses her, kisses her the way she seen Massa Jackson's nephew kiss his new wife, when he thought no one else was in the room. The way she seen a young buck kiss a housemaid after he walked 34 miles to be with her. The way she had never been kissed. Iron likes it. She is shocked at the aggression Bad Bell is showing. She decides to let Bad Bell do with

Then, There Was Iron

her, what she wants. She will give herself over completely. Bad Bell is now taking her hand, and leads her out of the tub, back to the mattress. Iron lays down while Bad Bell lays on top of her still kissing. Iron feels Bad Bell pushing, not like Massa, for Bad Bell had laid one leg in between hers, and one leg on the outside. Iron could feel her softness, rubbing against her own, and she loves it, she is pushing up to meet Bad Bell. She feels herself melting; she has never known that touching could be so sweet. Bad Bell is now kissing her breasts, and slowly moving down. Iron wonders what she is going to do. Bad Bell buries her head between Iron's legs. Iron feels her body define proportion. She has visions of people she has never met, riding rainbows on great big black horses. This was way better than she could ever imagine. She feels something in the pit of her stomach, and a strange tingling by the back, in that sacred part that Massa brought so much pain the first time. She thinks she is going to pass water. God, she hoped not, not with Bad Bell down there. God it feels like freedom. It feels like freedom, and that's what she screams when she explodes.

Most of the day was spent like that. Touching, talking, laughing, and licking. Iron had noticed 5 or 6 distinct changes in Bad Bell, in which her appearance, her voice, and her mannerisms seemed completely different. Sometimes Bad Bell appeared very childlike, shy and nervous. Other times she was like the bravest field hand, and still other times she was very soft, womanly, sweet and caring, ready to fulfill Iron's every need. It was the moment when Bad Bell appeared soft that she instructed Iron how to put her head between her legs, and lick exactly the way she had done. It took a few tries but Bad Bell exploded twice that Sunday. Iron herself counted 8 times. 5 times with the tough Bad Bell, and 3 times with the soft.

Iron thought that Bad Bell's ability to appear like completely different people, may have something to do with the fact that slaves claimed that she sounded like more than one person when she sang. Iron felt that Bad Bell was blessed with a most wonderful gift. The only drawback Iron saw, was the big gaps in Bad Bell's memory. She often forgot what she was saying just minutes before. When Iron showed the soft womanly Bad Bell her bible, she seemed shy and also amazed at the strange markings in it, after turning it over in her hands, if that is what they are to be called. She seemed very childlike again, and read it perfectly.

Childlike Bad Bell told Iron the names of the different letters, and agreed to help her learn to read. They spent hours that day on the alphabet, until Bad Bell got tough again and wanted more rubbing and touching. Iron loved the touching and rubbing, but wondered why when Bad Bell was tough she couldn't read a word. Bad Bell left late that night, soft, shy and womanly. Iron was completely confused. She wondered if anyone else noticed these changes in Bad Bell. Maybe she was marked by a ghost or a conjuere. Maybe Bad Bell was a witch or maybe she was just playing games with Iron. Whatever it was, she learnt more from Bad Bell that Sunday, than she had learned her whole life. She loved the company of Bad Bell, every single one of her.

Iron stayed up most of the night practicing to say the different letters of the alphabet. Now that she knew their names and the sounds they made, reading should be easy. She only hoped that on Bad Bell's next visit, she would spend more time in her childlike way, for Iron had a desire to learn to read as quickly as possible. She fell asleep with her bible in her hand. The next day, she spent the entire day studying her bible, only stopping to eat and wash up. Around midnight she heard Massa singing and hollering outside her cabin.

"I got Gravy. I got Gravy!"

Massa entered her cabin with the biggest smile she had ever seen on his face, and a jug in each hand.

"Come here girl, we got a lot of celebrating to do."

"What be delighting you so Massa?"

"Girl, you looking at the best poker player in all of the South. Ask me what I just won."

"What you win, Massa?"

"Gravy, girl. Gravy Dailey."

He picks up Iron and spins her around in a drunken glee. Iron hates this. She hates it when Massa is happy and looks to her to share her joy. She prefers the slaphappy miserable Massa, who does his business and gets out.

"Massa, you won Gravy Dailey? Why, he's the best field hand in all of South Caroliney!"

"Best? Girl, he is the best tobacco nigger in all of the South. Why he is the most valued slave, I ever heard of. Just last year a fellow came from up North. Had Gravy work in one of his factories in the off-season. He offered that stupid Edmond Dailey $4000.00 for

Then, There Was Iron

Gravy, and Edmond wouldn't sell. Now he has lost him to 4 aces. Girl, things be looking up around here. I'm gonna have the biggest, best crop, this land has ever seen."

"I sho is happy for ya Massa. Ise always heard that my Massa was one of the best poker players in this area. Now everyone knows it's true."

John grabs her and starts kissing her. Iron does not open her mouth, as she did with Bell, though she feels Massa's tongue poking at her lips. He has never kissed her in such a way before. She prays to God that he never does it again. The foul smell of liquor and tobacco, makes her want to turn her skin inside out. She wishes someone would tell him of the wonderful uses of baking soda. But she just lays back, and opens her legs.

CHAPTER 7

Seven days had brought many changes to the Cummings plantation. Iron felt left out, for she didn't know what they were. No one had came to see her all week, not Shelly, not Peaches, not Reuben, sadly not Bad Bell, and gratefully not Massa. This was the first time Iron could remember a week going by without a visit from Massa. She wished that Massa would buy a prized slave more often. She spent the week studying her bible, and wondering about Bad Bell. She felt that she had made great improvements with her letters and was anxious to share it with Bad Bell. Her body was also craving. She had tried using her hands and taking it away on her own. She was able to rub herself to conclusion, but she missed Bad Bell so much more afterwards. She had to admit that she was feeling lonely and decided to take a walk to slave row this evening, maybe sit with Mama Pearl. Iron began to prepare a special meal to take to Mama Pearl and Shelly.

As soon as the sun went down, Iron made her way to slave row. Pearl was already in the cabin.

"Girl, aren't you a gift to these tired eyes."

Iron walks over to give the older woman a hug.

"I brought you some dinner."

"You needn't be doin that. I gets plenty of food now, workin in the big house. You know that."

"Yes'm Mama, I know. But I also know that it's nice to have a hot meal ready for ya."

"Girl, that's the truth. Miss Mary be running us ragged all day. They havin lots of visitors these days, now that they got that fine Mr. Gravy Dailey."

Iron is shocked. She had never heard Mama Pearl call any man fine before. The idea that Mama Pearl could find a man fine was strange to her. Iron suddenly realized that not only did everyone need love; they wanted it.

"Hmmm. Fine Mr. Gravy Dailey, he be Gravy Cummings now."

"That man always be Gravy Dailey, cuz that's how often I like to see him."

The two women laugh, and Shelly enters the cabin exhausted.

Then, There Was Iron

"Lord, I am bone tired. Massa be workin us extra hard. The whip has been flying all day. I thank the Lord I didn't feel it today. I be digging down in me, how deep I don't even know, for the strength to keep up, and I finds it. Iron, you bring a taste?"

"Girl, Iron won't be bringing any whiskey to this here cabin."

"Sorry Pearl. It's just that after workin sun up, to pass sun down, a girl could use a taste."

"I brought some fried chicken, greens, and taters."

"That'll do."

Pearl gives the blessing on the food and the three women begin to eat.

"Shelly, you be out there working with Gravy, what he like?"

"I don't see too much of the great Gravy Dailey. He works less than a white man. All I ever see him do is talk to Massa, or talk to the ovaseer."

"Gravy be doing lots of work around here. Things be better now that he's around."

"Now Pearl, us field hands be workin harder than ever, now that he's here. That don't seem better to me. Maybe for you."

"What's that mean, maybe for me?"

"Just that you seem to be singing more lately, and there's a bounce in your step."

"Shelly, you leave Mama alone. But there's nothing like pouring a little gravy on top of a good meal."

Shelly laughs.

"Ya know the best gravy is brown and thick."

"Girls, now stop that talk. This is a good God loving cabin, and I won't have such talk in here."

Iron and Shelly lower their heads and continue eating in silence. Pearl watches the two young women. She has grown to love Shelly, and now took care of her, just as she did Iron. Trying to make her life, the life of a slave woman, a little easier. They kept glancing at each other, smiling with their eyes. They were both like daughters to her. Deep inside she was enjoying the teasing they were giving her. Pearl gets up.

"All I'm saying is pour it on before the meat gets too old."

Pearl starts to move her 250-pound frame in a little dance. The other two join her, all are laughing. The dancing stops when a tap is

47

heard coming from the door. The ladies look at each other in surprise. Pearl answers the door.

"Evening ladies. Pearl, I came by to return your cloth. Those were some mighty lovely biscuits you made. Remind me of my Mama's."

"Why thank you, Gravy. This here is Shelly, and this is Iron."

They all acknowledge each other with smiles and nods of the head.

"I be seeing Miss Shelly working in the field. That young lady work harder than any man on this place."

"I got no choice, if I don't wanna feel the lash. Why your Mama name you Gravy?"

"My mama say gravy is good, and my Daddy was too."

All the women laugh.

"Man, you is funnin with us."

"Miss Pearl, I'll always tell you the truth."

Sensing a certain excitement in the air, Iron asks Shelly to walk her back to the cabin. Shelly informs Iron that she is too tired for the walk and would like to talk to Mr. Gravy a little longer.

"Did you know both your Mama and your Daddy?"

"Yes I did, Miss Shelly. Lost my Daddy a few years back and I just lost my Mama last season. My mama was the cook and my Daddy the gardener on Dailey's place. Massa Dailey wasn't a man who liked to break up families. I had one sister but she died with the fever when she was still a little girl."

"You sho is a lucky man to know both of your parents and never be sole off. How come he sole you off now?"

"He don't sell me, he lost me playing poker. Massa Dailey done lose his head when his wife pass on last year. She had the sickness no doctor could fix. After she pass, Massa Dailey take to the whiskey all day. Spend his time with poor crackers just drinking. If I didn't take care of that place, he would have lost it. I live my whole life on that plantation I loved it. Even when I was hired out, I couldn't wait to get back home. But now with my Mama dead, the Missus dead, and the changes to Massa, I glad he done lost me. I especially glad to come to this place."

He gives a big smile to Pearl.

"So, Mr. Gravy, why you never married?"

"I am waiting till I'm a free man."

"How many children you make on that wait?"

Then, There Was Iron

Iron feels that Shelly is digging a little too deep. She whispers in her ear that she has a jug of whiskey back at her cabin.

"Well, nice to meet you Mr. Gravy. I be walking Iron back to her cabin."

"Also very nice to meet you two ladies."

When they leave, Pearl and Gravy look at each other and laugh.

"That girl practicing' to be a patroller?"

"Naw. She just likes to know people's business."

"The light one, she call you Mama, that your daughter?"

"Well, I been takin care of her since the moment she was born. She's a good girl. Massa got her locked away in one of those cabins in the woods. She makin do okay. Slave women, we ain't got much choices. I sho is glad my breedin days are done."

"I'm glad you out of the field."

"Why you glad about me not in the field?"

"Cuz Pearl, you is tired. I see it in your eyes. Woman, I'm tired too. I have been workin everyday of my life cept Christmas Day. I work every single Sunday, hire myself out for extra money."

"Massa Dailey, he let you keep the money?"

"Yes every cent, not like other Massa's. I know some niggers got to give half of the money they make; some got to give a lot more. Massa Dailey was a good man."

"He do sound like a good man. He should put that bottle down and turn to the Lord."

"Let's not talk about Massa Dailey, let's talk about you and me."

"You and me?"

"I would really like to take you on a picnic lunch on Sunday."

"I thought you work every day cept Christmas?"

"It sure feels like Christmas to me."

"Yes I would like that."

"Well I see you then."

Gravy walks out the door. Pearl continues her dance.

It took about 30 minutes for Iron and Shelly to reach Iron's cabin.

"Girl, it's getting late, you sure you won't be too tired for the field tomorrow?"

"Iron, tomorrow is Saturday. I could get up Saturday morning on no sleep at all. That's cuz I know I could sleep all day on Sunday. Where's that taste girl?"

Iron gets the jug and pours two cups. She did not feel like drinking. For some reason she did not want to see Shelly drinking alone.

"What do you think of that Gravy Dailey?"

"Been so long since I thought about happiness. I don't think I remember how it feels, if I ever known. That Miss Bad Bell seems to put a smile on your face."

"Yes we are very friendly. You ever notice anything funny about Bell?"

"I find her very sometimeish."

"Sometimeish?"

"Yea, sometimes she's very excited, sometimes she's very quiet, sometimes she speaks to ya, sometimes, she acts as if she don't know ya. Tell me what ya'll doing. The day when I surprised ya. Something seem like it was going on in here."

"We just sharing, learning, and teaching."

"Sharing, learning and teaching, eh? Girl, I seen it before."

"Seen what?"

"Some folks say you go to hell for it. My Massa's nephew back in Maryland. He was a girlie man. Look like a woman, dress, talk and act like one. One of the housemaids said she caught him all dressed up in one of the Missus dresses. The other white men treated him something terrible. He took to one of the field hands, who were also kinda girlie. They sure spent a lot of time alone together. Young Massa soon bought him, took him to New York and set him free. I heard even after his freedom, they stayed living together. I guess they be sharing, learning, and teaching too."

"Shelly, what you saying? You think I'm going to Hell?"

"Girl, we slaves. Slave women got the hardest life there is. I say whatever you need to do to be strong and survive, do it. Do what makes you feel right, what makes you stand tomorrow."

"You said, some folks say you go to Hell."

"White man say you go to Hell. You know how I feel about what the white man say. I think, why not? It just ain't for me though. So get that look out of your eye."

Iron laughs for she knows there's no special look in her eyes. She was also enjoying what Shelly was saying. Finding certain tenderness in knowing she and Bell were not the first ones who felt this way.

Then, There Was Iron

"Shelly, you know where to get whiskey? I gonna have to get another jug for Massa, this one is almost gone."

"How you gonna get whiskey?"

"I'll buy it. Ya know someone who sells it?"

"I know a man who sell $1 jugs. You got money?"

"Yes."

"I never had no money, ever."

Iron goes to her cookie canister, where she never kept cookies, and dug out the $5.00 she had slowly acquired from Massa, but didn't bother to bury yet.

"If I give you money, can you see the man to get me a jug?"

"Surely."

Iron puts the money in Shelly's hand. Shelly has the look of an old slave, getting new free papers.

"Shelly, I just need one jug, you can keep the rest."

"I can keep this here money, after buying you one jug?"

"Yes."

Shelly gets up and gives Iron a big hug, then walks out the door. Iron couldn't believe Shelly didn't even finish the whiskey in her cup, which was a first. She was so excited by the $5.00 that Iron had given her. Iron figured that Shelly would probably spend all of the first money she ever had received on whiskey. She wondered if Shelly were a free woman, would she drink so much? A question that she prayed one day she would know the answer.

Iron began to clean up. She considered studying her bible, but wasn't comfortable with the idea, because she did have a drink. She laid on her bed and thought of Bad Bell. She knew that she wasn't on one of her singing trips, so why hadn't she come to see her? Sometimeish, that was a good word to describe Bad Bell. Tomorrow, she would go looking for her. Iron fell asleep.

It tool Iron about 3 hours to reach the Jackson plantation. The actual walk took about 2 ½ hours. She had spent ½ hour with Peaches, getting directions and evading questions on why she couldn't come with her. Upon arriving at the plantation, which was a lot smaller than the Cummings place, it didn't take long to find an old Mammy who pointed out Bell's cabin.

She was completely surprised when entering; to see that Bad Bell's cabin was bigger than her own and she had better furniture and nicer curtains. Iron found Bell sitting under her table with a blank stare on her face.

"Hello Bell, remember me?"

"Don't let her put me in that. It hurts, it hurts."

Bad Bell was beginning to shake. Iron got under the table and tried to put her arms around Bad Bell to comfort her. Bad Bell kept pushing her hands away repeating the same line about it hurting.

"I won't let her hurt you. I'll stop her. I'll protect you."

Upon hearing this Bad Bell stops shaking and allowed Iron to hold her. They stayed that way for a few minutes. Suddenly Bad Bell trembled and said,

"What were we doing under the table?"

"You were sitting here when I came in, don't you remember?"

"Iron, I hardly ever remember anything at all."

"What?"

"I lose days, months, years."

"What?"

"Nothing."

Both women get up from under the table.

"Bell, please tell me."

"I never talked with anyone about it."

"About what?"

"Losing time."

"You lose time?"

"Sometimes I wake up and I'm in places I don't remember going. When I go to see you. I remember leaving, but I don't remember arriving, and sometimes I don't remember at all what we done."

"You don't remember what we do?"

Iron instantly looks very hurt. This causes Bad Bell to tremble and than look almost lost. Iron stares at her intensely and watches as Bad Bell's eyes change color, cheekbones appear to move higher, and she would swear that Bad Bell just got taller.

"You know some of us are in love with you."

Trembles and lost look again.

"It's breaking down the walls."

Iron is now scared. She has never known people's eyes to change color in a matter of seconds. Bad Bell's face is also going through a series of changes. When it finally stops she says,

"Ever see someone else's pictures through your eyes?"

Then, There Was Iron

"Someone else's pictures?"

Bad Bell than begins to laugh. She starts caressing Iron very slowly at first. In a matter of moments, they are making passionate love. Iron spent the day in Bell's cabin. Bad Bell came back to find herself standing naked at the door and Iron kissing her good bye. Iron had kissed her fully on the mouth, which she found strange; she also found her nakedness strange. What had they been doing? Bad Bell was used to losing time, since she was a little girl. She had never known when it would happen, for how long, or how often.

Lately it always happened during the time she spent with Iron. She loved Iron like the sister your Massa never sold. Iron was the only one she ever felt comfortable enough with, to tell about losing time. She remembered starting to tell Iron, but that was all she remembered. How long was Iron there? Why was she naked? She truly wished that she could remember what they did together, for she always felt physically elated after a visit.

Rose was resting. She had spent the entire day making love. Well, they had also cooked, sang, danced, laughed, and told stories. But it was the making love that stood out for Rose. The tenderness, the slow gentle touches. The longing. The desire. The feeling of falling. The passion. The explosions. The knowledge that she was what Iron wanted. Rose knew that Army was also making love with Iron. She knew that he was very rough with her. Rose felt that she was the only one who could give Iron what she really wanted. Not Army, and certainly not Massa Cummings.

It was Rose that first spotted Iron at the corn shucking. Her clothes, her mannerisms, her eyes. Rose knew they were alike. What they were, she was not sure. Today she had felt the anger of the others, for taking all the time with Iron. She felt that even Iron would appreciate the emergence of Baby, for another reading lesson. For only Baby and Clair could read. Clair had yet to meet Iron. But Rose wasn't moving. She was the one who had found Iron. If the others also fell in love with her that was their problem. Iron wanted her and didn't even know of the others. Rose didn't mind that Iron thought she was Bad Bell. She wanted Bad Bell gone. She wanted all of them gone. Familiar had come to her and said they were all necessary for survival. She explained that Bad Bell didn't even know they existed, and probably could never know. Rose said she just wanted Iron, and if

Ellen Barton

Army tried again to come out in their private time, she would kill him. Rose heard Army yell.

"I ain't afraid of you girl!"

She wasn't afraid of him either, even though he was not like the others at all. When Army came, he was already a man. They were all still children, some grew, some died, some stayed children, but it seemed that Army was always a man. Familiar knew everyone, and tried to keep them all happy, while protecting Bad Bell. Rose was tired of protecting Bad Bell. Why couldn't she know about them? Why couldn't they give her back her memories? Rose didn't want these memories anymore anyways. She felt Bell's confusion; it was strong. Bad Bell's feelings were so strong, it forced the other's out, and Rose couldn't get the body for days. That's why Iron came looking for her. Her. Not Bad Bell, not Army, not Clair, not Baby, not Familiar, not Peas, not Skinman, not Spacehead, not Doors, not Mud. These were the people she had to live with. She had to share the body with. How on earth could she rid herself of them?

CHAPTER 8

Iron was back at her cabin in no time at all. The walk back seemed a lot shorter than the walk there, probably because she had so much on her mind. Plus she also felt slightly drunk; from the things Bad Bell could do to her body.

This was the best time they had ever spent together physically. Iron thought that if Bad Bell kept doing these things to her, the need to be touched by Bad Bell might soon be beyond her control. But more importantly, what the hell was wrong with Bad Bell? How could she not remember what they did together? Would she remember this day? The most glorious of all days? How come she had such a fine cabin? It was the finest cabin Iron had ever seen belonging to a slave; finer than any housemaids, or breeder. Iron understood that Bad Bell was special slave. Known by many people and probably the most popular slave alive, so she understood why Bad Bell was given more than other slaves. But why did she look so impressed by the belongings of Iron? They still did not equal her own. She had heard of the goodness of Massa Jackson, but not to such extreme measures. Maybe it was the sister of Massa Jackson that supplied Bad Bell with so many luxuries that were not the usual custom of a slave. Could Bad Bell be doing things with Missus Jackson that she was doing with her?

Iron felt a tinge of jealousy. She wanted to ask Bad Bell. Not so much if she was doing anything with the sister of Massa Jackson, but if she was enjoying it. She of all people understood that whites could do anything they wanted to their slaves. These things one tried to make not count, not matter, for they were not of your choosing. So if the sister of Massa Jackson forced Bell to do things with her, nothing could be done about it. Iron's little dance with jealousy took her mind off the fact that Bad Bell's extreme mood changes were starting to mystify her. She decided not to ask Bad Bell what was going on with the sister of Massa Jackson. She didn't want to hear any questions about herself and her own Massa.

Even if she had asked Bad Bell if she was touching Miss Jackson, or not to her knowledge Rose, both would have replied, absolutely not. Rose would say the only way she would touch a white woman was by force. Bad Bell wouldn't even know it was possible for a

Ellen Barton

woman to lay with another woman. But if Doors would make an appearance, a member of Bad Bell's inner family, who had yet to present herself to Iron, she would admit to sleeping with Missus Jackson for years.

The sister of Massa Jackson, whose name was Sylvia, upon her first meeting with Bad Bell, was never the same again. Sylvia Jackson had enjoyed the wealth of her brothers and father, a long time before finding a suitable suitor. She was 35 years old when she finally agreed to wed. Many a young man had tried to hold Sylvia's hand through life. None were what Sylvia could imagine spending her life with. Neither her father, her mother nor her brothers could force her to do something she was not quite ready for. Sylvia had seen the countless numbers of bored, lonely Southern wives, who had no say, and subjected themselves to whatever their husband's commanded. Even if that meant, silently watching your husband breed a herd of mulatto slaves. Sylvia demanded a lot from a potential husband. Intelligence, understanding, and caring, not only to her but also to the world in which she lived. It was a long wait.

Finally after years and the death of her parents Sylvia found a man she could live with. Three months before she was to wed she met Bad Bell. Two months before she was to wed she met Doors. Once month before she was to wed she called it off. Sylvia was completely in love with Doors. A love like she never knew could exist. She secretly purchased Bell from her brother. Who surprisingly charged her a very high price. She paid for the education and care of Bad Bells daughter who lived as free child in New York with a cousin of the Jackson family. She brought Bad Bell gifts and gave her every single thing she ever asked for. She prayed Bad Bell would never ask for her freedom, which is why she never told that she had purchased her. She knew in her heart that if Bad Bell asked for her freedom she would give it to her and possibly lose her forever. She knew something was different about Bad Bell and once considered taking her to Northern doctors. She knew that Bad Bell was the most intelligent and creative person she had ever met. She knew that she would never love anyone the way she loved Bad Bell. She knew that such a way of living would never be accepted. She knew that Bad Bell brought her to such wonderful physical peaks that sometimes she swore she could see and talk directly to God afterwards. This would leave her brain fuzzy for

Then, There Was Iron

days and a feeling like her womanhood had gained enormous amounts of weight. She knew that she could not live without Bad Bell.

Sylvia tolerated the disappearances of Bad Bell. Who would sometimes be gone for days and upon her return act as if she never left. When it first happened Sylvia was extremely worried thinking Bad Bell had attempted to run away and was done horrible things by the poor white slave catchers. Sylvia was relieved when Bad Bell returned unharmed and unaware. Sylvia decided to write Bad Bell a pass that would allow her to go anywhere in the county anytime she wanted. She felt that having her stay in the county would assure that she would not run away. Unbeknownst to Sylvia, Clair the only white person in Bad Bells inner family and the only other one besides Baby that could read. Had been writing Bad Bell passes for years.

Clair had incredibly beautiful handwriting considering the condition of Bad Bells hands if that is what they are to be called. She once over heard one of the others stating that. Clair was completely surprised, after all the injury had not happened to her. Dumb nigras. Clair rarely spent anytime talking to them at all. She spent most of her time asleep. Not coming around much. Sometimes when traveling never on a train but sometimes on a boat or carriage rides. She often stood directly behind Doors. Doors was probably the only voice from the amount of voices that thundered next to Clairs brain, that she could stand to listen to. Once in a while Familiar also made sense to her. But Doors was her favorite and the fact that Sylvia Jackson loved Doors also endeared her to Clair.

Sometimes Clair would appear at the times that Doors and Sylvia were at their most intimate. She would never stay long just a few seconds after Doors exploded. Clair enjoyed the peaceful feeling she felt after the explosion of Doors. They were that close. Doors was so much like Clair; assertive aggressive, and a beautiful builder of words. Doors could recite a poem about anything at anytime of the day. Her gift was extraordinary. Doors and Mud were the most gifted poets of the group and made up most of the songs that Bad Bell sang.

They all admitted that Bad Bell had the most beautiful voice. Doors, Peas, Mud and sometimes Skinman also sang. Bad Bell wasn't aware when they sang with her only that her voice was sounding fuller. She didn't even wonder when a completed song arrived in her head. The songs were so beautifully written she assumed God gave them to her. When Clair wrote a song she would only tell it to Doors

Ellen Barton

who would incorporate it into one of her own. Clair did not mind she did not write as often as her friend. She felt what the nigras did to good music was to loud anyway.

Familiar did not know much about Clair. Only that she was an uppity white woman. She was the one that went into the kitchen and got the small cakes. Which made Missus nail them to the steps. Familiar held the most memories. And if she could hold Army, she could give them all her memories and introduce the ones that didn't know each other. Mainly Bad Bell to everyone else. This was something she always refused to do. She felt that if Bad Bell knew the truth she would break. Familiar was one year younger than Bad Bell. Unbeknownst to Bad Bell they had grown up together. Familiar had watched them all grow, while some stopped growing to early and some started growing to late. They ranged in ages from 5 to 35. Some also died but Familiar did not want to think about that. What she thought about was the arrival of Army who became the oldest.

Familiar recalled that Army was always a man, even when she was a child. Familiar stared at Army thinking of the first day he came. Missus nephew and one of his friends caught the little girl and held her down. They ripped off her clothes the child thought she knew what to expect until she saw the big green thing. The biggest tobacco worm ever created. They kept trying to push it. Push it. Bad Bell was screaming and kicking. They were always putting things there. Why. They always wanted to hurt her there. They were laughing, they put the worm to her face. One end was squashed. They wanted to put the other end in her mouth. It was moving. It had horns. Bad Bell screamed in terror. Army arrived; kicked, bit, and punched the boys with a ferocity so intense they allowed the 5 year old to run away. That was the last time Bad Bell felt any real fear. The others divided it up but Mud got most of it.

Bad Bell now lying in bed trying to get some sleep, is hearing her usual humming in the head. While Familiar is having her flashback, Bad Bell catches a glimpse of the memory. She doesn't know but Rose and Spacehead are giving it to her. Rose wants her gone and if Familiar thinks that if Bad Bell had all the memories it would damage her than why not give it a try. Spacehead also feels that it is time. The love between Iron and Rose was the first time the inner family felt love. Having it returned was changing everything. Spacehead knew this why didn't Familiar. It was time. Spacehead thought of the possibility of them sharing all thoughts and all memory. It was time. Spacehead felt Bad Bell deserved some peace in her life. It was time. Spacehead knew that some of the others must be gone. It was time. Spacehead knew that Rose had to be one of the inner family to disappear. Rose shouts

"We ain't ready yet."

Before Bad Bell falls asleep she decides to go and talk to Iron tomorrow. For the first time in her life she feels that she has someone she could trust. Iron is lying in her bed almost reading her bible when Bad Bell walks into her cabin in the early hours of the morning.

"What a beautiful surprise you are."

"Hi Iron."

Bad Bell crawls into bed with Iron fully dressed. Iron kisses her with her mouth closed for she has not used her baking soda as yet and is embarrassed by this. She lays her head on Bad Bells shoulder and cups one of Bad Bells breasts with her hand. Bad Bell is shocked, silent and motionless. She can't believe that her friend the woman she looked upon as a sister is slowly rubbing her breast. She can't believe how peaceful she feels at this moment. She wraps her arms around Iron and understands the word homesick.

"I wish we could lay like this forever."

"I wish we were back in Africa"

"Bell you know about Africa?"

"No."

She laughs.

"Why you say that?"

"I don't know. I do know that in Africa we were free and could do what we please."

"I wish we were free. Bell how come you never told me that you live in such a fine cabin?"

"It's not mine nothing in it belongs to me. I have nothing."

"You have me."

"Iron lately I've been seeing pictures."

"Someone else's pictures?"

"Yes."

"What you see?"

"A little girl."

"That's not so bad."

"A little girl scared, a little girl hurt, a little girl touched in a way I don't think you should touch little girls."
"Are you scared?"
"I don't think so."
"Do you know the little girl?"
"I think she might be me."
"Who hurt the little girl?"
"My ole Missus and the Nephew."
"What they do to her?"
"I've seen the little girl as a baby, just pass crawlin and she is tied up in the Missus big bedroom her mouth is covered. Missus is pushin her fingers in her. I've also seen the girl a little older and Missus is forcing her between her legs and making her lick as if it was candy."
"Are you asleep or awake when you see this?"
"I'm awake."
"Do you remember much when you were a little girl?"
"Not much at all. I've lost a lot of time."
"Where do you think that time go?"
"I don't know one second I could be here and the next second I'm miles away singing at some function. I never know what happened in between."
"I never heard nothing like that before. I wish I could lose time on those nights when Massa come around."
"Iron I've heard that my ole Massa and Missus had done horrible things to me and I have the scars on my body but I don't remember ever feeling pain. Nothing hurts me."
"You never feel pain?"
"Often I have a humming a thumping in my head I got a feeling it spost ta hurt but it don't. The other day I was in the kitchen of the big house. Pauline, Massa Jackson's head cook dropped some hot fat on me by accident. I didn't feel a thing. Everyone made a fuss like it should hurt so I pretended it did. But I felt nothing even as I watched the skin bubble and boil."

Iron has stopped caressing the breast of Bad Bell. While she is listening to the story she has decided to dig her fingernails into the thigh of Bad Bell as hard as she can. Bad Bell has no reaction and continues talking. Iron realizes that Bad Bell is telling the truth.

"What about pleasure? I know you feel pleasure."
"Pleasure?"

Then, There Was Iron

Upon saying this word Bad Bell trembles a bit and gets her lost look.

"Why don't you remind me?"

Rose pushes Irons head down to her favorite place. It didn't take long for Iron to taste all Rose had to offer, her completion was tremendous and shook her body violently.

Mud was watching, not too far away. She was appalled; she felt Rose to be a very filthy girl. So was Doors, and sometimes Army. Their actions with Sylvia and Iron, made Mud feel dirty. She prayed extra hard for these three. The idea of someone touching her, almost made her stomach come up in her mouth. Her skin was crawling; she was getting closer and stronger. Rose was getting weak now, almost asleep. Mud hurried in front of Rose. She jumped off the mattress and ran out the door.

Iron was laying on the mattress in disbelief. Bad Bell had never done that to her before. No good bye, no thank you, and worst of all, where was her turn? Iron did not know what she would do about Bad Bell. Someone else's pictures, losing time, changing eye color. She would try to help her. Help the slave. Be a friend. For a second she thinks about Jasper. She wonders if he made it.

Mud is running, where she doesn't know. Having never made the walk to or from Iron's cabin, she is slightly lost. How could she have been so close to that woman? Iron, what a silly name. Women were just as bad as men with their filthy longings. She remembers the Missus, and the nephew. Pushing, pulling, tasting. She heard the cries, the cries of a little girl. A girl who slept in a trunk with only three little holes for air, at the foot of her Missus bed, from age 1, till she was about 5. She also remembered spending a lot of her days in the trunk, only to be taken out to be rubbed between the Missus legs, or to be beaten. A girl who finally got a cot in the attic, after years of complaints by the Massa, of the moaning at the bottom of the bed. A girl who was happy when the Missus nephew came to live with them, for she had never seen a teenager before; nor a child for that matter. Her old Missus and Massa never had any. The children of the slaves were sold within days of their birth. A girl who was sad when she realized that the nephew of the Missus was a lot like the Missus herself. Though the thing he pushed in her, hurt more than the Missus fingers and was very pink. A girl who was angry, for she was too small and too black to protect herself from the Missus, whom she could satisfy with her mouth, or the nephew, who made use of every orifice in her 7 year old body. A girl who was skilled, for by the age of 12, she could satisfy both her Missus and the nephew at the same time, and have them completed in under 10 minutes. A girl who was lost, and everyday prayed to be saved by her Momma; a face she had never seen. A face that she made up in the back of her head when the pain got too much. A face she created before she was two. A face she was able to call upon anytime. A face that was now familiar.

Mud didn't want these thoughts right now. And where the hell was she? She was starting to walk in circles. Spacehead stepped in front of her. He would take them home. Spacehead filled the spaces between the others while giving them the space needed. He would only take them home, and then he decided to give the body to Doors. He knew that Sylvia wanted to see them today. He would let Bad Bell sleep for sometime. He knew that Skinman gave her some of Mud's memories. He had seen him holding Bad Bell in his arms, while Mud was remembering. As soon as Spacehead entered the cabin, he was gone and Doors was singing a gentle song.

CHAPTER 9

Iron had not heard anything from Bad Bell for days, not since that Sunday when Bad Bell had left her wanting and confused. She had wanted to go again and visit Bad Bell to make sure she was all right, but John had come 4 out of 5 nights this week. She guessed he was making up for the weeks before. She thanked God that his visits were getting shorter and shorter. She thought the 8 to 12 minutes he spent with her was barely worth the walk from the big house, which is probably why he rode his horse.

She remembered how one night Peaches had confided to her that Benjamin gave it to her all night long. She couldn't understand how Peaches enjoyed having a man sweat and grunt on top of her. Though the more she thought about it, the more she realized that Peaches probably couldn't understand the pleasure she shared with Bad Bell. Peaches said that Benjamin could give Massa John lessons any day of the week, especially growing lessons. Then she said maybe white men were better with white women. Iron laughed and said when do they have time for their own women? Peaches laughed harder and said it still wouldn't make it grow.

Iron enjoyed the laughing with Peaches about their sad predicament, though she didn't think she would ever be able to admit to Peaches, what she was doing with Bad Bell. She didn't know why, but having Shelly know, was enough.

It was Saturday night. Six days with no word from Bad Bell. Iron is sitting at her table, fighting to read her bible. Pearl and Gravy walk in.

"Hey girl."

"Hi Mama Pearl, Gravy."

Iron gets up and embraces Pearl.

"Mama, this is the first time you ever come to my cabin, and I must be here about 9 years."

"While Gravy and I out walking and we seen your candle burning. You reading."

Both women were completely secure in the company of Gravy. A slave trying to read is usually kept to oneself. Gravy is honored that neither woman attempts to hide the fact that Iron is trying to read. He

Ellen Barton

decides to tell them a secret he had hid from everyone except his mother, since he was a little boy.

"I can read."

"What?"

"I can read perfectly."

He takes the bible from Iron and reads to them, the creation of the earth. Pearl starts to get nervous.

"Your Massa Dailey know that you can read?"

"No, but it was his sons and nephew who taught me when I was a young boy coming up. I don't never get no chance to read though."

"Well, I sure can use some help with my letters. Maybe when we both get some time, maybe one night a week, you can come round and teach me. I don't never know when I got a free night though."

Gravy lowers his head because he knows the life Iron is living and he feels her shame not knowing what night Massa John would arrive at the cabin.

"Iron, we work something out."

"You two bes be careful."

"Don't worry, Mama Pearl, we be careful."

"Now Iron, you put that bible away."

"Massa give me this here bible, I don't have to hide it."

"Your Massa gave you that bible?"

"Yes. He think that I would never be able to understand it. He don't know me like he think he do."

"Massa John can't be that bad of a man."

"Gravy, you a drinking man."

"No, I don't trust no liquor. Never have."

"That's one of the reasons we here tonight. Shelly is all drunk up in the cabin. Someone gave her some whiskey. Iron, you know where she could have got that?"

"Can I get you some corn bread? Coffee?"

"Thanks Iron, that be mighty fine."

Iron gets up to prepare the snacks. Gravy is walking around the cabin, noticing things. Pearl is staring intensely at Iron, who is avoiding her eyes afraid she will be blamed for Shelly's drunkenness.

"Lord, I haven't been in this cabin for years."

"You been in this cabin before?"

"Long ago when this land was still owned by the father of Massa John. Massa Thomas Cummings, that be his name. He used to have

Then, There Was Iron

poor white trash as his overseers. One named Westley. Westley Calhoun, I think. He used to make corn liquor right here behind this cabin and hide it in the cellar."

"Ain't no cellar in this here cabin."

"It's a hidden cellar Massa Calhoun used to hide most of his corn liquor there. See, if Massa Cummings know about the corn liquor, he would have run him off."

"How did you know?"

"I know, because if you ever seen a slave with a coin to his name, he would often be here."

"Where's the cellar?"

"I was a young boy at the time. The field hands sometimes put their little coins together and send me here to pick them up a jug or two. It was about a half a days walk, and they often didn't have the time to make that walk themselves."

"Where's the cellar?"

"Massa Calhoun had a hidden trap door, right here by the window. It all covered up with dirt now. I'll dig it out for ya. Got a shovel?"

"Out behind the cabin."

Gravy leaves to get the shovel.

"Now girl, why you be interested in having a cellar in your cabin?"

"I just want to see it, that's all."

"Now Iron, you're scaring me, talk of reading and cellars. Girl, I couldn't stand to lose you."

"Don't worry Mama Pearl. You ain't gonna lose me."

Gravy returns and starts digging in the spot where he feels the cellar door is hidden.

"Now Iron, how you gonna explain a hole in this here floor to Massa?"

"Gravy, ya think that Massa know about the cellar?"

"Well, that was before Massa John was born. Westley Calhoun move on a long time before Massa John was around. But I can never be too sure on what a white man know. You just be careful girl."

"I will."

It didn't take long before Gravy had the small door in the floor revealed. It was very dark. Gravy carried down a candle to light the way for Iron and himself. Pearl wouldn't even go down to take a look. The small room was about 10 feet by 10 feet. They did not spend a lot of time looking at it. It seemed to Gravy as soon as Iron seen it, she was anxious to leave it and rushed him back up the rickety stairs.

"Now Miss Iron, what you plan to be hiding down there?"

"Mr. Gravy, I don't got nothing to hide."

Gravy noticed her beauty when she said this; he also noticed that she was lying. When Gravy went back out to return the shovel, Iron feigned tiredness to Pearl, because of her time of the month. She wanted to be alone with her new cellar. She was excited, for now she had a place to hide her friends, if they ever came calling. After Pearl and Gravy departed, Iron immediately began working on evening up her dirt floor. She would have to get a rug.

CHAPTER 10

Doors lay there looking at the sleeping Sylvia Jackson. They were in one of the small farms Sylvia owned but rented out to a sharecropper. The sharecropper and his wife were away for a week visiting family. Sylvia had sent the overseer on some all day errands, than she gave all the slaves the day off. She had no fear that they would run away without an overseer; this lot was a very compliant bunch. She enjoyed seeing the look on their faces when she told them that they could spend the day doing what they please.

She immediately led Bad Bell into the big house, went inside the guest room and locked themselves away for the day. Doors was tired of the hiding, the servitude. Relying on Sylvia for her survival. She couldn't stand being a slave anymore, waiting for a white face to call you and tell you what they wanted. She was Doors. How long did the others expect her to live like this? Pretending to be something she wasn't. She wasn't Bad Bell. Bad Bell was the perfect slave, full of ignorance. She was going to rid the world of Bad Bell. Hell she had created Bad Bell with the help of Familiar, Spacehead and Skinman. Familiar seemed to be the only one who wanted Bad Bell protected. Why, she could not understand. Life was hard for Bad Bell always walking in confusion. Doors was starting to feel sorry for her. It was time. It was time for some serious changes. Sylvia was starting to wake. Doors looked at her and said,

"Let's go to England."

Iron had enough. Who did Bad Bell think she was anyway? It had been months since Bad Bell had run out leaving her alone on the bed. Now she could understand if Bad Bell was away. Reuben had said that he had not heard of any white people parties and she knew the slaves were not having any celebrations this was one of the busiest times in the year. She had made two visits to the Jackson plantation both times she was told that Bad Bell was off with Sylvia Jackson. What Iron did not know was that Doors had the body for two months straight. Bad Bell had ceased to exist and Rose was enveloped by Skinman.

Sylvia and Doors were busy making plans for their trip. Despite warnings from Sylvias brother. He thought that Sylvia was insane taking her prized slave to England. Slavery had been abolished in

England for the last eleven years. Taking a property as valuable as Bad Bell to a free country was simple stupidity. Sylvia didn't care what her brother had to say. Since they started planning for the trip, Bad Bell had been by her side everyday and without her usual extreme moodiness. She had even stopped disappearing. These were the happiest days of Sylvia Jackson's life. For the first time she truly felt that Bad Bell was returning her love. She would allow Bad Bell her freedom. Give her the freedom to live a chosen life of mutual love. Yes they would move to England. Of course the true nature of their relationship would always be hidden. She did not care. What she suddenly cared about was knowing that Bad Bell was with her because she wanted to be not because the law said she must be.

Doors was watching Sylvia pack. The woman had so many things. She found it hard to believe that in six days she would be setting sail to freedom. She had done more for the family than any of the others. She had acquired their freedom. Of course Clair would exclaim that she had always been free. But Clair had not been around in a while. There had been great changes since it was decided to stop presenting Bad Bell to the world. Bad Bell had received memories from Skinman those memories were too hard for her to bare and she folded. Skinman then folded her until she got smaller and smaller so small she couldn't be opened. Oh well. As for Rose the fulfillment of her need for love simply made her not need to be. She was living in Skinman. They were one. Peas and Baby were children; they spent all their time listening to tales made up by Familiar. Tales that made them happy and laugh. All seemed well taken care of. Except Army, he was going to be a problem. She could hear him roaring next to her head. Something about going to see Iron that was the mulatto wench who Rose loved. Love and change everything.

Maybe she would pay a visit to this Iron. If it would keep Army quiet. Why didn't he go back where he came from? Wherever that was. Doors did not think he was related to them at all. He was so full of hate. It was Army that tried to kill Mud's baby. Doors had seen everything. She had seen the rape of Mud by the nephew and his friends, the beating. She had watched Mud throughout the entire pregnancy. Mud hated being pregnant. Hated being alone.

Left to herself all day in a bare cabin not far from slave row. Visited only by the Nephew and his drunken friends. Now that she was a young woman Missus had stopped troubling Bad Bell herself.

Then, There Was Iron

The overseer sometimes made visits. Though all the other slaves never bothered with her. They were afraid of her. At this time in her life Bad Bell was not known as yet for her voice. Doors remembered the day Mud was almost due. The Nephew came in; he forced her head between his legs. Not satisfied with this he beat her with a log from the fireplace. That day he broke her jaw, elbow and left her face swollen for two weeks straight. That night alone she had her baby and passed out. When she woke up someone had come in and washed the baby leaving her some water to drink. It was a girl. Army decided to kill it. He knew what was done to slave women. He was trying to smother the child when Massa Jackson ran into the cabin and stopped him.

Army felt the thought of Doors. What did Doors know about hate? Doors never worked seventeen hours in the fields. Doors never received five hundred lashes to her bareback. Doors was never chased through the swamps. Doors never listened at the window while a white man took your wife. Doors never saw her own heart being ripped out while a white man sold your wife and child. Doors had never hung from a tree until she felt peace. Peace like flying and floating. Peace and full of knowledge of love and forgiveness. Peace and what seemed like being warm forever. Peace and what seems like your less but you're alright. Peace and you can come back in dreams. Peace until one day you are rudely awaken from that dream, someone is calling you. Someone is screaming for you. She needs you She can't take the worm in her. You save her. You're a slave again and you're surrounded by all these voices. He swore if Doors wasn't getting them free he would knock her down forever.

Army needed to say good-bye. This was the only chance he ever had to say good-bye to a woman properly. A woman that opened herself to him. A woman that kept him warm and made him feel like a man. She deserved this. Army thought of other women that had been in his lives. Women that had been ripped away from him by auctioneers. Women that were just gone. One day you return from the fields and your woman was gone. Or having three or four white men hold you down while your woman is dragged away in chains. Yes, he must say good-bye to Iron. He wanted the feelings for Iron that Rose had. Feelings so strong they made her disappear. He wanted to disappear. He wanted to go back to the warm place. The place

Ellen Barton

between the hanging and the worm. He wanted the peace again. Maybe this time he would stay there forever.

Doors felt the thoughts of Army and decided that night to go visit Iron. Let him have his goodbye. It was very late when Doors arrived at Iron's cabin. She found Iron sitting outside in her rocking chair. Doors stands directly in front of the chair.

"To find a face that can hold so much beauty is indeed a rare and pleasurable treat."

Iron stares at the woman. This woman was not Bad Bell. She was tall and beautiful with a look in her eyes like she knew all secrets and a walk that instantly made you feel foolish. Doors was dressed exquisitely, she was wearing one of Sylvias dresses not an old one either. Iron gets up and walks into her cabin. Doors follows.

"Who are you?"

Doors is surprised by the question. For years she had wanted to yell her name from the highest tree. For she was bothered always being mistaken for Bad Bell. This woman was the first that was able to tell them apart. She understood why the family thought so much of Iron.

"My darling, I am Doors and you are much more beautiful than I imagined."

Army hears this and becomes angry. He does not want Iron to know about the family. He does not want to scare her. This is his chance to be a man. To say goodbye to his woman. He does not want Iron knowing how close he lives to other women. How hard he has to push to make it come out when she is lying under him. Army wants to be a man that feels the love of a woman. A love that can be appreciated by him without restrictions. Love between a man and a woman. Not a woman and a family. This was a love that he wanted to control. Needed to control and Doors was ruining everything. He was getting stronger. Damm Doors and her words he jumped in front of her. Iron watched the change. She recognized the tough Bell.

"I had to see you."

"I've missed you so much."

They begin to kiss passionately. Iron prefers the soft Bell. She was a more courteous lover, more passionate and their sessions lasted longer. Nevertheless tough Bell unlike who ever entered the cabin a moment ago was recognizable.

Then, There Was Iron

    Army lifted Iron up and carried her to the bed. He climbed on top of her and began squeezing her breasts while rubbing himself into her. Iron rolls over to reverse their positions. She begins gently lowering herself on Army's body so that her mouth can find its desired destination. Upon reaching it she begins the movements that bring tough Bell to fits of pleasure. She has long ago learnt that these movements are very different than those needed by soft Bell. Armys shakes; twitches and moans soon tell Iron that he is completed.

    Making the slow crawl up Bells body Iron discovers that the eyes of Bell are now sky blue. Iron is terrified. She screams and runs out of the room. She sits on a chair in the kitchen and begins a series of long interrupted breaths. Clair remains lying on the mattress. Wondering what is wrong with this crazy negra? She would only stay a moment she wanted to catch Armys peaceful feeling and this crazy negra is acting as if someone committed a murder. It was all so tiring.

    Familiar had watched the entire scene. Clair had always made problems for the family, right from the start. Familiar decided to take the body. She had only had it a four times before. She enjoyed the warm walls of life within the family plus she was slightly embarrassed by her appearance. Especially the crippled leg.

    Iron watched the woman get off the mattress and limp towards her. This woman was heavier than any one else that was supposed to be Bell. She seemed older and lighter in complexion. She looked the woman deep in the eyes. Thank God they were not blue. Though they were not the eyes of Bell. They were lighter and seemed to belong to a person more knowledgeable and more self-assured than Bell could ever be.

    "Don't be afraid."
    "What?"
    "Don't turn away."
    "What's wrong with you? What are you?"
    Familiar reaches to stroke Irons head. Iron slaps her hand away.
    "You the blue eyed devil."
    "No we are not. We would never hurt you Iron. We love you."
    "Your eyes. Your eyes were the color of the evil ones."
    "We are not evil. We created each other out of need, out of pain to live. Iron you have changed everything with us. You have broken walls forever and we will never be the same. Iron we want to thank

Ellen Barton

you. For loving us, for wanting us, for not hurting us. You opened us."

"Your talking mixed up. How many are you?"

Army is listening he will not let Familiar answer the question. Iron must see him as a man. A normal man that can give and receive love at his own choosing. He rushes in front of Familiar. He must say good-bye. He believes his proper good-bye will be a good-bye forever. Maybe like Rose if he achieves some control he could disappear. Go back to the place between the hanging and the worm. Let Doors have her own way forever. He wanted to be gone.

He is settled in front of Familiar. Which is not easy for she is very strong. He senses that she has allowed him to make the move. Possibly she also understands what he must do to be gone forever. Bad Bell did not exist the family was becoming smaller. It was time. He was not needed anymore.

"Girl it's only me, your man. Iron you did things for me that no one has ever done. You made me feel strong and in control. You made me feel like no one could ever take anything from me. You made me feel free. Now I gots to go. I done did what I came here for. I think the Lord is ready for me to move on. I will never forget you Iron cuz you freed me."

He holds Iron and trembles. Doors gathers her clothes and walks out the door. Iron remains sitting on the chair staring blankly into space with her mouth open. While the words, "your man" repeats in her head.

Then, There Was Iron

CHAPTER 11

It was her 32nd birthday. Iron was sitting at her table cold and wet. Her heart was beating rapidly. Her blood was rushing like it usually did after passengers left her station. These three were different. Different to her; a woman, her young daughter and her old mother. They had been riding the railroad for weeks, each day closer to freedom brought its weight in terror. A load so heavy it was now holding the woman down. She needed kicking. An expression Iron used when some of her passengers wanted to give up.

Iron herself led the trio about ten miles on their way to the next station. In the three years since she was working the railroad, she had never done this. She knew that it was very dangerous. More dangerous than harboring them in your cellar. Leading the trio in the rain she thought of the woman all the slaves and Miss Clara often talked about.

A little woman the people called Moses. This woman had escaped slavery went to the land of freedom but kept coming back to free more people. When Miss Clara first talked of the woman the words that kept replaying in Irons head were, she came back. Who after tasting freedom could come back to a land of slavery? Miss Clara had said that the cause was greater than ones life which was the probably the reason Iron never rode on the railroad in which she worked. Iron had to agree. She loved to listen to Miss Clara talk it was hard to believe she was Johns sister.

She wouldn't tell Miss Clara that she had led the women tonight. She knew Miss Clara would think it to dangerous. For a moment she felt like the little woman they called Moses. As her passengers looked to her for guidance. It was a powerful feeling.

Though one she did not want to experience again. Iron realized she had not the brains or the courage to be another Moses. While she sat at the table, sipping her whiskey. She decided to stick to her role on the railroad, and let others stick with theirs. She figured God puts us where he needs us.

Iron got up and undressed. She took a quick sponge bath with the hot water she was heating and crawled into bed. Before she slept she said a small prayer for Miss Tubman and whomever she was freeing tonight. She also said a prayer for her tiny group. She then thanked

Ellen Barton

God for sending people committed to freeing the slaves. She soon slept. She did not know it was her birthday.

That night Iron dreamt of Mama Pearl. She told Iron to stay strong and keep up the work she was doing. A day did not go by when Iron did not think about Mama Pearl and thanked God the woman now tasted freedom. Iron would never forget the look in Mama Pearls eyes, the day when Miss Mary pinned her lip to the top of her dress. Mama Pearl spent the entire day in that condition. Punishment for being too big and too slow. When Gravy made his nightly walk to her cabin his heart broke. When he saw what was done to Pearl.

Gravy immediately ran to Irons cabin to tell about Pearl. The two had grown close now that Gravy was giving her midnight reading lessons. He kept pacing the floor repeating over and over how he had to do something. When he left Iron went to tend Mama Pearl. Who said that it didn't hurt much. These words hurt Iron more than watching the swelling and the blistering on the mouth of the only person who was a mother to her. Mama Pearl did not want any fussing around her and told Iron to go back to her cabin for she would be fine. Iron did what she was told hoping Gravy would not create any danger for himself.

Days later Miss Clara arrived on the plantation. John Cummings loved his sister and was worried about her. Miss Clara was over 40 years old and still without a husband. John did everything in his power to play matchmaker, but Miss Clara was hard to please. Today she had good news for her brother. She had found a man in which she hoped to spend her life with. The man whose name was George Coleman was a recent widower from Florida. His family was not nearly as wealthy as the Cummings but he was a smart hardworking man. Clara claimed that she was tired of the dressmaking. She now wanted to plant crops. She did have plenty of land that was going to waste. For she could not claim parts of her fathers estate until she married. Her only problem George did not have tobacco experience. He needed a good tobacco man for his first crops. She then offered $4000.00 for Gravy and Pearl. John having absorbed everything Gravy knew about tobacco agreed to the sale, only upon meeting Mr. George Coleman.

Twelve days later the vagabond known as George Coleman was paid $100.00 for convincing John Cummings of his intentions in marrying Clara. Gravy and Pearl were given their free papers by Miss

Clara. They jumped the broom. Took on the new last name of Freeman (neither wanting the name of their masters past or present) and headed for Philadelphia. It broke Pearls heart to leave Iron, but Iron begged her to go. She wanted Pearls freedom more than she wanted her own.

That all happened about four summers ago. Not long after Bell left. She says Bells name smiles and rubs her hands through her wool. She wonders what Mama Pearl is doing exactly at this moment. She doesn't want to wonder about Bell. She feels it might make her angry. Free women. How do free women spend their time? One day she would know. She knew in her heart that one day she would be amongst those free women, with free time. Gravy and Pearl knew this also. Last summer Gravy sent Clara enough money to buy Irons freedom. John informed his sister he would never sell. Still brewing from the freedom given Gravy. John had never quite accepted the alibi that it was a spontaneous foolish act done because of a broken heart.

Other prominent South Carolinians did not accept this excuse either. Clara Cummings was too strong and independent a woman for such behavior. After the event Clara was watched more closely. By whites and blacks, especially by Iron. Who couldn't but remember Jasper. Looking for a friend. Looking for a white lady who was also a friend.

Clara Cummings was the only white woman Iron knew that controlled her own house. Clara Cummings was also the only slave owner Iron knew that never ever whipped any of her small group of slaves. Iron decided to spend more time on Clara's place. She knew Violet who was the house maid quite well maybe she could tell her more about Miss Clara Cummings.

As it turned out Iron did not need the assistance of Violet at all. Miss Clara enjoyed the almost daily visits of Iron and the two became fast friends, to Irons surprise. This was the first white person she did not hate. This was the first white person she was not disgusted by. This was the first white person she did not want to see fall in a giant hole that opened up in the earth so that Satan could open his arms and claim his own. This woman made Iron smile and smiled back at her. A smile that you could trust, a smile that understood. Iron truly liked Miss Clara and missed her when they were apart. She could listen to Miss Clara talk for hours for she was the smartest person Iron had ever met. Except maybe for Gravy. But Miss Clara seemed to know what was going to happen before it happened and more importantly she knew right from wrong.

Iron would never forget that night. Pearl and Gravy were gone almost 2 summers. It was so cold, only weeks before Christmas. Iron was sleeping when she heard the frantic banging on the door. It was Miss Clara herself her pig man Pierce, her personal maid Adele and group of the rattiest looking Negroes Iron had ever seen. Miss Clara was sharp and quick, she told Iron to quickly hide this group in her cellar for she felt her home was about to be raided. She left instantly saying she would send further instruction tomorrow.

Clara Cummings home was never searched. Iron was never certain if the threat was real. Or if it was Clara's way of starting Iron on the railroad. For after they're many afternoon conversations. Clara Cummings knew this is where Iron belonged. She also knew that Iron had a cellar. She also knew that Iron was given a lot of liberties not enjoyed by other slaves. Such as her time was not closely monitored and she had the courage to put that time to good use. Iron had the look. Miss Clara had not seen it often though when she did she knew that person could be trusted. All her slaves had it. She looked long and hard for her small group. Most had been with her for decades. A group so trustworthy and so discreet that they were not slaves at all. They were paid a small wage and all worked on the railroad. She had also seen this look in Gravy whom she would always consider a dear friend.

Miss Clara's heart went out that night Gravy showed up angrier than she had ever seen him. He was ready, he wanted a ticket on the railroad and he wanted Pearl to go with him. The more he talked with Clara about it. The more he realized Pearl was not the kind of woman to run away. Her fears ran to deep. Also a second fugitive slave law had just passed. Gravy would not live his life running. He would not start a new life with Pearl looking over his shoulder.

Gravy in his 51 years managed to save $3874.93, which Clara found to be an astronomical sum for a slave. But not for Gravy who was the hardest working and smartest man she knew. Gravy was also lucky to have a good master for most of his life that allowed him to keep all the money he earned on the off season. John Cummings wasn't quite the man Edmond Dailey was and took 50% of Gravy's earnings when he wasn't working on the Cummings plantation. John felt that he was treating Gravy with special care. For he took 100% of the earnings of his other slaves.

Gravy was saving one day to buy his own freedom. Because of John's greed it would take him longer than he had planed. He had hoped one day to offer John Cummings $4000.00 for himself and $500.00 for his first love Pearl. The twisted mind of Miss Mary had speeded up the plan. For late that night John and Miss Clara planned how to achieve his freedom along with Pearls legally and without hassle. To the marvel of all, the plan succeeded easily without a hitch.

Seemed like yesterday thought Iron as she made her way to her garden. Irons garden was now 50 times its original size. John had to clear land for its expansion. Iron was now required to supply food for about 1/3 of the slaves. A lot, which had also increased dramatically in size. The older slaves now came to Irons garden to help with its care. This made both John and the older slaves feel as though they were being useful. Expanding her garden and having the elderly tend it were both suggestions Iron had brought to John in which he granted.

John had also wanted to get more use out of Iron. Not visiting her so often anymore. His visits were down to once a month. If that. He now had a whole new set of cabins in the woods. Full of fresh young treats. Iron, Peaches, Doll and Lizzie were seldom troubled. Peaches, Doll and Lizzie were also required to work in the garden. Doll never ever showed up for work. Peaches and Lizzie came by a few days a week but mostly for conversation. John never checked on the work and they had no overseer watching. So they mostly talked about big strong black men. They were slaves of leisure. Though they now often irritated Iron, she loved them.

Iron picked up her hoe and began to work the earth. Last nights showers did the ground good.

"Mawnin Iron."

"Mawnin Miss Lydia. How ya feelin this fine day?"

"Child you always so happy. Someone should tell ya youse a slave."

Iron laughs and says her good morning to the others. She enjoyed looking in the faces of the old slaves. Each face had its own lines of pain. Each face had its own heartbreaking story. She heard them. Many times, from her passengers. She's heard suffering. These faces were different these faces were tired but relieved. Relieved to finally be away from the overseers whip. Relieved to know that the worst was over and all they had to do now was wait to finally meet Jesus. These faces were to tired to cry to old to care.

"Miss Lydia why don't you rest up in my cabin. I know how that rain always bring ya aches and pains."

"Ise alright child. I had the pains last night. Ise used ta workin. I can do my day. Child this ain't nothing. Now down in Georgia you should see whats I can do. I works harder than any of the mens. Right long side dem. Clearing trees. Sun up til sun down. Clearing trees. Youse wouldn't know it to look at me now. But I was a big strapping thing. Works all day sun up til sun down."

Miss Lydia is still repeating sun up till sun down as Iron walks away. She sees Peaches coming out of her cabin.

"Woman what is you doing in my cabin?"

"Sorry girl I thought that I just got my business and I need to take a look. Since when you get so private? You know I ain't stealing from ya."

'I just surprised to see ya that's all."

"Humph its not like ya ever have no man there early in the morning."

"You don't worry bout what I got where. What you doing out this early anyway?"

"Massa sleeping in my cabin."

"Massa sleeping in your cabin?"

"I don't know what kind of feelings he gonna have when he wakes up. So I gots on outta there."

"Lord I never know Massa to sleep til morning"

"He mighty whiskeyed up when he come over last night. Girl I was surprised Massa ain't come to by cabin in months. I thought he forgot he owned me. I was happy for it. Last night I heard that awful singing in the rain. I thought well time to earn my keep. I tell ya I turned my head and it was over. Then he fell asleep and he's still asleep."

"Well ya bes get a hoe cuz he might be around. Lord I sho hope he don't start sleeping in my cabin. This sho gonna set Miss Mary off."

"Off she ain't ever been on. Girl you hear about the school in the woods."

"Hear they took all day to kill that boy."

"Skinned him. Skin that boy for taking his brothers in the woods and teaching them to read. I tell ya that school been running a long time. I don't know who gave them up. But they should have terrible grief for the rest of their days. Ya can't do anything like that and have any kind of luck."

"What about white folks. Look at all they do and they still have luck."

"White folks are different. Us black folks we got to stick together. Not betray each other."

"That's the truth."

"Seem like now a days more Negroes trying to read than ever. Once we all know how to read there will be no stopping us. Everybody be writing their own passes."

"Peaches if every slave knew how to read we wouldn't need no pass."

"I like to see it when slaves don't need no pass to go places."

"The day we all know how to read be the day we free."

"Girl you think reading mean that much?"

"If it don't mean that much why don't the white man want us t do it?"

"Girl the white man look at you and know your black. He don't know if you can read or not. You a slave cuz you a Negro not cuz you can't read."

"Say what you want I know reading is the ticket."

"Ticket? Ha so now you workin on the railroad."

Iron laughs.

"Come on girl lets go in the cabin. I want to make coffee for everyone."

"I thought you don't drink coffee anymore."

"I don't but I want to make some for the folks. The rain last night gives a lot of them the aches and pains. I want to put something hot in them."

"How you get such a big heart anyway? Always helping always giving always thinking about others. You must want your name in the new bible."

"They writing a new bible?"

"Yeah but they trying t keep it quiet."

"Well who is gonna write it, white folks?"

"Be no white folks writing the new bible. God only wants the truth in there. And not the kind that changes everyday."

"So I guess black folks be writing it?"

"Guess so."

"See I told ya we all have to read or else how else could we write."

"Girl you always gotta be right."

Peaches chases her into the cabin.

Peaches spent all of the day with Iron and a small part of the night. As Iron prepared supper for the two of them. She postponed visiting Miss Clara until tomorrow. She needed her new schedule. She desperately wanted information on her last three. Though she knew it was to soon. They had walked all the way from Alabama. She didn't quite know where that was but she knew it was far. Imagine walking from Alabama to Canada covered in fear. She didn't quite know how far was Canada but it was more north than North. Iron didn't feel she had that kind of courage. The courage to run. Maybe if she lead the life of some of her passengers her courage would be greater. Maybe if she was beaten and starved, watched her loved ones sold away or worse watch them not sold but treated worse than a dog, watched your wife or daughter taken by a white man, watched your mother and father beaten by a white man. Maybe then your courage grows. How long does it take before you realize you are more than this and you do whatever it takes to prove it to yourself. Iron had no idea what Peaches was saying. She was lost. Lost in the footsteps of a runaway slave. She saw Shelly enter the cabin.

"What you doing here? Shouldn't you be preparing food for your man? Ya must just got out the field."

"I ain't preparing no food for that man tonight. He talking too much in my head. I needs a taste."

"Iron you got a taste?"

"Girl you know I got some whiskey. If I didn't keep a jug I never see Shelly. Peaches you know where I keep it. Shelly you hungry?"

"Girl I'm always hungry even when I'm asleep but especially right after I eat."

Iron laughs

"What that man going on about tonight?" Lord ya think he be happy Massa brought him from Massa Shakes. The whip be flying all day everyday on the Shakes place."

Then, There Was Iron

"Girl you should see his back it pains my heart every time. Lord I never think I jump the broom now I got me a mouth running man."

"Stop it Shelly, Paddy a good man. Last harvest when you jumped the broom was the happiest you ever been n your life. You know that."

"Paddy a good slave. He worse than white folks always telling me what I shouldn't do in case white folks catch me. Lord I had to get out of that cabin tonight. What you cookin Iron?"

"Fried chicken, taters, greens, corn, some biscuits"

"It's always a feast in this here cabin. Girl you living good."

"Funny slave woman eat everyday and its called good. I won't be happy until all my brothers and sisters are living good."

"I hear that."

"Amen."

The three women sit around the table to eat.

"Lord remember Mama Pearl's fried chicken?"

"Shelly you said Mama Pearl's name at the right time. We better bless this food."

Iron says a small prayer over the food and the women begin to eat.

"Shelly you didn't say what Paddy is going on about."

"Peaches maybe she don't want to say."

"Its alright. He's going on about that school in the woods."

"What about it?"

"I wanted us t go. I want to learn to read and I want Paddy to read to."

"Peaches and I was talking about that today. More Negroes want to read than ever."

"That's cuz they know it's coming"

"What coming?"

"Freedom coming and we gots t be ready."

"How you know freedom coming?"

"Cuz the times are changing. You hear more talk about those bolitionists."

"Abolitionists."

"Than ever before. Slavery is wrong. And God ain't putting up with it for much longer."

"Girl, you sound like Paddy's brother. What's dat man's name?"

"Alonzo."

81

"That's another sad story. Lord, I sho that they were gonna kill that man when they brought him back. How long was he gone?"

"He was gone two years. Two years in the land of freedom. He told me bout all the places he seen, and all the things he done. He tell me he saw a great big black man talking at one of those abolitionist meetings. Man name Fredrick Douglas. Talk just like white folks, but with a strong deep voice. Say this man actually got words that could put feelings in white people. Now I hear this man writes books bout slavery and I wants to read em."

"Now how you gonna get a book written by a black man around here?"

"First I learns to read, then I gets the book."

Iron, not comfortable with the keeping of the secret that she can read, from her closest friends, changes the subject back to Alonzo, although she knows plenty about him.

"That Alonzo, he ain't never been right since they brought him back."

"That damn figi slave law."

"Fugitive slave law."

"Yeh, that damn fugitive slave law. A man makes it all the way and sees freedom, and they drag him back. He alright though, he ain't off. They beat him for days, thought him dead for sho. But he alright now."

"You think he ever try running again?'

"No, they crippled him up a bit, but his head is alright. Anyways, he said with all those abolitionist working up Nawth, we just got to sit back and wait."

"Wait for freedom."

"Like your Mammy, and her Mammy, and her Mammy."

"Maybe we won't see freedom. Maybe we be dead by then."

"No Peaches, we will see it. It's in the air."

"Girl, I can smell it."

"What you smelling is whiskey. That cup ain't never far from your nose."

"Peaches, you leave Shelly alone, she knows what she's talking about."

"Iron, how you know Shelly right?"

"She got to be."

Then, There Was Iron

The three women debated on into the night. Iron did not allow them to stay late. She knew that Shelly had to get up early for the fields. There were a few occasions before Shelly jumped the broom, in which too much whiskey caused her to sleep past the horn, resulting in fifty lashes. Somehow Iron felt that those lashes hurt her more than they hurt Shelly. Now she always stressed that Shelly got to bed on time.

After the women left, Iron took out her bible and read Revelations. She had read it over and over, and could never understand it. She was dedicated in reading it until she understood every single word. She figured this might take a long time. But the bible being the only book she owned, she figured she had the time. She didn't feel that she needed to read a book written by a runaway slave. She had seen hundreds, and heard all their stories. One more may not make a difference. But to be able to put feelings in white people, that was something special. Let them read his books. They needed it more.

Iron was perplexed over if she should admit to Shelly that she could read and possibly give her reading lessons. She had never told those two of Bad Bell's or Gravy's secret reading lessons. Bad Bell because of what she did with Bad Bell, and Gravy, because Gravy did not want anyone knowing he could read. Could she trust these women? Her sisters? She feared her knowledge of letters would somehow reveal her work on the railroad. Secrecy is what made the railroad function with success. Maybe she would tell Shelly she could read, not Peaches. Peaches talked to everybody about everything. When people wanted information they came to see Peaches and believed every word she said. Peaches was a more reliable source to black people, than the newspaper was to white people. Iron knew that Peaches loved her and would do anything to protect her. She also knew that Peaches couldn't stop her mouth from working. This was her role, information handler. It was beyond her control. Iron would tell Shelly that this would have to be between them. Shelly may not want to tell Paddy anyway. Watching you're brother near whipped to death would make anyone walk carefully. Iron laid on her mattress with her bible in her hands. She wondered if Shelly noticed that she was the only one drinking. Iron drifted into sleep.

The next day it rained all morning and no one came to work on the garden. Iron was happy. She knew the joy brought to an old field hand not having to get up in the rain, having worked through so many wet days all their lives. Iron thought to walk to slave row, and have a talk with Reuben.

Reuben did not do much fiddling' anymore since Massa John purchased young Winston. Reuben and Winston had often played together until Reuben admitted the boy was more gifted than he was and started spending every day with John's cowmen. Reuben became an expert cowman and did everything from help with the births, to killing and cutting up. He said he was tired of watching white people try to dance and found cows to be better company. He said, unlike the white man, you could turn your back on them. Iron found Reuben in his cabin.

"Howdy, little sister. I sho love to see a beautiful woman in the morning."

"Why don't you get one of you own?"

"I don't want no slave woman, and no free woman want me."

"Sound like you can't win for losing."

"I gots you though."

Reuben grabs Iron and starts rubbing his knuckles on the top of her head. Iron screams and pulls away."

"How come you ain't at the barn?"

"Oh, I got nothing to do there until later on today. I got a nice piece of beef here though, you can have."

"Reuben, I'm always okay for food, why don't you give it to someone else?"

"I just might. So what's on your mind today? I know you a thinking woman, always got something to say."

"Reuben, you ever hear of Fredrick Douglas?"

"Heard of him sometime back. They say he's a thinking man. Like you."

"How you hear about him?"

"When I was still traveling, a few Negro's that been up North say he's a powerful man with words; just as strong as his fist. He's an abolitionist. Why you asking about Fredrick Douglas?"

"I just heard that he wrote a book is all. Runaway slaves, about slavery."

"Oh, so you want to read about slavery. I guess you feel that you don't know much about it."

Then, There Was Iron

"You a funny man Reuben. I just would like to know if he tells the truth about what is being done to us. I was thinking maybe some powerful people don't really know how bad slavery is, maybe if they knew, things would change."

"Girl, you don't remember all the fuss about Uncle Tom's cabin?"

"Who is Uncle Tom? Where does he live?"

"Uncle Tom's cabin is a book that came out a couple of summers ago, written by a white woman. I hear that book told all the truth about slavery. See girl, you right. Some white folks up North really didn't know how bad things were, and once they read that book they started making all kinds of noise. It be easier to find a field hand with a white wife, than to get a copy of that book down here. I don't go for it myself though."

"Go for what?"

"Slaves getting free and writing their own story. Fredrick Douglas ain't the only one. Men and women escaped to tell about it."

"Why don't you go for it?"

"Cuz, all the word and all the books will never tell you what it's like to have the skin rip from your back. And there ain't no words to tell about a woman who came in from the fields to find her children sold, and know she won't ever be able to see them again. You tell me the word I can use to tell about a man being held down while other men ripped the clothes off his wife and beat her nearly to death. I don't want to read about slavery, I live it. Me, I wants to know about freedom."

Iron knew a lot more than she was admitting to Reuben. She knew that many a runaway slave had told their stories. She knew that up North a man had started a newspaper dedicated to freedom. He was a white man named Garrison and he had started that paper when Iron was still a little girl. What she wanted from Reuben was if he knew the names of these runaways turned writers. Iron was hoping that maybe they were one of hers.

"Reuben, do you know the names of any of these runaways that write books?"

"Well, I sho heard more all my days while traveling. I used to know all the goings on. Now things different."

"Reuben, people still come to you. You know more people than anyone on this here plantation."

"Now that ain't true. Peaches the queen."

"Yeah Peaches may be the queen, but you know all the real important talk. You sure you don't remember any names?"

"Well, I heard the name Bibbs floating around, and another fellow called Wells Brown. Girl, I used to know more, but those two I remember from not too far back. Tell me you thinking about going down to the store and asking for copies of those fine books."

"I just like to know that my sisters and brothers are doing something for us, after they make it to the land of freedom. They remembering us who are still here, and they trying to bring us all to that land."

"Girl, you know we ain't gonna give up. We won't stop till we all free."

"You think that day coming soon Reuben?"

"I hope so."

"Shelly say she can smell it in the air."

"Shelly drink to much whiskey to smell anything."

"Stop it now, Shelly a good woman."

"Good and drunk."

"Reuben, you ever work in the field?"

"No."

"I think Shelly need that whiskey. Lord knows we all need something."

"That something don't have to be drunkenness."

"Reuben, look at our choices. Anyway, Shelly don't drink so much now that she's got Paddy."

"Yeah, that's the truth. Though last night I heard a lot of yelling from that cabin. Shelly too much woman for Paddy.

"I just hope the Lord choose to keep them safe and together. Don't know what would happen to that girl if they get separated."

"I don't even want that in my head. Massa John been real good about not selling slaves. Real good."

"Praise the Lord. I heard he's gonna buy a whole bunch more. Buying more land too."

"That's good. Slaves are safe here."

"How you mean safe?"

"Not a lot of whipping here. Not as bad as other plantations."

"That's the truth."

"Slaves also eat everyday here."

Then, There Was Iron

"Look at Paddy. Man near twice the man he was when he came. Massa Shakes have his slaves nothing but skin and bones. When Judgment Day comes I don't want to stand close to him, case what God plan for him, spill on me. Iron let me ask you, you talk to anybody bout these slave books?"

"Just Shelly, Paddy's brother Alonzo tole her about them; she ask me if I know anything."

"Girl, I know you smart enough not to tell people that you can read. You the only person in my whole life I told I know some letters, and that's how I like to keep it."

"Reuben, I ain't never been whipped and I don't want to try it now."

"You ain't never been whipped?"

"I had a few lashes when I was in the field, but never a real whipping."

"Girl, you better thank the Lord for that blessing everyday. You may be the only slave in the South that can say that."

Iron spent the day with Reuben. Sometimes she forgot how much she enjoyed his company. Always had. On her way home she stopped by the cabin of Shelly and Paddy. The two seemed to have made up fine. Shelly insisted that she stayed to eat with them. Iron did not really want to but it seemed as though it would insult her friend if she said no. Iron knew that she had so much more than Shelly. Shelly knew this too. In all the years that Iron had known Shelly, this was the first time she ate a meal that Shelly had prepared. She prayed to God that it would also be her last. For surprisingly, Shelly was a terrible cook. The look in Paddy's eyes said you got to be real hungry, to eat this mess.

Iron truly liked Paddy. Paddy wasn't a big man. He was half the size as some of them bucks. He was also a very nervous Negro. Most of the slaves on the Shakes plantation were. Beatings and starvation could change you like that. Other slaves would get edgy when they seen him coming, for he was always trying to keep the slaves in line. He was always trying to talk them out of something. He would never tell a secret to a white man, though he would beg you to follow the white man's rules. Some thought him weak. He was just a man, tired of seeing his people whipped. The sound of the whip would bring tears to his eyes and make him hide, or curl up like a baby.

Ellen Barton

Some said that it was because when he was a little boy, he watched the first Massa Shakes cut off his mother's ear, and force her to eat it. If she ate it all, still is unknown. Some say it was because the second Massa Shakes beat Paddy everyday for two years, until the Fugitive slave law brought back Paddy's runaway brother. Some say it was because he was held down while that same brother was nearly beaten to death. Anyway, Negro's close their mouths, put their heads down and look the other way when they see him coming, for no one wanted a long sermon from Paddy Shakes entitled "You better listen to your Massa, it ain't worth it." His stutter made the speech all the less enjoyable.

Iron felt almost sorry for Paddy, falling in love with a woman like Shelly. She thought if Paddy could choose whom he loved, his heart would have gone to another woman. One that didn't push him, yell, drink whiskey, or had dreams of the future. Iron knew that you couldn't control your heart. If she could, she surely would choose one of them bucks or hands that often showed her notice. But, she liked women; she could not help it. More than that, she wanted one to like her back, though she hardly thought about that anymore.

Paddy was very excited, for he had gotten Shelly and himself out of the field for a few weeks. Having carpentry experience, Massa John needed him to build a few more cabins, for he was planning to increase his stock. Paddy had asked if Shelly could assist him and Massa John agreed, knowing that Shelly had the strength of a man. John had also said that Paddy and Shelly could pick any one of the new cabins if they wanted to move. They both did. Paddy kept repeating, "that Massa John, a good man." Maybe he was comparing him to Massa Shakes, thought Iron. John Cummings gave a little more food, and a few less whippings compared to other Massa's, but he sold his own children into slavery and forced his dirty ways on creatures he considered animals. She guessed he was good for a Massa that being as good as it gets.

Paddy and Shelly were exchanging looks that said they were happy, they were lucky, and they were in love. Iron left them to celebrate alone. Slave couples don't get many moments like that. She was happy just to witness a little of the emotion. It gave her a feeling of hope. As she walked back to her cabin, she found herself humming a song Mama Pearl used to sing to her when she was a little girl. She looked at the stars and screamed, "Hi Mama." Free Mama. She

Then, There Was Iron

thought of Bell. She wanted to be touched. She needed to be touched. God, how she hated Bell, for not being with her. For giving her things to remember. For making her see how life could be. How could one be happy just lying in each other's arms? She started running before her brain relived the explosions.

The next morning was Sunday, and nobody was coming to work in the garden. Iron decided to make the walk to Miss Clara's house. The walk would take 2 ½ hours, so Iron ate a hearty breakfast and went on her way. She stuck to the woods, not wanting to run into any white folks. Since John's visits became infrequent, Iron had become nervous about not traveling with a pass. She thought about asking him to write one for all occasions, but hadn't done this yet.

Iron had an image of Lenox, one of her first passengers. Lenox was a hard worker and had managed to save enough money to buy his freedom. When he approached his Massa, urprisingly his Massa had agreed and gave him a reasonable price. His Massa took the money, and sent him on his way with a paper that read, "this nigger can't read." Then the man hired some Negro catchers and claimed the man a runaway. Lenox had been free two days before the dogs were upon him. He was taken back to his master and severely punished. None of the whites that were beating him, believed or cared about his story. Lenox was beaten so badly it took him an entire season to partially heal. After that incident, he took a ride on the railroad. Iron hoped that he was seeing freedom this minute. She hoped that he would learn to read.

Sitting down having a tea with Miss Clara, Iron asked about Fredrick Douglas.

"Great man. I had the pleasure of hearing him speak, about 10 years ago, in my travels up North. Why do you ask?"

"I heard he wrote a book."

"Well, I think he just had his second book published. Such novels are hard to find in the South. However, many written works of slaves can be found in the North and abroad. The narratives of runaways for decades have made great contributions to our cause."

"Have you read these slave books?"

"In the North years ago, I read the Liberator. I would not have these things here. If anyone happened to see them, so much would be lost. Maybe one day I will write my own memoirs."

"Truly Miss Clara?"

"No. My place shall be forgotten, and my reward silence. My role is a dedication for righteousness. I do not expect to be remembered by name. Just one of the many doing God's work."

"The lives you changed Miss Clara, I think you'll be remembered by name."

"Child, I never use my real name."

Iron spent the afternoon with Miss Clara and left just before dinner. Miss Clara was having company for dinner and a Negress sipping tea in her parlor was hard to explain. Miss Clara actually never said these words to Iron and it truly pained her that she lived in a world in which such words were necessary. Miss Clara hated the South, but made a decision never to leave it. She was needed here more than she could ever be needed anywhere else. Iron had seen all this in her eyes, and then said she had to be going.

On the long walk home, Iron relived her afternoon chat with Miss Clara. Though she truly cared for Miss Clara, she still found it strange talking comfortably to a white person. She wondered if it would always be like that, or if it mattered. She long since gave up waiting for Miss Clara to change on her, the way white people often do. God, she trusted a white person. How could she? Why was Miss Clara so different? The Quakers, and the white abolitionists? Why did they have to make it so hard? She wanted to despise white people with every pound of her body, but she could not. Yes, we were capable of liking one or two. But, all of them? Their stiff bodies, their underdeveloped men, their ugly babies, and their foolish beliefs that blacks thought as much of them as they thought of themselves. Could blacks ever truly care about all white people as a group? Probably not, but what did it matter for though she cared and wanted to help every single slave, she knew she would be lying if she said she liked everyone she ever met. So many were completely ignorant, the kind of stupid that an education couldn't help. Hating all whites and loving all blacks, she thought it foolish and impossible.

CHAPTER 12

Christmas time was upon them once again. Iron's greatest gift was a beautiful handkerchief sent by Gravy and Pearl Freeman. She loved saying their names. It also came with a letter written by Gravy saying both were doing fine. Gravy had gone into lumber. The letter was sent through the postmaster to Miss Clara's house. Pearl was doing work at the black orphanage, though she wasn't getting paid. After Miss Clara explained to Iron what an orphan was, she realized that she was one also, so were most of the slaves she knew, even her own children. It was a sad thought but Iron realized Mama Pearl was just that to every orphan. A smile crossed her lips to know that more children will grow up loving her Mama Pearl.

Gravy and Pearl were still suggesting ways to get Iron out of slavery, neither knowing of her work on the railroad. They did not realize that she felt she must stay where she was, even if they did come up with an accomplishable plan. Knowing that no one could ever hurt Mama Pearl again, gave Iron a light inside the kind that never goes out. Iron's moment of joy, was interrupted by Peaches bursting into her cabin.

"Girl, they here!"

"Whose here?"

"The new hands. You ain't notice that this place has been all stirred up cuz Massa got new slaves coming?"

"Yes, I did know that. I just didn't think they be here until after Christmas."

"Well they here now. I think there is about hundred of them."

"Hundred new slaves, girl that's a lot. Massa John be much bigger than the Smith plantation now. Can't be that much? What they all gonna do?"

"Well you know Massa just bought a lot more land."

"I didn't know."

"Yeah, he tole me. Came to see me three nights last week, all we did was talk."

"Massa John came to you just to talk?"

"Yeah, he say Peaches you an old girl. We been together a long time. I can always count on you to make sense. He was asking what I thought about tobacco prices, and cotton prices over there in England. I say Massa; I don't know nothing about that. Then he laugh."

"Was he drunk?"

"As Shelly on a Saturday night."

"Girl, don't talk like that."

"I just mean Massa acting funny. He come to see you?"

"Not in months, thank the good Lord."

"If I was you, I be spectin a visit pretty soon. Now come girl, let's go see the new stock."

"They got chains on?"

"Some of em, not all."

"I don't want to see no Negro's in chains."

"Now girl, don't be getting uppity. We slaves. Sometimes we be in chains. I think you should have been born free."

"I was. We all were."

"Girl, please don't start that preaching about slavery today. I want to go see if there are any fine bucks."

"Fine bucks? What about Benjamin? You two have been all over each other, as long as I can remember. Now you want to see fine bucks."

"Girl, you can eat chicken everyday of your life, sometimes you need a piece of beef."

"I don't want to hear this. Benjamin a good man."

"Well, he ain't ever asked me to jump the broom."

"How he gonna ask you to jump the broom? He knows what we do here. We ain't no housemaids, cooks, or field hands. We in these here cabins for one reason, and Benjamin knows what it is. Peaches, don't do that to him."

"Benjamin always the same everyday. Drink two glasses of whiskey, then he all over me. Once a week we go on a picnic. Girl, I need something new, before I gets to old."

"How old are you Peaches? Do you know?"

"Well I thinks I'm 40. But I'm not sure somewhere around there. Come on girl, let's go."

Peaches grabs Irons arms and drags her out the cabin. They run to slave row Iron thinks Peaches runs pretty fast for a woman older than she is. Peaches doesn't appear to tire as easily. Iron knew that she did not have the strength as most slaves and today for a moment it bothers her.

Then, There Was Iron

    These thoughts are quickly forgotten as Iron sees everyone on the plantation gathered around. Paddy is yelling out cabin assignments and Shelly is looking mighty proud of that. Iron and Peaches go over to Shelly.
    "Ssth, they a scraggily looking bunch."
    "I think Massa got so much for a special price."
    "How far they come?"
    "I dunno."
    "God, some have no shoes. At least they're not in chains."
    "Girl, you act like you ain't never seen no nigger with no shoes before."
    "I don't like it, specially this time of year."
    Iron was getting angry inside when she seen her. The woman that stepped up when Paddy yelled, "Ch, Ch, Chloe."
    "You, you, you'll be going with Mi, Miss Ch, Ch, Chaney."
    Some say that Chaney was older than dirt. No one knew for sure. She was still truly gifted at healing the sick and midwifery, it just took her a lot longer to get to you, plus she was becoming extremely forgetful. John knew that someone was needed to replace her, for years.
    The woman was not too tall. A rich earth brown, with a long braid down her back. Her nose was straight, and a little long as it relaxed on her face. Her lips were full, like a rose in bloom. Her eyes were slightly slanted up, and almost black in color. She had the straightest, strongest jaw line that Iron had ever laid her eyes on. She looked to be almost Iron's age, and was the most beautiful creature Iron had ever seen. She instantly felt water flowing through her body, as she forgot how to breathe. She grasped her chest and started to fall slowly backwards until Peaches took hold of her arm.
    "Girl, what's wrong with you?"
    "Look like she having one of those white women fainting spells."
    "I alright. I just gotta go back to my cabin."
    Iron takes off running and Peaches and Shelly look strangely at each other. It takes about seventeen minutes to run back to the cabin. She doesn't know, but it's record time. She has to get a pair of shoes for Chloe. She had noticed the woman's feet were wrapped in well-worn cloth. She needed shoes. Iron had five or six extra pairs. She was frantically examining ones to find a perfect pair for Chloe. She was wishing that she had more to choose from, though seven pairs of

shoes for one slave, was never seen. Iron would go to the old men on the plantation that made the shoes, and give them little extras like food, coins, and cloth ribbons for their wives and daughters, so they could make and sneak her extra shoes. She gave them to her passengers that were without any. The old men didn't ask any questions, they knew, everyone knew that Iron was a gift giver. When she found the shoes that she felt perfect for Chloe, she then thought the woman might also be hungry. Miss Chaney was given even less rations than the field workers. Who knew the last time Chloe had anything to eat? Feeding a slave was never high on John's list of things that must be done.

Iron stewed catfish with onions, and then she boiled turnips and potatoes. Iron arranged it all nicely on a plate, covered it with a cloth, and was on her way to present herself to Chloe, when she remembered that she should also bring something for Chaney. How could she forget this woman? The woman who birthed all her babies. Iron wondered what was happening to her. Was it the thunderbolt? Peaches talked about it. The thunderbolt was when you see someone for the first time, and that person never leaves your mind. All you ever want is to be with that person. Could this be it finally? What she had heard talk about all these years? She had never felt this strange, even with Bell. Iron prepared another plate and made her way to Chaney's cabin. She was out of breath when she reached the cabin, and tapped on the door.

"Who dat?"

"Chaney, it's me Iron."

"Well girl, nice to see ya. How ya feelins?"

"I'm alright Miss Chaney."

"Girl, this here is Chloe. She be doing prenticeship with me. Chloe, this here Iron."

Chloe looks at Iron. Iron says hello.

"I got this here for ya. Are you hungry?"

"Well, Ise know Ise hungry. Iron, what you got?"

"Miss Chaney, I got some catfish, taters and turnip."

"Woo, woo, that's good eatins. Iron set that up for us."

Iron unwraps the plates for the two women. Chloe has yet to say a word to her, even when Iron gives her the shoes. The two women dig into their meals with ravenous hunger.

Then, There Was Iron

"Girl, you gon like it around here. Not much whipping, praise the Lord. Got three overseers, two white, one black. Black man whip ya more, ya ask me. But nobody ask me."

"Where you from girl?"

"Georgia."

"That not too far. Yor Massa before, he a good man?"

Chloe laughs. Iron cannot take her eyes off Chloe; no matter how hard she tries. Chloe finally looks at her.

"So, what do you do around here?"

"I runs the garden."

"Oh, you run that big garden I seen in the front?"

"No, I runs another garden further back in the woods. It bout just as big though. You want I fetch you some water so you can wash up after your travels."

"That be nice."

As Iron goes for the water she hears Chaney filling Chloe in on how many little white slaves Iron has given John. Chaney's whispering abilities have deteriorated with age. Iron is embarrassed; she knew that Chloe would find out sooner or later. As she reenters the cabin, Chaney is repeating "She a good girl, though."

"Iron, this food here is mighty fine. You sure always had skills in the kitchen. Her Mama's fried chicken bring the dead to life. Thank God she's free."

Chaney lays her head back and closes her eyes.

"Whose free?"

"My Mama."

"How she get free?"

"Miss Clara gave it to her. Her and Gravy."

"I think there is more to the story than that, Miss Chaney."

"You don't want to hear all that on your first day here. You must be tired."

"Oh, I'm alright. Tell me, did Massa send you with these shoes?"

"No."

"I think I'll go in the other room and wash up."

Iron listens carefully, as carefully as she can over Chaney's interruptions about freedom, good food, and Georgia. She tried hard to hear Chloe take off her clothes, breathe, and step into the tub of water, but it was hard. Should she leave? Should she be there when Chloe returned? What would Chloe think of her, she had nothing to do there? She didn't even say thank you for the clothing or the food. She didn't even give a blessing to God. She better leave. Chaney was sleeping. Chloe was probably also tired. Did they all walk from Georgia? They might have been walking for weeks. She really needed shoes. How could she not say thank you? New slaves were always so strange. Some had to be tied for the first few weeks. Thank God Chloe did not need to be tied. Anyway, that was mostly men. She would leave. Chloe must need some time. New slaves always needed time. Time to realize they won't see their loved ones again. Time to fear their new home. She would leave, and go find Paddy and Shelly for more information.

Chloe listened to the strange woman leave. To call her high yella would be giving her too much color. She slips into the tub and thinks about Ruth, her beautiful daughter. God how she prayed the child wasn't hurting. This was the second time she had been sold since being parted from her daughter. She heard the screaming at the auctioneers. Hers and her child's as they realized they were being sold apart. She felt the pain again in her head from the auctioneer slamming his pistol into her, to keep her quiet. The tears started to fall again as she realized that the last time her daughter seen her, she was passed out on the ground with blood pouring out of her head.

Maybe the picture would give Ruth strength. The kind needed to get up North. Maybe Ruth would run away up North and become one of those abolitionists; she sure was a special child. Chloe slid her body lower in the water. It had been a long time since she had a bath. She thanked God for a tub big enough for her to sit in. On her last plantation, she could only stand up in it. She thanked God for the shoes. It had been about two years since she had a pair. These ones fit perfectly. She also thanked God for that meal; she hadn't had a meal like that even longer than since she had shoes. Her last plantation the Massa got so poor, slaves only got two pounds of bacon and a cup of flour each Sunday. How she had known hunger. Things may be better here, but without Ruth, how could they?

She remembers the words of her mother. "Make do, make do cuz you a slave and if a day comes that you ain't bleeding, then that's a good day." Chloe shrugs and figures she is bleeding inside. Chloe in her thirty years had given birth to seven babies. She had no idea where these children were, what they looked like today, or if they had any memory of her. The one that pained her the most was Ruth, for

Then, There Was Iron

her master had allowed her to keep Ruth till she was nine years of age. Ruth was her best friend. A child, her best friend. She said a prayer to God asking him not to allow the white man to hurt her too badly. She got out of the tub mumbling; make do cuz you a slave.

When Iron arrived at Shelly's cabin there appeared to be a party going on. Even Reuben had gotten the old fiddle out. Iron was happy to see Peaches and Benjamin dancing together. She pulled Shelly aside.

"Today Christmas and nobody tole me?"

"Nah, we celebrating cuz Massa told Paddy he gon use him as a overseer!"

Shelly screams and jumps up and down holding both of Iron's arms.

"You serious?"

"As a poor white cracker hunting a nigger for $50.00."

"Shelly, that beautiful."

"Girl, I know my man overseer. Lord, that sound good. The best part is Massa John say with all these new slaves, he be needing more women to make clothes and what not. Tend to the providing of slaves. Girl, Paddy said he get more women together. Girl, I'm out the field. Iron, Ise out the field!"

Shelly continues to scream, dance and laugh; Iron has never seen her so happy. Lord, she hoped it would last.

"So, Massa John gonna have four overseers now."

"I dunno. He bought a slave just for that, some big black buck. Reuben know him from way back, says he a good man. Massa also got rid of that William, the other nigger overseer, but he keep the two white men. White William and John. I tell you I take the white William over the black William, any day. That nigger had a heart of stone. I'm sure glad he's gone. I hope he drop dead on the way out the gate."

"Shelly."

"That man put enough marks on me. No, I don't hope he drop dead, I hope it takes him longer than that to die. I hope it's long and painful."

"Massa sole black William?"

"Traded him, I thinks."

"Traded him for what?"

"Plow and some mules, I thinks, ask Paddy."

"Where's Paddy?"

"He's somewhere drinking whiskey and chewing tobacco."

"That don't sound like Paddy."

"Oh, he does it every Christmas Day. Just the one day a year the man have a taste. Lord, what kind of man I got."

"The kind you need."

"Anyway Paddy celebrating today like it was Christmas Day, cuz it's Christmas for us. Iron, Iron, I out the field! My man got me out the field!"

"Girl, I so happy for ya. I'm going looking for Paddy."

Iron surprisingly found Paddy out back sitting under a tree, not drinking or chewing tobacco at all.

"Man, dat how you celebrate?"

"I, I, Iron, I'm not a dr, dr, drinking ma, man."

"Well Shelly think you're out here celebrating with the men."

"Ov ov ovaseer or or not. Sl slave men d d don't care much fo fo my company."

"I sure happy for ya Paddy."

"You know any of these new ones Massa buy?"

"N n no. But Re Re Reuben know a couple"

"Sure you don't want no taste now?"

"Yeah I dr drink only one d day a year. Sh Sh Shelly want me to have a taste so ba bad, I told her I would. But Iron that ain't me."

"That alright Paddy. Ain't nothing wrong with not being a drinking man. Best slave man I know never touch no liquor. I don't see nothing good in drunkeness."

"You have a ta taste sometimes though?"

"Yeah but I don't ever get drunk."

"Lord I wi wish Shelly was like that."

"I think she be a little different now, she out the field"

"Lord I sho hope so."

"Paddy why don't you go in and dance with your wife."

"Iron dat a good idea."

The two get up and go into the cabin. Paddy immediately grabs Shelly and they start moving together. Iron reaches for Reuben. Who has sat his fiddle down and allowed young Winston to accompany the many singers in the cabin. Iron leads Reuben outside.

"Girl why you bring me outside, I wanna dance."

"Man you to ole to dance. You should be happy you can walk."

"Oh you a funny girl. Now what you want, thinking woman?"
"You know anything about that woman in Miss Chaneys cabin?"
"What's her name?"
"Chloe."
"Where she from?"
"Georgia."
"Well girl you know more than me."
"Reuben you know everyone."
"Girl I don't know where you got them beliefs but they ain't all and entirely true."
"Come now Reuben you must know something bout her?"
"I know that she a good healing woman. Benjamin tole me that. Said she get you fixed up better than any white doctor. She know things even Miss Chaney don't know."
"How she learn so much about doctoring?"
"I duuno you gonna have to ask Benjamin about that. Or you could ask the woman herself."
"Well she don't seem to like much talking. Lord only know what she been through. Some don't like talking much about their past. It hurt them with the remembering."
"Yeh dat true. Why you so curious about this woman?"
"Reuben I don't know. I seen her and I felt like I known her forever."
"Maybe she your kin. Sometimes that happen you know."
"What happen?"
"You find your people. Maybe she your aunt or your sister."

Iron stayed quite long after her talk with Reuben. She was hoping that Chloe would hear the jubilations and come join the others. This did not happen. The celebrations were still going strong, when she left. Iron quickly dismissed Reuben's idea that this woman might be family. Shelly and Peaches they were her sisters and they sure didn't make her feel like this. True they were not her blood sisters, but they were the only sisters she had ever known and they were family. Mama Pearl was family too and she never made Iron forget to breath. This was no sisterly feeling. This was her Bell feeling but much stronger, much much stronger.

Tomorrow she would go back and visit Miss Chaney see if there was anything else Chloe needed. But would she frighten the woman, being so nice. Maybe she should go the day after tomorrow. What if

Ellen Barton

she doesn't receive rations? She'll have nothing to eat tomorrow. What's wrong with John? Why don't he think about feeding his slaves? He even let them have a party in the middle of the day. Niggers dancing, laughing, singing. Must be cause it was so close to Christmas. Lord what would she give Chloe for Christmas? Why can't she stop thinking about this woman? She didn't even say thank you. Iron slept.

The next morning on her walk to Chaney's cabin with two plates of ham, eggs and biscuits. Iron wondered what the hell she was doing. To late she was at the door.

"Who dat?"

"It's me Iron."

"Mawnin Iron. Wat bring you down here?"

"I brought you some breakfast."

"Lord Iron you gonna get this ole woman custom to things that ain't always so."

"Well I know you busy teaching Chloe all about the healing. Where is she anyway?"

"She gawn to look at plants and bushes. I say girl you see the snow. But she gawn out anyway."

"She a nice girl? Quiet?'

"Yeah she seem nice."

"Lord Iron you should come and visit ole Chaney mo often. Two days with good food. God bless you chile."

"Well I can't stay long Miss Chaney. I come back for my plates later."

"I see ya den."

Iron leaves she can't believe Chloe is not there. At least she has a reason to return. Iron decides to walk through the woods to look for Chloe. She could show her around the plantation. Show her how to get to her cabin. If only she could find her.

Chloe watches the yella woman. She watched her hurry into Chaney's cabin and leave shortly afterward. The woman had two plates in her hand. Thank God cuz Chaney's dry cornmeal for breakfast was already wearing off. The yella woman was a great cook. But why did she feed them? Why did she give her the shoes? Why was she racing all over the plantation? Chloe had been following her for about an hour. What was wrong with this woman? Chloe thought maybe she had known her. Maybe they had shared a pen. She

Then, There Was Iron

couldn't remember. Maybe she should yell to her. Ask her did they share a pen. Wasn't that you who lost your son the day I lost my daughter? Wasn't that you who rubbed my head the day it was filled with blood and tears? Wasn't that you who brought me food and gave me my first pair of brand new shoes? She was about to yell and ask all this when she realizes the yella woman is looking for her. Why?

What does this woman want from her? Does she really want to know? Chloe turns around and heads back to the cabin for a closer examination of those covered plates. When Chloe arrives back at the cabin. A semi plump bright-eyed woman with a beautiful smile was sitting in one of the chairs.

"Chloe ya back. Dis here is Shelly. Shelly dis here Chloe. Shelly husband the new ovaseer. Chloe here doin preniceship with me."

"Well Miss Chaney I hope you show her how to make your special save me tea."

"Save me tea. I ain't never heard of that."

"Lord with out Miss Chaneys save me tea, my back be more scarred up than it is now."

"How you mean?"

"Say you had to much whiskey in the night. Next day you better have a save me tea or your head feel like it be nailed to a board."

Chloe laughs and decides she likes this woman.

"You didn't hear the celebrations last night. Girl you should have come out. Make your acquaintances."

"I was so tired. That yella girl made us a feast that knocked me out. I went right to sleep after washing up."

"Yella girl?"

"She mean Iron. Iron bring us food last night and breakfast today. You know how she like ta take care. Ise happy now she taking care of ole Chaney."

"She a funny woman."

"Lord girl, Iron like my own sister, her Mama like my own Mama."

"You mean her Mama that now free?"

"Yes, Mama Pearl. She took care of me like no other. See, I never knew my own Mama. Nobody ever cook for me, wash for me; just care. Make sure I'm okay. Lord, I loved that woman. Thank God, thank God."

"Mama Pearl ain't Iron's real mother."

Ellen Barton

"No?"

"Mama Pearl took over Iron. Iron's real Mama was beaten to death. With her last bit of life, she push out Iron. Mama Pearl seen all that and took on Iron as her own. They were sold here together when Iron was just a baby. I remember the day she come. Shelly, you didn't hear about that."

"I know Mama Pearl was not Iron's blood mother. She ain't mine either. She still the only mother we ever known."

"So they beat on Iron's mother with her big belly?"

"They say Iron fell right in the dirt."

"Maybe that's why she a little funny."

"Girl, there ain't nothing wrong with Iron. Why you think that?"

"She give me these here new shoes. She made the best meal I had in years. I dunno, there's something about her."

"Girl, if you think someone who shows you kindness is funny, I sorry for what you must of been through. I tell ya, Iron like my flesh and blood sister, ain't a better woman on this here plantation. You want to take a walk to her cabin? She always a got taste."

"Shelly, you going for a taste this time of day? And you come here for my save me tea?"

"Well Miss Chaney, sometimes all that can save me is another taste."

"Iron say she be back later for the plates anyhow. And I gots some things to show Chloe. You dreamin if you think Massa gonna let two days go by with no niggers working."

"You right on that Miss Chaney. Chloe, I come by later and we go to Iron's cabin. Girl, you gonna love it. Once you walk in her cabin, you feel like you not a slave anymore."

"What?"

"You can do whatever you want there. Always a lot of food, a lot of whiskey, and Lord I remember the day when Bad Bell was always there. Lord, the music beautiful. Dem was the days."

"Lord, Bad Bell used to go to Iron's place; how I loved that woman's voice. I heard her sing three times, and I will never forget it. I hear she's free now."

"She went over there to England. Her Massa's sister took her over. I think her name Sylvia Jackson. She died on the boat."

"What?"

Then, There Was Iron

"Miss Chaney, you didn't hear that? Miss Jackson, she never made it to England. Fell overboard before the ship got there."

"Oh yes, yes I did hear dat. Just slips my mind."

"Well, I gots to go. But I be back, we go to Iron's."

"I be ready."

Shelly came back well after dark to pick up Chloe. The two women laughed and talked on their walk to Iron's cabin. Shelly deeply enjoyed the new woman's company. She loved the idea of a new friend that had a reputation for healing; that with a new job for her and her husband. She felt her life improving. Upon arriving at Iron's, they found her sitting outside in her rocking chair covered in at least five blankets. Chloe whispers,

"I tole you she funny."

"Girl, why you sitting out here in all this cold?"

"I needing some air is all."

She doesn't want to explain that Miss Clara had got word to her that she might be receiving a few passengers this week.

"We brought your plates from Miss Chaney to save you a trip."

Iron now notices who is with Shelly, and she forces herself to breathe normally.

"Girl, I thought I show Chloe your place. You know, Chloe always also likes a taste every now and then."

"Come in, come in. Ya'll hungry? Ise just fried up some chicken and I got some fresh biscuits."

"Nah, Paddy cooked a heap of food this evening. That man sho love to cook."

Iron figures he has no choice.

"I a little hungry. Massa don't give out no extra rations."

"Massa don't give out no extra rations, yet what he expect ya'll to eat? Have a seat, Iron fix you up."

Chloe stares at Iron. Iron thinks that she is looking through, right into her very spirit.

"If it wasn't for you these last days, I nearly starve to death. Thank you."

Finally thought Iron.

"Well, I like to help folks. Massa done give me some extras. I don't like to see no one hungry. The shoes fitting?"

"Perfect."

Shelly is watching the two women. She thinks something is going on here. She has never in the seventeen years she has known Iron, seen her so nervous. Chloe seems more careful than she did on their walk over. She is talking much more slowly and appears to be examining Iron.

"I never heard a name like Iron before."

Iron is thinking, and I have never seen a face so beautiful, but she says,

"I don't even know who gave it to me."

"It's a lovely name."

Iron sighs. Shelly is staring at Iron in confusion. Iron sits the food in front of Chloe, and the jug in front of Shelly.

"Chloe, you want some whiskey?"

"A little bit and some cold water."

"Iron, where's Peaches tonight?"

"Benjamin over there tonight."

"Who is Peaches?"

"You gonna love her. She our own Negro newspaper got all the information."

"Iron, this here some good chicken. Lord, I haven't eaten like this in years. I be over here every night."

Iron exhales loudly and Shelly figures out exactly what is going on. It's the woman woman business. Iron is watching Chloe the way Paddy used to watch her. Lord, she hoped Chloe was like that. Not many people were and Iron truly needed some love in her life. Maybe she could help.

"Iron, I was telling Chloe bout the good days we had when Bad Bell used to come around."

Iron instantly stiffens.

"Lord, that Iron and Bad Bell, were two of the tightest friends. They always together. You ever have a friend like that Chloe?"

Iron is making strange faces and gestures at Shelly, hoping she would change the subject.

"No."

"Have you ever been married?"

"Yes. It seems like a lifetime ago. He dead now."

The mood in the room had changed. Shelly jumps up.

"Iron, have a drink girl. You needs to loosen up."

Then, There Was Iron

Iron pours herself one. God knows she needed it. She is watching Chloe. Taking a small sip of whiskey and a large gulp of water. She had eaten her food extremely rapidly. Iron wanted to witness her every motion, her every move. She wanted to share her skin, to taste every word that went through her head. She settled on asking,

"You want more chicken?"

"No, I'm alright. This whiskey here is good for me. Been so long since I had me some whiskey, I think it must be bout five years."

"Lord, five years without a taste, I just die."

"My last plantation, whiskey was the last thing on your mind. You think more about eating, staying warm, and staying away from that whip."

"Things a lot different here. Massa Cummings he slow to feed ya, but he ain't quick on whipping niggers. Other plantations round here, the whip be flying a lot more. He whip, they all do, but he don't whip to kill ya, and not as often. He told Paddy that niggers cost money and he got no money to waste. Seems like the older Massa Cummings get, the better man he is."

"More Massa's should be like that."

"But if more Massa's was like that, maybe we wouldn't try so hard to get free. Wouldn't be no abolitionists, no railroad maybe."

"I think no matter how good your Massa is, we still be fighting to be free, cuz we supposed to be free. We stolen people and we won't stop till we put things back the way God wanted things."

Iron loves what Chloe is saying.

"How long you been in this here cabin?"

"About seventeen summers."

"You should say years."

"Yeh, seventeen years."

Talking to Chloe was completely opposite than talking to Shelly or Peaches. She always had to be the one to tell them the proper words. Now someone was doing it to her. They were so much alike. How come Chloe didn't see it? Iron finishes her whiskey in one swallow, and pours another one.

"Lord, Iron I can't remember the last time I seen you drink like that. What's in you girl?"

"Trying to get out a chill. You want some mo?"

"Girl, when you ever see me say no? Maybe only when my ma, ma, man around."

"Stop that Shelly, that ain't right."
"What ain't right?"
"She's doing Paddy's stutter."
"Do you always do what's right?"
"Sometimes I don't even know what's right. I know you shouldn't laugh at your own husband."
"Iron, you ever jump the broom?"
Shelly laughs. Iron glares at her.
"The way Massa got me here, I couldn't jump the broom."
"Did you ever want to?"
"Yes."
Iron doesn't add only once, only now, only with you.
Chloe doesn't pry on the subject any further. She knew the life of slaves. It was best not to ask too many questions about the past. Memories could be horrifying. Hers were. She still thought this woman a little strange. Extremely kind, but a little strange. Why is she always watching her? Why does she pretend she is not watching her?
"You ever been to Georgia?"
"No."
"How many times you been sold?"
"Only once, when I was a baby. You?"
"Been sold three times."
"How come you know so much about healing?"
"My mother learned it from her mother, who learned it from her mother."
"You knew your Mama?"
"Yes."
"Did she look like you?"
"Yes."
"Did you know your father too?"
"Yes."
Shelly over hearing the conversation sits back down at the table and stops doing her little sway while humming a little song.
"Chloe, you say you knew both your Mama and your Daddy?"
"Yes."
"They nice folks."
"They the best folks there ever were."
Chloe begins to feel sympathy for the two women. They are both staring at her in awe. For some reason she never realized how few

Then, There Was Iron

slaves grow up with both their parents. This brings to mind her children and she starts to feel the sadness, the one that held her for years.

"Lord, I always thinking bout my Mama. Wondering how many babies she have, did she get to keep any? I wondering if she ever wondering bout me. We should not be talking bout all this. I bring Chloe here so we could enjoy this evening."

"Shelly right, some things a slave woman should try not to let in her head."

"I can't think about my Mama. I just can't."

"I think I'll have some more whiskey."

Iron pours Chloe another cup.

"You want some more water?"

"Thank ya."

"Iron, remember that song Bad Bell used to sing all the time?"

"Girl, Bell sang so many songs."

"You know the one."

Shelly begins to clap her hands and stomp her feet, she sings,

"I am a King and they don't know it,

I'm a King, but I won't show it,

I'll take my place in front of the race,

I'm a King and with you,

I can do anything."

Iron and Chloe join in on the clapping and stomping. Chloe is smiling and Iron is melting. Shelly gets up to dance, holding her faithful partner, a little brown jug. She is singing another one of Bell's songs. Iron is amazed Shelly remembers the words to these songs, knowing Shelly was always drunk when she heard them.

Chloe gets up to dance with Shelly. Though she is clapping and stomping Iron has never felt more paralyzed. She has never seen one move with such smoothness. Shelly pulls her up.

"Girl now you know you can't be sitting down around me."

Shelly has put down the jug and is stomping, clapping and singing loudly. Chloe looks happy. The happiest Iron has seen her since she arrived. Chloe takes both of Irons hands and pulls her closer so that they can dance together. Iron thinks that all her blood had just turned to coldest of ice water. She can't look up; she keeps her eyes down staring at Chloes feet. She fears that Chloe is staring at her. She peaks up. Chloe is.

Ellen Barton

Why is she doing this to her? Does she know? Does she know that Iron is using all her concentration not to fall into her? Fall completely into her. She doesn't want this night ever to end. She is so close to Chloe she can smell her. She wants Chloe to stay there forever. If she must go could she at least leave all her clothes so that Iron could sleep with and hold them all night long. Iron looks up again. Chloe is still staring. What is she thinking? Is she thinking about the things Iron knows she could do to her? The pleasure they can share together, probably not?

Chloe is watching the yella woman. Iron. She figures she should stop calling her the yella woman. She was uncertain, if Iron would be fond of that name. Chloe had the feeling that she could do anything to Iron. Anything at all. She wasn't sure if it was the whiskey, but she wanted to. Wanted to what, she didn't know. But Iron gave her a feeling of power. At first she didn't know what the feeling was, never having it before. At this moment, on this day, in this time of her life Chloe was enjoying the feeling. She was going to do something about it. She pulls Iron even closer. So close that they are touching. She feels Irons deep exhale. Their hips are semi circling each other to Shelly's slow thumping beats.

Chloe feels lost and found. Lost in a space where nothing seems to matter. She hears Shelly's voice in her head repeating you feel like you not a slave anymore. Found by something that was looking for her. Something she knew she deserved. Something she was waiting for. Is she too close to this woman? Their breasts are touching. God they just touched again. Where was Shelly? Was she watching? How come she couldn't see Shelly anymore? What's going on here? Chloe looks over and sees Shelly in the corner still making the music to keep the dancing going. Though not paying any attention to the two women. Chloe is relieved. Why doesn't she want Shelly to see? God their breasts touched again. Oh oh now she feels the yella woman. Iron. She feels her on her upper leg. She knows what that is. She better back away. Who are Shelly and the yella woman? Do they do this to all the new slaves. But she started it. She pulled Iron close first. It's not some plan. Yes she better back away. She can now feel herself pressing against Irons leg. It feels to good. It isn't right.

Chloe takes a couple of steps back. Iron hangs her head a little lower. But doesn't stop the dance. She can't let Chloe know how much this means to her. Not yet. Shelly from the corner of her eye is

Then, There Was Iron

watching the whole story. She is now only humming and stomping and doing a slow bang on some pots. In her head the words, look like Iron finally getting some are being repeated over and over. Chloe stops dancing and goes to refill her cup. Iron follows.

"I haven't felt like that in so long."
"Like what?'
Chloe quickly turns her head and stares at Iron intensely.
"Like I was alive."
Shelly runs over with her own empty cup.
"See tole ya. You like it here."
Chloe staring deep into Irons eyes says
"I like it very much, but we should be leaving it's getting late."
"Must you leave already?'
"Yeah not like any of us going to the field tomorrow. Girl its just a few day till Christmas. It's celebration season."
"Miss Chaney and I got a lot of work tomorrow and I drank way more than my fill of whiskey."
"You want me to make you a plate for breakfast?"
"I'll be alright for breakfast."
"How bout lunch or supper?'
Chloe smiles and says will see.
"Lord you worser than Paddy and Massa. Wanna go already."
Chloe ignores Shelly's protests and Irons eyes; she prepares to leave. Shelly follows behind her.
"See ya tomorrow."
"See ya."
"Bye thanks."

Iron follows them to the porch and stays out there until she can't see or hear them anymore. When she goes back inside she stands in the middle of the floor for a minute staring.

Staring at the spot where Chloe was. Staring at Chloe's empty cup. Staring at the space where they danced. She continues dancing. She sings and twirls around her cabin as she cleans up. She doesn't remember ever feeling so happy. This kind of happiness was terrifying. Were slaves supposed to feel such joy? Was this a feeling only intended for the free? Iron thought even if she were free she would probably feel no different. She felt as if Chloe now owned her. Owned her in way Massa would never know. She felt as if her whole life depended on Chloe. Chloe was in charge now. Chloe was all that mattered. It seemed her entire happiness now depended on the way Chloe treated her. She prayed Chloe felt the same way.

On their walk home Shelly was trying to find out just that.

"Look like you warming up to Iron?"

"She warming up to me."

"You two look like you were having a grand ole time."

"Where you watching?"

"Well I'm not one to stare. I just notices when people happy that's all. And yall look happy together."

"Happy together? Shelly what ya saying."

"I'm saying take happiness anyway it comes. Do you like her?"

"Why of course I like her. She fed me the best meals I had in years. She gave me the only new pair of shoes I ever received in my whole life. Lord it cold out here."

"Yeah its cold. Whiskey in your belly warm you up though."

"Dat true. Why you talk so much on Iron?"

"Iron different than other women."

"I ain't never seen her in no women's clothes. How come she always dress like a man?"

"You bes ask her that yourself. Chloe you never seen a woman that dress like a man before?"

"No. But we slaves, not like we got a lot of choices in clothes. Lord I wore the same dress everyday for two years."

"What about white women. They got all the clothes they wants still you never see a white woman in long pants."

"Why you think that is?"

"I duuno. Maybe white man won't let em."

"Why does Massa let Iron dress like that?"

"Massa let Iron do what she want. Hell she feed most of his slaves."

"Iron feed that many people?'

"Has been for years. Wait till the season come. You see how big her garden is. She also fish, catch rabbit. You name it. Iron always feeding people."

"I ain't never heard of no slave like that."

"I tell ya Iron special. You should spend more time with her. She can make you forget."

"Forget what?'

"All that needs forgetting."

"Some things I don't think anybody can make me forget."

"She done it for me. Lord when I first come here. I had the scars inside and outside. But that woman can put a light inside of ya."

"You see how she look at me?"

"Yes."

"You think that's right?'

"It's right for Iron."

"Maybe I go back tomorrow night."

"I think you should."

CHAPTER 13

Chloe did not go visit Iron the next day. Sipping a cup of save me tea, she blamed the entire experience on too much whiskey, and made a small promise to herself not to drink that much again. She did not feel shame for her behavior. Telling herself that she needed it, a night of feeling free. She would love to do it again, and again, and again. But she was too close to that yella woman. Iron. Once was definitely enough when rubbing up against a stranger. How could she look at the yella woman again? Lord, she hoped she won't be bringing any food today, even if Massa don't give out any rations.

Iron was busy preparing a feast; enough food for seven hungry people who had not eaten in days. She was praying that no one would come around that afternoon. Her passengers had arrived in the middle of the night. Miss Clara's pig man, Pierce, led them. He said that Miss Clara's house was full. He couldn't remember the last time he saw so many people coming through. Iron's stomach was working. That was what she called it when she felt twisted inside. She usually got this feeling when her cellar was full of runaways. Happy because she was helping slaves to get free, but filled with fear that at any moment she could get caught. This feeling had been keeping her alive, until she met Chloe. Now what she wanted was to take Chloe's hand and ride the railroad together. But was Chloe a running slave? Some slaves can't run. Some slaves can't stop.

The four men in her cellar were runners. Strong, smart. The women with them were tired. Iron had seen it all before. Women that just wanted to get love and keep love, men that wanted to be strong. Wanted to protect, wanted to take care of their families. Men ran away more often than women. Iron didn't know if it was because they were stronger, or if the feeling of "I can't take this anymore", hit them faster. Women were more willing to accept their role and make do with it. Maybe they found it harder to leave their families, if they were lucky enough to have any with them. Iron felt every slave had their reason for doing what they did not do. She could only pray they made it to their destination.

Could she make it, all the way to Canada? That's a long walk. Could Chloe make it? Maybe she should take some of the food to Chloe and Chaney. She never left slaves in her cellar before, but she

Then, There Was Iron

was sure they would be fine. She had to see Chloe after last night. Feeling her. She felt her pressing. She was not dreaming. It was the most wonderful feeling, and it left her with a strong desire for more. How could you stop with one so beautiful? When she was not looking at Chloe, her eyes felt almost as if they were not working; not being used to their full working ability. How was she supposed to survive the day without seeing Chloe? No, she didn't think it could be done.

Hours later Iron descends the cellar steps.

"I got enough food for all ya. Got a bucket a water too. Ise gots to go out for a bit. Yall stay down here and stay quiet. No one should come in here. But if they do, don't worry, cuz no one knows about this cellar."

"We be alright."

"God bless you, Miss Iron."

"God bless you."

"Thank ya, now you all be quiet. When I come home, I'll stamp two times to let you know it's me. But yall got to stay here for the rest of the night, and not make a word. And I won't be coming back down, till it's time for you all to go. So if ya needs anything, tell me now."

"No, Miss Iron, we be just fine. You go on, don't worry bout us."

"All right."

Iron runs out to take supper to Chaney and Chloe. She can't believe she is doing this, leaving passengers alone. But she doesn't have a choice. Chloe could be hungry; Chloe could be cold. Chloe might allow their bodies to touch again. Chloe might want to tell her that she can't live without her. She definitely had no choice.

Chloe did not feel the same way. She barely noticed Iron at all. She did not look her in the eye, and she again did not say thank you for the food. All of Iron's attempts to engage in conversation, brush up against her, smell her hair, or even listen to her breathing, were shrugged off and ignored. It hurt. Not like things Massa said to you as he pushed your face in the pillow, and did unspeakable things while lying on your back, not like hearing his boot steps coming closer to your cabin door and knowing he can do these things, because he owns you, not like feeling you will never touch, or touch anybody ever again because your only ever changing lover who you were slightly afraid of, has set sail to freedom, not like knowing the idea of you setting sail to freedom with her, was never even thought about, or possible. This hurt a lot more.

In the back of her head she knew that she should not have come. But she didn't listen. She should have stayed with her passengers. That's what the voice said. Stay with your passengers and you will not be hurt. Stay with your passengers and air will continue to exist for you. But she didn't listen and now she wanted to crawl home screaming why. Why do I always get the sometimeish ones?

Instead she walked home. A walk that felt much longer and much colder than it actually was. She thought a lot of Bell. Though she rarely ever thought of her anymore. Not since she started working the railroad. She felt the railroad saved her. After Bell left Iron found herself turning to whiskey and had many nights just sitting on the floor staring blankly and clutching a jug. It didn't last very long. Getting close to Miss Clara was Gods help. Miss Clara took away the dreams. Dreams of Bell with seven other people living inside of her. Seven completely different people. Dreams of seeing Bells head open up and seven little heads inside. Iron hated those dreams and for a long time she hated Bell for leaving her, not asking her to go, teaching her, scaring her. When she heard the news that Sylvia Jackson fell over the boat. For some reason she felt better. Bell would not be doing to Sylvia Jackson what she had done to her. Whoever or whatever Bell was anyway.

Now Chloe looked to be heading the same way. One day one way the next day another. At least she still looked the same. Lord if her eyes changed color, Iron swore she would try a field hand, cuz woman were off. Why couldn't she find a woman just like Reuben? And she wasn't going to cry either. Nope, not going to cry in this here cold. Chloe might just be putting her to a test. She wasn't like Bell. No one could ever be like Bell.

Chloe was like her but no one ever told her. Chloe would come around. She knew it. She could always tell. The ones like her. She didn't see many but she could always tell. Couple girls came through last harvest season they were like her she could see it in their eyes, in their hands. A young man came through three times more girlie than she herself could ever be. Lord he was funny. She seen it three or four times but she could always tell. Most people didn't know about such things, would never do it and probably thought it wrong. Chloe wasn't one of those people. No one could press that hard and rub the good places so close together and not give it a try.

Then, There Was Iron

That's all she needed was a try. Then, then Chloe would understand that God himself must want them to be together. He had to. Why would he give one person a strong feeling and not the other? Then she would have her chance to pour everything she had within her into Chloe. And once Chloe received what Iron had to give she would have to feel the same way. This she hoped. In her heart she knew things did not work that way. Living was not that easy or always that beautiful. If only two people could always feel the same way for each other at the same time. If only people could stay together holding that feeling. No she has heard about, talked about, and seen to many tears for that to be the truth. Sometimes one person gets hurt. She thought why does it again have to be me.

Iron found no joy in the season of celebration. Chloe barely gave her the time of day but had gotten rather close to Shelly. The New Year came in and Iron made a promise to God to do her best in the freeing of her people. She held a lot of hope for the year ahead. 1856. Reuben told her that was they year and though she had kept track of her age she never considered keeping track of the year. Reuben had said that 1856 was going to be a good year. One year closer to freedom.

As the year wore halfway through. Iron saw Reuben's words coming true for her passengers but not for her. The railroad kept her together while Chloe was pretending she did not exist. Iron had more passengers going through her cabin than ever before. She knew the greater the numbers the greater the danger. But she could not stop herself she kept going to Miss Clara and asking for even more. Miss Clara had informed her that she was doing the best that she could. But a certain level of discretion was necessary. Iron was now hiding food all over the woods. She had five or six excellent hiding places where she would stash food, hoping runaways would find it. She informed Pierce and Adele and only Pierce and Adele of her selected spots. They would tell the runaways where to find something if they were hungry.

Iron would often spend an entire day planting food. Up in trees, buried in holes, under water, in a cave above a stream. She would always leave a special sign for the runaway to find. Adele couldn't believe that no animal ever found the food, but Iron was excellent in keeping things hidden. She felt that she might have learned this from Bell, or from Mama Pearl. Don't allow them to hurt you girl. Don't show them you. How can they hurt you if they can't find you? The words of Mama Pearl. Would she like Chloe?

Iron had given Chloe a beautiful new dress for Christmas. She also gave one to Peaches and Shelly. Chloe did not say thank you but had tears in her eyes. She walked out of Shelly's cabin and wasn't seen for days afterwards. At first she did not take the dress with her. Though weeks later Iron saw her wearing it. Peaches explained to Iron that some slaves find it hard to take things. Since most were never given anything. She said that Chloe would come around; she got to first get over her hard memories. Iron accepted this. She had seen slaves that came from plantations where they were beaten everyday. You can't start out being kind to these slaves. It took some time before they trusted you.

Chloe did eventually come to the cabin one night much later and said thank you. That was the first time they were alone together. Iron replayed the evening over in her head many times. They did not drink, they did not kiss, they did not touch they only talked deep into the hours of the night. Chloe told her more about her parents, about healing, about her last plantation. A place more close to hell than any other place Iron had heard of. A small plantation owned by a poor cracker who had a little money only once in his life. He starved his slaves and beat them regularly and severely, this made Irons heart break. When Chloe said she had never talked about these things before. Iron felt blessed. Chloe had chosen her to tell her worst experiences. Though Chloe appeared to enjoy the company of Shelly or Peaches over Iron. She chose to tell the most painful memories to Iron. Iron knew it had to mean something. She would be patient.

The next few days Chloe again acted as if their night never happened. Going back to her usual ways, serious and deep in thought. Chloe was a thinking woman that is what Reuben would call her. She rarely laughed. Iron could count on one hand the number of times she had seen Chloe laugh or smile. This she felt was a great robbery to life. For when Chloe was happy it opened up heaven. She would make Chloe laugh again. She would teach her true happiness. All she had to do was suffer through today for tomorrow Chloe would love her. It just seemed that tomorrow took so long to arrive.

They were losing time. Precious time. One morning after tossing and turning all night, she took a walk to Miss Chaney and Chloe's

Then, There Was Iron

cabin. Miss Chaney was resting and Chloe was cooking when she arrived.

"Who dat?"

"Miss Chaney, it's Iron, just come calling to see how ya doing."

"Ise fine girl, though my eyes ain't wat dey used ta. Thank the good Lord for Chloe. She takin care of me just fine. Don't know what I'd do without her."

"Well if you need anything just tell me Miss Chaney, I try my best to get it for ya."

"Thank ya child. I gots to catch some sleep now. You visit with Chloe."

Miss Chaney gets out of her chair and goes to the back room.

"What you cooking?"

"Just brewing some herbs for Miss Chaney. It knock her fever out."

"How she doing?"

"I don't think she long for this world. You know how ole she is?"

"No. Don't think anybody does."

"Well, she real old. I think she could be 100."

"That old? I ain't never seen no slave that old."

"Well, we hardly know our own ages. But she sho full of memories. That old woman got a lot of stories. She remember when this land was full of Indians. I think she might have been the first slave ever."

Iron laughs.

"She ain't that old."

"How old are you Iron?"

"33, you?"

"I'm 35."

"I guess it's good to know your age."

"I guess."

"Chloe, you want to come to my cabin this evening for supper?"

"Yeh. Shelly coming? Peaches?"

"If you want."

"It's your cabin, so it's not if I want."

"I'm just asking you."

"Just me and you."

"Yes."

"I'll be there Iron."

Ellen Barton

"I'll see you later."

"Bye."

Iron could have flown back to her cabin. So that she was not disappointed she didn't try. Lord, what was she going to prepare? Was it too late to catch a fish? Maybe she'll kill a chicken. She decided since she was on the row, to go and visit Reuben, and get a nice piece of beef. She could roast it with onions and potatoes. She also would make some biscuits, brown gravy and bake a pie. Pumpkin. She hadn't had pumpkin pie in the longest. She also remembered that Chloe said one of the greatest things from the days when she was a little girl, was her mother's pumpkin pie. She must hurry; she had so much to do.

It took Iron hours to prepare everything. All the cooking, plus she scrubbed the entire cabin, though it did not need it. She put on what she considered her nicest clothes. All hand me downs from Massa, but she liked the way she looked in his pants and shirts after the necessary alterations. She had two cups of whiskey before Chloe arrived. Her stomach was working. Working harder than it ever had before. She was about to pour her third cup when she heard the tap at the door. It was Chloe. Iron could not put into words the feeling she had when Chloe walked into her cabin. She felt as if God was blessing her, as if he chose that very moment to give her life. Chloe looked wonderful in a black dress Iron had never seen before.

"That's a lovely dress."

"Peaches gave it to me."

"I'm sure it never looked that good on Peaches."

"You always got nice things to say to me."

"I can't help it. You don't mind it do you?"

"No, I think I like it. I hadn't heard nice words in a long time."

"You hungry? I got some beef in gravy, some biscuits, some taters and a pumpkin pie."

"Lord, I never seen a slave that make meals like you do. Lord, pumpkin pie, last time I had pumpkin pie, my belly didn't even get big yet."

"You got babies?"

Chloe glares at her.

"What slave woman don't have babies?"

"I shouldn't ask you that. I'm sorry."

Then, There Was Iron

"Don't be sorry. I got to learn to be proud of my babies, even if I don't know where they is. Lord, I just can't stop thinking of my one girl."

"What's her name?"

"Ruth. I had her till she was nine years old. Lord, she always on my mind."

"I never looked at my babies."

"You never looked at your babies? How many you have?"

"5."

"All by Massa?"

"Yes. How many babies you have?"

"7."

"By your husband?"

"3 by my husband, 4 by white men. How come you never looked at your babies?"

"I didn't want to see their faces in my dreams at night."

"You think you did the right thing?"

"I don't know."

"Neither do I. You ever think about all those babies?"

"All the time."

Iron begins to cry, softly at first. When she realizes that she could not hide her tears from Chloe, they poured out.

"I'm sorry. I wanted us to have a nice dinner."

"That's not what you wanted."

"What?"

Iron has stopped crying and is wiping her tears. She is surprised by Chloe's words.

"You wanted me to love you."

Chloe can't believe she is saying this. The talk of children; the smell of pumpkin pie; the tears of Iron. She needed to be honest. She knew for months how Iron felt. She sees the way Iron looks at her. She repeats it.

"You wanted me to love you."

"I want you to be happy."

"Happy, what's that?"

"Let me show you."

Iron kisses Chloe with a passion that she didn't know existed. Chloe kisses her back with the same hunger. Was it possible to taste life in the flesh of another? To understand why, ah, that's why I had to get up in the morning. That's why I must sleep everyday. That is why I must eat. Iron thought so for at this moment, she knew why she must live to be old and one day die some way. This was it, and even if it wasn't it, this was all she needed. All she needed to survive.

Iron slowly massages Chloe's hips while pulling her closer. She hesitates for a moment. She wants to give Chloe the chance to stop. She wants to make sure that this is what Chloe wants. She stops for a moment and pulls away so that she can look Chloe deep in her eyes. Chloe says, "don't you stop, don't you ever stop," and kisses her again. Their lovemaking is desperate, clumsy and strong. Iron is slowly climbing back up Chloe's body. Chloe is convulsing rapidly, having just experienced her first orgasm ever. Iron lies next to her and watches the movements die down.

"Lord, then in walked Jesus!"

Iron laughs.

"That was beautiful."

"I never felt anything like that before. I thought I was dying."

"What a way to go."

"I got the sticky stuff, like a man."

"You never had it before."

"I didn't know woman could get the sticky stuff. I didn't know you could put your mouth there on a woman."

"Did you like it?"

"I loved it, I can't wait to do it again."

"You don't have to wait a long time."

Iron again kisses her. This time with more tenderness. Her movements are much slower. She caresses every inch of Chloe's body. She turns her over and rubs her back. At first she is appalled and angry at the amount of scars that cover Chloe's back. She kisses each of them. Both women are softly crying. Not wanting the other to know. Chloe has the most beautiful body Iron has ever seen. Even with the scars, if anyone ever hurt her. Iron doesn't know what she would do.

"Chloe you ever think about running away?"

"Tried it once. Didn't make it."

Iron thinks this is the most casual manner in which Chloe has ever spoke. She has absolutely no emotion in her voice.

"How long you gone?"

"Four days."

Then, There Was Iron

"What's it like being free?"

"Everybody talk like freedom the best thing in the world. It's spose ta be the greatest feeling ever. It wasn't like that for me. I was so scared. I never ever been more scared in my life. Every second thinkin they gonna catch us. Freedom was not that good for me."

"If you could be free and not be scared than freedom be good. Where you alone?'

"Had my husband and my little girl."

"Ruth?"

"Yeh."

"Chloe you sure you wanna keep talkin?"

"I'm alright. It was the fourth night. I was settling up a place for Ruth to sleep. I was making a spot in the leaves for my child to sleep."

Her voice breaks as Iron hears her tears, her shame, her anger.

"Then I heard them. The dogs. The dogs that eat slaves. The dogs that would eat your children. I hear Nelson say run. I grab Ruth and I start running. I don't get to far. She nine. Heavy. I put her down but we running next to each other. I don't look back. I hear the dogs growling. I don't look back. I hear Nelson screaming. I don't look back. He screaming run run. I can hear the dogs ripping flesh, breaking bone. Then I don't hear Nelson no mo. I never know if he gave himself to those dogs so we could get away. They catch us. Wasn't long they were on our trail. Told Ruth climb a tree. That way they couldn't eat us. They sure to catch us anyhow. They left Nelson there. Didn't bury him. Nothing. Had us walk by what was left of him on the way back. I told Ruth to close her eyes. But I seen him. Had 5 babies with Nelson. The only one they let me keep pass crawlin was Ruth. I married with Nelson 10 years. Married him right off. Few months after I was sold to his plantation."

"Did they beat Ruth?"

"No praise the Lord. They didn't whip her. They sold us apart. We spend two nights in a jail. Tied me like a dog. My daughter she see me tied like a dog. Can't do nothing for her. Iron what is wrong with white people?"

"I don't know. But you can find some good ones."

"Good ones. Ssth. There were no good ones when they drag us out the jail and put us on the block. There was no good ones when they drag me kicking and screaming from the only person I had left. My child. How do they do it? Sometimes I think they all got some kind of disease in the head. In the heart. We could never do to them what they do to us. Lord knows they not strong enough to take it. White women faint all the time. Got to spend six days in bed if she hear her daddy sick. Or her husband don't listen to her. Or her daughter to old to marry. Lord what happen if you sold them away from everyone they love? Or starve them or beat them unmercifully? Lord they just die. I never seen no white man as big and strong as a buck. Never. I tell ya they all ain't no good."

"Chloe I know most of them real bad. Trust me there are good ones."

"Quakers. I heard of em."

"Some of them running the railroad. Abolitionists up North."

"I just never meet any good white person. How you tell the difference from the bad ones?

Iron laughs.

"What's so funny?"

"I remember asking someone the same thing a long time ago."

"Did they have an answer?"

"No. Chloe you think freedom coming?"

"Iron it got to. God don't want this."

"Been slavery forever. Lots of slaves in the bible."

"How old is the bible?'

"I don't know."

"I wish I had a bible."

"I got one."

"Can you read?"

"Yes. Can you?"

"Yes."

"Who teach you?'

"Massa kids on my first plantation. Who teach you?'

"Gravy and Bell."

"Who is Gravy?"

"Gravy's the man that married Mama Pearl."

"Bad Bell teach you to read. You two real close eh?"

"Yes we were. You can take the bible. But don't let Chaney see it. She scared of anything with words on it."

"Old slaves always like that. Too many whippings."

"You think more slaves try to read now than ever before?"

Then, There Was Iron

"I don't know. My last place, I didn't see or hear too much. I hope so."

"So do I. I'm near starving. You hungry?"

"I get used to being hungry. I can go days without food."

"Don't say that."

"Why?"

"I don't like hearing it. I'll heat the food."

"I forgot all about that pumpkin pie. I can't wait to get into it."

"I hope you like it. I only made 2 or 3 in my life. So I don't know if it's good."

"I'm sure it's good."

"Chloe why don't you stay all night with me?"

"What if Massa come around?'

"Massa ain't been here in over a year. He thinks I'm old."

"You ain't old."

"I'm old for what Massa likes."

"He still go see Peaches. She tole me."

"He like talking to Peaches. Everybody does. But he don't bother with her no more. Massa leaves me alone. He don't come around here cuz I feed most his slaves so he think I'm doing my part. Massa just want to know that you giving something to him or the plantation. Then he leave you alone."

"I really don't want him waking us up."

"He ain't gonna come. I know him well. Chloe I would like to wake up and see you that's all."

"I'll stay Iron. Lord I hope Miss Chaney won't think I try to run away."

"If you go back early she probably won't even know you were gone all night."

"Lord Shelly was right."

"Shelly right about what."

"She said you feel free when you come to this cabin"

"Shelly said that?"

"Yes."

"Do you feel scared?"

"I feel better than I ever felt before."

"Chloe I'm so happy."

The two women ate the feast Iron had earlier prepared. They talked a little longer before they made love throughout the night. Love much different from their earlier session. This time they both took the time to explore every inch of each others body. Chloe was surprised Iron had no scars. She said that Iron was the first slave she had ever known who had never been whipped. She marveled at the smoothness of Irons body. This time their lovemaking was slow and sensuous. They asked each other questions and compared their good places. As Iron liked to call it. She showed Chloe the exact spot to touch to achieve the feeling she had earlier. Chloe said that no one had ever touched her there before. They would go down further to the small hole. When Iron asked why didn't she try to touch herself there. Chloe said she had never had the time. It was the most extraordinary night of Irons life. As Chloe slept and Iron lay with her arms wrapped around her. She wept because she knew the night would end.

Chloe woke up first. Then woke Iron with gentle kisses. She wanted Iron to relax while she prepared breakfast for her. She fried ham and eggs and served it to Iron while she was still in bed. They washed each other and made love for a third time. Iron was actually surprised that Chloe wanted to make love before she left. Iron enjoyed this session immensely more than the other two. Though it was much shorter. This time Chloe initiated it and was more aggressive than she had been the night before. Iron loved it. Iron loved hearing Chloe urge we got time. She loved knowing that Chloe wanted her. She wanted them to spend the whole day in bed together but she reminded Chloe to get to Miss Chaney's. She didn't want Chloe to be assumed missing. She didn't want Chloe whipped and she didn't want Chloe sold off. She would rather die. For a quick instant she understood Nelson. To have a woman so great so beautiful you would give your own life before you let something happen to her. She didn't like him having ten years with Chloe. Ten years of waking up to Chloe. What an honor. No she didn't like him at all, even if he was dead. But she understood him.

Watching Chloe walk back to the row. Iron thought I would do anything for this woman. I will never say no to her. Could they share love as slaves? There were slave couples that lived together all their lives. There were also couples that had no idea where the other was. Sharing a cabin with Chloe. Is there anything more sweet? But what if John did come around again? What if John wanted to take Chloe? Lord knows they would hang her for what she would do to him. No, Chloe was to dark, to old for John. Thank you Jesus. What about the

Then, There Was Iron

railroad? She had completely forgotten about it. She didn't want to run a station anymore. It was time to ride.

Up North. Up North with Chloe. They could stay with Mama Pearl and Gravy. Find work. Chloe might run. It's different now, the railroad get you north safely. Well more safe than running on your own. Oh, the fugitive slave law. They couldn't stay with Mama Pearl and Gravy. They would have to go to Canada. Irons mind was racing to fast. All she was certain of was she wanted to be with Chloe every minute of every day. How she was going to do that? She would have to figure it out. But that is how it must be. Iron wondered how much John paid for Chloe. Maybe she should collect her money from her various hiding spots and see if she could purchase Chloe's freedom. They couldn't live together all year but Chloe be free.

This was also unlikely; Massa did not often sell his slaves. Especially, so that they could obtain their freedom. He was still angry over Gravy. What could she do? She must tell Chloe about her station on the railroad. Thoughts of the future were put aside when Iron heard terrible screams.

She quickly threw on her coat and went running in the direction of the screams, praying all the way it wasn't Chloe. It was one of the housemaids being severely whipped by Miss Mary. A small group of slaves had gathered to watch, Chloe was one of them. She looked at Iron, than instantly put her head down. Iron felt that Chloe was only there because she would have to tend the girl after the whipping. John Cummings appeared.

"Mary, how many is that?"

"Well John, I haven't been counting."

"I think it's enough. That wench won't be good for nothing for weeks."

"John, I know how to handle these niggers. It isn't enough until the ground is red. That is how you teach a nigger."

"Women, are you saying, that I don't know how to run this plantation?"

"No John."

"Then when I say that's enough, that's enough. You two come untie this girl. Take her to Chaney's cabin."

While the girl was being untied, Iron slowly sneaked away. She did not want to be seen by Miss Mary. In all the years she had been on the Cummings plantation she could count only 6 or 7 times she had been in the presence of Miss Mary. Most of these times she was a youngster getting started in the field. John Cummings tried his best to keep his breeding wenches away from his wife. Grateful to his immense success, Iron had nothing but hate and terror for Miss Mary. She quickly snuck to Chloe's cabin. No one had yet arrived.

"Who dat?"

"It's me, Iron."

"What's all the fussin I hear? Who getting whipped?"

"A housemaid. One of the new ones. They be here soon."

Chloe enters with her new patient who is being carried by two field hands. Surprisingly the girl is still conscious.

"Lay her down on her chest over there. Iron, get me some lard."

Iron does as she's told. She watches Chloe, the tender way she touches her patient. She loves the way Chloe takes control of the entire situation. Barking orders at everyone. The girl is saying,

"Don't waste your time on me, I wants to die."

"Hush child, you don't know what you are saying."

"I'm saying I wants to die. I can't be no slave no mo. I can't, I can't!"

The girl passes out while Chloe continues working on her back, as Iron quietly watches. When she is finished Chloe finally looks at Iron. Iron feels relieved.

"So, that's Miss Mary?"

"Yes."

"I heard lots about her since I been here."

"Thank God she don't leave that house too often anymore. She just lock herself up in there. Don't go visitin. Don't receive visitors. She sure hard on her house slaves."

"Look like it."

"I seen her kill a girl."

"Whip her to death?"

"Took a few days for the girl to die. But she die cuz a whipping by Miss Mary. It Miss Mary that pinned my Mama's lip down. That's why my Mama free to this day, Gravy couldn't stand her serving Miss Mary."

"Then I guess we can thank Miss Mary for something."

"I guess we can."

Then, There Was Iron

"Must be hard knowing that your husband is sleeping with a Negro woman every night. Knowing that he rather be with a Negro woman, than be with you."

"She don't think we women, she think we animals anyway."

"Then it must be hard watching your husband go lay with an animal, instead of laying with you."

"Chloe, you trying to have sympathy for white people?"

"I'm trying to understand them now."

"So, you don't think they all got a disease in the head anymore?"

"I don't got it all worked out yet. Let me ask you something. If you were married to a man and every night he went to the barn, to lay with a cow, what would you do to the cow?"

"Well, he wouldn't be my man too long. As soon as I found out he was laying with a cow, he'd be gone and there be meat for everybody."

"Iron, you ever lay with a black man?"

"No."

"You never wanted to?"

"I tried to, wanted to years back, but I couldn't. I don't think it be much different than a white man. Though Peaches say they bigger and last longer."

"That's the truth."

"So you prefer black men cause they bigger and last longer?"

"I prefer touching someone I care about. I had black men that come in and take me cuz Massa say so. Cuz Massa want me to breed. Girl, if you don't feel nothing, it don't matter if they white or black. Well, sometimes you rather a white man cuz it faster. But no matter how long it takes; you left with the same feeling. Like you never can be clean."

"Lord, I know that feeling."

"You don't think that you will ever try with a black man?"

"You want me to?"

"I'm not saying that. I'm just asking if you think one day, you be curious?"

"All I'm curious about is how long you gonna want me."

"Thank God. Iron I don't know what you did to me. I don't know what I'm gonna do."

"You don't gotta do nothing. Lie back and let me do everything."

Chloe laughs and the two women embrace.

"You better go. I got a lot of tending to do on this poor girl."
"You need anything?"
"No. I got everything I need."
"She gonna be okay?"
"She be fine in a few days."
"You comin around tonight?"
"You sure it's alright?"
"Yeh, I'll cook you supper."
"Woman, you spoiling me."
"You should be spoiled. How bout some fish?"
"I got a taste for your chicken."
"I'll have some chicken ready when you get there."
"That's not all I want you to have ready."
Iron laughs and walks out the door.

CHAPTER 14

Chloe came by late that night and every night. The two were inseparable. Most of the slaves on the plantation and the neighboring plantations knew what they were up to, although no slave ever told any white person. Both women were very happy about this. They had no idea what the reaction of John would be if he knew. They feared, like a percentage of the field hands, he would want to crawl in between them, or he would want to watch. For the first months they were together, when the rumors were still flying, most able-bodied men in South Carolina asked them just that. The reply was always no. Iron felt no black man told any white person because a white man did not need to ask. He just took what wasn't his. This Iron knew angered the black men. They must have felt that if they couldn't crawl in the middle, a white man shouldn't either. Iron was very grateful for this.

Iron thought black women just didn't care. It meant two less wenches after their men. Iron and Chloe were also very popular. Iron because she was known to give the clothes off her back, and Chloe because she was a superb healer. She was so good, that neighboring plantations called for her services. White people would call John Cummings to see if his girl Chloe was busy, before they called their own doctor. It was getting to the point where the doctor was losing a large amount of his clients. He than made an offer to John Cummings, to purchase Chloe. John wouldn't sell. Iron felt almost love for John that day. Chloe didn't; she hated John.

She would never forget that night. The sounds. She was taking her usual nightly walk to be with Iron. She was just about to open the cabin door, when she heard him. She heard John saying vile things to Iron. She heard the sound of the mattress squeaking. They had been together about six months. Iron had sworn that Massa never came to see her anymore. That night Chloe wanted to kill John, but she didn't. She wanted to run away, but she didn't. She only made the long tearful walk back to her and Chaney's cabin. She did not want to see Chaney, and wondered why the old woman wouldn't die. She was completely blind, and partially deaf. At least she wouldn't see her crying. She thought that she might also hate Iron. Lying to her and telling her that Massa don't come around anymore. That is probably the reason why some nights Iron came to see her. Claiming she wanted to save Chloe the walk, or she wanted to bring food for Miss Chaney. Chloe had a feeling on those nights; Iron did not want Chloe in her cabin. Now she knew why.

Two days after the night she had heard John with Iron, Iron came to see her.

"How come you ain't been by?"

"I don't want to bother you is all."

"Bother me? What are you talking about?"

"I know you a busy woman. I don't want to take all your time. Others may need it."

"Chloe, what are you saying?"

"You still seeing Massa, and you told me that you don't. You lied to me."

"Chloe, I ain't never lied to you."

"I heard him. I heard him the other night."

"What do you want me to do Chloe? Say not tonight Massa, I is busy? Not tonight Massa, I already made plans? Try me again another time? Chloe, he owns me. What you want me to do?"

"How often he come by?"

"I swear to you, that was the first time in years."

"How come sometimes you don't want me at your cabin? Like today, you walk down here before I get a chance to see you. You spectin him tonight, aren't ya?"

"Lord, I pray not. You don't believe me, do you?"

"I don't know what to believe."

"Alright Chloe, you want the truth? Come on."

Iron walks briskly to her cabin. Chloe walks a few steps behind, neither woman saying a word. As soon as they enter the cabin, Iron clears the floor to reveal the secret cellar door. Chloe is shocked. Iron leads Chloe down the stairs to the frightful eyes of five runaway slaves. Chloe studies them, doesn't say a word, than goes back upstairs.

"You are a conductor."

"Have been for years."

"How come you never tell me?"

"I can't tell no one around here. That's how the railroad works. We gotta keep quiet."

"Oh, Iron."

Then, There Was Iron

The two women kiss passionately. They are about to make love when they remember the five people downstairs that could hear every word.

Massa never again visited Iron after that night. But that visit left her belly big. To her surprise Chloe was not angry because her belly was big with Massa's child. Chloe took extra care of her and tried to satisfy Iron's every need. When the time came, Chloe was the one who delivered the baby. Upon hearing Chloe say the words, "he's beautiful," Iron for the first time, looked at one of her babies. She screamed, "Oh my God, he's so white!" Chloe was shocked to hear this, after all Iron was one of thee lightest slaves she had ever seen, and John Cummings was a white man; what did she expect? The boy was named Lenox. Iron did not hold him. John sold him immediately.

Chloe was surprised at Iron's complete coldness when it came to her children. But she didn't say anything about it. She couldn't imagine having all her children by white men. She couldn't imagine being tucked away, a plaything for a white man. Yes, white men had taken her, but this was not her only purpose. If it was, she may be at the same place where she couldn't look at her children. She admitted to herself that she loved her children created by Nelson, but the four children forced upon her by white men, she never thought of. Maybe this was wrong. Maybe she should have enough pain and suffering for children of all colors.

After the birth of Lenox, the woman's love affair continued with no talk about children. Except the two nights when Chloe laid in Iron's arms and cried for Ruth. Iron felt heartbroken, and completely powerless. On these nights she wanted to talk about running away. Running away from a life that took your children away from you. She was scared; she didn't know how to suggest this to Chloe. It was running away that caused her to lose Ruth. Since working on the railroad, Chloe had never suggested riding it their selves. Iron had to know, would Chloe be willing to leave with her? One night while lying in bed, she could no longer take it.

"Chloe, you awake?"
"Yes, ummm, you wanna go again?"
"I don't think I could. I wanna talk to ya."
"I'm listening."
"I been thinking about Canada."
"Don't Iron."

Ellen Barton

Chloe turns around and embraces Iron like she is holding on for dear life. She is gently crying while giving Iron light kisses.

"Lord, please don't, Lord please, oh Lord please, don't please!"

"Alright Chloe, it's alright."

"Iron, I couldn't lose you. I can't, I can't Iron, I can't lose anyone else, I can't!"

"Chloe, it don't mean you gonna lose me."

"Don't Lord, please, Lord please!"

"Chloe, Chloe, we could go together. You see all the people we got going through here? You doctored them. Don't you think they gonna make it?"

"Some might, some won't."

"I like to think they all make it. Most do."

"How you know?"

"I know. Chloe we could make it."

"Iron, Lord if we got caught. We could be sold to the deep South. We could be worked to death, and our breeding years ain't over. Iron terrible things could happen. Iron, I can't lose you, I can't, I can't!"

"It's alright. You ain't gonna lose me. I'll be here for you."

Iron embraces her and returns the light kisses.

"You wouldn't run without me?"

"Never."

"You got running in your head."

"I got loving you in my head. I want to do it right. I want to be free to love you."

"Your words are beautiful."

"Your face is beautiful."

The lovers slowly fall asleep in each other's arms.

CHAPTER 15

The next few years flew by almost overnight. Miss Clara said she didn't like it. There seemed to be a nervous tension in the air. Iron was enjoying life at a level she did not even understand, or try to. Chloe was her very air. The slaves she helped were her food and drink. Her cellar was constantly full. She was amazed at the amount of slaves that arrived at her door. The amount of new Canadians that included in their prayers, the two women from South Carolina who fed them, doctored them and helped in any way they could, was astonishing. Iron was amazed that Chloe would take on so many risks assisting on the railroad, though she wouldn't make the voyage herself. One day Iron wanted to say, "if you get caught, you would suffer the same fate, or worse, than if you ran yourself." But she did not.

There were a few occasions when Iron had worked up the nerve to ask Chloe to run away again. The results were always the same, fear, and sheer panic. Iron thought she would give up asking for a while. Reuben said it wouldn't be a long while, because freedom was now so close, you could taste it. Iron thought the man was getting old. Freedom. He could taste it. Shelly could smell it. Chloe was afraid of it. Paddy could barely say it. All Iron wanted, was to know that Chloe wouldn't be sold away from her. That Chloe wouldn't be given to a man. That Chloe would never be whipped. That Chloe would never be hungry, or alone. Freedom.

It was coming. Peaches said a poor white man wrote a book, saying slavery was terrible because it kept the poor whites, just that. She said the rich Massa's thought the poor whites, may cause trouble.

"Poor whites always trouble."

"But Chloe, this time they won't be giving trouble to us."

"They always giving trouble to us."

"Ladies I saying that they gonna cause an uproar with the rich whites."

"How you hurt a rich white man?"

"Kill all his slaves."

"You two never wanna hear no good news."

"Oh that's good news."

"Pray she don't got no bad news."

Ellen Barton

"I just thought you two like to know is all. I know ya like to talk about those abolitionists and fighting against slavery. So I come over this fine evening to tell ya what I heard today."

"But this man who wrote the book he ain't no abolitionist?"

"Well he against slavery."

"But he don't care about us."

"Look he against slavery. That's an abolitionist right?"

"Yeh. Yes"

"Does it matter why you want slavery to end as long as you want it to end?"

"I guess. But he don't like black folks do he?"

"I don't know for sure. Didn't sound like it."

"Peaches right, he an abolitionist if he wants to end slavery. If he ended slavery and we all be free. You think we stop and say. But he didn't like black folks. W say bye see you in Philadelphia."

"You want to go to Philadelphia?"

"Mama Pearl there."

"You never told me you wanted to got to Philadelphia."

"It's just someplace I would go if I was free."

"Chloe don't you have someplace you would go. I suppose you follow Iron to Philadelphia."

"I never thought about it."

"You never thought about being free?'

"Peaches you want a taste? Got a new jug."

"No I don't, thanks. So Chloe you never thought about being free?"

"Want some food? Cooked up some good food last night."

"I'm not hungry thanks. Talking about food. I gotta go. I told Benjamin I cook him up something special tonight."

"You got some celebrations?"

"Yeh he won some money on a cock fight. See ya tomorrow."

"Bye."

"You know how to get Peaches mind a changing."

"I just don't want you getting upset."

"Why I got to get upset?"

"Oh nothing."

"Must be something."

"I love you is all."

"Oh that. I love you too."

Then, There Was Iron

The next day Iron received a message to go visit Miss Clara. Chloe didn't mind for she was occupied, tending a dying Chaney. Usually she hated the time Iron spent with Miss Clara always mumbling why she must see that white woman so often. Eventually Iron admitted to Chloe that it was Miss Clara who organized the passengers on the railroad and it was important that they communicate often. Still Chloe wasn't happy about it.

"Afternoon Miss Clara."

"Iron how many times have I told you that Clara is fine. Call me Clara."

"It's hard to break habits."

"I know dear. You must break them soon. The times are about to change."

"What do you mean?"

"Abraham Lincoln is running for president."

"President?"

"He is not a man that believes in slavery. If Mr. Lincoln is elected from what I've heard the South will go it's own way."

"What you saying Miss Clara? Clara."

"The South will secede"

"Succeed, sound like they lose if Mr. Lincoln not a slavery man."

"Not succeed Iron secede. Which means they will become their own country."

"You mean the South will be one country and the North another."

"Yes but I don't think it will last."

"What do you think gonna happen?"

"As John Brown said, what must happen. Bloodshed."

"We slaves been shedding enough blood."

"White bloodshed dear. I'm fearing a war."

"A war?"

"Iron there is no possibility of the South claiming victory in a war. The North has a much greater population, developed industry. Iron the reason I called you today, is to ask if you had any money?"

"I got a little, I been saving."

"Iron I will soon move north. I will not remain on Southern soil during a war. I have plans to buy extensive properties in Philadelphia possibly New York. I have managed to correspond with Gravy, through messenger. He shall partner with me. I suggest you join us."

"Why?"

"Southern currency shall be worth nothing if there is a war. Trust me. I can help you arrange to have something in the future. Listen to me, if you don't do this all your savings shall be worthless paper."

"I trust you Clara you always seem to know what's right."

"In a few days I am having a lawyer look over my affairs. What I suggest is you bring all your money to me. I will have the bankers think it's mine. After the exchange I shall give you the deeds. This is the only way you will have something after the war."

"Clara you sure there will be a war?"

"If Lincoln is elected there will be one."

"You think he got a chance of being elected?'

"I've never seen the man myself. I know he served terms in state legislature and in congress. I have heard talk of him before. I did not pay it that much mind. What I am aware of is. If the South hates Abraham Lincoln, then he must be a good man. Keep your eyes and ears open Iron."

"I will Clara. I'll come back tomorrow with my money."

Irons walk home was anxious. Wait till Chloe hears. It was coming. It was really coming. Should she tell Chloe that she was going to hand over all the money she had managed to save over the years. She had never even told Chloe that she had money. She wasn't hiding the fact. It just never came up. Chloe would not trust Miss Clara. Imagine owning properties. Somewhere to go when freedom came. Owning properties in Philadelphia. Iron started running.

When she arrived home she was surprised to see it full of people. Reuben was there with Peaches and Shelly. Chloe appeared to be making coffee. Iron often wondered how no ever realized that neither she nor Chloe drank coffee. They kept it for the runaways. Most thought it a luxury.

"Chloe how's Miss Chaney?"

"She was sleeping. I think she getting some of her sight back. But her head going. When I'm there she don't really know it's me. She calling me different names all the time."

"Her time to be with Jesus."

"It way past her time. I don't know how that woman holding on."

"Peaches don't talk like that. What yall doin here anyway?"

"Girl you don't hear the news. Massa Lincoln gonna run for President."

"I just heard that."

Then, There Was Iron

"Lord Iron you getting the news faster than Peaches. What we gonna do with Peaches now."

"Shut your mouth Shelly. Things are going to be hell around here. White folks hate Lincoln."

"White folks in the South. White folks up North gonna make enough votes for Lincoln to win."

"How you know this Reuben?"

"Everybody tired of slavery. America a beautiful place, it's had enough of the terrible injustices on this land."

"Terrible injustices. Man, America was created on terrible injustices. It was Indian land. You all know what they did to the Indian. And stealing us from Africa. Well that is the smartest thing the white man ever did. That's his greatest accomplishment."

"Chloe you sure full of sunshine this morning."

"I heard if Massa Lincoln be president. There probably be a war."

"Like the Mexican war. Lord I remember that. I seen the soldiers marching off."

"It be like the Mexican War. But it be fought in the South. Right here."

"To end slavery?"

"Seem like it."

"We don't know if Massa Lincoln gonna win. If he lose everyday be just like yesterday."

"Peaches he gonna win."

"How you so sure?"

"God told us. He told me and he told my daddy and he told my momma. He telling my children too. Wherever they are. God say Reuben fret not. For your people shall be free."

"God said, fret not?"

"God call you by your name?"

"Maybe he don't call me by my name. But how long black folks been praying to God? How long we been suffering? We been waiting for our chance to make our own lives. Our chance to show what we can do. Not for the white man. But for each other."

"We do love to step fine in front of each other."

"Once we free there's no stopping us. Cuz as soon as one black man get good paying work. Another black man gonna want better paying work. Gonna pull ourselves up. Make it better and better. Our grand babies and their grand babies when they know what we went through. They gonna work harder. Cuz it's their hard work that's gonna say thank you to us. When we cold in the ground."

"Reuben I hope you right."

"You really think that our grand babies and their grand babies gonna care what we went through?"

"We making a life for them. We stolen people. Stolen and made to work. Not allowed to own our own children. Make other men rich from our blood. We help make this America. We were forced to be Americans; well we can't go back now. The time is coming when we take back what's ours and we give it to our children and their children."

"Now you starting to sound like those white folks that say if you give black folks freedom we will make them the slaves."

"They scared fools. We don't got that in us, to do what white folks do. Freedom come we start to get education. We will take what's ours with ease and time. And a sad thing with no pain to white folks."

"Why you say a sad thing?"

"Cuz they do got some pain coming to them."

"If war comes. They will get plenty of pain. Believe me."

"We don't know for sure if war coming. Let's not get anxious."

"Anxious?"

"Let's not talk ahead. No one knows tomorrow. All we hearing now is talk. Things maybe even worse for black folks. Why everyone think things be better, if Lincoln win or if there be war. I got a good life now. I'm not ready for changes."

"Chloe we need changes. We can't live like this forever. Don't you wanna be free?"

"My children already gone. You think freedom gonna bring back my children?"

"Chloe freedom probably won't bring back your children. But that feeling you had when your children were sold. Freedom make sure you children never feel that."

"Lord I better get back to the row."

"Me too."

"We all got things need doing. Sitting around here like we already free."

"I think we should keep this talk among us."

All agree. Everyone leaves except Chloe.

"You going down to check on Miss Chaney?"

"Soon. It's that white woman?"
"Miss Clara."
"Told you war was coming?"
"Yes."
"You think she right?"
"Since I known her, she been right about everything. That woman see tomorrow. Always has."
"Why she tell you?"
"She gonna take her money and buy properties in Philadelphia. She say if a war come. Southern money won't be worth nothing. So it's best to buy properties now."
"If a war come. How she know her property won't be ruined."
"She said the war is sure to be fought in the South."
"Where we living?"
"Think so."
"Why she telling you all this business?"
"She is gonna help Gravy buy some property to. She think I should take my money and put it with her and Gravy's and we all buy property together."
"You got money?"
"Yes."
"How much?"
"I don't know."
"Where is it?"
"All over."
"You gonna do it?"
"What you think?"
"Do you trust her?"
"Yes."
"You sure?"
"Yes."
"You got that much money, you can buy property?
"No. That's why we putting our money together. Miss Clara really helping Gravy and me. She said that she will even put everything in Gravy's name."
"Not yours?"
"No one knows I have money. Gravy already in Philadelphia. This way he can take care of things. When freedom comes, we have somewhere to go."

Ellen Barton

"Oh, you taking me?"

"Don't you want to be with me?"

"Yes."

"If we were free, and you could be anywhere you wanted, would you want to be with me?"

"Iron, I love you. I'll always love you, as a slave woman, or as a free woman."

"I love you too. I'm doing this for us. I want us to live together, have a life together."

"Iron, you think it be that easy?"

"I don't think it be easy at all."

"Give your money to the white woman."

"Miss Clara."

"Yeah, Miss Clara. If you trust her, I trust her. You right, we gonna need a place to stay. Once we got that, we have to find some work is all."

"You sure you fine with all this?"

"I'll take it day by day. First we see if that Massa Lincoln gonna win and be President. Then we see if that white woman,"

"Miss Clara."

"Yeah, we see if Miss Clara right. If the South becomes it's own country."

"I tell ya, she always right."

"Well I heard talk about the South becoming it's own country. Must be about ten years back, and it never happened."

"You know, I remember that. All white folks in an uproar. Maybe they tired of talking and they gonna do something about it."

"Iron, let's say Miss Clara right. Is she sure the South would not win a war?"

"Miss Clara said the South don't got enough people to win a war."

"Maybe they get help."

"From who?"

"I don't know. You right in telling everybody not to mention this. You really like that Miss Clara, don't you?"

"Yes. She the best white person I ever met."

"She never lie to you, or cause you harm?"

"No."

"Does she make you do things?"

"Things?"

"Like we do."

"God, no. Chloe, she wouldn't even think of it. It's Miss Clara that got me started on the railroad. You know Miss Clara working on the railroad, and you still don't trust her."

"She still white."

"But she so good to black folk."

"I expect her to change, show a side of herself more like other whites."

"I been waiting for that change for a long time. I finally realized it ain't coming."

"Lord, I hope so. I best get back to the row; quite a few sick these days."

"Come back later and help me count my money."

"See you later."

The women kiss and Chloe leaves. Iron stares into space wondering what is happening out there.

Ellen Barton

CHAPTER16

What was happening? Near the Alabama Georgia border, on the Joplin plantation, a large number of slaves were being loaded off wagons. It was planting season and they were weeks behind. This was one of the reasons he had to go out and buy more slaves. He had picked 20 of the strongest looking ones. He only wished that they could last longer. It seemed they were always sick or dying.

Lewis Joplin remembered the words of the preacher who had came around a few years back. Give them more food, better clothes and use the whip less often, this would help them to last longer. Lewis had used all his strength not to punch the man full in the face. Tell him how to handle his slaves. He knew the solution when one died. Buy another one. They were worth the money. The only nigger he could stand was David. The boy was as white as he was. If he hadn't purchased David himself, he would swear David was a white man. Didn't even have any wool. His hair was as straight as any white mans. Nope, you would never know his mother was a slave.

This was one of the reasons David was chief overseer on the plantation. This, and Lewis Joplin loved him like a son. He had brought David in South Carolina not long after his own infant son had died. When he seen that white baby boy, he would have paid anything for him, though Mr. Cummings gave him a rather fair price. Lewis wanted to raise him as a white child, kept him in the house, but did not allow him an education. David was after all a nigger; he couldn't change that. He blamed David's unusual smarts, honesty, and loyalty, (loyal because David could have left and easily lived the life of a white man) on David's white blood. Plus David was an excellent overseer.

David had his own cabin with four rooms. He owned fine clothes, and never went without anything, including his pick of any woman he wanted on slave row. David would surely like this lot; it included some fine wenches. Maybe he should get David out of the field to inspect them. But he heard the whip flying and the screams. David was hard at work; he would wait before he showed off his new purchases.

"Hello Massa, got some new slaves?"

"Yes."

Then, There Was Iron

It was Squirrelly. Lord, she was more hated by Lewis, than all his other slaves. He really wanted to kill her, but he was afraid. Seemed like she could put spells on people. Lord knows what she would do to him from beyond the grave. It started years ago, about three. David had just been made head overseer. He wasn't even out of his teens. He gave Rowena a whipping so bad; people thought she was dead. She remained completely unconscious for about three days. When she woke up, one of her eyes constantly trembled and still does to this day. After that whipping people started calling her Squirrelly, probably because of the eye. Squirrelly did something to David and Lewis that had them sick in bed for months. Every time after that when they punished her, something would happen to one of them. When Lewis finally decided to sell her, the man who bought her, mysteriously died after raping her. Squirrelly walked back to the Joplin plantation. No one would ever buy her again. These days she helped the older woman who made clothes for everybody.

"Rowena, shouldn't you be working?"

"I always working Massa, always working on something."

She then turns around and heads on the opposite direction of were she should be. Damn, that was an uppity nigger. They fix her. They fix her yet. His boy David would think of something. Squirrelly would not be walking around here forever, like she owned the place. He got on his horse and rode into the field.

"David, how's it going?"

"Going good. We should get a lot done today. Keep em in the fields till the sun goes down."

"Well, I just picked up the new ones."

"How they looking?"

"Got some strong backs out there. We have done real good this year. Real good."

"They all for the field?"

"Got a couple of breeders. Why don't you come and take a look?"

"I'll do that later. I want to stay up on these ones here. As soon as I go, they get real slow."

"I'll send one of the housemaids with some food for you."

"Good."

David's day was like every other; beating and yelling. He never tired of it. He never tired of the look in the slaves eyes when they seen him coming. Or the sound they made when his whip hit their back. He was probably the most hated man for miles. Some say he was so cruel, because his mother never looked at him when he was a baby. That was the story they heard from the old man that was sold with him. That man, long since dead, told the other slaves that David's mother was a breeder who never looked at her children. Most slaves accepted this as a reasonable excuse. That, and he was white.

David stayed in the field until sundown, although it was not necessary. He felt it was completely up to him to get the crops in. The other overseers could not be trusted to stay up on the slaves. He went to bed as soon as he reached his cabin. Ready for another long day tomorrow.

David was giving his usual 17 lashes to an old woman. He liked to start with the old get his rhythm going. By the middle of the day he could easily give slave after slave 25 to 40 lashes without his arm getting tired. His whip flew all day. Then it happened, David was punched in the face by God. This took the form of a woman about 22 years old. She screamed.

"What are you doing?'

She didn't know he was a black man. New slaves on the plantation always first thought him white. She did not care. She glared at him with a hate that made him feel three inches tall. David would never be the same again. Her name was Nicey she was what was meant when one used the word beautiful. He immediately lowered his whip and understood shame.

The other slaves were shocked. David who was believed to be the son of Satan himself. David who had whipped many a slave to death. David who was known to have performed the most violent of rapes on three generations, of women belonging to the same family. David who would spit in your food. David who kicked a woman to the ground when her belly was big with child. David got on his horse and rode out of the field. He didn't know what else to do.

"Gal how ya talk to the ovaseer like dat?"

"Dats David he kill ya soon as he look at ya."

"Gal wats yo name?"

"Nicey."

"No one talk to David like dat."

"You bes stay on the look out."

"I ain't scare a nobody. I ain't scare ta die."

"Girl where ya from?"

Then, There Was Iron

"Don't know."
"Wat ya las Massa named?"
"Devil."
"Yo las Massa name devil?"
"Massa Devil he ran a plantation in hell. I was his servant."
"Gal ya still in hell. Dis the worses plantation I know."
"If I'm still in hell den I'm ready for it."
"You something."
"Hope you don get us all in trouble."
"I'll take all the trouble. I ain't scared. I'll never be scared."
"You don't know David. I'll never forgets when he was just a boy he made a kitten tree."
"Kitten tree?'
"Was a time here we had lots of cats. Now quite a few of them were ready for birthing. Now time come this place full of kittens. One night you hear all kinds of small squeaking but you don't get up ta look. Ya so tired. Mawning come one dem big trees full of kittens. He hung em all by the neck. Mus be 25, 30 kittens. He was jus a boy. He only grow to get worse. I never forget that kitten tree."
"I tole ya I done met the devil himself. I ready for anything."
"God Bless you chile."
"She gawn need more than Gods blessing."
"I don't need nothin thank ya. God will bless me if he wants to. David will get me if he wants to. What ever happen I don't care."

Some of the others look at each other as if Nicey had seen times worst than theirs. If that was possible. Nicey is still helping the old woman.

"You be alright Missy."
"Thanx chile. I use ta da beatings. Don't trouble over me. He be on my back gin tomorrow. I don't mind none. He taken me ta Jesus."

The woman smiles and looks Nicey deep in her eyes. Nicey is lost for a moment deep inside the old woman eyes. The endless depth of pain there. The smothered pride. Layers and layers of hurt so thick and strong it turned into happiness. Happiness, that you are closer to death. Happiness in knowing one day the pain will surely be over.

Nicey knew that place. Where they can't hurt me no more. I won't let them hurt me no more. But they do. Would Nicey have that look in her eyes? Far in the years. She probably had it now. But her layers were not that thick yet. Do they get thicker when you accept that you

Ellen Barton

be beaten to death. Beaten to death. Beat me to death. Nicey wants to scream this. She wants to die before her layers got to thick. That devil white boy, maybe he can do it.

David arrives back at his plantation completely out of breath. He doesn't know why. He doesn't know why he stopped when that wench yelled at him. God she was beautiful. He had never seen a woman more beautiful in all his life. What was her name? He didn't know. She thought him a beast. He was. She had seen him. She had seen him beating that old woman. Why did she have to see him? They will tell her. They will tell her the things he has done. If only he could cut out all their tongues. He laughs. What does he care. What does he care what she thinks. He is David. He could do anything he wanted anytime of any day. She was a field wench. He could have her. He could go in the field and take her now.

David takes off out of his cabin and jumps on his horse. He rides back to the field even faster than he rode out.

"See m comin?"

"Dats it."

"Nice ta know ya gal."

"I'll memba ya name if I ever see ya peoples. Nicey from the devil plantation right?"

"Right."

"What's all this standing around talking? Get back to work."

"Yes'm Massa David."

"All you old folks don't have to work today. Come in. Tell all the old folks come in today. That's all"

David turns on his horse and rides out.

"Lawd hav mercy."

"I never seen dat since Ise been here."

"Lord we work in rain, storm everything"

"Just get 3 days off for Christmas."

"Other folks get a week."

"The man said come in. Lawd hav mercy."

"Something wrong."

"Day mus gawn kill em all while we in da fiel."

"Yeh dey gawn kill em all."

"Why kill em? Dey still can work."

"Dey dawn work so good."

Then, There Was Iron

"Dey can work in the garden. Dey can tend children. Make clothes. Dey can do sumpen out da fiel. I dawn think dey gawn kill em."

"I think they want to die."

"Maybe girl you right."

"Dey all tired."

"Yall stop, dey ain'ts dying today."

"Get on working, here come John."

"Whose John?"

"Udder ovaseer. He ain't as bad as David."

"Where all them old ones going?"

"David tole em to go on in."

John turns around and rides off to go find David.

"David, what are you doing?"

"Don't worry what I'm doing."

"Mr. Joplin ain't gonna like you calling all them in."

"I'll deal with Lewis."

David rides off. He didn't feel like listening to John anyways. He was sure John hated him; being a slave giving orders to a free man; both being of the same complexion. Being a slave didn't bother David at all. He knew in his heart that he could leave and live the life of a white man. Every looking glass told him this. This was not necessary, as David enjoyed the life of a King. He felt more power in his 20 years, than most men would ever see in their entire lives. He enjoyed the liberty of abusing this power, abusing other slaves, until today.

What was he doing? Calling all the old slaves in. What would he tell Lewis? It didn't matter, what mattered was she seen him. She has seen him call them in. Now she wouldn't think him such a beast. He would also get her out of the field. No, she isn't any field slave. She isn't a slave. What if he bought her? What if Lewis gave her to him? Give her to me. He didn't like it. He didn't like that she had to be given. What if he just took her and left? How far could he get? Would they ever be caught? Why hadn't Lewis ever offered him his freedom? Why hadn't he ever thought of this before? Lewis often said he loved him like a son. What kind of son? A son you owned? A son you attacked women with? A son you killed with? A son you wouldn't send to school? A son you wouldn't allow to eat at your table if your wife was in the house? A son who would not receive your vast fortune when you died.

Lewis was beginning to look a tad less admirable. Not the great man David adored his entire life. The only person in the world that cared about him. Cared. Didn't treat him like a slave. Was that enough? Enough. To be given all the food and clothing you want? To have the biggest cabin on the plantation? To be put in charge of others? It wasn't enough. David, for the first time in his life, hated slavery. He hated being owned. He hated what could be done to a beautiful girl in the field. God, he had to find out her name. He didn't see or hear Lewis approaching.

"David."

"Yes?"

"What are you doing with the slaves?"

"I'm trying something new."

"You sure this the right time to be trying? All the fields not even planted yet."

"Lewis, trust me. Have I ever let you down?"

"Alright. Go ahead. You always know what you are doing, but I don't want to start seeing lazy niggers around here."

"You don't have to worry about that. How many women you buy this time?"

"About six."

"You got em all in the field?"

"Just two in the field; got two for the house; and I got two real dark ones for breeding. Figure I can sell off the babies for good money. I always said you get a real black wench, and a big strong buck, you get the best market pups."

"Yeah. Ah, two field girls, what's their names?"

"I think one name Kate, she a mulatto, light, light girl, and one name Nicey. Why you want to know? If you fancy one, you don't need to know their names."

"I don't fancy em. I seen one scratching herself, hard. She may have some woman problems."

"Which one?"

"Sound like Nicey. I wouldn't try her. I don't want no aches and burning."

"No, don't want that. Thanks for telling me because I was going to give a couple of them a try tonight. You up to a little fun?"

"Not tonight. I can't have fun till the crops get in."

Then, There Was Iron

"That's what I love about you David. Always working. I'll see you later then."

"Right."

Woman problems that should keep Lewis away until David could figure things out. He thought of the things they had done to other women. God, if anybody did those things to Nicey, he would rip out their hearts. He had to get this woman out of his head. This wasn't right. This wasn't the man he had become. Maybe this was the man he was supposed to be. A man that needed a woman. A man that wanted to be held in the night by a woman. Would he still be King? Would he still be the great David? He feels he would be even greater. Ah, what he could do for the reward of Nicey. Nicey. Nicey. He liked the way it sounded. He would go see her tonight.

It seemed to take forever for the sun to go down. He couldn't pull her out of the field today. Not after what he had done with the old folks. Tomorrow he would arrange for her to have other work on the plantation; making shoes maybe. He knew help was needed for that. That is what he will tell her tonight. That is the reason for his visit. David knocks on the door.

"Come in."

"Hello."

"It's you."

Nicey turns around, leans against the wall, and starts to lift her dress.

"What are you doing?"

"What do you want?"

"I was coming around to tell you, you won't be in the field tomorrow."

"Where I gonna be?"

"We not sure yet."

David looks around the cabin. There is some hay in the corner with an old horse blanket, and a chair. In the middle of the cabin there is a fire pit. She can't live like this.

"You got food for the night?"

"I got a piece of bacon. I got to get some firewood."

"Where did you get the bacon?"

"Massa gave us all some when we got here."

"Why don't you come by my cabin? Cook brought me up some real good food."

Ellen Barton

"Why you care so much about what I'm eating? Every slave on this plantation hungry tonight. Man, if you want it, take it. I got no time for talking with a white man. Just gonna get troubles."

"I just thought being new here, you might need some things. I thought I could help you."

"Help? I didn't know you were my helper man."

"Look, you want me to go over to my place and fix you up some food?"

"That would be lovely."

"You kind of a funny girl."

"Yeh, funny."

"How old are you?"

"I dunno. I thought your first question would be, what's my name?"

"I know your name."

"Oh? How far you live?"

"Not too far. I guess you're tired. Long day in the field today."

"I'm alright for now. I guess I be a lot more tired later."

"Why you think that?"

"This walk we taking now; go to your cabin, get food. I'm sposin your cabin full of white men ready to do things to me. Hurt me. Make me bleed."

David stops walking and faces Nicey.

"How could you say that? I would never do anything to hurt you. Never."

"Yes, Mr. Ovaseer. You just want to feed me. Thank you Mr. White man. Well you gonna keep walking? I'm ready. I'm ready for anything."

"Yes, and you will see. Plus I'm not a white man."

"Yeh, and I am not a field hand. I'm president of Merica. I just look like a field hand."

"Umph, you sure you hungry now?"

"Yeah, I'm hungry for everything."

The two keep on walking in silence. When they reach David's cabin, he enters first, and lights a few candles. He latches the door behind Nicey.

"See, no one here. No great plan to attack you. Now don't you feel foolish?"

"The nights young."

Then, There Was Iron

"There's food in the kitchen, through those doors. You can find everything you need. Go ahead and prepare something nice for us."

Nicey stares at David. Then she walks through the doors to the kitchen. David has a beautiful cabin. Not a white man umph. A slave. His cabin sure didn't look like the cabins of the other slaves. She has seen slaves on the row, 5 or 6 in one room. Big holes in the ceiling. You can see right through the cracks in the walls. No furniture. Lord, it looked like he had 4 or 5 rooms, and a kitchen with everything. Loaded with food. Lord, a jug of whiskey. Should she take some? Yes, especially if he would take her tonight. Foul white man. Wanna be black. Lord, she heard about him. She heard from the others the son of the devil himself. Yeah, she take a big cup. Then she go to work on the fish and potatoes.

David could smell the food cooking. It was wonderful. He was sitting back in his favorite chair. Listening to Nicey prepare dinner. She came out about an hour later. Slightly staggering but carrying a plate of what looked to be a beautiful feast.

"Where's yours?"

"I left mine in the kitchen."

"Why?"

"I never eat with white folks."

"Nicey I'm not a white man. I'm a slave like you."

"I prefer to have my food in the kitchen."

"Then I'll come to the kitchen and eat with you."

"Suit yourself."

David follows Nicey into the kitchen. He sees that she prepared for herself an even larger portion than she prepared for him. She also had some wrapped in her pocket to take home, plus she finished his jug of whiskey. None of these things bothered him.

"This food is excellent. You ever work as a cook?"

"I did mos the cooking on my last plantation. I did mos everything."

"Small plantation?"

"Only had 3 slaves."

"Why they sell you?"

"Got a younger one."

"Your not old."

"But I'm worn out."

"You don't look close to being worn out"

Ellen Barton

"You planning to speed that along."

"Woman why you so sure I'm going to do you harm."

"Look at you. Look at me. You were made to do me harm. I was made to take it."

"Can not a man simply offer a woman kindness?"

"Ah, like courting. You courting me Mr. Ovaseer?"

"Please stop calling me Mr. Ovaseer."

"Why? That is what you are."

"I'm thinking to change that."

"So you don't want to be an ovaseer no more. Wore out your arm did ya? You gonna bring that snowflake skin and that head full of thread out to the field are ya? Work side by side with your brothers and sisters. Somehow I just don't see it."

"What do you see?"

"Nothing."

"There was a time I look for tomorrow and I didn't not see anything myself."

"Now you see something?"

"Now I want to see something?"

"What?'

"A life far away from here."

"I can't look for tomorrow. I don't got no say in it, so why look to it"

"What if you had a say?"

"How I'm gonna have a say I a slave woman."

"I'm a slave man but I will have a say."

"You a white man."

"My mother was a breeder. My father was most likely her owner. I was brought when I was a baby by Lewis."

"Whose Lewis?"

"Massa Joplin. He brought me right after his own infant son died. He treated me special because I'm so light. Still he owns me. I don't want to be owned anymore."

"Why don't you run away? I sure you hear about the railroad. People probably think you a spy though if you tried to ride it."

"Why didn't you ever try the railroad?"

"I would if had a chance. So many nights I lay there listening for Moses hoping she come to my place and take me away."

Then, There Was Iron

"I heard about her myself. Mind you when I thought she was doing a terrible thing. Stealing property. I'm now beginning to think slavery is wrong."

"You telling me all evening that you not a white man. Now you telling me you just realized slavery is wrong. What kind of fool are you?"

"The worst kind"

"What is the worst kind?"

"An ignorant child in a mans body."

"I never heard no one talk like that. You start to sound like it's coming from the heart."

"And you Nicey. You ever talk from the heart?"

"Heart. My heart is made of stone. I don't feel nothing, no more. They took my heart out years ago. I don't think I will ever get it back."

"Nicey don't say that."

"Why not it's true. Nicey Stone that's me"

"I can help you."

"Help me what?"

"Feel again. Like you helped me."

"I helped you."

"You changed my life. You opened my eyes."

"God, we are courting"

"Would that be so bad?"

"Like I told you, Nicey Stone. I'll go through the movements but don't expect me to feel anything. Specially with a white man."

"How many times must I say I'm not white?"

"Of course you aren't"

The two talked and bickered most of the night. By the end of the evening David was convinced he was in love. Nicey was convinced that this white man was only trying to trick her. So that she would believe he was nice, he was different. Once she was convinced of this, he would do her harm. She knew the plan had to be coming. It always did. This was one of the reasons she agreed to sleep in his cabin. He said that he would provide a new cabin for her in the morning. Meanwhile he would sleep on his spare mattress while she used the bed. Nicey figured he would come in and do vulgar things to her in the night. The sooner it was over the better.

Ellen Barton

To her surprise she woke up peacefully to the sound of David preparing breakfast. So he didn't attack her in the night. The attack was sure to come. She knew it. They were all alike. They could not change that quickly. She would not believe it. She crawled out of bed.

"Mawnin."

"Good morning."

"Did I miss the horn?"

"Yes. So did I."

"I gots me some trouble now."

"You got no trouble. I'm the overseer remember."

"Yeh I remember. What's gonna happen?"

"Nothing. I told you, you would not be working in the field any more."

"You sure?"

"Yes."

"All last night you telling me how you just a slave. Now you makin the decisions of a massa. What I'm spose ta believe?"

"Believe everything I tell you. You hungry?"

"Yes."

"Well I'm no cook. Just fried up some ham and eggs."

"It smells good."

"Ham and eggs is the only thing I ever cook. I get my other meals from the big house."

"Sound like a good life."

"I think it will only get better."

"This is good. I can't tell you the last time I had ham and eggs."

"See your life getting better also."

"Whatever you say."

"You sleep good last night?"

"Yes. That's a might fine bed you have."

"It's an old one from the big house. Couple years back Missus was redecorating."

"Redecorating?"

"That's when white women throw all their old stuff out and want new things. She was going to throw out that bed from their guest room. Lewis brought it down to me. That's how I got all this stuff."

"You are treated well. Even for a white ovaseer."

"Lewis always kept me close. Since he brought me after his own infant son died."

"They never had another son?"
"Never had another baby."
"I guess that's lucky for you."
"Why?"
"Well if they had another baby. He wouldn't show you so much attention. He give it all to his child."
"You had babies?'
"No."
"You never made babies."
"Belly got big a couple of times. Baby didn't make it."
"Did you want the babies."
"They were not mine to want. Massa put em in me. Massa owns those babies. I was happy they would not see the life I'm living. The life I would pass to them. Specially if they girls. I'd rather a dead baby girl than a slave baby girl."
"Maybe that's why my mother never looked at me?"
"I heard something like that."
"What did they tell you?"
"You want to know zactly?"
"Yes."
"They said you were the son of the devil himself. They said you were a beast and probably cuz your mother wouldn't even look at you when you was a baby. Said you were a man so evil your own mother didn't want to see you. Said the devil kicked you out of hell cuz he didn't want to see you. Said."
"That's enough I get the idea."
"You said you wanted to know zactly. Shouldn't you be getting to the field?"
"I'm alright. There are four other overseers"
"You the big one?"
"Yes.
"So you think your mother didn't look at you cuz she didn't want to make a slave child?"
"I never thought before about how women feel not owning what is growing inside of them. How it must feel to make a baby just to sell it. A baby that was most likely forced into them."
"It ain't easy on the slave man either. Finding a woman you can't protect. It ain't easy on the man or woman."
"I thought you hated men?"

"I don't hate men. I've known great men. My daddy was one of them."

"The way you talk, I just thought you hated everything."

"I hate white people. I hate life; I hate slavery. But I don't hate all men."

"You don't hate black men?"

"I don't hate black women either."

"You hate me."

"Well, you keep saying you ain't a white man. So I guess I don't hate you."

"You just don't trust me."

"Now, how you know that?"

"I wouldn't trust me either. I better go. I got to find you some work."

"What should I do?"

"You stay here. No one will come in here. Maybe you can clean up a bit."

"It is a mess in here."

"I'll bring you in some water before I go, so you can wash up. I'll be back about noon."

"Now, don't get used to me in your cabin waiting on you. I Nicey Stone remember."

"I remember, Miss Stone."

David leaves the cabin feeling better than he ever had. God, he talked about his mother. He talked about his mother with Nicey. He had never talked about her before, though he had heard the rumors. What kind of woman, would not look at her own child? That was mostly what he heard. This was usually followed by, "I can't stand looking at him either." Was she beautiful? Old man says she was. Very light skinned. She must have been. He heard her name was Iron. He once thought it an extremely unusual name. Then he never thought about it again. The mother that didn't even look at him. The father that sold him. Maybe the slaves were right. Maybe this was the reason he was such an animal. A vicious animal. Just like Lewis called the slaves. Maybe Lewis was wrong. More and more he realized, he and Lewis were the animals, the slaves were just trying to survive. Today he would have a talk with Lewis. He wanted his freedom. He wanted a new life. A life far away from here, a life that included Nicey. North, he would go north and make a new life with Nicey.

Then, There Was Iron

Nicey started cleaning the kitchen. She had never seen so many plates, bowls and cups, all dirty. She would wash everything. This sure was better than the field. She didn't know what this man wanted from her, but she would go along with him. Maybe even be a little more pleasant with him, though it was hard, for the very sight of him repulsed her. But she would try. If he was sincere, if he really cared about her as much as he appeared to, maybe he could help her have freedom. Than she was heading North. Find herself a black man. A black man that did not care about scars. A black man that understood. No one looking like David could truly understand her. She made up her mind that she would take all she could from David, than she would be gone.

David was happy all morning. He couldn't wait for noon so that he could get back to her. He'd see if he could move her into his cabin permanently, until they were ready to go. She would love him. He would make her. He saw Lewis galloping up on his horse.

"Morning David."

"Morning. How was your night? Find some bed warmers?"

"I gave one of those new wenches a try. She just as good as the others."

"Which one?"

"You'll see her. She the one walking funny."

Lewis then laughs. David knew that he was expected to, but he did not find this line as amusing as he used to.

"Son, I heard that Abraham Lincoln gonna run for president."

"I don't know Abraham Lincoln."

"He's an enemy of the South. He ain't a slavery man."

"You think he gonna try to end slavery?"

"I don't know. He might not even win the election. What I heard about him is that he has no appreciation of the fine institution that makes the South what it is."

"Some of these bucks, Lord if it wasn't for slavery, what they do? Find food for themselves, make money for themselves, I don't think they make it. But others I think they could make it. The smarter ones."

"Smarter ones? I have never seen a smart slave. You know that you got to tell them exactly what to do, or they be lost."

"Lewis, you forgetting I'm a slave."

"I always forgot that. David, I always say you a son to me. You can have your freedom papers, anytime you want."

"What?"

"I mean it. I draw up the papers today, if you want it. But I don't want you to leave. I need you here. You know this land. You know how to work it. In the last couple of years, it was your brains that made me all the money I got. I made more money in the last three years, than I made all my life. If I said it wasn't because of you, I'd be a dishonest man."

"I do want my papers Lewis. I feel like a better man."

"That's no problem, son. I want your word, you stay on."

"You saying, all I got to do is give my word?"

"All the years I raised you, that would be about twenty years, you never lied to me. I don't think you'll start now. If having your papers makes you feel like a man, you got it."

"You got my word."

"I'll bring the papers to your cabin later tonight."

"Good, that's good. I'll see you later."

"Fine."

David could not wait until noon. He rushed back to his cabin to share the news with Nicey. He runs into the cabin out of breath.

"Nicey, Nicey!"

"I'm in here. Lord, what you so cited about?"

"Nicey, Nicey!"

"Calm down, catch your air. Take your time."

"Nicey!"

"Yes?"

"I'm getting my freedom!"

"What?"

"I just talked to Lewis. He said I could have my freedom anytime. I just didn't ask. Nicey, I'm free. I could start to save some money. Than I buy your freedom."

"You gonna buy my freedom?"

"Yes. You know what Massa paid for you?"

"I got $450.00 on the block."

"You were on the auction block?"

"Yes."

"I'm sorry."

"Why you sorry?"

Then, There Was Iron

David falls to his knees; he has his arms wrapped around Nicey. She thinks he might be crying. Lord she guessed she could suffer through this, if it meant her freedom. He is burying his head between her legs repeating the words, "I'm sorry." She also drops to her knees and puts her arms around him. He kisses her and massages her gently. Nicey is thinking, Lord, the man wants sweet love from me. Sweet love like it mean something. She only gives that to black men. Slow sweet love. Well if it meant her freedom, she guessed she could do it. She accepted his kisses and his gentle touches. She even let out a small moan to make it look real. He started to undress her. Then he stopped and gasped.

20% of Nicey's torso was covered in bite marks. Both of her nipples were almost completely bitten off. David started to cry again.

"It's alright, it don't hurt no more."

"Who did this to you?"

"My last Massa."

"What's his name?"

"Why?"

"Because I am going to find him, and kill him."

"You a free man. You kill another man you go to jail. Then what about us?"

"Nicey, I'm sorry."

"Don't be sorry for what you didn't do."

"I've done terrible things."

"David, we gonna have a new life, let's forget yesterday."

He is crying again, holding her tightly.

"I just want to hold you."

"You don't want me no more. You hate the way I look."

"I love the way you look. I just need to feel you in my arms. Let's lay down."

"The two lay on the mattress. David is holding her tightly."

"You don't want love?"

"I got love."

David slowly caresses Nicey's body. He seemed to be enjoying touching every inch of her. Nicey thinks she is going to be sick. The man makes her stomach rise in her mouth. His crying has got to stop. Lord, she hoped she could survive just until he bought her freedom. She would prefer if he just took her. Rough. Fast. But this touching slowly with care, she couldn't stand it. What was he thinking?

Ellen Barton

Freedom together. Lord, he was a white man. Falling in love with a field wench, would not give him color. She could not wake up every morning, to a white man in her bed. She had seen him. She had seen him whipping that old woman. She had seen that look in his eye. The look her old Massa used to have. The look that said I work better when I'm surrounded by blood. I love to see it pour. Who knew how long before he was beating on her? Maybe he would even want babies. What black woman would want to make babies for a white man if they had a choice? She surely wouldn't. Lord, will he stop crying?

David finally got it together and went back to the fields, after he repeatedly confessed his true undying love to Nicey, to her complete disgust. He also mentioned that he had about $280.00, to her complete joy. He told her he would be back early that evening since Lewis was coming to bring him his freedom papers. He than bid on his way leaving her with a vast amount of domestic chores, which included having a wonderful supper waiting for him when he returned. Nicey smiled, kissed him, and sent him off. She wondered if all this was real. Nicey spent the rest of the day cooking and cleaning. She had prepared him a wonderful feast. Surprisingly, she found herself enjoying cooking for them. Maybe just cooking. She had never had so much food at her disposal to prepare. She didn't know if she would ever again. She spent a wonderful day thinking of her future, working at her leisure. This must be what freedom was like. She soon would know. God was finally going to give her the turn she deserved to have peace. Peace and no pain. Peace and no blood, no tears, though she had stopped crying years ago. She heard David come in. He had another jug.

"Nicey."

"You are back early."

"Look what I have. I thought we had a reason to celebrate."

"You were right."

"It smells wonderful, and it looks great."

"Thank you. I'll get you a cup."

"No. I do not want any now. I'm starving."

"I'll fix you some food."

Nicey goes into the kitchen to prepare David a plate. She hears Lewis enter.

"Lewis, I didn't expect you so early."

"Yeah, I'm riding into town for a poker game. So, I thought I get this to you."

"You want some whiskey?"

"Love some."

David goes into the kitchen for some cups. He motions to Nicey to stay there and stay quiet.

"You want to come to the game?"

"No. I got a nice field girl coming over tonight."

"Now, what I brought you was the original bill of sale, I received when I purchased you. I thought that would be better than freedom papers. See, you could rip these up and then it would never look like you were a slave. You pass for a white man any day. Find yourself a white wife. Probably a poor cracker woman, but she be white. Raise kids, you could have a great life David."

"I don't know about a white wife. This field girl I'm really fond of, she really likes me."

"Now David, you grown to be a smart man. I take pride in helping you with this. Let me tell you, I'm not giving you these papers so you will make the wrong choices. Marry a white woman; it's best for you. Keep the wench on the side. If you marry a wench, your kids will be slaves. Now you have kids with a white woman, you can send those kids to school."

"I can't just start living like a white man."

"Why not? You as white as me. I never told anyone I bought you as a slave. Everyone knows you as my chief overseer. So what a bunch of slaves say you one of them. Who believes them over me?"

"Lewis, you right. I just keep the wench on the side."

Nicey was in the kitchen listening carefully to every word. She knew it would happen. She figured they be in the kitchen any minute to beat her, to take her. What was she thinking, freedom? She was fooled. For a few minutes she allowed him to fool her. Buy her freedom. What white man would buy her freedom? Trying to convince her that he loved her. Listen to him. She lay back against the wall and drifted off in her head, off to the place where she floated on her back in the water. She would go there when the pain got too much. The night the devil tried to bite her to death. She could still hear most of her nipple being ripped from her breast. Though later she admitted to herself the sound probably wasn't as loud as she remembered. After that night she rarely felt pain. She would just go off to her place. She never even closed her eyes but she could see the sky as she was floating on her back, the few clouds, sensing the hot sun in the corner. She would never see the face of the devil though it was often right above her.

"Nicey, Nicey."

"What?"

"You okay?"

Nicey was drooling with her eyes rolled back.

"Nicey, it's alright, he's gone."

"He's gone?"

"You were afraid, afraid because of what I said. I seen it in your face. Nicey, don't worry; I was only talking to get him to leave. I want him to think I can still be trusted. Nicey, I would never leave you. Never hide you away."

David wraps his arms around her and leads her out of the kitchen. She is surprised he doesn't see her skin crawling.

The next few months Nicey lived in his cabin, though she kept saying she wanted one of her own. She didn't seem to notice that everyday he put it off. David could not imagine not waking up to Nicey, though she would not allow him to sleep in the same bed with her, and was surprised when he didn't protest. She said that was something that had to be done, after they jumped the broom. She would not jump the broom as a slave woman. This left David working hard to save money. After Lewis got his fields planted David hired himself out, adding to his $280.00 savings. He figured it would not be long before he had the money to purchase Nicey, plus some starting out money. Then they could marry and head north. He would find a job, and come home to a hot meal, and a good woman.

Nicey could not believe the man David had turned into. He had not forced himself upon her and agreed they should not sleep together before they were wed. She had heard of white people doing this, so she shouldn't have been surprised if that statement worked on a white man. For that is what he was, even if he didn't admit it. Now, she never heard of a black woman waiting for marriage before they lay with a man. They never had the chance. Maybe they would want to, if some white man were not forcing them. Maybe they would hold off relations until they could find the perfect man to spend their life with. Who knows? Nicey imagined being a young girl, finding the perfect match, and waiting till the beautiful night of marriage, to give

Then, There Was Iron

yourself to him. White men sure ruined that dream. Black men never received anything new. By the time they had the chance with their own women, a white man had already opened her up. Lord, she hated white people. This monster she was living with, she hated him too. God, couldn't he work faster? Everyday she was with him, she felt further from God.

David was praying. He now prayed hundreds of times a day. He would take a few seconds and ask for forgiveness, or he would ask for blessing on his enslaved people. He even snuck into the woods on Sunday afternoons; stood way back and listened to the black folk prayer meeting. He didn't go up for he didn't feel he would be welcomed there. He felt God had forgiven him. The slaves he didn't think would ever forgive him. He could not blame them either. He had done horrible things and he knew it. His shame consumed him. When his old desires came floating, he tried to drown them out with a prayer. He now treated certain slaves with incredible kindness. But they still didn't trust him, and he didn't blame them. Last week when giving Squirrelly extra rations, she looked him in the eye and said, "You can try this now Massa David, but your day is coming." When he asked what she meant, she just kept saying, "Your day is coming." It scared him a little. Everyone was scared of Squirrelly. Though this was the first time he admitted it to himself.

Lately there were a lot of things he was admitting to himself. One that stuck in his mind daily was that he wanted to meet his mother. Cummings. That was the name on the Bill of Sale. The Cummings plantation of South Carolina. He memorized it before he destroyed the paper; that advice he did take from Lewis. Iron Cummings, he wanted to meet her. He wanted to ask her why she did not look at him. If she did, would he have been different the first 21 years of his life? He wanted to be wrapped in her arms and hear her say, "It's alright son, all is forgiven." On his way North, he would stop in South Carolina. He was sure Nicey would not mind. Might help her to meet his slave mother. Sometimes he felt she still looked at him as a white man. But her love for him was growing. How could it not? He would provide her with everything she needed, everything she ever wanted. As long as he was with her, no one would ever hurt her again.

Nicey was taking a hot bath. She was not needed to make clothes today, and she spent most of it relaxing, and just laying around. She knew she better not get used to this life, but she was enjoying it while she can. Her hands kept playing with her nipples. Nipple stumps. She hated the way they looked now. But she had to admit since that night the devil tried to bite her to death. They were a lot more sensitive. She missed the touch of a man. A black man. Though her body was yearning for attention. She could not give herself to David. Not the way he wanted. If he wanted it rough, quick even beat her a little or a lot that she could do. David wanted affection, caring, meaning which would never happen. Jesus, how long does it take one man to raise $350.00. She better get out and begin to prepare his supper. He loved having a hot meal waiting when he comes home. She got to work on the food for that was the only hot thing she would ever willingly give him. The sun had gone down and David was late. He had said something this morning about going into town. Maybe he went to buy her a new dress he had been saying that she needed one. From the kitchen Nicey heard someone enter.

"David you took long."

"It ain't David."

Lewis enters the kitchen.

"Nicey, right."

"Yes."

"What are you doing in this cabin."

"Massa David likes me to come and prepare his supper."

"Well it sure smells good."

"Thank you sir."

Lewis is watching her strangely. Nicey knows what is about to happen she has seen the look in the eyes of white men many times.

"David be back soon sir. He should be here by now."

"You don't have to worry about David we share everything. Now come over here."

Nicey lowers her eyes and begins to walk close to Lewis. She is thinking the only good thing about white men they are quick. She hoped the pink thing was small, so she couldn't feel it. She seen that he had dropped his pants. Thank god it was.

"Get on your knees girl."

In her mouth, now she would have to smell it. Why did they always want to put it in her mouth? She hesitates. He punches her in the face. He would have to punch her again for she has decided not to take it in her mouth. He smelled like the barn. He would have to take her the other way, or no way at all. For she swore to die biting. She

Then, There Was Iron

was not taking that stinky little pink thing in her mouth. She could lean against the wall and lift up her dress. For when there was a white man behind her she had no feeling at all. While she was thinking all this Lewis continued punching her. He was screaming something about her taking it. David rushed in.

"What are you doing? Leave her."

David pulls Lewis from Nicey. Pushing him to the floor. He comforts her, wiping the blood from her face. He doesn't see Lewis reaching for his pistol. Lewis fires one shot directly through Nicey's head. She dies instantly. While still in David's arms. He screams and looks at Lewis.

"What have you done?"

He is trying to wake up Nicey saying everything will be fine. Lewis walks over to him.

"Stop son she's dead."

He sits down next to David pulls the dead Nicey out of his arms and wraps his own arms around David.

"Son I had to do it. Look to me like you were going to let that wench come between us."

David gives him a look of pure hate.

"David I brought you directly after losing my own infant son to Cholera. You know that. You know my story. When I first saw you, you reminded me of him. A beautiful white baby boy. I never treated you like a slave. Never took a whip to you. Gave you everything you needed. Hell I look to you as my flesh and blood son. Now I just lost $350.00 for you. To show you don't let anything come between us. Especially some field wench it ain't worth it."

David doesn't say a word he only stares at Lewis. Then he hits him. Lewis is shocked. The two men fight with intense ferocity. David being bigger and stronger doesn't take long before he wrestles Lewis to the cabin floor. He repeatedly bangs his head on the ground until the skull is completely crushed.

David looks down to see that he is covered in blood. Some of it belonging to Nicey some to Lewis. Nicey he goes back to cradle her. His future. His love. He rocks her and begins to cry. She was beginning to love him. She loved him. He knew it and now she was gone. He picked her up and carried her outside. Making sure that no one could see him. He begins walking into the woods.

Ellen Barton

After walking for a while he finds a nice spot near a stream. He puts Nicey down using the shovel he grabbed; he begins to dig her grave. He buried her then sits next to the grave well into the night. Remembering the mess he left on his cabin floor he makes his way back. He knew he could not stay there. He had killed a white man. His master. He changes his clothes and throws the bloody ones in the oven. As he lit the fire he looks over at Lewis. What a mess. What a smell. He searches Lewis; finds another pistol somewhat smaller and a large knife. He also finds $500.00, which he adds to his $320.00. He looks at the money and begins crying again. He was so close, so close to $350.00. Why didn't he ask Lewis if he would accept $320.00 for Nicey? He was stupid, to stupid to protect a woman. Nicey didn't think him stupid. Nicey thought him a great man and he let her down.

David was surprised his heart was still beating. How could it? How could it continue to beat knowing that he would never see Nicey again? Shouldn't it stop? David looked at Lewis. He couldn't leave him there. It would be obvious that he killed him. He checks outside the cabin. Again no one was looking. He drags the body of Lewis into the woods and buries it. Not as far as he buried Nicey. He then retraces his steps covering the marks of a dragged body. He jumps on his horse and begins riding. Having no clue as to where he was going. Maybe South Carolina.

Then, There Was Iron

CHAPTER 17

Iron was having a great time. She was dancing slow and close up against Chloe. She loved the way the woman moved. No matter how long they were together, she never tired of watching her. It was a time of celebration. Lizzie and Marcus had finally jumped the broom. John had also agreed to purchase Marcus. John never visited Lizzie anymore, so he gave his permission to the tired couple. The two had been lovers for around 30 years. They were elated that they could now live together. It seemed that most of the higher slaves were having the time of their lives.

Higher slaves. That is what Shelly called them, only to herself. She was now a member of this select group, and was very proud of the position. Her husband was an overseer. Her best friends were the ones that did the doctoring and that fed most everybody. No one in this selected group worked in the field. They were even above the house slaves. Shelly loved this; being a field hand all her life. Watching the few slaves that got the little extras. The ones who had more than one dress, who were never hungry, who were never whipped, she was now one of these. Though she was nearly drunk, she took a minute to look around the room, and thank God.

Lizzie's cabin was full. So was her yard. She swore that she did not invite so many people. The only person who did not appear was Doll. No one was surprised. In the 37 years that Doll had been on the plantation, the amount of times she socialized with the other slaves could be counted on one hand. She kept to herself doing her carvings. Lizzie thought she might come out today. It was a special day. She was the first of the breeders to jump the broom. Though it sometimes looked as if Chloe and Iron had jumped hundreds of years ago. She wasn't quite comfortable with what they were doing. Marcus, Peaches and Shelly told her, not think about it then.

She tried not to. But it wasn't right. The good Lord just might punish them. She cared for the two women deeply. She did not spend the amount of time with them that Peaches did, but she called them friends. It just didn't seem right. Both women were beautiful. Probably could pick any man they wanted for miles and miles. Why would they choose to be together like that? Shelly said you can't pick who you love. If you could, Marcus would surely have picked

Ellen Barton

someone else. Shelly and Peaches both thought this to be very funny. Lizzie didn't. She wondered what the two women did together anyway. What could they do without the right parts? Peaches laughed and mentioned, they must have had something figured out, for they smile more than anyone on the plantation.

Lizzie was staring at the two women. They did look happy and they had given the newly married couple a beautiful new mattress. Lizzie had no idea how or where they got the mattress. But it was the most wonderful gift they had received all day. She didn't have to sleep with Marcus on that old mattress, which was full of memories of Massa John. Yes, maybe she should stop thinking about what Chloe and Iron do. God, she can't she stop staring at them? Why couldn't she be a fly on the wall? One day, one night she had to see how it was done.

"Girl, your cup empty. You can't have no empty cup on this day."

"Thanks Shelly. You having a good time?"

"Lord, this is just like Christmas. I couldn't ask for a better day."

"Tell me Shelly, you know where Iron and Chloe get that mattress?"

"I have no idea. You know those two always got their secrets. Always talking quiet together. Lord, I was surprised to see it."

"Me too."

"You like it?"

"It was just what we needed. I want to thank you and Paddy for that pot also. I'll cook Marcus some wonderful meals in it."

"I'm happy for ya Lizzie. You sure got a nice turn out."

"Yeah, everybody come, and then some."

"Well, you know it's always like that."

"Doll didn't come. I didn't think she would though. I was just hopin."

"You know, all the years I been here, I only see that woman once."

"That's once more than most folks."

"I even seen her from far away. Never seen that woman up close. Don't rightly know what she looks like. Lord, I see her work everywhere though. The woman can work some wood. I never in all my life see things like she do."

"Yeah, you see the new one?"

"By the creek?"

Then, There Was Iron

"Yeah, she made that old tree look like a woman growing out of the ground."

"Lord, I lost my breath when I seen it. I would have liked it if she came today."

"I don't know how she live. Imagine the only one you talk to is Massa."

The women look at each other and laugh.

"You know she older than me, so Massa surely don't go see her no more."

"So that woman, don't talk to anyone at all?"

"Probably for years."

"Lord."

"Can't even go over there. Few tried years back, but she chases you off with stones."

"Well, I ain't trying. She do wonders with wood. But I ain't the one to be disturbin those who don't want to be disturbed."

"I hear you."

"I hear a drink."

"Iron, Chloe, Lord, you two is makin the room hot. Come have a drink with an old married woman."

"Love too; Iron wearing me out."

"You love it."

"You two sure look like you having a good time. Where you get that mattress?"

"I don't know. Iron brought it home. Said it was for the two of you."

"I ain't talking. You like it?"

"I love it. It was just what we needed. Thank ya so much."

"We happy to please you. Bout time you and Marcus jumped the broom. How long you all been together anyway?"

"Bout 20 years."

"That's a long time."

"Yeah, I thought I better hurry before the man too old to jump the broom."

"20 years. How long you been on this plantation?"

"Bout the same time. Marcus and I started up right away. The first time I seen him, I was gone. We had some hard times together, but I think things be looking good now."

169

"Everything looking good now. I think the hardest times are over."

"Cuz, Massa Lincoln gonna win the election."

"We don't know if he win."

"Even if he won, don't mean things better for black folks."

"Now Chloe, don't you start."

"I'm just saying, most black folks can't read, and got no money. Let's say they all free tomorrow, what they all gonna do?"

"Chloe, they find something. Now this is a celebration. Iron, you got no control on this here woman?"

"None at all."

"I see that."

"Oh, she got control on me, when I needs controlling."

"That don't seem too often."

"3 or 4 times a week."

All the women laugh, understanding what Chloe is really talking about. Iron is blushing. She is proud; proud to be the one Chloe is with. Proud to be the one Chloe returns to when her body is aching. She is even proud of Chloe's seriousness. The woman was perfect, and everyday she thanked Jesus for bringing Chloe into her life. At that moment Chloe looked at her and smiled. Iron thought she was melting. How she would love to spend 35 years loving Chloe.

"Now this drink is for true love. We thank God we have it in our lives."

"Alright Shelly, to true love."

The four women drink. Chloe is mischievously smiling at Iron. Iron knows what is going on in Chloe's head. She can't wait to get back to her cabin. Whenever Chloe gets that look in her eyes, Iron is guaranteed a wonderful evening.

"Ya know I kinda tired."

"Iron, you can't leave so quick."

"Lord, we haven't even brought out the food."

"It looks beautiful."

"Yeah, most folks bring something. I don't know how or where they get the food, but they bring something. Specially the ones I don't invite, that just show up. They don't show up empty."

"It's great that everyone made it."

"Everyone cept Doll."

"Well, you know she wouldn't come."

Then, There Was Iron

"Iron, you ever see that woman?"

"Once or twice. Once years back, not long after Massa first move me back here. I caught her looking at me with pure hate in her eyes."

"What?"

"Yeah, she was peeking right through my cabin window. Lord, the look in that woman's eyes, told me to stay away from her. That's what I did. That woman don't like me."

"Don't like you? Everybody likes you."

"Now Chloe, everybody can't like me."

"Why not?"

"It just can't be. Somebody must not like me. That somebody is Doll."

"What you ever do to her?"

"Nothing."

"Maybe she didn't like that Massa brought you out here."

Only Lizzie and Iron laugh at what Shelly says.

"Girl, you happy when Massa bring another woman out here. That's less time he gonna have with you. Lord, when I first saw Iron, I thanked God. I also thanked God when I first saw Peaches."

"Who was first, you or Doll?"

"Doll was first and I don't remember her looking at me with hate. We even talked a few times, but she don't like people. I just thought she might come today."

"Maybe she don't come cuz Iron here."

"Don't say that. Everyone likes Iron."

"Alright Chloe, everyone likes Iron."

"Well, how could they not? She gives the clothes off her back. The food out of her mouth. She always there with a kind word. Always trying to make it easier for someone."

"Alright Chloe, we done said everybody likes Iron."

"Except Doll."

"Iron, you must be makin a mistake. How could that woman not like you when she don't even know you? I'm sure you made a mistake."

"I'm sure that woman hate me. She talked to Peaches. She talked to Lizzie. I'm the only one the woman never talked to. Why?"

"Well Iron, I think your right. She don't like you."

"Shelly, I'm telling you, everyone loves Iron. All they got to do is get to know her. If Doll took some time with Iron, she love her too."

Peaches, Iron, and Lizzie at the same time all say, "Alright Chloe!"

Chloe rolls her eyes. In her heart she knows it is impossible not to like Iron. The woman was smart, beautiful, and kind. There had to be something wrong with Doll.

Iron made a few more hints on it being late, or her being tired, everyone ignored them. No matter what she said, she couldn't get Chloe home. So she sat back and watched Chloe laughing, Chloe dancing, Chloe singing, and Chloe eating. Chloe wasn't getting any bigger over the years, like a lot of other women were doing but she ate like a horse. Iron loved this also. Though she didn't like it when Chloe took too much whiskey. If it looked like a night when Chloe was going to drink a lot, Iron didn't drink at all, for she knew how those nights would end; with Chloe crying in her arms for her long lost daughter Ruth. Iron thanked God; Chloe was beginning to slow down. When she finally came to her and said she was getting tired, Iron was relieved. The two made their good byes, and started on their short walk back to Iron's cabin.

"You never did tell me where you got that mattress."

"Miss Clara gave it to me. She said I could use it but I thought it would be better for Marcus and Lizzie."

"Yes, it was really nice. You get all your papers settled?"

"It be settled soon. I'm going back to see her the day after tomorrow. She should have papers for me. She called them deeds."

"Deeds?"

"Yeah, we get those deeds, then we have our place to go in Philadelphia."

"Lord, I'm gonna miss everybody."

"Me too. Peaches, Shelly, they like my very own sisters. But we gots to move on. When the time come for everybody to break up, Peaches go with Benjamin, Shelly and Paddy, Lizzie and Marcus."

"You and me."

"We got to make our own lives."

"You right. Maybe they all go to Philadelphia."

"Maybe. I know Shelly love to see Mama Pearl again."

"Iron, you ever see two women jump the broom?"

"Never."

"You think they can?"

"I don't know. I can't see myself asking Massa if I can jump the broom with you."

"Lord, knows what he do."

"You want to jump the broom? Have all our friends over? Have a big celebration?"

"You think it's wrong?"

"You know I don't think it's wrong. I'm just saying I never seen it done. I don't know how folks would act. Then the white folks hear about it, Lord knows what they do."

"They may break us up."

"We could jump the broom alone. Just you and me."

"We could say a few words."

"You want to?"

"Yes."

When Chloe and Iron arrive back at Iron's cabin, Iron quickly gets the broom and lays it across the floor. Chloe is staring at her as if looking for leadership. Iron take a deep breathe and says,

"I Iron, before God will promise to love Chloe always, and work hard to keep us together, and happy."

"I Chloe, before God, will promise to love Iron, and work hard to keep us together and happy."

Then they jumped. They got real silly after that. Running around the cabin, insisting on doing everything that is to be done after a couple jumps the broom. First they sang and danced, and then one would yell, "food!" Then they would stuff their mouths for a few minutes. Then one would yell, "more dancing!" One would yell, "speech!" They combined a half a days celebration in under an hour. And loved every minute of it.

After that they made love. An intense grasp to save what they had. Terrifying touches that made them want to be connected forever. Be sewn together. Love so true they needed to drink of each other until they were one. They never wanted to let go. Chloe cried. She was scared something so good, could not last forever. She knew this. Iron didn't. Iron thought they would move to Philadelphia and live happy lives. Chloe knew things were not so easy. They never were. They were black women. They would have to pay their dues. Of course she had paid again, and again, and again. Iron hadn't. How could a slave have so much luck? It would have to end sometime. Chloe hoped no matter what happened they would face everything together. Together.

Ellen Barton

Forever. She made a silent prayer they would always be. She fell asleep in Irons arms.

The next morning they were awoken early by a young field hand.

"Miss Chaney dead, Miss Chaney dead."

"Hear that?"

"Yeh, I heard it."

"We better get up."

"I gots to wash the body."

"She free now."

"Yeh, I wished she had seen freedom in her days."

"She was old. She wouldn't know what to do with freedom."

"No, she talked more about Jesus."

"She with him now. Want some breakfast?"

"I better hurry up and go."

"Why? She already dead."

"Iron. I thought you cared more than that. I remember all the food you cooked her."

"I was cooking for you. She was a good woman and I gonna miss her but I was ready for this."

"So was I."

"It easier when you ready."

"Yeh. So you were never that close to her?"

"Well she delivered all my babies, cept the last one."

"What you name your babies?"

"What?"

"What are the names of all your children?"

"Why you askin that?"

"We jumped the broom. I spose to know everything."

"First one named David, then: Janus, William, Henry, Quincey and Lenox."

"Umph David, Janus, William, Henry, Quincey. I'll always remember Lenox."

"I don't."

"I remember him cuz I birthed him."

"Have you birthed many babies?"

"Hundreds and hundreds. See more babies than dead people. Thank God, I think."

"You think?"

"God only knows what happens to our children?"

Then, There Was Iron

"God only knows what happens to the dead?"
"But they free."
"That's true."
"You want to tell me the names of your children?"
"Edward, Louis, Richard, James, Sampson, Cato and Ruth."
"We both only ever had one girl."
"One is all you need. I better go."
"Stay and have breakfast with me. You feel better."
"Not much though. Maybe just some dry biscuits like Miss Chaney used to make."
"I got biscuits but they ain't dry."
"They do."

The women eat their breakfast in silence. Iron knows Chloe is thinking about Ruth. Why did she have to ask about the names of children? Why did she have to talk about it? She wished there was something she could do to ease Chloe's pain. Some folks said time made you feel better. Somehow she thought Chloe would never feel better. Iron sometimes thought of her own children as dead. It was hard but it was easier then thinking of them being whipped, being starved, being slaves. She didn't know how to say this to Chloe. How to say, do what I do think they dead. Best not to say anything. Just hold her when she need holding.

"You want me to go with you to tend Miss Chaney?"
"You ever do it before?"
"No."
"Then I bes do it myself."
"You don't get scared?"
"Scared of what? Dead folks can't hurt you. It's the ones breathing you got to worry about."
"I love you."
"I love you to."

Chloe walks out the door. It was getting cold. Christmas be on them soon. Another year gone. Reuben would say another year closer to freedom. Sure was for Miss Chaney. Chloe wondered how old the woman was. She was the oldest woman Chloe had ever known. Her pain was finally over, Chloe was happy for that. But she was truly going to miss the old girl.

Iron was sitting at home thinking about Miss Chaney. She was a real nice old woman. Mama Pearl be sad to hear of her passing. Best not to send her word by postmaster. Things going north shouldn't be to often, Miss Clara would say. She tell Mama Pearl when she see her. She should have gone with Chloe. She had a feeling Chloe shouldn't be alone. She was looking sad when she left, not sadness for Miss Chaney but sadness for her children. The worst kind of sadness the one you could do nothing about. How could she find Chloe's children? It was impossible all slaves knew that. They lived with that. She would give her life for Chloe's happiness. But it wasn't enough.

Nothing could be done about the yesterday. All she could do was take care of tomorrow. Making sure they had a place to live was a good start. Miss Clara said they had done real good. They could even rent out rooms. Iron fully did not understand all Miss Clara had said. She would ask more questions tomorrow. It did sound as if they could make some money. Miss Clara had used the word income. She said that was money coming in regular. Regular. When she had told Chloe this a few weeks ago Chloe had said, like an ass whipping.

She guessed it would take some folks awhile to get used to getting paid in money instead of pain. She found it both sad and funny. But she kept this to herself and only gave Chloe a strange look. She wondered if Chloe could work at healing in Philadelphia. Maybe she would have to go to school. A nice life it was coming. A nice life, they could have it together. Last night they jumped the broom. It was Chloe's idea that meant she wanted to stay with Iron forever.

She needed to be with her right now. This was the first day. They shouldn't be apart for a second of it. Should she go help her prepare Miss Chaney for the ground? Start off their new life together saying good-bye to an old one. Is that good? She didn't know. Maybe she should wait and prepare a lunch for Chloe. But what do you eat when preparing the dead. Iron kept thinking vegetables. Just vegetables. No she would not take anything. She would just walk down. If Chloe wanted to be alone, she would spend some time Reuben. That is if he felt alright? He was into the whiskey quite heavy last night. Surprisingly for he was a not a heavy drinking man. Everybody had to forget life sometimes. That's what Shelly would say. Iron wondered why Shelly never mentioned learning to read again. She should. Maybe Iron would bring it up. She wait and see, maybe Paddy changed her mind. Iron hoped not. She got dressed and left.

Arriving at the row, Iron found about 35 slaves gathered at Miss Chaney's cabin. The music had already begun; slow, deep, sad.

Haunting voices. Times like this, she often thought of Bell. Whenever she heard sweet music. Being happy or sad. She quickly shook Bell out of her head. Wasn't right to think about Bell, the day after she jumped the broom. What could Bell be doing now? Free, and in England. Months back, maybe a year, Miss Clara told her she had heard Bell published a book of poetry. She said these poems would be impossible to get in the South. She had heard of them through a cousin in the North. The cousin wanted to know if Miss Clara knew this ex-slave coming from the same region. Iron was desperate to read these poems, having never read a poem in her life. Miss Clara showed her a few poems. Iron did not really like them. She preferred the book of Psalms in her bible. She asked Miss Clara if the book of Psalms was poetry. Miss Clara replied with a hesitant yes. That was enough poetry for Iron. The poems of love that Miss Clara showed her, she could not associate with. She did love Chloe, but her love was different. Love without bounded obstacles. Bell's poems would probably be different. Bell could write poems she could understand. The life and love of the slave. The anger of the slave. This would be better for her than versus about a rich white man waiting for the attention of a spoiled white woman. She couldn't believe Miss Clara wasted her time on anything that uninteresting.

When she went home and told Chloe, of course Chloe said, she is a white woman. With all their freedom, they don't enjoy life as much as we do. White folks they funny, but they no fun. Iron had told Chloe that Bell was now a writer. She told everyone. People were happy to hear it. She was still their Queen and they were still proud of her even if she left them. She also admitted to Chloe the nature of her relationship with Bell. When Chloe asked if she loved her. She replied she had no idea what love was until they had met. She admitted to Chloe that she was afraid of Bell.

"Why?"
"She was different. She kept changing."
"Lot's of people change."
"Chloe, you ever see people nice some days, and mean the next?"
"Like white folks?"
"Kinda like white folks."
"You mean their mood keeps changing?"
"Your eyes change color; you get taller or shorter; your whole face changes."

"I have never seen that, don't mean it ain't possible."

"That's how it was with Bell. It was like she was more than one person. After she left, I had dreams that there was more than one person living inside her."

"You believe that?"

"The last time I ever seen her, she said she was a man."

"A man? So you think there was more than one person living in Bell, and one was a man?"

"Sometimes she could read, sometimes she couldn't."

"You talking the truth?"

"I swear. I been thinking about it for years. Chloe, ever pretend that you were free? Maybe that you were someone else?"

"Yeah, when I was littler."

"What if you pretended so much, it happened?"

"You say if you a little slave girl and you pretended you a little white girl, you turn into a little white girl?"

"Just in your head."

"I don't know. It don't sound right."

"Bell had no memories."

"What?"

"She hardly remembered anything. She would forget what she did yesterday. I think was one of her pretend people living. Doing stuff. That's why she couldn't remember what she do. Because she didn't do it."

"I do know one thing, the few times I heard her sing, I could swear it was more than one person singing. I never heard anything like that before. One person could sound like 3 or 4 people singing."

"What did you think when you heard her?"

"Well, I didn't think she had more than one person inside. I thought the Lord blessed her."

"He did."

"You miss her?"

"No."

"You sure?"

"I was afraid of her in the end. I tell you something else, I think she pushed that white woman over the boat."

"You ever tell anyone all this, about the more than one person?"

"No."

"I don't think you should. They might think something wrong with your head."

"Is that what you think?"

"I believe every word you say. I tired of talking about Bell though. Considering."

"What I had with Bell is nothing to what I have with you."

"I still tired."

They never talked about Bell again. Iron thought funny she doesn't get tired when talking about Nelson. Nelson was dead; Bell wasn't. Maybe that was the difference. Chloe had also loved Nelson. Iron realized that she had never loved Bell, which was also a difference. One that Chloe couldn't see. She never stopped Chloe when talking about Nelson. She listened, even if she really, really didn't want to hear it. She knew Chloe needed to talk about her past sometimes. She had to be there for her, no matter how much it hurt. Please Chloe. Satisfy Chloe. This is what she was living for even if Chloe at times thought only of herself. Most people did. Iron was different and knew it. Just because she loved Chloe, it wouldn't make Chloe different.

Iron saw her talking to Reuben. Iron liked watching Chloe from a distance. The way she moved her hands, and rolled her eyes. Sometimes, she would hold people by the arm. Iron loved all this. She enjoyed that people wanted to be around Chloe, felt good in her presence. She also enjoyed that a lot of men desired Chloe. It made her all that much more proud. She walks over to them.

"Iron, I didn't think you were coming down."

"Had to."

"You alright?"

"I'm alright Reuben. I was spectin this day."

"We all were. She was a good woman."

"You know how old she was?"

"Nobody knows. She lived a long life."

"She free now."

"Praise Jesus."

"Where are Shelly and Paddy?"

"Paddy went somewhere with Massa. Shelly sleeping."

"Sleeping?"

"I tried to get her up."

"She say Chaney still be dead when she get up."

Ellen Barton

"Lord, that woman!"
"Well, she did some celebrating yesterday."
"Thank God, it's Sunday."
"Yeah, I saw you quite often with that jug."
"Well, jumping the broom is a special thing."
Chloe catches Iron's eye, they along with her lips are smiling.
"It sure is."

CHAPTER 18

David had been riding for weeks. His attempts to make it to South Carolina were not recognized, not knowing which direction to ride in not knowing how to read. He was never stopped for papers and he bedded down in some of the finer establishments. With no questions asked, he soon found himself in Tennessee, than Kentucky.

It was 30 days after he left the Joplin plantation and he found himself in Chicago. He rented a room, and found a job in a factory by day, and paid the young son of his widowed landlady, to teach him to read at night. He felt lonely, but not alone.

He could not bring himself to even look at a woman. He didn't want to. Life in Chicago was showing him that blacks were not particularly loved in this location either. They may not be slaves, but they were not far from it.

He never talked to the widow on her views on blacks. He did know that none were allowed to rent rooms in her home. Would she hate him if she knew he was the child of a slave? Should he care? Was he wrong to rent a room with a sign in the window that read, no blacks? Was it wrong of him? If Nicey were alive, he would of never walked up those steps. He should be proud. He should be proud of his mother. But he wasn't. He wanted the best of both worlds; he wanted all the luxuries and comforts that were given to whites, plus the strength and determination of blacks.

Live the life of a white man. He remembered Nicey saying, "If you look white, than you white." Sad but true. He would keep working, a job that he would have never received if not for his complexion. What would his mother think? Denying her. Denying the her in him. It had to be done. David Cummings. He didn't like it. David Joplin, he liked it less. When asked by his new employer, "What's your name, son?" Thinking of Nicey, he quickly responded with David Stone.

CHAPTER 19

"Iron, Iron, Chloe!!"

Iron hears Peaches screaming her name outside.

"Lincoln won, Lincoln won!!"

Iron can't believe the news. She wishes Chloe was there but John loaned her to another plantation, which had a lot of slaves getting sick. She would probably be gone for days. Peaches burst into the cabin.

"He won. Massa Lincoln won."

"I heard you."

"Girl, aren't you excited? Where's Chloe?"

"Massa took her away for a few days."

"Ah, that's why you look down."

Peaches wished Chloe were there. Chloe always seemed to get more out of good news than Iron. She was a screamer, the type that liked to jump up and down. Iron was they type that only smiled. Peaches wanted someone to jump up and down with.

"Lord, where's Shelly? Girl, we got some celebrating to do. I'm going to get Shelly, I'll be back."

Peaches takes off running out the cabin. Iron goes outside and watches her. She thinks Peaches runs pretty fast for a woman her age. They won't have to run no more. They could stop running. She was ready. She had her place waiting for her. Waiting for Chloe. When Miss Clara gave Iron the deeds, she wrote all the information on a separate paper and gave it to Chloe.

"What's this?"

"That's our place in Philadelphia. You keep it and hold it dear."

"Hold it dear?"

"Everything on that paper you study, just in case it get lost. I just saying hold it dear."

"Why? What you got planned?"

"I got nothing planned. I just feel better if you have the paper is all."

"I got you, why I need this paper?"

"Chloe, it's best we be safe."

"How am I spose to be safe walking around with words on paper? What would happen to me if someone find it?"

"Then put it in your head, and burn the paper. I don't care. But you best know those words in your head, just in case. I'm going to do the same thing. That way no matter what happen, we know where to find each other."

"What going to happen? You going to run, aren't ya? Don't Iron. Don't leave me. Please don't run Iron, you don't know what could happen."

"Chloe, I ain't gonna run. Just do what I say please."

"Alright, I hold it dear."

Iron thinks about that night as she watches Peaches disappear. It was a warm day for this time of year, a beautiful day. Iron sees another figure walking through the woods. She barely recognizes the person. Looked like an old woman. As the woman got closer, Iron realized it was Doll. She had not seen Doll in years. She appeared to be walking toward Iron. Iron thinks Massa Lincoln bring out everybody.

"Ya think it dat easy."

Was Doll talking to her? Maybe she was talking to herself.

"Ya think it dat easy?"

"What?"

"Ya thinks things come dat easy?"

"What things?"

"Sweet life. Easy life ya got here."

"I'm sorry. I don't understand."

"Sorry, ha. Sorry. You be sorry. I been keeping my eyes on you all these years. Since the cursed day Pearl bring you on this here place."

"What are you talking about?"

"I'm talking about you. Devil woman. Running round here like you own this place. Doing anything you want. Anytime you want to. Working on the railroad."

"I don't know what you're talking about. You mistaken."

"I ain't making no mistakes. It's time. It's time to stop you. Things shouldn't be so easy for you. No, I won't let it, can't change nothing, can't change nothing now. No can't change nothing."

Doll seems to be talking more to herself than to Iron.

"Yesterday gone. But I ain't gwan let you live like that. Not after."

"Doll, please tell me what you are talking about."

Ellen Barton

Doll loses her patience and begins screaming at Iron.

"It was you crying! It wasn't my beautiful baby girl. God, she was a quiet baby. You, you wouldn't stop! Ovaseer thought it was my girl, but it was you!"

"Oh dear lord."

Iron begins to understand what Doll is saying. They must have been bought in the same lot. It was her crying. But the overseer killed Doll's baby, by throwing it against the boat, and letting it fall in the water.

"It was not my fault! I was just a baby."

"A crying baby. You be crying again."

Iron falls to her knees. Tears are running down her cheeks.

"That's right, crying again."

Doll turns around and walks away. Iron is about to scream something at her when she sees three white men riding up on horses. She runs into the cabin. She is looking around the cabin frantically. She remembers the deeds, shoves them down the front of her shirt, and lays them under her breast.

"Come out wench!"

"Yeah, we will show you what happens to thieving niggers!"

Iron begins to cry, silently thinking of Chloe. Chloe will not be able to handle this. She could. She walks out the door.

"You Iron?"

"Yes."

Swoosh. She felt it. For the first time since being taken out of the fields, Iron felt the sting of the whip. She fell to the ground. She lay there staring up into the sky. One man continued whipping her while the two others ran into the cabin. They found the cellar in no time. Iron was thinking of Chloe's face, her touch, her laugh. She would not let her mind sway from the image of Chloe's face, Chloe's smile; if she did she would surely die, for this man was peeling her. She heard John's voice.

"That's enough!"

"Now sir, I can't tell you how to handle your business, but if this here wench working the railroad, stealing property, we got to set an example with her."

"Sir, you are correct. You can't tell me how to handle my business. Now take her to jail until I decide what to do with her."

Then, There Was Iron

Iron is chained hand and foot. One of the men holds the end of the chains. He gets on his horse and expects Iron to trot behind him. She is sore and bruised, but she manages to keep up. They take her past the row.

"Aaahhhgh!"

Iron hears Shelly scream. Shelly and Peaches come running.

"Where are they taking you?"

"Jail. You black bitches don't stay back, you going there too."

Peaches spots Massa John.

"Why Massa? Tell Peaches. Iron don't do nothing, she a good girl. Listen to Peaches, Massa she a good girl!"

"Stop it Peaches! She was working on the railroad."

"She never done nothing to you Massa. She never take nothing from you Massa. Lord, she help make this plantation what it is!"

"Peaches, we can't have no one on this place working the railroad. Now let me be."

Peaches thought it best to listen to John. She work on him later. She couldn't try to convince him of anything in front of three white men. It wouldn't look good on him. She left him and ran to Iron. Shelly was crying and running alongside the horses. She had received several stinging lashes from the whip, but would not stop.

"I tell you wenches, get back or I'll shoot!"

One of the men pulls a gun.

"It's alright. I'll be alright. Tell Chloe to hold it dear."

"What?"

"She will understand. Tell her I will see her there."

"See her where?"

"I said, get back!"

They are almost off John's property. John screams at the women.

"You two better not leave that gate!"

"Please tell her to hold it dear!"

"We will tell her Iron. Hold it dear. You will see her there."

"Thank you."

Shelly and Peaches make the sad walk back to the row. John disappears inside the big house. The news of Lincoln's election suddenly means nothing. Iron was gone. How where they going to tell Chloe?

Iron walked for hours before being thrown into the jail. She never fell once, and took a strange pride in that. Chloe never left her mind.

Ellen Barton

What would she do? What happened to her did not seem important compared to what would happen to Chloe. The only reason she wanted to live, was for Chloe. To be with her, she did not think Chloe was strong enough to accept her death. She had to live. She had to get back to Chloe.

"Well girl, we going to have some fun tonight."

Iron is thrown into a tiny, dirty cell. The smell almost made her want to pass out. Sweat, excrement, urine, and vomit mingled in the air through hints of death and fear. She expected everything.

To her surprise the men left her alone. She took this as a sign to quickly dig a hole in the corner. She safely planted the deeds and covered them again. She felt they would be safe there, until she had an idea of what would happen to her. The look in two of the men's eyes told her, the papers would not be safe on her person. She sits and waits.

Hours later, one of the original men return with a cracker Iron knows as a famous nigger breaker. They have whips, paddles, and something in a bucket. She knows what is coming. Iron looks at the men and begins taking off her clothes. She knew this cracker liked to whip his women completely naked. Others only made them strip to the waist. But not this fella. She would not give him the joy of ripping off her clothes. She had seen him do it to a young woman once before. She did not stay to witness the whipping. But she had watched the same man rip off a woman's clothes. She knew from his eyes how much that part meant to him. She leaned against the wall. They started with the paddle. 50 strokes, than the whip. 50 lashes than the paddle again. Iron was making sounds she did not know possible. She wanted to scream Chloe's name. But if they heard it, Chloe might be in this position. Iron thought better her than Chloe. She was going to die. She knew it. She had never seen her babies, her beautiful babies. She could hear them crying. She could hear them screaming along with her. She smelt the blood; she tasted it. She was going to die and never see Chloe again. Her beautiful babies, they continued to scream. Lord, why don't they kill her? Why don't they stop, and kill her right now? She wants to fall, but they have tied her so she is forced to stand. She feels her knees buckling. Chloe, Chloe, I love you. She sees Chloe lying on her pillow, smiling, laughing. I love you too, Iron. Hold it dear. Why? What have you got planned? I got nothing planned. Promise you'll hold it dear. I promise. Her babies are crying louder

Then, There Was Iron

than Chloe is talking. She can't take it any longer. She must be dead. Yes, she is dead. She raises her head and screams, "Mama!!!"

Iron passes out.

"We wasting our time now. She can't feel anything."

"Should we untie her?"

"Why not."

The men untie Iron. She slumps lifelessly to the floor.

"Think we gone too far?"

"She ain't dead."

"Yeah, but Mr. Cummings didn't say to beat her."

"He didn't say not to. You the one that come and got me anyhow."

"I didn't think it would be so bad. I thought we would start with this, than take a different approach. She is a fine looking wench."

"She doesn't look too fine right now. Besides, I don't lay with niggers."

"Never?"

"Never."

"My friend that is one of the luxuries of being a Southern man."

"You have your luxuries, I had mine."

"What do you think Mr. Cummings will say when he sees her?"

"I do not care what he says. He's too easy on his niggers. They run his place."

"I've never heard that. John Cummings is a fine man; a great planter."

"Let's turn this wench on her belly. Move her to the corner. Beautiful."

"What?"

"Beautiful. No marks on her."

"Now you saying she was beautiful."

"Not the wench. Her back. Not a mark on it. I love working on a flawless back. Makes me feel better, you know?"

"Ah, let's get out of here."

The two men gather their belongings than they leave. Iron silently watches them through one eye. She heard every word. She wasn't as lost as they thought. She had seen some whippings. The quicker you pass out, the quicker they would stop. She knew any longer, she would be dead. The pain. It was worse than childbirth. Something she never thought possible. She was certain there was no more skin left on

Ellen Barton

her back. She now had the marks that most of her friends had. Chloe had them; though not as bad as others she had seen. Not as bad as Shelly, certainly not as bad as Bad Bell or Paddy. Bad Bell had them all over her body. Now she had them. They never did use what was in that bucket. Thank the Lord; it smelled like turpentine. Turpentine. Iron passes out, this time for real.

She wakes up 18 hours later, but doesn't know it. She doesn't know that Peaches and Shelly sneak into town in the middle of the night. See her through the little window of the cell, lying unconscious in a pool of blood. Think she is dead. Cry all the way home. Fear, for they cannot tell Massa that they snuck off the plantation. Beg Paddy, because neither can knock on the big house door, to wake John, for the jailers have killed Iron. Realize Paddy is too afraid to wake John up with the news. He fears John would figure out his wife slipped off the plantation. Continue to cry all night until Paddy finally tells John of a rumor that the jailers have killed Iron.

"Well, how do you know this?"

"Sl, sl slaves told me."

"How they know?"

"Sa, sa sa someone seen."

"Who has seen?"

"Na, na, not someone from he, he, here si, si, sir."

"I will look into it Paddy. Tell the others not to worry. I never gave orders for her to be killed."

"Da, da, da, that don't mean sh, sh, sh, she ain't de, de, dead sir."

"Well, it bloody well should!"

John leaves; gets on his horse and rides into town. It doesn't take him long to reach the jailhouse.

"Where's my wench?"

"Which one? Got a few wenches here sir."

"Don't play games with me. The one you got off my property yesterday!"

"The light, light wench?"

"That's the one."

"Follow me."

John is horrified at what he sees. He was never a friend of the slave, but he did not believe in cruel whippings. Slaves were property; paid for with good money. Property should not be abused. It didn't make sense to him.

Then, There Was Iron

"My Lord, what have you done?"
"I have done nothing, sir."
"Who has beaten her in such a manner?"
"I do not know, sir."
"Lord, just when my healing wench is away."

Healing wench. Iron barely hears these words. Chloe. My healer. Iron thanked God Chloe was away. She did not want Chloe to see her like this.

"Send for a doctor."
"Doctor never comes here."
"Tell him John Cummings is waiting for him with a handful of dollars. Get me something to cover her. Don't you have a better cell? One with a mattress?"
"Beg your pardon sir, but this is a jailhouse."
"I don't care what it is. Now I paid good money for this here wench, I will not watch her die naked on a dirt floor."

The man goes to get Iron something to cover herself. John rubs Iron's hair and says some kind words, gently in her ear. Though he doesn't want to be, he is moved. He had what he considered good times with Iron. She was a good slave. She had single handedly took on the burden of feeding most of the slaves, off his shoulders. She gave great back rubs, listened to him, plus she was beautiful. He hadn't visited her cabin in a long time, for his tastes were getting younger and younger. Iron was probably the most beautiful woman he had ever been with, even if she was a slave. Times he pretended she wasn't; she was so light. He remembered those nights, years and years ago. His escape from his miserable wife, who just kept getting bigger and bigger. Peaches was right. Iron was a good woman. She never helped any of his slaves to run away. What was he to do? To his surprise, he did not want Iron to die. He thought he might even start visiting her again. Lord, she was beautiful, even now.

"I got some blankets."
"Put one down on the floor and we will roll her on that."

The two men roll Iron on her stomach. She moans.
"Massa?"
"Yes, Iron?"
"Massa?"

Iron reaches out and holds John's hand. He gently rubs her hair. The jailer looks at them confused.

"I told you to get the doctor!"
"Right away, sir."
The man runs out of the room.
"Iron, you will be alright. You a strong girl."
"Massa, it hurts so."
"The doctor will be here shortly."
"You taking me home?"
"I only brought my horse. I don't think you are in any condition to ride."
"Massa, you gonna sell me?"
"I'm not one for selling slaves."
"You gonna leave me here?"
"I don't know what I'm going to do as of yet Iron."
"Massa, I'm so hungry."
"They didn't give you anything to eat last night?"
"They were busy."
"I'll get you some food in an instant. Now tell me the truth, have you been working on the Underground Railroad?"
"No sir."
"They found a cellar in your cabin."
"Sir, I didn't even know it was there."

Iron is having a hard time talking. She is speaking very slowly, wincing between words.

"Sir, if you had a station on your very own plantation, how come none of your slaves never run away?"
"I have been asking myself that very question."
"All these years I never lied to you. I been a good slave to you Massa. I tried to do my part."

The doctor walks in.

"Sir, you know I don't rush for niggers."
"Doctor this here is a good wench, one of my best. I don't want to lose money on her. She is very valuable and I'll pay whatever it takes."
"Looks like some crackers had some fun with her."
"That depends on your definition of fun."
"Sir you are going soft on us. We will need every good Southern gentleman we can find. Now that Lincoln is president."
"Doctor, it is not the time for talk of politics. Will you look at my wench?"

Then, There Was Iron

The doctor rubs something on Iron's back, and then wraps her in bandages, from the top of her breast, to the bottom of her stomach.

"There you are. Never seen a man make such a fuss for a wench."

"Like I said, she is valuable."

"I heard she was working on the railroad. Bad time to be caught for a crime like that. Fire eaters talking of secession."

"I have heard such talks most of my life."

"I think the time has come when talks will turn into action."

"We shall see."

"John are you in favor of secession?"

"Most definitely. Do not think that taking care of my property makes me less of a Southerner. Is this not what we stand for? If we are willing to stand for the rights to own slaves, should we not care for them? Our distinct society is based on our superiority over Negro. If we do not take care of them, are we to expect that they can take care of themselves? We know this is not possible."

"Of course. You only appear quite eager."

"Oh good day doctor."

"Good day sir."

"I will have one of my hands come round with the bill."

"As you please."

The men are interrupted by the voice of a woman giving orders. Iron thinks, Miss Clara. Who always seemed alive when telling others what to do, in a pressure situation in which she had to work very fast. Iron loved watching her at those moments.

"Bring that in here. Yes. Yes with the food. I do not care. Haul it in."

The doctor leaves, John rushes to the hall to see all the commotion. He finds his sister her pig man Pierce and Adele. Carrying a large mattress, clothing and other provisions.

"Clara what is all this?"

"I've brought it for Iron."

"What do you care about Iron?"

"You know that she has been helping me with my sewing for years. After I heard the dreadful news of what you had done to her. I knew she would be needing a few things."

"Clara this is not a hotel. I thought you were going abroad. Have your planes changed?"

"Slightly, I will be leaving a few days earlier. By train to Boston then I set sail for England. I would like Iron to accompany me."

"You wish to buy her then set her free. Never not after the catastrophe with Gravy."

"I will pay whatever you desire. I still have property I am wishing to sell. I will trade all for Iron."

"You are willing to trade property for Iron only so that you can set her free. Never."

"John do not be such a heartless man. She has served you well."

"She is mine, to use as I please. She will stay with me always. She is quite necessary in the maintaining of my farm."

"Why to give you sons to sell?"

"How dare you speak to me in such a manner?"

"I will speak how I wish."

Adele and Pierce are fixing up the room for Iron they lay her on the mattress and are trying to make the cell as pleasant as possible. Both are quiet. Acing as if they are not listening to the argument between brother and sister though they (including Iron) are hanging on every word.

"You are my younger sister, you will show me respect."

"Respect for what. Quietly selling your own children. How many John 50, 100? Under the nose of your miserable wife. This I should respect? Having one of the smartest women I know lying in a filthy cell, letting crackers abuse her. I am afraid to look at groups of Negro children, fearing how many are my own nieces and nephews."

"How dare you?"

"Oh how dare I nothing. I am only speaking the truth. Why don't you leave here I have to talk with Iron."

"What kind of talking must you do with my slave?"

"It's women's affairs."

"Please I'm so hungry."

"Prepare the food for her."

"Scuse me Miss Clara with all the commotion to leave we forgot the food."

"John will you take Pierce to purchase food for Iron."

"What? I am not a man for errands."

"Please John it will save me the trouble of writing a pass. Like I said we must discuss women issues. Who knows what those crackers did to her."

"Alright, alright."

John leaves with Pierce. Adele quietly stands in the corner of the room watching the two women.

"Oh my poor girl."

"I'll be fine Miss Clara."

"Please Iron."

"Clara."

"Does it hurt much?"

"Yes."

"I'm so sorry."

"It's not your fault."

"How did he find out?"

"Doll."

"Whose Doll?"

"Don't matter. I can convince him that she is lying."

"Iron I didn't think he sell you, but I had to try. I made arrangements for you to ride the railroad in ten days. I figure that will give you time to heal. You know where to go?"

"Yes."

"Promise me you will."

"I promise. Thank you Clara."

"Everything should go fine. As long as we move fast. The South is headed for a storm. I plan to be abroad when it hits. Adele and I will be sailing to England but I will make several trips to Philadelphia. So I will see you again in a much more pleasant situation. I know you will make it Iron. There is so much waiting for you. Do you still have the deeds?"

"Yes."

"They are your future. I will be sending a trusted friend to check on you. Though I wish, I can not change my plans for you. It would appear peculiar."

"I understand. Thank you Clara."

"Don't thank me. You have done as much for me as I for you."

"I'm going to miss you."

"As I you."

Clara leans in on Iron, hugs her for a few moments then walks out the room. Adele comes over smiles squeezes Irons hand and silently follows. Iron watches Clara's red hair disappear for what she imagines would be a very long time. She hears Clara and John saying good-bye. She hears all boarding the carriage, then the sound of horses leaving. John reenters.

"She always had been a pistol."

He sits next to Iron holding her food.

"Can you manage?"

"I think so."

John watches Iron try and fail terribly at feeding herself.

"Let me do it."

Iron doesn't say a word. Massa feeding her. This has got to be a first. She can't look at him. He can't look at her, only her mouth. Clara's words repeat in his ears. Was he wrong in selling her babies? He knew some men that would shave the heads of certain slave children. So that no one would notice a resemblance. It never worked. Though nothing was ever mentioned about it. He was protecting Mary; the years had made her more fragile, but only in the head.

"Chloe come back Massa?"

"Chloe?"

"Your healing girl."

"I will send Benjamin to retrieve her tomorrow night. You two are quite close?'

"Yes."

"She is very good at what she does."

"Yes she is."

"She would probably have tended you better than the doctor, and with no bill."

"I be fine Massa."

"Why would someone lie on you, Iron?"

"Maybe they don't like me."

"You are honest. Always have been."

"Always will be Massa."

"I will bring you back home in a few days. I'll let you heal up in here. Probably be best not to move you. Clara has turned this place into a boarding house. You will be fine here."

"What if those men come back?"

"I shall leave orders whoever touches my wench shall answer to me."

"Thank you Massa."

John gives Iron the last few bites. When she is finished he doesn't say a word only walks out the door. He is feeling very strange. He

Then, There Was Iron

thinks it might be guilt. Has he been wrong all these years? Seeing Iron in that condition did not sit right with him. She did not deserve such treatment. He did not believe Doll anymore. Having a cellar in your cabin did not necessarily mean one was working on the railroad. He believed Iron did not know it was there. He would move Doll to the field or sell her. He couldn't imagine that he would get a good price for her. Her best years were over. As he rode his horse John began to feel a slight pain in his left arm. Damn Clara she was always trying to change his heart. He was a good master he did not starve his slaves. The whip barely flew on his plantation. Why did Clara always want to set his slaves free? His brother was much harder on his slaves. They were running away over there all the time. He must lose a buck every few weeks. He never ever got them back. God the pain was getting stronger. Set Iron free. What would she do with freedom? Go north, start a garden. Iron was best with him. He knew what was right. Damm Clara. The pain was almost unbearable it was moving to his chest. Maybe he should stop for water. As he tried to direct his horse to the side of the road. John Cummings fell over and died.

CHAPTER 20

"Dear God no! I do not deserve this. Why me God? Why me?"

Such screaming was heard from the big house as patrollers brought the lifeless body of John Cummings home. Miss Mary was not taking it well. Her 250-pound body was bellowing, breaking everything in sight and slapping any slave in arms reach.

"You damn niggers. I knew you would be the death of him."

"What will you do Mrs. Cummings?"

"Sell them. Sell them all."

One of the housemaids tried to sneak out, so that she could share the news with the row.

"Where are you going?"

"Ise goin no where Missus."

"That's right. Clean up this mess."

"Now Mrs. Cummings if your seriously thinking of selling off some slaves. I know some spectators just arrived in town. Friends of mine, they like to stock up on the off-season. Then take them deep South for planting time."

"They pay a fair price?"

"I've heard no complaints. I could rush into town, bring them back here for you."

"That's a good idea, the sooner the better. Alright, off with you then."

"I'll be back shortly."

The two patrollers who found the body of John Cummings dashed off. Moans and spiritual were softly heard from the row. Slaves mourned their master. Most thought him a good man. He owned them and would never have given any of them their freedom. He starved most of them and barely allowed them enough clothes for decency. But the whip on the Cummings plantation rarely flew. More importantly families were rarely torn apart. Which was what the slaves feared most.

"Lord that ain't good."

"Reuben what ain't good?"

"White folks running. Massa ain't even in the ground; Miss Mary got white men running. Lord knows what gonna happen round here. Someone better go check on Iron."

"Miss Mary comin out the house."
"That ain't good."
"Reuben stop saying that."
"All you niggers better line up and be counted. I'm making some changes around here."

Most slaves start running towards her immediately. When Miss Mary demanded something it was done.

"We better go."

Reuben and Shelly join the others. Roughly 159 slaves gather around Miss Mary.

"I want you all to stand right here."

Miss Mary goes back into the house. She is amused at having all the slaves standing in the cold waiting to be told what to do. She would leave them there until the spectators arrive. She didn't think they would try to run. Hell most had no shoes. Where would they go? She didn't care anyway. She was tired of niggers. This is what John wanted, to be a great planter. Now he was gone. Bastard. Did he love her? Did he ever love her? He hadn't touched her in years. Seemed like he hadn't really talked to her in just as many. Now he was gone. She would move. Open a shop. Sell the plantation. A lovely Southern shop with lovely Southern things. Fragile pieces. Pieces she could have shipped from Europe. Art. Culture. The best of society. The widow Cummings would do just fine. Just fine. The more she thought on the idea the more she liked it. Ah but first funeral arrangements.

"Lord how long you think she gonna keep us here?"
"Sh Sh Shelly don't wo wo worry, it it wont be long."
"I'm so cold."
"Take my co coat."
"What about you?'
"I'm fine."
"Who dat riding up?"
"Don't know."
"It's Chloe."

Chloe gets down off a horse behind a young black man.

"Thanx Willy. What you all doin here?"
"Miss Mary made us all lineup. Chloe Massa dead."
"What?"
"Died today."
"Dear Jesus. Where's Iron?"

"Chloe."
"What? Where's Iron?"
"Chloe."
"Stop saying my name and tell me where's Iron."
"She's in jail."
"What?"
"She's in jail."
"Massa heard she was workin on the railroad and he had some crackers take her away."
"She comin back?"
Peaches and Shelly stare at her.
"She's comin back ain't she. She alright? Lord tell me she alright. I'm going."
"Chloe you can't go now. Miss Mary said stay here."
"I don't give a damm bout Miss Mary I'm going."
"Chloe, Iron tole me to tell you, hold it dear."
"Hold it dear?'
"Yes."
"I'm going."
Peaches is holding her arm.
"Girl you want to be in jail with her?"
"Yes. Yes I want to be in jail with her. I'm going. I want to be with her."
Chloe falls to her knees and begins crying. Shelly and Peaches try to comfort her.
"Go Chloe. Miss Mary don't know you back yet."
Chloe stands up hugs Shelly and begins to walk off. She doesn't get very far when she sees white men riding up to the gate. Miss Mary appears out of the house. Chloe eases back in with the rest. Miss Mary and the men talk about 15 minutes then all walk up to the group of slaves.
"That's quite a nice lot you have Mrs. Cummings."
"Call me Mary."
"I take them all if I had the finances."
"Take all you can afford. I won't be needing them."
The spectators walk between the rows of slaves. Looking in their mouths, checking their backs for scars, searching for gray hairs, squeezing the muscles of men the breasts of women. More then half the slaves are crying mostly the women and children. The pleas to

Then, There Was Iron

keep families together have already started. Shelly is clinging to Paddy. Peaches to Benjamin. Reuben is staring at the sky. Chloe is in shock.

She watches one man buy Lizzie another Marcus. She hears Lizzie scream watches the man beat Lizzie on the head. It didn't seem real. Another man took Peaches and Benjamin. They were together. Someone was squeezing her breasts. Yes it felt like hands. Hands on her breasts. There was a white man her face.

"I'll take this here one."

"The white man was pushing her."

She was now on a wagon. Where did the wagons come from? Shelly, Paddy and Reuben were with her. About 10 other field hands were there. She couldn't remember their names, if she knew them at all. The wagon was moving. How long was she on it? Shelly was lying in Paddy's arms.

"It be alright. We ta ta ta together."

"How you know it be alright? They spectators. We going to the block."

"Sh Sh Shelly. Wh whatever happens I love you."

"Love me. Love me. We shoulda ran. We shoulda ran a long time ago. Now we going to the block. We going deep South. Deep South Paddy. I can't go back to the fields. I can't."

The wagon stops.

"Yall making to much noise back there."

"We're going to have to put chains on you."

"I heard your place had a railroad stop on it. Be no running from us."

Chloe watches the three men prepare their chains and wrist irons. Iron. I'll hold it dear. You better. I will. What you got planned. I got nothing planned. Irons voice dances in her head. The men begin their work. Three men. Where did they come from? Half the wagon was already chained. Shelly is next, then Paddy then her. She hadn't been chained in a long time. Iron.

"I ain't going back to the field. I ain't wearing no chains."

Shelly is yelling, screaming and kicking.

"Ja just listen to em Shelly. It be best."

"That's right do as your told. Now hold out your arms."

"I ain't going. Dem days are gone."

Ellen Barton

"They just beginning. Now do as your told or I'll put a ball in you."

Two men hold Shelly down. They put an iron bracelet around each of her wrists then slip a chain through them.

"Sh Sh Shelly let dem do."

"I will not. I ain't going back to the fields."

Shelly wraps the chain between her wrists around the neck of one of the men. She begins choking him. All the slaves are yelling. Another man raises his pistol in Shelly's direction. Reuben knocks him down. Shelly continues choking. Paddy tries to pull Shelly of the spectator. Other slaves knock him off of her. The third spectator pulls his pistol and shoots Shelly through the head. Paddy yells and attacks the man with an intense ferocity. Shelly is dead all the slaves are wailing. No one notices Chloe running for the woods.

Go go go. Don't look back. Run. Run. Jesus Shelly is dead. She free now. No Shelly you aren't going back to the field. You free now. Go go go. Right in the head. Ball right in the head. Nothing can be done for her. Jesus Shelly. Go go go. Run run. Shelly you free. This minute you free. I love you. I love you Shelly.

Chloe is replaying Shelly's death in her head over and over. She is running at an unbelievably rapid pace. Unbelievable to her. She never thought that she would run again. She decided when Shelly said to Paddy that they should have run a long time ago. Iron had often talked of them running, they probably would have made it. She was sure most of her passengers did. She was scared. She could hear the sounds of teeth going through Nelsons bones. She could still hear the wailing of her daughter as they were separated. Run, she swore never again. It wasn't worth it. Not until now. She would hold it dear. She swore she would make it to Philadelphia and she would be free. Or die trying.

Chloe thanked God she still had her bag from her stay on the Lynn plantation. She did not remember until she thought about the thud that was repeatedly hitting her lower back. She had food in there, a knife and a few changes of clothes. She was ready. She had strong boots and a good winter coat. A coat Iron gave her. Probably got it from that white woman. Miss Clara. Boots, Iron paid God knows what to have made for her. Iron. We should have run a long time ago. Warm. Warm. Warm feet. That was most important. Chloe seen this from the slaves that went through Irons.

Then, There Was Iron

She couldn't shake the eyes of a young girl, about 2 ½ years old. The girl had a sister 4 and a little brother 9 months. They were on a long walk to Canada with their parents. Chloe would never forget the feet of those girls. It wasn't the way God had intended the feet of children to look. Blistered. Swollen. Chloe could cry thinking about it. Those girls didn't cry. Didn't make a sound just looked. Looked at her with big brown innocent eyes. If those children could run, why couldn't she? She had seen that in Irons eyes after they had left. Though Iron didn't say a word about it. That night they held each other all night long. Silently wondering why. She hoped they made it. They had to. They had to.

Chloe stops for a minute out of pure exhaustion. She had been running for nearly an hour. Without looking back. She falls to her knees. Raises her hands to the sky, makes a fist, clenches it, stretches out her fingers, clenches it, stretches out her fingers. Lets out a silent scream. Looks around nervously gets up and keeps running.

Weeks pass. She did not hear the sounds of dogs. She did not see the shapes of white men. For a while she thought if it wasn't for the complete and total loneliness, the starvation and the cold, living in the woods for the winter months wasn't so bad. Most things she ate she either stole or caught. She spent a few nights in barns. But mostly she found shelter outside. Daring to make a fire when the two blankets she stole were not enough. It was getting colder and colder.

Chloe figured they must be a few days until Christmas. Earlier in the year she wondered what she would give Iron for Christmas. She cried when she realized that this dilemma was sadly solved. When she found herself in North Carolina she felt sure she make it to Philadelphia. Iron would meet her there. She didn't know how Iron would make it, probably that white woman. Miss Clara. If Iron needed help at all? She was so smart. Everyday Chloe thanked God that Iron made her memorize the place in Philadelphia. All she had to do was keep moving. Keep walking. Stay alive and the good times will be back. The good times. She will have them again. She refused to have anyone or anything else taken away from her. She didn't deserve it. She will have what belonged to her. Iron. What could she be doing at this moment?

CHAPTER 21

Iron was mad. Mad at time for not standing still on the good days, and for moving to slow on the bad. Love with Chloe; laughter with Shelly and Peaches. Talks with Reuben and Miss Clara. Clara. The food, the song, and the feeling of belonging. The pure moments of life. Sharing. Sharing each other. They should of stopped for a second and screamed, "these are the times of our lives!" The times we will need to remember. Damn time for taking it all away so quickly. For making it all pass. Time went on and left those moments behind. Iron's only comfort is that one-day this time will also be behind her; and she would joyfully forget every second of it.

She had been in jail, by her estimation, about 6 weeks. 6 weeks. No word again from Massa, Shelly, Peaches, and especially Chloe. Something was wrong. No one would say anything to her, and no one would answer her questions. Someone just came twice a day with a little piece of pork, and some corn bread. She could see outside, see people rushing in the streets. They did not pay her no mind. She was alone. Completely. Her brain imagined the worse, for only the worse could keep Chloe away. She prayed Chloe was on her way to Philadelphia. Why wouldn't she stop and say good-bye? I'll see you there; I love you. Something was definitely wrong. She felt it. Felt it in inside.

Iron stops daydreaming for an instant to listen to the sounds of jubilation coming from the streets. Fireworks were exploding. She could hear Dixie being sung. White people seemed to be going out of their heads. She had never seen white folks looking and sounding so joyous. She calls out to the guard that she can't see, but knows is there.

"Sir, please."
"Shut your mouth."
"Please sir, tell me the reason for the celebrations."
"You'll find out soon enough."
"Please, sir."
"South Carolina has seceded from the union."
Iron thinks Clara is right again.
"Congratulations."

Then, There Was Iron

Iron walks to her little window. She watches for most of the night. There was quite a lot of drunkenness. A few white men yelled terrible things through her little window. She hid back in the corner and sang Bell's whipping song. Bell called it her whipping song because she often sang it to grown men lying on their chests covered in rags soaked with blood. The song was actually written and always performed by Baby.

"Don't be scared,
Just believe in God,
Don't be scared,
Just believe in God,
I'm not scared,
I lean on God,
I'm not scared,
I lean on God,
When I get weak,
He holds me up,
When I fall down,
He picks me up,
Never go empty,
He will fill my cup,
Don't be scared,
Just believe in God,
Don't be scared,
Just believe in God."

She sang the song over and over, but was still scared. Scared of tomorrow. Miss Clara. Clara said that first the South would secede, and then there would be war. What would happen to a slave woman in prison during the war? She shuddered at the thought. She had to escape. Clara's plans for her to ride the railroad were gone. The time had passed weeks ago. Where was her friend that was supposed to come and check on her? Where was Chloe? Iron began to cry, silently on the floor of her cell as the fireworks and the jubilations roared outside. While her tears poured she took the great risk of digging up her deeds. She held them in her arms like a newborn baby, curled up on the mattress and went to sleep. She awoke to the loud screaming of a mad female. Miss Mary.

"I say they all ran away!"
"Widow Cummings that is a terrible thing."

Widow Cummings. Widow Cummings. Iron is repeating this in her head over and over.

"Call me Mary. Anyway, 20 of them. I only left 20, and sold off the rest. I felt I needed just to maintain the place, until I could sell it."

"That is quite understandable."

"Of course it is. Anyway I had some neighbors over last night. I don't usually entertain, especially since my husband's recent passing. But the excitement of a great country that's of our own, well it brought out folks. We stayed up well into the night. Being a Southern hostess, I offered rooms for the night; they refused and rode off quite late, causing me to sleep until well past sunrise. Anyway, when I awoke, I found the place strangely quiet. I called on my girl. No answer. I go outside to check things. I find my overseer tied up in the barn, and not a nigger on the plantation."

"20, you say?"

"Yes. Now I want to post some bills for their return. I also need to hire some men. I got my overseer, but they already tied him up. What's next? Anyway he informed me I had another girl just wasting away in jail. Plus I was paying for her to stay here. So I will be taking her home today."

"What about the charges?"

"Charges? What charges? She ever harm a white in South Carolina?"

"Not to my knowledge."

"Then release her, she's mine."

Iron is listening to the entire conversation in complete and utter disbelief. Massa John was dead. All the slaves sold except 20 who ran away last night. She had to assume that Chloe, Shelly, Peaches, and Reuben had already been sold, for if they ran away last night, they would surely have found a way to come by her window. Sold, Chloe was sold. Dear Jesus, Iron prayed she was running. She heard Miss Mary and the guard coming toward her cell.

"To think I had to drive the wagon here myself!"

"No."

"Yes."

"A fine Southern woman as you."

"Yes."

Then, There Was Iron

They stood looking at her. The skinny guard who never forced himself on her, (and for this Iron was truly grateful); and the devil's big fat daughter.

"You got irons for her?"

"Yes, we got everything you need here."

"Cause I don't want no more running niggers. Put leg iron on her and handcuffs. Put a good space of chain between them, cuz she is going to work in that condition."

"I'll go and get the blacksmith."

"I'll wait for you."

The guard hurries off leaving Miss Mary and Iron staring at each other.

"What's your name girl?"

"Iron."

"That's a strange name. How come I never seen you before?"

"I worked in the garden."

"Oh yes, I remember you now. Last time I seen you though, I swear you were just a child. I thought John had sold you."

"Massa didn't like selling much."

"Yes. Unfortunately. You all I got left now. So there's a lot of work for you to do."

"You going to buy someone else?"

"That's my concern girl. Who taught you to ask white folks questions?"

"Sorry, Miss Mary."

"What you in here for?"

"Nother slave lied on me."

"What did they say?"

"Said I was working on the railroad. Massa didn't believe it though."

"If he didn't believe it, how come he put you here?"

"He put me here till he checked it all out. He was about to release me, then I never hear nothing."

"That's because he died."

"He was a good man."

"Yes, coming from you, that means a lot. What you know about a good man?"

"I know he was a great planter. Everyone said so."

"Yes. Well things different now. I'm selling the place."

"Like you sold all the slaves?"
"All but the filthy animals that ran."
"Who you had left?"
"Well, I'm going to have to teach you a few things. What did I say about questions?"
"I'm sorry. I was just wondering about my friends and family."
"Lord, ain't no such thing as friends and family for niggers. Keep sniffing, you will find more."

Iron hated this woman. She had a quick image of biting the woman in the neck until she tasted blood. Sitting back and watching her bleed to death. She quickly shakes this image. This was not her. Miss Mary was still one of God's children. The bible says love your enemies. She thought, "God Bless you bitch, I hope you die like a dog." That should be alright. Miss Mary was still talking. She tuned back in.

"They were mostly my house girls. You listening?"
"Yes Miss Mary. Chloe?"
"What?"
"Chloe. Massa John bought her for doctoring."
"I don't recall any Chloe. Oh yes, yes. She was quite a good healer wasn't she? John used to lend her out quite a bit."
"Yes, yes that's her."
"Sold. Sold her more than a month ago."

The casualness in which Miss Mary ripped Iron's heart out was unimaginable. The guard soon returned with the blacksmith. They prepared handcuffs and leg irons. Miss Mary insisted on a two-foot chain between Iron's feet and hands. She than hitched Iron to the back of the buggy; climbed to the front of the wagon, and made her way home. Iron trotted behind.

If the wagon hadn't stopped, Iron would have never recognized the plantation. She had never spent much time near the big house, but it never looked like this. Lonely, the land looked lonely. There was not a person on the place, the great farm that once housed the activities of at least 150 people a day. It didn't look right. It didn't feel right. Iron looked out to the fields. She could see Mama Pearl working, urging her on. The first day she met Shelly; the spot where Reuben used to fiddle. She was so young. She used to love to dance. That was all before she moved to the woods. This place wasn't right. How could she stay here? How could she stay here without Chloe? If

Then, There Was Iron

there was a here without Chloe. Without Chloe, here did not exist. Iron is awakened by a slap in the back of the head.

"Stop your dreaming girl. There is a lot of work to do."

Iron wipes the tears from her face. Follows Miss Mary into the house trying desperately to erase the hate from her heart. She has a strong feeling her and Miss Mary were not going to last too long.

CHAPTER 22

He seen her. Walking through the woods as if she did not have a care in the world. He seen her; she looked like $400.00. Yeah, he was sure he could get $400.00 for her. He would not even bother to find out whom she belonged to. Just grab her. Grab her and sell her. Hell, it was Christmas Day. He had to get up to his wife and two daughters, and have nothing for them. Nothing. Absolutely nothing. Lord, they were lucky if they had something to eat today. He had to get out of the house. He grabbed his rifle, and called his hound. Then he seen her. Francis Malone was not a stupid man. He was just an unlucky man. Poor cracker. That is what he was called. That is what his Daddy was called.

The only work his father ever got was catching runaways, or as an overseer. Francis remembered growing up moving from plantation to plantation. He remembered the fights between his parents. Once, his mother called his father a nigger. This was the first time he saw his father hit his mother. Francis remembered thinking maybe she was right. The rich white kids treated him no better than they treated their slaves. They would even play with the slave children, but not him. Their parents wouldn't allow it. The parents rather they spend their time with slaves, instead of those dirty cracker kids. He swore he wouldn't be the man his father was. He wasn't. He was less. His father always put food on the table. His father always had something to give on Christmas. His father never looked into the eyes of a hopeless woman and hungry kids. But not today. Today he would go home and he will have something to give his wife. He will have food and toys for his beautiful girls. All he had to do was stay quiet and stay back. Ease up on them quietly. Then jump. That's what his daddy used to say. That's what he was doing.

Chloe knew he was there. She didn't turn around to see how far back. But she knew he was there. He had been following her for about half an hour. She knew he had a dog; she wasn't sure how many. Probably one. If he had more than one, he would have set them on her. One dog had a good chance of being killed. One woman, being followed by a man with one dog. She did not increase her pace. She did not run. This man just might have one gun. Surprisingly, she was not afraid. She did not know what she was going to do. But she was certain that she would never be a slave again. After this decision was made, she was quite at ease. Living in the woods had changed her. Seven weeks of scrounging for food like an animal. Seven weeks of winter weather with no shelter. Seven weeks with no one to talk to. She was a different woman. She had tasted a live animal. She had felt the blood dripping down her chin; so surprised to have caught the small wild pig, she bit into it.

She had just started her woman business and had terrible pains in her stomach that combined with the hunger and loneliness. She grabbed the animal and bit it. Of course after the initial bite, she realized what she was doing and killed the animal. She had gone 5 days without food and had eaten raw meat before, on the plantation before she was sold to John Cummings. Lord, she could never tell Iron this, could she? First she would have to be in Iron's arms to find out. That was where she was walking to and one man with one dog and one gun were not strong enough to stop her.

She was getting a little too far ahead. He was going to have to speed up. He wasn't losing this one. Not a woman. Though some of those nigger wenches were strong as men. This one looked strong though she was slender and dark. Dark ones sometimes you could sell for a little more, as a breeder. Now she was reaching in that sack she had on her back. If she had a gun he would shoot her in the shoulder. Ah, no weapon. Looked like she was getting something to eat.

Chloe got the tiny cloth of pepper. She had brought it for Iron with a few other spices she was going to surprise her with. The cook gave them to her, a small gesture for healing her son, the days that Chloe was away. Chloe thanked God now. It would also be a nice gift for that hound. She pretended she put something in her mouth and began chewing, while she hid the tiny sack in her hand.

Eating. How could she eat when he was so hungry? He had biscuits for 6 days straight. That's all. Biscuits. Breakfast, lunch and supper. What kind of meal are biscuits for a man? A man comes home from looking for work, looking for food, sits down and eats two biscuits. It wasn't right. He eat good today. Blessed Jesus. He will have some meat today.

As the woods get thicker, Chloe decides to start running. It would be hard to get a good shot and to keep up with her through the trees. Francis also begins to run. He sends his hound ahead, in case he loses sight of her. Chloe turns back, doesn't see him. She takes a second to open the tiny pouch and sprinkles it all over the ground. Then she takes off again. She hears the dog running not far behind her. Barking. Lord, she thinks of Nelson. Go, go, go! Run, run, run! Don't stop. Don't stop. She now hears the dog sneezing. Don't look back. Go, go, go. Jump, dodge, go, go, go! She's scared, damn it! She didn't want to be scared. She didn't want to be scared ever again. She's crying. She sees Iron. Iron is holding out her arms. Run, run, run. She'll kill him. A shot. A bullet hits the trees. She's covered in fear. Go, go, go. Don't look back. God, she could hear him. Reach for the knife. Should she reach for the knife? Another bullet. She's screaming. Why can't she stop screaming? He can follow her voice. She tries to stop screaming but finds she can't. She makes it to the road. She's dead now. She knows it. She grabs the knife and waits for him. She is aware that she probably looks like an animal, out of breathe and hungry for blood. A buggy pulls up; she did not hear its approach.

"Dear lady, dear lady, get in. I'm a friend."

Christmas Day. Iron spent it vomiting. She was sick. Not physically. She was disgusted, disgusted by Miss Mary. The few days she had spent with her. She understood why John had so many cabins in the woods. The woman was lazy, loud, and unpleasant to look at. Always yelling orders. Always slapping. Always completely unsatisfied and looking for sympathy. Iron looked at her and thought the last time my stomach came up this much; I was carrying your husband's child. But she did not say it. Miss Mary might not take that so well. She hated Iron as it was. At least she appeared to.

Miss Mary was off to spend the day with her cousin. She came into Iron's room the night before. Drunk. Laughing. Asking Iron, "Would you prefer to be chained in the house, or go along with me?" Iron chose chained in the house. She had stolen a small bottle of laudanum from Miss Mary's cabinet. She preferred to sit alone with it, instead of celebrating Christmas cheer without the one she loved. How could she go in chains anyway? No other slave would wear chains on Christmas Day. She didn't want the embarrassment. One of the slaves from Miss Mary's cousin's plantation came to pick her up. Miss Mary had him install extra heavy chains on Iron. He didn't look at her, or she at him. She had already taken several swigs of the laudanum, and was just beginning her journey into desired self-pity. As they pulled out the drive, Iron screamed, "Merry Christmas, you demented white bitch!" She took another swig and added, "God bless

Then, There Was Iron

you." That should be alright. Now to see if she could reach the liquor cabinet. She could. How long would it take her to get to the place where she didn't hear voices? How much would she have to consume? Was this better than jail? She did not wake up and see bars. Was that better? What she hated most about being in jail, was waking up. In her dreams she was with Chloe. Not always free, just together. Then she would awaken, and look at the bars. Every morning she almost cried. Was this better; no bars to look at? Only empty spaces where love had once been.

Why? Why her? Why her heart to be ripped out of her chest? Was it beating too hard, too strong? Was it causing too much attention? Was her love too loud? Making too much noise at a time when love was not allowed? Quiet. Not recommended. Not in your best interest. Ah, don't love girl. It just makes things worse. Just get through. Get through. If only, that could happen. If only you could get through your life and not love. Probably have more belongings. Never learn to care. You hear the news. Man's been beaten to death. You think, "I don't care." I'm not going to jail over it. Let em be beaten to death. Let em starve. Let em freeze. I don't care. I'm not going to jail over it. I'm not going to get whipped. I'm not going to be taken from Chloe. I love her. I care. I got feelings; I'm no animal. Why the hell am I in chains? She begins rattling them.

Iron passes most of the day in this state. She finishes a bottle and a half of whiskey, and quite a few swigs of laudanum. She laughs, cries, sings, dances, crawls, pleads with God, and then passes out. Only to awaken 6 hours later feeling much worse than she had when she began.

Christmas Day and Chloe was soaking in a tub. She had to thank God. She had to. She had been living in the woods close to two months. She knew it because she had bled once, and her body told her she was soon to bleed again. Nearly two months without a bath. It being winter weather she rarely found water she could wash with. She was filthy and she smelt bad. She could smell it herself. An odor she never wanted to experience again. The smell of being hunted.

CHAPTER 23

David had continuously asked questions about the Cummings plantation of South Carolina. It was more difficult than he thought. Someone told him South Carolina was a big state. There were quite a few Cummings plantations in South Carolina, but they were not the ones he wanted. Having spent a fair amount of money, he decided to give up the search for a while. As the days wore on, the idea of finding his mother appeared less in his head, till eventually it did not appear at all.

What did appear in his head were extreme colors of hate. Rage he tried to swallow. He was mad at the world. Mad at his life, mad at his boss, mad at his job, mad at the men he worked with, mad at the food he ate. The only comfort he received was his late night reading lessons. He was coming along at an average rate, though he thought it was extraordinary. Andrew was a good child, polite; knew his place, despite being raised by his mother. With her gaze that screamed, "Impregnate me!" and the fact that she always seemed to be in his way. She appalled him. Her niceness. Her never-ending search to find another husband. The only thing David saw that she had going for her, was the color of her skin. A woman of nearly below average looks, with below average hair, below average intelligence, and a below average bank account. She had the house, but her late husband left her deeply in debt.

She was miserable. Mary began insulting blacks in front of him slowly at first. Now they were at a point where she was saying derogatory remarks 10 to 15 times a day. She believed in slavery. Though the country was doing just fine the way it was; half slave and half free. She believed in the fugitive slave law and didn't think blacks should be allowed to vote. When David talked to her he could barely control the desire to punch her squarely in the face. He understood her misery. A poor white woman, she had to look down on blacks. If not blacks, she would have to choose another group. Any group. She had to look down on someone. It was all she had to feel better about herself. That's the kind of person she was, stupid thing.

David knew she had dreams of them possibly marrying. His dreams were quite different. His dreams involved ropes, flesh and blood. Biting. Nicey was bit. Pain and pleasure. He could see it. Hear her screams, taste her fear. She wanted to please him. She wanted to be there to satisfy all his needs. Well he had some needs that she didn't understand. He had some needs that would terrify her. He would readily show them to her. If she didn't make him so sick.

He was thinking about smashing a glass in her face while sitting down to a tasteless bird surrounded by other colorful items he was expected to chew and swallow. Mary was going on about shots fired on Fort Sumter. He attempted to smile at her during the appropriate pauses. Wondering how anybody could be so unperceptive. Mary said the country was heading for full out war. Then she giggled, saying such conversation should be left to gentlemen and she did not know much on the subject. But she did, plus she had a normal citizen's concern. She pretended to be ignorant on such matters and shrugged them off because she was a woman. Thinking that was what he wanted, because he was a man, only made David hate her more. As soon as he finished his supper, he rushed out for a walk.

David walked most of the night before he accepted that he needed it to live. He went to a prostitute. He choose a white one. He had the urge to beat her, but he didn't. He instead shoved her, bit her, and pulled her hair. He was rough as he could be without completely terrifying her. She did not enjoy the session, and tried her best to have him perform in the way she was accustomed to. He could not. This caused her some more fear. He had seen it in her eyes. The unknown. He felt her relief when she said, "Get out." He appreciated it. The next morning Lincoln issued a call for 75,000 soldiers. He answered it.

It was a lot easier than David expected. A thump on the chest and a count of the extremities, David found himself raising his right hand and swearing an oath of allegiance. He thought his Southern accent would run him into difficulties, but he was wrong. David Stone was now a soldier of the United States army. He couldn't wait to kill.

CHAPTER 24

Miss Mary and Iron were on their way for supplies. The doctor came by late last night and informed Miss Mary of a Northern blockade of seaports. He told her she should stock up on some items, for they may soon be hard to come by. It wouldn't last long. He said the South would whip the North in three months. Iron listening from the kitchen thought the man a fool. Did he not know anything about the population, or the strength of the North? She was just a slave and he a doctor. She knew. Miss Clara had taught her many things. How come no one told him? Just look at what's in front of you. It seemed Southern men have been beating slaves too long. They had gotten drunk on their power. They now thought they could beat anything. Iron let out a sympathy sigh, and poured herself another whiskey.

Iron drank quite a bit, as did Miss Mary. Miss Mary drank so much, she did not notice how much Iron drank. She enjoyed playing the sick widow spending most of her time in bed, occasionally receiving a cousin, niece, or old friend. She had a terrible cough and complained about feeling weak. Visitors waived it off saying she would be up and about very shortly. Iron thought they were wrong and only being kind. She knew that cough, it never got better and it only came before death. Miss Mary did have what some would call her good days, and this was one of them.

"Now I don't care what the doctor said, I ain't spending lots of money buying up the town."

"Yes, Miss Mary."

"We are closer to North Carolina then Charleston. How will a sea blockade affect me? People getting in an uproar. Such foolishness."

"Well, it is a war Miss Mary."

"Watch your tone. I know it's a war. It be over before you know it. The North will get a taste of what they are up against. They will come to their senses and mind their own business."

"Spect your right, Miss Mary."

"I am right. Here we are. Iron, you wait here, and I'll go in."

"Yes, Miss Mary."

Iron was relieved not to go into the store. She had been shopping there for a week using passes she had wrote herself, using money she had stolen from John Cummings private office. Hidden in the cut out pages of a book. She was sure Miss Mary did not know of the nearly two thousand dollars. She also found a surprisingly large amount of cash in various slave cabins. She found either hundreds of dollars, or no money at all. There did not seem to be a middle ground amongst the field hands. She left all their money intact, thinking they may one day make their way back for it.

Even more blacks were running away these days, now there was a war. She read it in the newspapers. She heard it from the guests of Miss Mary. They all said that Miss Mary was lucky to have such an obedient hand in Iron. Miss Mary, to Iron's bewilderment, often agreed. Sometimes saying, "I wish I had her working in the house years ago." This was always followed by, "she's dumb, but she ain't lazy." Iron never minded such talk. She actually took pride in it. She wanted Miss Mary thinking she was dumb. She spoke in the dialect of most of the slaves from the Deep South, the manner in which nearly all her passengers spoke. Whenever Miss Mary asked her questions of matters, which usually would not concern a slave, Iron pleaded ignorance. Though she wasn't. She also agreed with everything Miss Mary said, and completed every task given to her in a short time with efficiency. Miss Mary liked her, as much as she could like any slave woman. This was a major accomplishment, for Miss Mary naturally hated blacks. Had since she was a little girl.

Iron also hated Miss Mary. Mostly for the things Miss Mary had done in the past. She had to admit Miss Mary's treatment of her was not that harsh as expected. Once you had gotten over the fact she kept Iron in chains for the last 5 months. She didn't seem interested with what Iron did with her time, as long as her chores were completed.

Miss Mary was also now consuming large amounts of opium. She was not the same person capable of past atrocities. Her mind and body had suffered too much deterioration. She relied on Iron. She needed her; almost trusted her. Almost. Miss Mary could not stand to have another overseer around. She detested that class of people. She did not want to spend the money on purchasing other slaves. She found contentment having only Iron in the house.

The days she spent lying in bed, coming in and out of consciousness, she was not aware of the doings of her slave. But when she was back to her old self, everything appeared in order. Iron did not even appear to steal, and Miss Mary had set a few tests for her, which Iron passed. She must have the only slave in the South that did not steal. It was so in their nature. It must be because of her color. This was one of the lightest slaves Miss Mary had ever owned. Terrible. It was just terrible what some Southern men were doing. Slaves were getting lighter with every new litter. How she hated it. She was a firm believer in not mixing the races. So was Iron, and like Miss Mary, she did not have a say.

"Come on girl. I'm ready."

"Yes Miss Mary. Let me get that. You sure didn't get a lot."

"I got what I needed. Having some company over tomorrow. Want a special dinner."

"Anything you want Miss Mary. I prepare something wonderful."

"Good, good. You are quite handy in the kitchen. Even with them chains on. How come you never asked me to take them off? Never. Not one complaint. How come?"

"I figure you know when it's time to take them off Miss Mary."

"Umph. My. So many men gone. You can see it."

"They be back shortly, Miss Mary."

"Jeff Davis, he have our men back soon. Praise him."

"Praise him, Miss Mary."

Praise him? Praise Jefferson Davis? Bless him, maybe. God should bless every man. But praise, she thought not. President of a country whose firm belief was blacks should be owned by whites? Iron knew enough intelligent black people and ignorant white people, to conclude this was not the best reason to form a country. Any other, maybe. But not this one. Poor Southerners did not know what lay ahead for them. Iron did; which is why she began shopping weeks ago. She had also killed pigs and beef, and salted down the meat. She had a major supply room in her old cellar.

It had almost ripped her apart going back to the cabin. The cabin she shared with Chloe. To look at their bed, to see Chloe's clothes. None held her smell. Another stab. She lay in their bed a long time. Crying. She only did this once. Then she never went to the back room again.

CHAPTER 25

David's urge to kill had to be put on hold. Hold while he practiced endless drills. Hold, as he learned hundreds, or what appeared to be hundreds of bugle calls. Hold, while he memorized instruction from drums and the sound of angry voices. Drill, drill, and more drill. Why couldn't they hear his urgent need? His need for battle, his need for life.

Talking to other men. (Which in his heart he hated to do.) He would like to live a life and not talk at all. He really did not care for these men or about them. He only talked, for they expected answers to their time killing questions. Where are your people? What is your occupation? Where did you study? Did you study? Did you farm down there? Good land there. Oh, how he didn't care. But he had to talk. He had to appear somewhat social. A voice told him it was necessary. He had found out that not every man fought this war to end slavery. Some did not give a damn about slavery. Some men were fighting to preserve the union. They had a belief that America was a great country, and should remain so. Others were fighting for the pay and three meals a day, which was something David could not understand, for the food started out awful and had continually grown worse. What surprised David the most, were the men who had brothers on the other side, cousins, life long friends. Family and friends they were willing to take a gun to. All in the name of war. Brother killing brother, father selling son. The country was dirty. He didn't know how long would it take to clean it up.

One man asked him why he was fighting this war. He stood up and said for the right to love a black woman. There was some laughter, than not a word. The majority of the men did want slavery to end. They just didn't want to live amongst the blacks once they were free. So much had to change. David was surprised at the vast amount of officers committed to equality of all people. A higher percentage held this view, compared to the soldier. All men are created equal. This was often heard from various campfire debates. The officers stood proudly for a country claiming they were willing to kill or be killed for it.

David had no plans of being killed. He felt completely invincible. He was different. He knew it. He was not as stupid, as boring, or as

Ellen Barton

pathetic as the others. He was stronger, smarter, and his need to tell no one only proved it more. He did not even get ill, as did most of the men. Stomach ailments haunted almost everyone, but not him. Personally he thought it was because he drank large amounts of boiled water, never coffee. The other men drank coffee. He would never touch it, though he had drank it every other day of his adult life. The coffee supplied by the union army, or what the men could forge for themselves was so awful he just stopped drinking it, and started drinking plain boiled water. Loving it, he imagined how it was washing him inside. He soon felt a strong desire to drink it all the time. Anyway he never got sick. Watching the other men vomit, have diarrhea, and suffer with the cramps; he knew he should share his secret, but he never did.

David was not willing to give up knowledge of any kind. As far as he was concerned, the men were too needy. They needed sweethearts back home. They needed to write letters to these sweethearts. They had a booth set up where a photographer was taking pictures of them to insert in these letters to their sweethearts. They needed to talk about these sweethearts, and to hear about other sweethearts. They needed food and rest to sustain their bodies, for their return to these sweethearts. They needed guns and pain and suffering as not to appear as cowards to these sweethearts. Needy.

They were all too needy for David. He did not see their necessity of trivial conversation. He couldn't stand it. The atmosphere when the postman came about also slightly annoyed him. How the men turned anxious. How some were even moved to tears when nothing came in their names. Nothing ever came for David. He accepted this. He did not write letters, thus felt no surprise when he did not receive any. He certainly would not cry if the postmaster never screamed his name. Needy. He looked at it as a sign of weakness.

He was not weak. Not in any manner. He almost was. Almost. Weak and foolish, as the other men. How they could not see their complete dullness. The dullness of the lives they left behind. Joining the army was the only thing they appeared to do that mattered. That would give them strength. They did not know it. David knew it. The chance to kill. This would put some meaning in their lives. They needed meaning. They needed purpose. He has seen it. They needed a leader, someone to point them in the right direction. The direction of life. For a while he was one of them. He knew this. Not making a

Then, There Was Iron

mark on the world. Factory worker, easily replaceable. He saw where his life was heading. Work everyday; come home to a loving wife, adoring children. Working man. Work like a dog to pay the bills until you die. Dull.

He had seen it in the widow's eyes, the hope for dullness. The hope to make everyday exactly like the day before. How he thought about flogging her. His days as an overseer sometimes came back in his dreams. He did not regret these dreams at all. Usually the widow or his old Missus was his victim. He still remembered his boyhood; the things she used to do to him. He hardly ever dreamt about slaves. His favorite dreams occurred when he was awake sitting away from other men, thinking of things he could do to old Mrs. Joplin. He would of liked to have her alone for days. He would need days. Days for cutting and chopping. These thoughts were occurring to him more frequently. At first he thought they were only reactions because of the delay to the battlefield. Now he looked at them as something all together different. Something he felt he had to explore. Someone had to clean up the country. So many were dirty. Dirty and dull.

Why hadn't anyone told them? How come they couldn't see it for themselves? Why was it he who was chosen? Chosen to be bored. Chosen for a hunger he could not quite as yet put his finger on. David sat back and watched the men. They were singing. Dancing. They certainly tried to enjoy their evenings after long days of endless drills. David felt sure most would make excellent soldiers. Religious, high patriotic men they were. That combined with bravery, David felt comfortable he was in the right army. Soldiers, they were excellent. Men. He didn't know where to begin. David found the more he looked at people the more they sickened him. He leaned back and closed his eyes.

"Stone, Stone. You sleeping?"
"No."
"It sounds like we finally moving out."
"I have been hearing that for weeks."
"Think the time has finally come."
"Have there been orders?"
"Not officially. You want some whiskey?"
"Where you get that?"
"Won it playing poker."
"No, not tonight."

"You must. It's a lucky jug."
"Alright."
"You sure aren't a drinking man, are you Stone?"
"Used to be."
"You must be a lot older than you look."
"No. I'm still a young man. It's only whiskey and the army are not a mix for me."
"I understand."
"But this being such a grand occasion, I will make an exception."
"Funny man, Stone. Enjoy."
"Thank you sir. Umm, that's fine. What did you beat him with?"
"Full house. Ace high."
"Ace high. Well, it is a lucky jug."
"Makes for a nice start on our way to Washington."
"Washington?"
"That is to be our destination."
"To protect the capital?"
"Or to take Richmond. I'm unsure."
"Both are smart moves."
"That they are."
"Stone, Snow. I see you are both still able to enjoy the finer things in life."
"Snow here won a jug of whiskey playing poker."
"Honor us."
"I love to."
"Gentlemen, excuse me."

David was relieved the other man arrived. It made his escape all the more easier. Politeness. He was losing patience with it. The waiting. Waiting for the opportunity to escape. Just the precise moment. The proper break in a conversation. At times they were so long in coming. David wanted to get to bed early. He retired before most men, and was awake before them. He had a certain habits he didn't like to disturb. Personal hygiene, walking, eating. He liked to do these things alone before the duties of the union army called him. He settled in and went to sleep.

The next morning proved Snow's rumors to be true. At first light they were on their way to Washington. It took a few days to arrive traveling partially by train, and partially on foot. It took another half

Then, There Was Iron

day to pitch all the tents and get what David guessed somewhat organized. He was looking over a newspaper when Snow entered.

"Stone, do not tell me you are staying in."

"Those were my plans."

"We will be seeing battle in a few days. Who knows what will happen to us? Stone, we must go into town. Visit the ladies. They love soldiers. Haven't you heard the stories? This is Washington."

"Yes, I have heard all the stories. The women in those stories who love men as you say, all have a price."

"What is wrong with that?"

David stops and thinks for a moment.

"Nothing."

"Then, let's go."

As they walk into town, Snow's endless jabbering makes David wonder if he should try this, another time. But he can't resist. It doesn't take that long to reach the area where most of the ladies frequent. They are, as Snow suggested, in love with soldiers. David doesn't think it has anything to do with the uniform; they were businesswomen. The soldiers are paying customers; like any paying customer. David allows Snow to choose first. They agree to meet at a designated area in one hour. David doesn't want Snow to see the woman he chooses. He doesn't select until Snow is completely out of sight. Then he chooses one of the more sickly looking women, with black hair, and what David imagines to be only a handful of fat.

The woman obviously had problems. She appeared very absent-minded. Only stared at the ground and continually chewed on the same piece of hair.

"Do you want a room?"

"Outside will be fine."

"Outside for an hour?"

"It won't take an hour."

"It never does."

David leads the woman away into a wooded area. He is sure no one has seen him. She wasn't standing with the others. A small distance away. No one saw him walk with her. He was certain. They walk for about 15 minutes.

"How far are we going? I'll have to get back."

"This is fine."

"What would you like?"

"Just the normal."
The woman reaches in to touch him.
"No, no. Just lie down on your back."
"Should I remove my clothes?"
"Doesn't matter."
"Doesn't matter?"
"Just your under things."
David lies on her.
"Your not quite ready yet. Let me help you."

She lowers her hands and before they reach their destination, David grabs her throat and begins squeezing. The woman appears shocked at first, terrified, and then somewhat relieved. He wanted to bite off her lips. He had thought about it as soon as he seen her. But he hadn't taken off his shirt, and he didn't want to get blood on it. Damn. He might have his knife on him. He thinks he does. Maybe he will cut them off; he wanted those lips. He couldn't believe how thin they were, almost nonexistent. He is staring at her mouth when he realizes the woman is not kicking or making that funny gasping noise anymore.

He gets off her. He has a seat next to her and looks at her for a few moments. He then reaches for his knife and proceeds to cut off her lips. He begins with the bottom and it takes longer than he had thought, so he doesn't bother with the top. For an instant he has a vision of Mistress Joplin. Sees her pink lips yelling at him, cursing him always, always when Lewis wasn't home. Why couldn't he take him on those business trips? Why did he have to leave him in the big house with her? David put the lip in his mouth, and swallows. He rolls down his sleeves; wipes the knife clean on the prostitutes dress, and begins walking back. Before he reaches the area he is supposed to meet Snow, he encounters another young lady.

"Well, hello soldier."
"Hello. How much for twenty minutes in that there hotel?"
"$1.00."
"$1.00. Is it worth it?"
"It's guaranteed."
"Well, let's go."

They walk in what David knows to be the direction Snow will be waiting.

Then, There Was Iron

"There's my buddy. I can't make it tonight. Listen, here's the dollar, why don't you give me a nice kiss, and we call that even?"

"That's fine with me."

They kiss passionately for a moment, and then both go off in their separate directions. Him feeling better than he had in a long time. Her thinking he had the worst breath she had ever encountered.

"You're a bit late. I can understand why. But your not supposed to pay her out in the street. How come she didn't take the money first?"

"Oh, that was a tip. Well deserved, I might add."

They walk back, in what David was wishing to be silence. But as always, Snow's mouth continued to run. David easily tuned him out. His mind was focused on his evening. Scattered with quick reflections of growing up on the Joplin plantation. He had visions of his childhood while freeing the prostitute. Mostly animals. Animals he killed when he was a boy. Mostly rabbits. He used to squeeze them to death. He always preferred petting them after they were dead. He had done that for a long time. Until he got old enough to beat the slaves, rape the slaves. The only time he had ever penetrated. He had never made love. Never made love with Nicey. He couldn't. Yes, yes he let her believe that they would wait until married. But the truth be known, he did not have the stirrings. The necessary stirrings needed by men. He was hoping they would come. When he went to touch her, nothing moved. He had enjoyed kissing her, and holding her. What he loved more was staring at her. Her beauty. Like none he had ever seen. He wanted to own that beauty; make it his. His forever. Sometimes he wished he saved her smile.

"My Stone, you are quiet tonight."

"It's women."

"What?"

"They weaken me."

The next morning, they were on their way out. Marching for hours, probably days. David was exhausted. He tried not to let it affect him. He could not sleep the night before. He was still exhilarated. He had killed his first white woman. He had killed many black men, a few black women, but never a white one. They died pretty much the same way. There was no difference in the end of life. Another good reason to end slavery. Another good reason to march off to war. Skin made no difference when you were chocking on your last breath. David had spent the night replaying his murder over in his

Ellen Barton

head. So many things he would have done different, and he definitely needed more time.

Slaves, he used them for days. He had the time; he had the place. He had no fear of getting caught. He did not like rushing. It wasn't the same. Marching, marching closer to battle, he had a hunger for blood. It seemed to be growing at an alarming rate. The only time he could not remember feeling this hunger, was his time with Nicey. What did she do to him? How long could it have lasted? His days with Nicey, he did not kill, did not rape, did not torture. He did not feel like himself at all. His only desire at the time was to stare at Nicey. Just watch her. The most beautiful creature ever created. How could he leave her? Ever let her go. That was decided for him. He still had visions of shoveling the dirt on Nicey. She looked so peaceful. The part of her that was left. He had never seen her so peaceful.

Remembering back, he never felt so close to her. It was their most honest time together. He began feeling the stirrings. The stirrings that would not come when Nicey was alive. The stirrings that only came when he gave pain. These stirrings were now for Nicey. In the ground Nicey. So quiet. So cold. He had taken women when they were passed out. Knocked out by him. This was his best time. David knew that this might not be enough anymore. Last night with the prostitute, he did not have any stirrings, until she was at peace. Then he did not have the time, or the proper cover. Yes, next time would be very different.

Other men were complaining about the heat. The endless marching. Their thirst. David barely heard them. He could not stop fantasizing about another chance. Another prostitute. Again he had her in the woods. This time she put up more of a fight. He had seen himself holding the woman down. Her kicking and screaming. Terrified. Terrified of him. He gets her on the ground, gets his hands around her neck, and looks into her eyes. She knees him in the groin and gets away. He gets up and chases her. Catches her. Punches her repeatedly in the face. This subdues her. He lays on top of her and looks her again in the eyes, and begins strangling. The punches have weakened her and the fight is not as strong. It doesn't take long for him, to take her life. He wants to cut her now. He wants to open her up. He feels the stirrings.

"Stone, Stone! Wait up. My you appear deep in thought."

"Anxious for battle."

"As I."

Then, There Was Iron

"I hear we are marching to Manassas Junction."

"It does not matter to me where we fight as long as we fight."

The soldier looks into Stone's eyes, than rushes ahead to talk with another. David did not care about the name where the battle would take place. Names did not matter to him. He had heard other soldiers talk about generals, lieutenants. He was not interested in who was giving the order as long as the order was to shoot. They seemed to be walking forever. When would the war begin?

They marched all that day and much of the next. He had heard it was only 25 miles. He was not impressed with the time the men needed to march 25 miles. They should be better organized. Finally they reached their destination, which now he heard was called Bull Run. Again he didn't care what they called it. Only point him in the direction of the enemy. The battle was close now. He felt that they would be fighting in a matter of hours. Surprisingly David had noticed a great amount of civilians had come out to witness the spectacle. This he liked. What he did not like was his fellow union soldiers did not appear to be as prepared as he was. He watched them stopping to pick blackberries; thinking this was definitely not the time for fruit.

Finally the call came to move into action. He was ready. They were moving closer to the enemy. The spectators were cheering them on. He couldn't truly hear them but he could see their apparent joy. What he could hear was a strange yelping cry the kind that tickled your spine. Then he saw them. Confederate soldiers, waiting to die. The orders came, he fired. He reloaded and fired, reloaded and fired. There were lots of smoke and plenty of confusion. The two sides appeared to be dressed the same. It was hard to tell who was the union, and who was the confederate. David swore he saw people shooting their own men. The heat was unbearable for some, but not to David; he was on a mission.

While his fellow soldiers were running away, he kept fighting. When they were shot directly next to him, he kept fighting. When they stopped and ran to look for water, he kept fighting. He would not stop until slavery was abolished. Slavery was not polite. He saw Nicey lying in her grave every time he leveled another rebel soldier. He loved it.

His one-man war against the confederates was not enough. The North was forced further back. His fellow union soldiers looked whipped. Whipped good. Seemed like most of the men he had started with, were gone. Dead, taken prisoner, run-off. He didn't know, but they were gone. All the civilians were gone. Seemed like everyone was running. Running back to Washington. There was no organization, only thousands of soldiers making their way back. They looked terrible, and felt worse. The talk on the walk back was about arranging some kind of surrender, striking a deal with the South. David did not agree with this talk. Neither did Abraham Lincoln, for the next day he issued a call for 75,000 men for three years. David was happy and looked forward to his next battle.

CHAPTER 26

Chloe watched the entire battle from a position much closer than she would have preferred. Her companions, two male runaway slaves, one named Anderson, the other Isaiah, appeared more frightened than she. She guessed they had not completely as yet decided in their heads, never to be slaves again, where as she had. Anderson she had known for 5 months. He was already amongst the Quakers when she had arrived. Isaiah they just happened upon a few weeks ago. Chloe didn't trust him. With Anderson, she was developing a kind of sisterly love.

When she had arrived amongst the Quakers, Anderson was the only black face in the bunch. He explained things to her that of the Quaker way of life. Said he had been with them for years, working on the railroad. He was a runaway who after arriving at this station traveled no more. Thought he could be more useful there, than any place else. He was probably right. Their station was highly efficient. Chloe understood why Anderson did not want to move on. They were extremely kind people.

It took Chloe a little while to trust white people. Eventually she did; at least these ones. The first time a white woman looked her in the eye and called her Miss, Chloe thought she would fall over, but she didn't show it. She now understood Iron all these years saying there were good white people, for she now had shared their homes. She guessed Iron was correct in her declaring Miss Clara a good white person, though she was never comfortable with all the time they spent together. These people were special in a time when special was so necessary. These people talked to her and listened to her opinions. All they asked was that she pulled her weight, and she could also have stayed as long as she liked. She loved their fairness; their understanding of good and evil. She wished more whites were like them, more blacks at that.

Chloe appreciated their hospitality, but she had to get to Philadelphia. Iron was waiting. The Quakers made all the necessary arrangements on the railroad. Chloe gave them the same heart felt thanks that she herself had received so many times. Everything was going perfectly. Chloe felt truly free until they arrived in Virginia. The Quakers had warned the two that this was not the perfect time to

Ellen Barton

be traveling on the railroad because of the war, but they would probably make it. Chloe and Anderson were the very last two passengers to leave this Quaker station, a station that had been in operation for over 20 years. A station that had seen nearly 3000 passengers pass through it.

There was a certainty amongst the Quakers that the North would surely win the war. The need for an underground railroad would be no more. To the dismay of the three runaways hiding in the bushes, the railroad appeared to have broken up just a few stops before they reached their destination.

"Wot we gwan do?"

"We going to stay here till the fighting stops."

"Den wot?"

"Then I think we should try to join the North."

"Join the army? Wot black faces gwan do in the army?"

"Isaiah, I don't think he means join the fighting, but get with the side of the North. They probably will protect us."

"White men protect us? I don't think so."

"What you think they fighting about?"

"Freein nigas. Ise knows, but Ise ain't bouts ta go up ta no group of white men."

"I'll go."

"Now Chloe, I don't think you should go alone. We will wait it out, and then we will all go. And Isaiah, you got to get over that fear of white people. They fear you just as much."

"But Ise don'ts whips dem!"

Chloe and Anderson laugh.

"Isaiah, you know there is some good white folks. I just came from some."

"Dats good fa you. Ise ain't never seen no good white folks."

"I used to be just like you, believe me. I hated white people; hated their look; hated their smell; hated when they talked, hated when they didn't talk."

"Ise thinks Ise would liked ya better den."

"Look! One sides running."

"Which side?"

"Looks like our side."

"Damn."

"Lawd, da South done whip da North."

Then, There Was Iron

"They are not whipped yet."
"Deys running."
"This is only one fight, plenty more to come."
"Well, Ise hopes de next fight don't see da Nawth runnin."
"Anderson, it don't look good."
"It be alright Chloe."
"Wot we spose to do now?"
"We just stay put."
"Ise can't stay here with all dese white folks runnin around. Dey gwan find us and take us back."
"Isaiah, you hush now. They are not all running. We wait here until things clear up. If there are any Northern soldiers left after a while, we will go up to them."
"Sounds good Chloe sounds good."
"Youse two off in da head. Dey gwan find us. Look ebey bodies runnin."
"Let em run. If they all run away, we hide here for days if we have to. Then we continue."

The three stayed hidden for most of the day and part of the night, until Chloe heard the moans; the cries of the wounded on the battlefield. She couldn't stand it. Chloe had a healer's heart and listening to those men beg for help was ripping it apart. It looked like they were setting up some kind of tent to care for the wounded. Chloe wanted to help.

"I think it's time we make our move."
"Why you think it's time Chloe?"
"How wese know those souljas the Nawth?"
"Cuz we done watch the South already drag off their injured. The men left on the field are from the North. Let's see if they need help."
"Help? You want to help those white men? Lawd. Ise don know why Ise run into youse two. Must be the most mixed up nigas I ever seen. Lawd. Help the white folks."

Chloe rolls her eyes, gets up and starts running. Anderson is right behind her. Isaiah doesn't move, deciding to wait to see what happens to the two cracker lovers before making any move. The two run onto what was hours before, a battlefield. It being nighttime Isaiah is losing sight of the events.

"Soldier, soldier, you need our help?"
"Who are you two?"

"Sir, is this the Northern army?"

"Yes it is. Come out of Washington. Now who are you two?"

"We come to help."

"Wait here."

The soldier goes off to talk to his commanding officer. He returns very shortly.

"The man can help pull the wounded off the field. I don't know about you."

"Sir, I been healing all my life. I can tend wounds."

"I don't know about that."

"Sir, I been healing slaves for over 20 years. Ain't no wounds worse than what I seen."

"Okay. Go in that tent and see if there is of any use for you."

Chloe heads for the tent running at top speed. Anderson heads back on the battlefield with other soldiers to drag in the wounded. The first thing Chloe notices when entering the large tent, was a pile of legs about two feet high. Cut off just below the knee with the foot intact. Chloe had seen a lot of things all her years of healing slaves, but she had never seen no pile of legs before. She had seen men beaten to death. Men who wished they were beaten to death; backs tore open to the bone. She had seen women used so badly by gangs of crackers, she couldn't look them in the eye. Slaves whom had handsaws taken to them. One man who had his private parts cut off. Three women who had one or both breasts ripped off. She had seen heads broken open. She had seen the insides of a woman sliced open by an angry overseer. She had seen a young boy about 5 or 6, dead. Had been dead for days; half his head was crushed. An older girl (Chloe was about 10 at the time) told her a white man swung him in a tree, holding the boy by his feet. It was spectators going through with a gang of slaves. The boy probably couldn't keep up. The other girl had pointed to his foot. Said he must have been a cripple. Chloe still had nightmares of his face, half a face. That was the day young Chloe took an interest in her mother's skills. That was the day she decided she wanted to heal.

Waking up one night next to Iron, after that particular bad dream, she related the story to Iron. Iron had comforted her. Saying it was that boy that gave her the need to heal. Iron said the thousands of slaves Chloe had worked on over the years, all she probably was doing, was trying to fix that boy's leg. Now there was a pile of them.

Then, There Was Iron

White ones at that. Now she had seen everything. She knows this. The next thing to catch her notice was the stench and screaming. There appeared to be some commotion in one corner of the tent, and Chloe follows it. A man is holding a pistol to a surgeon's head.

"You will not take my leg off."

"I beg your pardon sir; lower your pistol, I am a trained professional."

"You are a drunken fool desperate to show off your skills as a surgeon. I will wait till I arrive back in Washington."

"Man, there is no time for that! I am trying to save your life."

"Well, it's going to cost you yours."

All able-bodied persons inside have rushed over to the scene. Chloe waits patiently in the back. Curious as to what will be the result, but trying to stay out of the way. Chloe notices one doctor calling for help; he is working fanatically on what appears to be a dying man. No one is paying him any attention, though his cries for assistance are quite clamorous. Chloe rushes over to help.

"Who are you?"

"I was told to come in here and help, sir."

"Alright, press here."

"How come you are not with the others?"

"Others?"

"Negroes. They have about 10 or 15 in the back, under guard."

"They told me to come in here and see if I could help."

"Why you?"

"I tended thousands of slaves over the years, plenty white folks too."

"You ever lose any?"

"Some. Saved more though."

"As I."

"Can you get the bullet?"

"I think so. I don't want to amputate."

"Amputate?"

"Cut off his arm."

"Like that other doctor?"

"That's Dr. Bates, I think he gets carried away."

"So does that soldier."

"What's your name?"

"Chloe."

"I'm Dr. Samuel Collins. Can you come put your fingers here?"

"Yes sir. Can you reach it?"

"I got it."

"Good sir. I can wrap him up."

"When you're done that, check the men one by one. Do the best you can with our limited resources."

"Resources, sir?"

"Supplies."

"Don't worry I know how to make do."

"Most of these men are waiting for transportation to our Washington hospital."

"Yes, sir."

"If anyone says anything to you, tell them you received your orders from Dr. Collins."

"Yes sir. Thank you sir."

"Chloe?"

"Yes sir?"

"You can call me Samuel"

With that the doctor smiled and walked away. Chloe watched him walk over to the stubborn soldier still holding the gun to the other doctor's head. More spectators were now witnessing the show including quite a few able-bodied soldiers. Chloe watches as Dr. Collins talks the man into handing him the pistol. She then proceeds to bandage the man they retrieved the bullet from.

Chloe's night was exhausting, going from patient to patient; wrapping bandages, administering whiskey and chloroform. She even held down a couple of patients who desperately needed amputations that instant. Dr. Collins, not Dr. Bates, who was given the remainder of the evening off to rest, performed the procedure. Dr. Collins called on Chloe the whole night. Not 5 minutes would go by where she didn't hear him call her name. No one asked again where she came from. All the staff were grateful for the help. The load was almost unbearable.

Just past sunrise, Chloe finally received a break. She goes outside to eat some corn beef and potatoes Dr. Collins had presented her with. She hadn't realized how hungry she was. She finds Anderson sitting on a bug rock also eating, though he has ham and eggs.

"Who gave you the food?"

"One of them soldiers. Who gave you that food?"

"Doctor. They alright to you?"

"Yeah, they real nice. I think they just glad to have the help."

"Yeah, they real busy in there. They got some runaways in the back under guard."

"I heard that."

"Soldiers say that they won't send em back."

"That's good. Probably use them for work."

"War do bring plenty of that. Lord these fields terrible."

"I see em when you bring em in."

"Thank God you don't see the ones we leave there."

"I can only imagine."

"I never seen men in such a mess. And I seen some slaves worked over."

"Lord, I hope this war over soon."

"Soldiers say it going to last a lot longer than the people thought at first."

"How long you think?"

"I don't know. Soldier say Lincoln want men to sign up for three years. I can't be pulling around pieces of men for three years."

"Anderson, did you see the runaways they got in the back?"

"No. Why?"

"I was wondering if Isaiah is there."

"I done forgot about him. I'll go check later. Chloe, what you fitting to do?"

"You know I'm going to Philadelphia."

"When you leaving?"

"As soon as I can."

"You know how close we are to Washington?"

"No."

"Woman we free."

"I have been free for months. You have for years."

"I never felt this free before. Few days walk from free soil. Lord, it's something."

"It sure is."

"How is that corn beef?"

"Lord, it's terrible. I don't know how they can ruin corn beef, but they did. What they should do is pull some of those slave women from under guard and have them do the cooking. It doing the job though. How's your breakfast?"

"Like you said, it's doing the job."

Both of them laugh. Chloe had heard Anderson laugh quite often in the last few months she had known him. But she never heard him laugh quite like this. It was a free laugh. A laugh that carried no burdens. She loved the sound of it. Dr. Collins came out to join them.

"Enjoying your food Chloe?"

"Yes, sir."

"Is this your husband?"

"No, sir. This is Anderson, he a friend of mine."

The men shake hands.

"This is Dr. Collins."

"I seen you working all night Anderson. How those fields looking?"

"We finally got them all in sir."

"Lot's of dead men out there?"

"Unfortunately sir."

"Well Chloe, some wagons should be here shortly to carry the men inside off to Washington. You about ready to go?"

"Washington, sir?"

"No, I'm not going to Washington. I'm a field doctor; I follow the fighting. I'm going to need you by my side. Your work is exceptional. The North would surely fair better with you tending it's wounded. Anderson, I hope you stay with us. All help is greatly needed. As we go, I'm sure you will find more Negro's will lend their hand to the side of the North. You will see a great many more runaways. I guarantee that. Runaways that the Northern army will need. I must go in now and gather my things. See you shortly."

Anderson and Chloe stare at each other for an instant.

"Follow the fighting? That man said follow the fighting. Lord, I can't be dragging around pieces of white men for three years. Damn."

"I don't think we have to. I think we got a choice. Who is to stop us right now from leaving? We are not under guard. We could start walking and not look back. You know we make it."

"Yes I know. You don't sound so sure."

"I'm not. I got to get to Philadelphia. It's all I been thinking about since I started running. But this here war will end slavery. I got children in slavery. I don't know where they is. I don't want my children seeing what I had to see. Doing what I had to do. I could make it to Philadelphia. Live a free life with someone who loves me.

Then, There Was Iron

Loves me! What kind of life could I make knowing I had a chance to help end slavery, and I thought about my own happiness? Not the happiness of my children. Grandchildren I'll never know. I have a chance right now to end their suffering. To fall asleep knowing my children are safe wherever they are."

"You staying with the doctor, aren't you Chloe?"

"I must."

"You trust his intentions Chloe?"

"You think he wants to mess with me?"

"He just met you. Now he needs you at his side."

"I don't know the man to trust him, but together in there we saved dozens of lives. Some that can live to fight another day. I will do everything I can to help them win. I do mean everything I can. I could work to free myself, or I could work to free my people. Anderson, it is not a hard decision."

"Chloe, I hear what your saying. I giving many years to the railroad. Helping thousands to freedom. But I need my chance, my chance for life. I think I would do more good in Washington, than dragging around the bodies of white men."

"I understand."

"I'll never forget you Chloe. You a special woman."

Anderson gets up and hugs Chloe. They embrace for about 5 minutes. Then he turns around and walks away, straight through the forest, not looking back. Chloe knows that she will never see him again. She knows that he will make it. She knows that he deserves it. Chloe goes back into the tent.

"Chloe, you got your things together?"

"I just got the one bag sir."

"Please Chloe, call me Samuel."

"Samuel."

"Our wagon will be here soon. We will have some rest for a few days and believe me, take advantage of it, for it will not happen too often. Than the next battle."

"Let me understand Samuel, all we do is follow the fighting?"

"Battle after battle."

CHAPTER 27

After battle after battle Iron stayed in her chains. It must have been close to a year and a half now since Miss Mary took her out of prison. Iron barely remembered; like Miss Mary she was still heavily dependant on whiskey and opium. Because of the war, these items were hard to get. Miss Mary made arrangements with local boat runners to have these things and other luxury items delivered to her once a month. Miss Mary at the beginning of the war was a woman of incredible wealth. The sale alone of all her slaves had brought her close to $300,000.00, on top of what was made by John Cummings. Iron watched this wealth diminish at an abnormal speed. It seemed like overnight goods had gotten more expensive. More paper money was also needed at every outing for purchases. It had gotten to a point where Iron was carrying large sacks of money for fewer goods. Even in the South, Southern currency was not wanted. Lincoln had issued something called greenbacks. This was the currency that was in demand. Miss Mary had none.

She had also lost all her livestock, wagons, valuables, and most everything the army could carry. Only the Southern army had been through the Cummings plantation to the surprise of Iron. She had read in newspapers how the Northern army went through various Southern plantations and all the slaves followed them, when they left. She did not have such luck. She did not even have newspapers anymore. The last few copies she read were printed on wallpaper. Now they were extremely hard to find. Miss Mary did not care about the lack of newspapers or the devalue of her money as long as the boat runners supplied her with whiskey and opium. She did not even care that she was out of food. Doubling up on her orders of chocolate and caviar from the runners. Iron did not think this was a proper way to eat. But she did not share the vast amount of food she had stored in her cabin.

Sitting alone in her cabin one night eating biscuits and fried chicken. Iron couldn't help wonder where the time went. How did it all go by so fast? Iron now spent quite a bit of time in the various slave cabins. Especially that of Peaches, she felt comfortable there. Mary never cared about her absences from the big house. She was usually in her bed barely aware of what was going on around her. The only time Miss Mary made her presence felt was when she was out of her various medications. She grew very nasty and would throw things at Iron. She always missed. Iron felt particularly lonely this evening, thinking about Chloe even more than usual. She heads to the big house for her medicine.

Iron realizes there is no whiskey left. They were also down to just one bottle of opium. Which sat comfortably on Miss Mary's nightstand. She goes to bed. She lies there gently rattling her chains. A year and a half she had been in them. How could this happen? When did she settle? When did she give up? When did she choose whiskey and medicines over life? Over love? Making everyday a cloudy day. Every day a day she didn't care, didn't dare. Wasting time. Wasting life. Was this supposed to be everyday? Drinking. Ingesting medicines until past sun down. Would she do this until she was in the ground? Wasted flesh. Taking space that was all she was doing. Taking space.

Her life was now nothing. She was not helping anybody, especially herself. She was occupied, numbing her life. She realizes a numb life is no life at all. She would get out of the chains. She felt what she was doing to her body was stronger than the chains. The whiskey. The medicines. They had a lock on her stronger than any chain binding her wrists and ankles. Theses were chains she put on herself. These were the chains that were holding her back. She was keeping herself a slave. It was now time for freedom. Iron decides never to touch them again. At least not until she arrived in Philadelphia.

Philadelphia and Chloe. Chloe, could she be there waiting for her? At this very moment waiting for her. Waiting for her, a year in a half maybe more. Iron was quite close to her third Christmas in shackles. Not this Christmas. No. She will get out of her chains and begin her journey. A path she should have been on a long time ago. But somewhere she got lost. She will be lost no more. She will fight it. The feeling in her head told her it would be a fight long and strong.

Inside her body someone was screaming for their medicine. She could. She could sneak inside Miss Mary's bedroom and retrieve the opium. If Miss Mary were asleep it would require barely any effort at all. Iron tosses and turns. She laughed and thinks she needs an underground railroad. Help I'm trapped by whiskey and medicines. It's keeping me from the one I love. It's keeping me from the life I deserve. It's keeping me from life itself. While she is thinking this she is grateful that she hasn't moved to give in to the opium. One instant at a time. She would have to live one moment at a time. Hoping in that moment not to fall weak to her destructive desires. She touches herself hoping it would help her fall asleep. It does.

"Iron. Iron."

Iron awakes to the bellowing of Miss Mary. She jumps out of bed and hurries to her room.

"Where have you been I must have called you 20 times."

"I was sleeping Miss Mary."

"Well it's way past sunrise. I better see some improvement, or I will have you whipped. Understand?"

"Yes. Miss Mary."

"I want you to go into town. I need some supplies."

"What you need, Miss Mary?"

"The usual girl. Do not pester me this morning."

"Sorry, Miss Mary. If you want me to find those running men, it's hard in the daytime. They be coming in three days anyway, Miss Mary. They come twice a month now, always the same time."

"I know that. But I'm out of medicine. You expect me to wait three days for my medicine?"

"No, Miss Mary."

"Now you take this pass, and hurry back."

"Yes, Miss Mary. Miss Mary?"

"What now?"

"I been a good servant to you."

"What do you want?"

"You said in the past when I prove myself, you take the chains off. Miss Mary, I think I done prove myself, many many times."

"If you can find my medicine, I'll unchain you. Now go."

"Thank you Miss Mary."

Iron runs out of the room. She is elated. She rushes to her room to freshen up a bit and heads to town. The elevation does not last very long, for she cannot find the boat runners anywhere. She does manage to produce two jugs of whiskey. She hoped this would last Miss Mary three days. It was a strong home brew. She may water it down. With her not drinking it, the odds were better. She was strongly tempted to taste it. Just one sip; instead she fastened her mind to the image of Chloe. Pictured being with her. Together, free in Philadelphia. She hurried home.

"I couldn't find them Miss Mary."
"What?"
"I found these though."
"Well, that's better than nothing. Fix me a glass."
"Yes, Miss Mary."
"You can leave them right here on the stand."
"Yes, Miss Mary."
"You know that is not my medicine."
"Yes, Miss Mary."
"Remind me again in a few days about the chains. I must remember where I left that key."
"Yes Miss Mary."

Iron leaves the room. She realizes that Miss Mary is playing a game with her. Probably having no intention on freeing Iron of her shackles. Iron doesn't mind. The assistance of Miss Mary was never something she counted on. The woman simply couldn't be trusted. She would have to do this herself. She could forge a note and find a blacksmith to release her and never look back. That would not be a problem. She had been practicing her writing everyday, now having access to the utensils. She could sign Miss Mary's name just as fine as Miss Mary herself. She thinks of these things as she walks to her old cabin for a hearty breakfast.

Miss Mary had not eaten for days. She had not even enquired about food. It must have been the medicine combined with the sickness. Miss Mary still hadn't shaken her cough, though she wasn't as sick as she made herself out to be. Iron couldn't remember the last time she seen that woman stand up. No one came to visit anymore. Most of the men were gone. Women. White Southern women to Iron's surprise were now working in the field. No one had time or energy for visiting.

Iron was even now more disgusted by Miss Mary. Her constant yelling, her complete idleness; but mostly her smell. Iron had to talk long and hard to get that woman to take up some soap and water. A few times she almost felt sorry for her. She remembered one night not too long ago, Miss Mary on one of her few occasions, was hungry. Iron could find absolutely no food to give her. She had gone into town but no supplies could be bought, for none had arrived to the local merchants. They said to come back in 2 or 3 days. Iron of course had her own supplies. When eating that night in her cabin, she felt she could not let Miss Mary starve. It wasn't right to allow anyone to go hungry, no matter who that person was, or what they had done in their past. Iron fixed Miss Mary a plate. She was going to say someone left it on the back porch. Just as she was leaving her cabin she stumbled a bit and all the food fell to the floor, leaving Iron with the empty plate in her hand. Iron took that as a sign from God and never attempted to feed Miss Mary again.

"Mamm, Mamm."

Iron is shaken from her memories as she listens to the voice of a young woman. She turns around to see a slender black woman running in her direction. The girl arrives in front of her, out of breath.

"Is this the Cummings plantation?"

"Yes, it is."

"Is there a Chloe here?"

"She sold away. Why?"

"I'm her daughter."

Iron screams in jubilation. She hugs the young woman, pulls her in and holds her tight. She does not demonstrate any desire to ever let go.

"Your name Ruth?"

"Yes."

Iron screams again and holds the woman even tighter.

"Miss, miss, I can't breathe!"

"Sorry."

"Do you know where my Mama sole to?"

"No, but I do know she be on her way to Philadelphia."

"Philadelphia?"

"We have property there."

"Property?"

Iron is aware that she is conversing with the young woman, but just barely. Her eyes cannot stop from drinking the woman in. She looks so much like Chloe, only younger. Her skin is the same earth brown. Her eyes are as dark but appear more intense than Chloe's. Her nose is thin like Chloe's; so are her lips. Ruth, like her mother was extremely beautiful.

"Mamm, mamm. You listening to me?"

"Excuse me, I was thinking how much you look like your mother."

Then, There Was Iron

"I be so happy to see her face again. I been looking for her a mighty long time."

"How long you been walking, child?"

"Bout 16 months, since my Massa gave me my freedom."

"You free?"

"Yes, most everybody free. You the first slave I seen in chains in a long while. What your name?"

"Iron."

"You and my mother was close?"

"She's my heart."

"Well Aunty Iron, you got any food?"

"I was on my way to fix breakfast. When's the last time you ate?"

"3 days ago. Union soldiers gave us some bacon."

"You must be starved, come on. Ain't too far. My cabin's in the woods. I stocked up the cellar. Have a good meal for you in no time."

"Aunty Iron, you heading for Philadelphia?"

"Yes."

"I got a horse."

"You got a horse?"

"Yes, I left him tied by the road."

"Well, we go get him after we eat. How you get a horse?"

"I bought him. Massa gave us all money with our freedom. I used all mine cept $50.00 for the horse."

"He give you greenbacks?"

"Yes."

"Sounds like a good Massa."

"He was alright. Might as well give us our freedom. We would all run anyway. Aunty Iron, you should see all the slaves in the woods, and the swamps. Things change and they ain't never going back."

The two women continue their walk in silence. Ruth wondering how this woman managed to be the last slave in chains. There did not seem to be anyone else about. What was wrong with this woman, though she seemed friendly enough. Why didn't she get herself free, and be on her way? Though, if she had done that, Ruth would have no knowledge of her mother. Iron keeps watching the woman out of the corner of her eyes; she has a lot of the movements of Chloe. She had called her Aunty quickly, and without invitation, Iron liked it. She had never been called Aunty before. It sounded right. They arrived at the cabin. Iron leads Ruth to the cellar.

"My God! I ain't never seen this much food in all my life!"
"Well, you take whatever you want."
"Lord, you got beef meat! I sure miss a nice piece of beef."
"I'll go up and get a fire going."
"How you get all this food?"
"I been saving. Had a glimpse of what was to be."
"Anyone know about this?"
"Just you and me. Your mother and I used to use this cellar to hide slaves."
"My mother worked on the railroad?"
"Yes, she did."
"I tried so long to find some of those railroad people, never did."
"Well, at least your Master gave you your freedom."
"Not really. I mean I got the papers. What happened was one of the housemaids over heard my ole Massa telling his young nephew when he die, he gonna leave all his slaves free in a will. So then they poisoned him."
"What?"
"Yep, they done kill him. Would have run anyway, with this war. Everybody running. How come you didn't run?"
"Imagine I was waiting for you."
"Well I here now. We got to get you out of those chains. How many white folks up there, cuz I only got four bullets."

Ruth reaches under her dress and pulls out a pistol. Iron continues seasoning the meat, as if the pistol does not shock her.

"Where you get that?"
"Took it off a dead soldier. Wished I could get more."
"Only one woman in the big house."
"Any guns there?"
"Some rifles, they in a glass case. I don't got the key."
"We break the glass."
"You think we be needing rifles?"
"It's a war out there Aunty Iron. Some soldiers far away from their women. Aunty Iron, there are some things I decided never to let happen to me again."

Iron lowers her head. She doesn't want to think what possibly could have been done to Chloe's daughter. She knows what has been done to her. Punishment. Punishment for the crime of being a woman. She decides they need the rifles and everything else they can carry.

Then, There Was Iron

She also had things she would never allow to be done to her. She thinks these things are sadly the same as Ruth's. Then she wonders why she never thought of breaking the glass. Miss Mary could probably remember where she left the key, if she was looking down the barrel of a gun.

But that wasn't her. She was not a violent creature. She was more likely to forge a note from Miss Mary and go searching for a blacksmith. She was the type to secretly for months and months master Miss Mary's handwriting. Then one day disappear. She was more patient, more calculating than the average slave, chained up in war times hoping to make it to the one they love. She knew this. There was also the medicated months. She wanted to forget this. None of these things she felt like explaining to Ruth, the darling child of the one she loved. Ruth, now Ruth seemed like the violent type.

"You say soldiers gave you bacon?"

"Yes."

"They must be pretty close."

"I ran into them about a week back. I was saving the bacon."

"But they still close."

"I seen them close to Charleston."

"They ain't never come through here. I heard they gone everywhere, but not here."

"How the place get so deserted?"

"The Southern soldiers come through. They take everything. Horses, livestock, wagons and cleared the vegetable garden. Told me I better tend that garden, they be coming back for more. Lord, you see the size of that garden? I can't work it all by myself, and me chained up."

"What you do?"

"I wrote a note from Miss Mary, say she need me to tend her."

"Don't they ask her?"

"She so drugged up that day, they couldn't ask her anything."

"What she like?"

"Fat, lazy, and evil."

"Well, I'll be making my introduction as soon as I'm full up. This used to be your cabin?"

"Yes."

"It sure is big."

"I was one of Massa's favorites."

Ellen Barton

"Sorry."

"Me too. Got some of your mother's things in the back. Get some water, you can bathe and put on one of her dresses."

Ruth gets up and goes into the back room. Iron concentrates on the meal. Ruth is very quiet. Every few moments she would ask, "Was this her brush?" "Was this her mirror?" And so on. Iron smiled as she answered. It was nice having someone around. Someone she shared a common bond with. Love. Love of an exceptional woman. Iron began on the biscuits.

Ruth ate with the same dedication and appetite her mother had. Watching her, Iron thought she ate with such ravenous commitment, not because she hadn't eaten in a few days, but probably always ate like that. She demonstrated a certain respect for food. Iron fixed her some stewed beef, rice and biscuits. She used her last two onions, though she was well stocked with flour, sugar, meat, soap, rice and a few other things she called necessary, such as tooth powder. She hadn't eaten a fruit or vegetable in months.

"Aunty Iron, I hadn't had such a fine meal since my mother used to cook for me."

"Thank you."

"What do you reckon we should do with all your supplies in the cellar? We can't take it with us."

"Well, maybe I'll take it to the next plantation over, they got a few slaves left there and they seeing some mighty bad times."

"Hard to believe some slaves left."

"They dedicated to their Massa."

"Fools."

"They think they had a good Massa, and they don't want to leave their Missus now the men gone."

"You dedicated to your Missus?"

"I hate her. She pinned my Mama's lip down. I had my setbacks. Now that you're here I can't see no reason for sitting on time."

"I can't believe you lasted this long."

"Neither can I child. Feel like I been asleep."

"You awake now?"

"Awake and ready to get up."

"What should we do first?"

"You go get the horse. Will load him up. Times like this we can't leave food wasting. Then we see about that key. Then we on our way

Then, There Was Iron

to Philadelphia and your Momma. You sure you can find your way back?"

"She ain't too far from the big house, be no problem."

"You make it back to this here cabin."

"Don't worry Aunty Iron, I done a lot of traveling all by myself. I can find my way back to your cabin."

"Alright, I'll pack up."

Ruth went off to retrieve the horse. Iron went to the back room. A room she had only visited once since her return. She had thought to take a few things; a few things of Chloe's. Standing in the middle of the room, she immediately changed her mind. She did not want tokens of her slave days. She did not need small things to remind her of Chloe. She noticed that Ruth had pocketed most of Chloe's meager possessions. Funny, she was not carrying them when she left. Slaves, they sure did know how to conceal.

She headed for the cellar. It didn't take long to bring up all her supplies. By the time she had finished, Ruth returned with the horse.

"Nice animal."

"She strong too."

"Let's load him up."

"People sure be happy to see us coming. Seem like everybody hungry. Whites, blacks, soldiers and slaves."

"That's the truth. I never thought I see a day when money don't mean much in stores."

"Money don't matter when there ain't nothing to buy."

"That be everything. Just got some papers to get out of the big house."

"These papers don't matter. All the patrollers gone. Swamp, roads loaded with slaves."

"Not freedom papers. Property papers. Got the numbers on it for where your Mama is."

"Numbers?"

"House number in Philadelphia. Deeds. Say we own the property."

"I ain't never seen no slave own property."

"I ain't a slave no more."

The two women walk back to the big house in silence. Both are thinking of the woman they loved; the same woman. The woman they felt incomplete without. The woman they would do anything to get to.

They wondered how long their journey would take, neither knowing the distance to Philadelphia. Neither truly caring, they would walk years if they had to.

"So, how you think we should handle this Aunty Iron? Pull out the pistol and demand the keys? Fast and easy?"

"Nothing with Miss Mary is fast and easy. You don't got to hurt her. Let me tell ya, she got a mouth on her. So try to stay calm."

"Calm? I thought you said she an evil woman?"

"She is."

"She ever whip my Mama?"

"No."

"She ever whip you?"

"No. I seen her whip a girl to death. Years, years ago. She couldn't do that now. Medicine got her."

"Medicine? She sickly?"

"Yeah. But she taking opium."

"Opium? What's that?"

"A medicine that weakens you, until you need it everyday."

Ruth wanted to hear more about the weak medicine, but they arrived at the house and she was starting to feel it. Iron watched the young woman, her whole face changed. Iron had a quick remembrance of Bad Bell, though this was not as drastic. Ruth's eyes got slightly darker, her brows began to meet, and she looked extremely serious.

"This looks like a house filled with spirits."

"Every house look like that now. Maybe they are. Old slave spirits."

"You sleep in here now?"

"I got a room right next to Miss Mary's. I'll go get my papers."

"All this is yours Aunty Iron. We can take whatever we want."

"I don't want nothing from here."

"Where's the old Missus?"

"Maybe I go in first and talk to her, see how that go, then you come in."

"I wait right outside the door. When you ready for me, cough. Alright?"

"Iron, that you? Stop talking to yourself girl. You woke me. Iron. Iron, come here."

"Coming Miss Mary."

Then, There Was Iron

"Where you been?"

"Just walking the grounds."

"You better walk into town and see about those runners."

"Miss Mary, you know I ain't gonna find those men."

"Girl, you better listen to me. I'll have someone over here double quick to rip a strip down you. Fix me a drink."

"Yes Miss Mary. Miss Mary, bout these chains, my skin chaffing something awful."

Ruth is vaguely listening outside the door. She thinks Iron is being much too polite, that was probably the older woman's problem. Niceness. What kind of slave stays in chains guarded by only one woman? Ruth wanders into the office, sits in John Cummings chair, and lights one of his cigars. She is feeling pretty good. Better than she had in years. She felt a certain peace. She received her freedom. She has found a dear friend of her mothers and she will soon be with her. So much joy, she could barely contain herself. She jumps out of the chair and runs back towards Miss Mary's room, where she bursts in without knocking.

"What is going on here?"

"Good day. I am from the association of I hate white people. I'm here to tell you that you better give up that key, and set this woman free."

"What?"

"Is there a problem with your ears? I said, you better give up that key and set this woman free."

"Get out of my room and get rid of that filthy cigar! Who do you think you are? This is my house!"

"And this is my pistol. Now where is that key?"

"You filthy animal! You do not give me orders!"

Iron quietly watches the exchange between Ruth and Miss Mary. She is quite entertained not spending very much time in the company of others since her return from jail; she thoroughly enjoys the verbal battle of wills. It took all she could not to laugh out loud when Ruth jumped directly on top of Miss Mary. She had the cigar flame aiming at Miss Mary's eye.

"You gawn tell me where is that key."

"You get off me this instant. I'll have the hide from your back."

"Whose gawn take it? You? Ha. I'll have the hide from your back."

"Well I never."

"Tonight you will."

Ruth jams the cigar into Miss Mary's eye. Miss Mary raises her hand to cover the damage while unleashing a terrifying howl. Iron rushes to the bed.

"Ruth."

"She will keep us here all night. We got no time for fooling. Now you want to lose the other eye fat girl?"

Miss Mary is crying hysterically.

"Iron you still got cow hide here?"

"Yeh. In the barn."

"Will you go get them? If you got a bit, bring it."

"We got some with bells. So you hear all the movements and they can't lay down."

"I know those well. It be perfect."

Iron runs to the barn. She isn't sure leaving Ruth alone with Miss Mary was the best idea. Ruth might kill her before they had the keys. Lord she going to take the cow hide to Miss Mary. Could life turn inside out? Iron didn't think she could stick a cigar in the eye of anybody. The noise alone made her skin crawl. The smell (sort of like ass and bacon) was no more pleasant. It didn't faze Ruth at all. She had never seen a woman like Ruth. No wonder Chloe could not forget her. She guessed hearing your father eaten alive only hours before you are separated from your mother. For what you imagine is forever. Sold to a strange place. God knows what happened to her there. Iron guessed all that might do something to a girl. Iron wondered what kind of woman Ruth might have been if she was allowed to grow up peacefully with her mother and father. Would she be the kind of woman that could burn out eyes? Iron hears a scream that sounds of complete joy.

"Aunty Iron. Aunty Iron I got it."

"What?"

"I got the key."

"What?"

"I got the key."

Iron is surprised to hear herself scream. Iron was surprised Ruth jumped in her arms and they were twirling around and jumping up and down. This was so unlike her.

"What about Miss Mary?"

"She dead."

"You kill her."

"She just dead. Made a wheezing noise and was gone. Must have been the excitement. Few seconds after she told me where the keys was. I cursed her all they way. Said she bes not be lying being dead and all."

"Yeh. I can see where that could have brought problems. Where was it?"

"In her drawers drawer."

"Drawers drawer?"

"Where she keep her big ole white drawers. It was tuck underneath, way in the back. Had to pull the whole drawer out."

"We got to bury her and say a few words."

"What?"

"We got to give her a proper burial."

"The ground to cold and I don't want to drag that cow downstairs. I ain't a slave no more I don't need to be dragging around heavy weight."

"Give me the key."

Iron undid her wrists rubbed them than she bent down to undo her ankle bracelets. She stared at the skin; it was harder, darker, raw, dead. She felt almost whole. Iron had an urge to cry but standing next to Ruth she swallowed it back she took her first step and immediately fell on her face.

"Aunty Iron. Aunty Iron you alright?"

"I'm alright just weakened up a bit. Run back to the house and get me an old dress."

"Miss Mary dress?"

"Any dress."

"Your dress?"

"Just a dress."

"I really don't want to go back into Miss Mary's room."

"Go get me the table cloth."

Ruth runs back into the house. Iron crawls around and gathers some palm size stones.

"What you gwan do?"

"I'm going to rip some cloth and tie it round my ankles. Put some stones in em. Everyday, I'm going to take out a stone, until I have no problem walking at all. I do the same with my wrists."

"You think you can leave today, or do you want to wait until tomorrow?"

"Today's fine. I waited long enough. Can't wait no more."

"You want to bury Miss Mary today?"

"We got to."

"You certain?"

"Yes."

"Lot's of work digging a grave. Your wrists weak."

"I be alright. We won't dig it that deep."

Iron finishes wrapping, then they head off to the big house. Iron gasps when she walks into Miss Mary's room. Ruth had beaten her pretty well. She did lose the other eye. Iron took a close look at Miss Mary. Went into John's office, found his property ledger; wrote her name and the word sold next to it, under so many other names. She then went into her room, gathered her deeds, walked by Ruth and said,

"Let's go. By the way, what did you do at your old plantation?"

"I was a housemaid."

"Thought so."

CHAPTER 28

Chloe leaned over the soldier. Holding his hand was not enough; he kept pulling her closer with a death-like grip. This was one of her duties; holding the hand of a soldier as the doctor sawed off the limb. As he gripped into her, his agonizing screams made Chloe think of the sounds she had fallen into. The sounds of the soldier, the sounds of the slave. A saw through bone, a whip through flesh. Sounds that made her pray. The weeping, the pain, was all the same. The soldier passed out. Samuel looked into her eyes. A look that did not belong to blacks or whites. A look of pain and suffering.

"Chloe, why don't you get some rest?"

"I'm alright."

"When is the last time you slept?"

"Yesterday morning."

"Chloe, you work better when your rested, we all do. Get something to eat first."

"Samuel, I can go a little longer. I need to change some bandages, those men that came in 3 days ago. I'll make a few rounds, then I'll lie down."

"Don't forget to eat."

Samuel walked away. Chloe headed out to change bandages. The one good thing about having too many patients and not enough doctors and nurses were they did not get around to changing bandages that often. This caused maggots and they ate up most of the rotting flesh. Chloe pointed this out to the entire staff, the healing power of maggots. Working all her life on slaves, she had seen the times when some masters had allowed her to treat their slaves once, then not come back for weeks. She found that maggots appeared and did most of the work for her. They were great healers as long as the patient could stand it.

Most of the soldiers were able to suffer the tiny predators eating away their flesh. Chloe had an entire new respect for whites. Now that she had seen the war, their bravery touched her, tore her. Even the Southerners; she had watched them walk into rifle fire, run into it. Whites were stronger than she had previously thought. Kinder. And most of them were not evil. Of course still so many were, evil, off in the head, untrustworthy. Lord, they were making it bad for the others.

Even a few Southerners impressed her; the ones who did not believe in slavery but were fighting purely for a country of their own. She had listened to their arguments though she could never bring herself to tend to a man in a confederate uniform. She left that to the white women.

"Chloe, Chloe, you eat?"

"I'm going right this minute."

Damn that man was good at sneaking up on her. She wasn't ready to leave yet. She had to be half starved to eat and ready to pass out before she lay down to sleep. Reason being the food went beyond awful last year, and so did her yearning for Iron. If she didn't remain completely occupied every second of her day, sometimes her breath became short and quick in its search to share with Iron. Her air was looking for Iron; her air was not quite right, when it was not combining with Iron. It was getting harder and harder. She goes talk to Judson. That man always made her feel better.

Judson was one of hundreds of slaves, following. Following the soldiers. Following the battles. Following the food. Seemed to be more with everyday. When a Northern army took a town, they seemed to take all the slaves with them. Chloe did not associate much with the other blacks, not until Lincoln freed everybody. She joined the party that night. Found an old hand from the Cummings plantation. John had sold him a few years before they were all sold.

"Chloe, Chloe, girl you got a taste?"

"Judson, you know I got no whiskey for you. We have to save that for the soldiers. Seems like supplies take longer and longer to get here."

"Dat be changing soon."

"Why?"

"Ise hear we heading Nawth. Mos dese here Negroes, dey be stayin dere."

"Staying where?"

"Nawth."

Chloe was still impressed by the Negro grapevine. Even during war times they seemed to receive information not yet made open.

"Where you hear we moving?"

"Pensavania."

"Pensavania? I ain't never heard no place named Pensavania."

Then, There Was Iron

"Well, its Nawth. Ole Davis he think he gawn attack the Nawth. Dem Yankees be heading out ta proteck it. Mos us slaves, we be staying. Thankin dem fer gettins us dere in safety. Girl, you should stay too. You always dog tired."

"I got my duties."

"Duties? Lincoln done freed ebeybody."

"The war not over."

"Girl, you know the Nawth gwan whip the Sawth. Just matter of time."

"That is the truth. You eat?"

"Piece of hartack and some bully beef. Got a piece of hartack left. You want it?"

"No. I'll get something later. I got to go. Talk to you tomorrow."

"Yeah girl. You bes think bout makin some changes."

Chloe walks through the Negro camp. She enjoys the feeling of calm in the air. Some were half starved, but all seemed happy. There was music and dancing. Laughter flowing from every corner as they huddled together for talks of the future. Chloe loved this but being amongst groups of blacks made her think of her own family, her friends, mostly of Iron. She rushed back to the soldier's quarters.

"Chloe, there you are."

"Samuel, I was looking for you."

"I was looking for you too. Time to pack up."

"Where we going?"

"Pennsylvania. I'm not exactly sure which part."

"Pennsylvania is that North?"

"Yes it is."

"I ain't never been North before. You been to Pennsylvania before?"

"Well, I been to Philadelphia."

"Philadelphia?"

"Yes, it's in Pennsylvania. But I don't think we will get very close to it."

"But we be close?"

"Why?"

"I got people in Philadelphia."

"Well, don't worry. They are safe. Now you eat and get some rest, we are leaving at first light tomorrow. Good night Chloe."

"Good night Samuel."

CHAPTER 29

It didn't take long to reach Gettysburg, coming from Fredrick, Maryland. The men had marched long and hard, most without food. David had two pieces of hardtack, which he wanted to fry in some grease to make cush, but they hadn't really stopped long enough for cooking. Rumor was Lee was planning an invasion of the North. Rumor was, again that a new General was leading them. David still didn't pay much attention to facts and never developed an interest in his fellow soldiers or the words coming out of their mouths. Though lately he had to admit that he was interested in the General shuffle. He was also looking for a man that could end the war. This new General's name was Meade. David wondered if he was the man for the job.

David's hope for the wars end had a lot to do with his fears of it. He wanted to tell the war when it was time to end, as opposed to it being surprised on him. His attempts to end the war on his own terms made him an exceptional killing machine. He flourished in the smoke and confusion. He thought better when using the bodies of the dead for protection, living in a hail of bullets. He had seen terrifying battles. Every single man he had started with, was gone. Killed in battle, deserted, taken prisoner, or died of a stomach disease. Such things passed him by. He was never ever wounded.

David was looking forward to this battle with the cockiness of the invincible. He was certain of victory. The soldiers had greatly improved since the first battle. They ran no more, but fought with courage and determination. Even the battles they lost, David did not feel it was any failure on the part of the Union soldier. They just could not win them all. This one. This was theirs. He enjoyed the look of the land. He knew the enemy would soon be approaching, he could see it. He could see the fields covered in bodies. He could hear the moaning. He hoped they attacked slowly. He hoped that he could get close enough to throw down his gun and fight with his hands. Kill up in their faces. Fight like a man, using pure strength. Something about guns he found slightly cowardly. A child could squeeze the trigger. The physical battle he much more enjoyed. He was becoming lost in his thoughts when he heard the order, "Forward, double quick! Load at will!"

Then, There Was Iron

The men were now running. He could hear it. He could feel it inside of him, straight up his spine. The air was getting thick. He could smell death. Over a fence, he could see it. Up a hill, he could taste it. Through a narrow valley, they kept running; fragments everywhere, shells from Confederate guns. "Double quick! Double quick!" They kept running. In a short time they were in the line of battle. The enemy was visible. They began to advance; bullets were as thick as mosquitoes in a swamp. Then he felt it; his arm exploded. David fell back and grabbed his left shoulder and squeezed. Nothing was done about him. He laid there for minutes as his fellow soldiers ran around and over him. Though the pain was extraordinary David got to his feet, stood in a spot for a few seconds deciding whether to go for medical help, if any was available, or to go on in the battle. That was when his leg exploded. David fell to the ground. The bullet hit his calf muscle. He was about to examine the other side, to see if it went through, when someone began to drag him back. He passed out.

David woke up on a cot. There were about twenty to twenty-five other men in the room, all on cots. Some were moaning, and some looked to be in much worse shape than he was. At least they sounded like it. His wounds were bandaged, but the pain was intense. There appeared to be four doctors. Two were performing amputations, while the other two appeared to be causing more harm to their patients. David counted eight nurses, seven white and one black. The black one did not have the uniform of the other nurses, though she seemed to carry more authority. David watched her giving the white women orders. The white women following dutifully, as if they had respect for the woman. David enjoyed looking at the woman. She was in command, and comfortable with the position.

Chloe was racing around frantically. Patients had already begun coming in. They only had twenty-three now, but they were not completely set up yet. Word was this was going to be a long battle. Chloe prayed she had the strength to handle it all.

"Chloe, Chloe!"

Chloe looks up to see Judson's head peaking inside the tent. He is frantically beckoning for her to go outside.

"Judson, I can't talk now. Man, I thought you were gone. We North, I thought you was leaving."

"Ise leavins. Lord, Ise done left. But I gots Iron's boy."

"What?"

"Ise gots Iron's boy. Got em for you."

"What you mean, you got Iron's boy?"

"Alright, Ise come right back."

Judson heads back through the woods. Chloe stands there watching him. She worries about him running around with such an intense battle going on. She prays the Southern soldiers don't catch him. If lucky, they would kill him. If not, they would send him back south. She thought he might have been going off in the head. Got Iron's boy. As soon as her brain forms the name, Iron, she rushes back into the tent. She has to be busy. She rushes to one of the soldiers. Then she sees him, Iron's son. Got Iron's boy. She rushes to the man. Under his cot was a sack with his belongings. Chloe quickly goes through it until she comes to a small card containing the name David Stone. "My first boy named David," Chloe heard Iron's voice. It had to be him. He looked exactly like her. Exactly. Except without the wool. She stares at his face. Cradles it, and then begins to cry. She walks briskly out of the tent.

She is pacing and crying and feeling more incomplete than she ever had in her whole life. She thinks about Ruth. She hears Judson's voice, "got Iron's boy." Did he shoot him? How did he get him?

"Chloe."

Chloe looks up to see Judson coming towards her holding the hand of a young boy.

"Chloe, Chloe, got Iron's boy."

Chloe looked into the face of the child. For the second time in less than 20 minutes, she has seen the face of her lover. The child also looks exactly like Iron. Exactly like the soldier lying on the cot; only he was browner. He was brown, a beautiful light brown. Not the pale white of his brother lying on the cot.

"Chloe, dis here Lenox."

Chloe wipes her eyes and falls to her knees. She embraces the boy passionately.

"I delivered you."

"What, Mame?"

"I delivered you, when your Mama had you."

"I don't got no Mama."

"Everybody got a Mama. Judson, how you find him?"

"Ran into some folks on da road with him. Say dey gwan take him to a place mo Nawth, fa chilun wid no famlee. Ise say Ise knos dat

Then, There Was Iron

boy. Massa Cummings sole him wid me when he a baby. Ise wuz on the same plantation wid him till he was bout 4 years ole. Ise say Ise take him. Ise bring him to you. Ise remembers how youse and Iron was. Just like sisters."

"Well, I know where his Mama is."

"Alright Chloe, let the Lord bless you."

"Bye Judson."

"You know my Mama?"

"Yes I do."

"Her name Iron?"

"Yes it is. You heard about her?"

"Just her name, and if she got two biscuits, she give you two biscuits."

"Do you know how old you are?"

"I heard I about 5 or 6."

"You seem to be a smart little boy."

"I heard that too, and my name is Just Lenox."

"That's what Judson called you, Lenox?"

"Not Lenox. Just Lenox."

"Oh, Just Lenox."

"Yes."

"Well, Just Lenox, you hungry?"

"I always hungry Miss Chloe."

"You can call me Chloe."

"I always hungry, Chloe."

"Well, let's go find you some food. We got to be real careful; big battle going on here."

Chloe takes Just Lenox's hand and they go off to find food. She does not go back to the hospital tent, taking time a few feet off into the woods to make a fire. She does not want to give the boy only hardtack. She starts to feel bad for she does not have much to feed the boy. She thinks of her last few hours with Ruth, the feeling when you can't supply or protect a child. She thinks of a whipping, inside out; the kind that takes longer to heal. She decides to go to Samuel, to see if he had extra rations. Hell, he was always trying to feed her.

"Now, Just Lenox, you stay here and tend this fire. Don't move, alright?"

"Alright. You coming back?"

"I just going to that tent to get something to put on this fire. You'll be able to see me."

"Alright."

The look on his face broke her heart. Slave children are always ready for the worst. He looked so much like Iron when Chloe had to go off to another plantation to tend someone, that look of hopelessness. Lord, the boy was handsome. She wondered how he got so brown. Iron wouldn't. Iron couldn't. She couldn't think like that. She and Iron were together constantly when Iron got big with that child. John Cummings had to be the father. Running into the tent, seeing David, who was now awake; she thought David could easily be mistaken for that child's father. The resemblance was remarkable. She thinks that she better keep Just Lenox, out of sight. She sees Samuel.

"Samuel, Samuel."

"Yes, Chloe?"

"I need rations."

"Chloe, this is no time to eat, they are coming in fast now."

"It's not for me, it's for a child."

"A child here?"

"One of the old slaves brought him to me. He is my friend's son."

"Well, he can't stay here, it's too dangerous."

"I know. But I go to give him some food."

"I go some pickled beef in my belongings in the back."

"Thank you Samuel."

"Chloe, we need you."

"I be back soon. Let me feed the boy."

Chloe attains the beef, some grease and a frying pan. She also takes his canteen with fresh water. She also stops for her canteen, bowl, and spoons; all gifts from Samuel.

"See how fast I'm back?"

"Fires doing fine."

"I see that. You did a good job. When's the last time you ate?"

"Yesterday, I had some cush."

"Well, we going to fry up this hardtack in grease with some bully beef."

"I hate the way that beef smells."

"Me too, but when your hungry sometimes it's best to hold your nose."

Then, There Was Iron

Just Lenox laughs and decides he really likes her. After stuffing him with every morsel of food she could find, Chloe brought the child to the tent the hospital staff set up for them to take a rest. It included four or five cots. All twelve members of the staff never slept at the same time. Just Lenox was tired and excited to lie on a cot, even though it was not yet nightfall. Chloe tucked him and told him not to move, no matter what. She was anxious to get back to the hospital tent. She wanted to talk to David Stone. Could this be the first child of Iron? Could she possibly have found Iron's first and last child in the same day, in the same hour? She had seen slave families finding each other amongst the thousands that followed the soldiers. She always had hope. When Judson informed her that a new batch of slaves came in as they followed various divisions, she would take a quick walk through the Negro camps, looking for Ruth. She never stayed long, though she was happy families were finding each other, she was also jealous.

Now she had Iron's son. The one she delivered. Was this a miracle? Was God telling her that she had done enough in this war? Take the child to Philadelphia now. Now, when they were so close. And David? David would surely be relieved of his duties considering his wounds. God sent her two of Iron's children, on the same day, so close to Philadelphia. She must talk to him. Make certain it was of whom he was. But he was living as a white man. He was a white man. Did he know of his slave mother? Would he want to know? Lord, he looked like Iron. As soon as she enters the tent, she rushes to his cot.

"Hello."

"Hello."

"How ya feeling?"

"Been better."

"I got some whiskey. Here. You keep it."

"Thank you."

"You lucky those two bullets missed the bone. No need for amputation."

"What's your name?"

"Chloe."

"Yours?"

"David."

"You sound like a Southern man."

"I am."

"How come you're not fighting for the South?"
"I don't believe in slavery."
"Why not?"

David laughed the best he could. He had not laughed in a very long time. He was enjoying talking to the woman. He was enjoying being in a hospital tent, the screaming, the blood. He felt more contented than he had in years, well probably since Nicey. He felt at peace, at home. He looked at the woman and decided there was something about her that made him sure he could never kill her. Her eyes were dashing off his face, quickly darting back and forth, as if it was a crime to look him in the eyes. As everything moved frantically around him, they were having a quiet conversation. Though he despised trivial questions, he wanted to tell her all about himself. Well, not everything. Not the dreams. Not the realities.

"That's a strange question coming from a woman such as yourself."

"I suppose it is. You ever been to Philadelphia?"
"No, why?"
"I thought you might know the way."
"You going to Philadelphia?"
"I'm thinking on it. I got some people there."
"Well, I heard it's a city full of opportunities."
"Chloe, Chloe, thank God your back. How's the boy?"
"He's fine. I got him sleeping in our tent."
"That's alright. Lee's sending them back in pieces now. Come Chloe, three men in the back. I need you to take their bullets out."
"I'll be right there."
"Did you take my bullets out?"
"No. I real busy now, but I like to talk to you more later. Actually I think you do better outside. More air; help you heal. You don't seem to be in as much pain as the other men."
"I know how to take pain."
"I'll have someone move you outside, alright?"
"I kind of like it in here."
"It be better for you."
"Alright."
"Now you keep that little flask out of sight. I suppose to use that amount of whiskey on five men."
"Why you give it to me?"

Then, There Was Iron

"You resemble someone I love."
"Do I?"
"Yes, and I'm going to her."
"A woman? I have the face of a woman?"
"This woman. Yes. You are the very image of her."
"Well, what's this woman's name?"
"Iron."

Then she knew. She was certain this was Iron's son. She saw it in his eyes. The struggle. The struggle not to reveal that he knew his mother's name. It was hinted with a splash of shame and a dash of fear. Would she tell that he was a black man? Black men would be fighting soon enough anyway. She heard about them training for months. She had even run into field hands who said they were going to volunteer. Seemed to be taking a long time though. Chloe could not understand the hesitance in having black soldiers in battle. Hell, she thought it was their fight anyway, nice of the white man to want to do it for them. She figured that they got them into this trouble; they wanted to get them out of it.

"What do you want?"
"Nothing. I am not out to hurt anybody. Just saying you got a resemblance, is all."
"Resemblance, hah!"
"I make no troubles. You never get a problem from me."

David watches the woman as she walks around his cot, shifting the blanket. Wiping things off that are not there. She still has a problem looking him in the face. Something about her, he wants to protect her. A woman old enough to be his mother. She doesn't look it, but you can tell she is. The wisdom in her step, the pause in her grace. She was probably in her late forties. There was no sexual attraction, but he found her beautiful. He wanted her to teach him. He wanted her to teach him about women. He wanted to understand them. He wanted to stand them. He hoped that would stop his fearful passion of wanting to butter their skin.

"Probably lots of pleasant young women in Philadelphia."
"Probably. I'll go see about getting you moved outside. I'll see you later."
"Alright."

Chloe had to get away from this man quickly. She felt the smile start in the center of her chest, move out her body, and was about to burst through her skin. She didn't want him to see that. Chloe walks briskly outside, and then she remembers the three men with the balls in them, and walks back. On her way she see two men who are bringing in the wounded, and asks them to move David outside. She finds her patients quickly, and performed her duties admirably. She would miss this. The pace. The feeling that she was working like a dog, to do something right, something that would make a difference. But she had to go.

It was time to be with her "big heart love." Everything pointed to it. God said, "You gave, and gave your all. Here. Big heart love." That was what her mother called it. This was not her father. Though they appeared happy, as happy as a slave couple could be. Both loved her. Chloe knew this and she loved them. She loved spending time with them. She loved talking to her mother. Her mother talked to her as if every day could be the last day they spent together. She was right. Her mother talked about her big heart love. A gardener she knew way back on another plantation. By the time Chloe was sold, her mother had been encouraged to marry four times, and had eleven babies. But only one man held her "big heart love."

Chloe thinks of her marriage of the two or three field hands that she had grown accustomed to visiting her in the different stages of her life. None ever remained on her mind as Iron. Iron was it. This was it. Maybe you only got it once. Probably. Now was the time to take little Lenox, and go to Philadelphia. Ask David. She hoped he would come. If not to live, but only to meet his mother. But she would have a family with Iron and little Lenox. A safe family; a free family with no worries of being sold. With no sound of your Massa, having the one you love. She was free. She wanted to kiss Iron. Free. She wanted to hold Iron, free. Now that she finally owned her body: her hands, her breasts, her legs, her head. It all belonged to her. Like it was meant to be. She could not wait to give it to Iron.

CHAPTER 30

The trip was longer and more peaceful than expected. Iron and Ruth arrived in Philadelphia late February 1863. They had no problems as long as they kept out of sight from Southern soldiers or sympathizers. Iron insisted they give the horse away when they arrived in Virginia. They encountered a woman on her own with five children. The children were so tattered and cold Iron felt her heart break. Ruth, unlike her mother, did not seem to have a high degree of sympathy and complained about it for nearly ten days. Iron had grown to love the young woman who had the amazing ability to find anything they needed: food, money, clothing. She say you just wait here Aunty Iron. She always returned with what she had set out to retrieve. After a while, Iron stopped asking questions.

They walked in the city, tired, hungry, and broke. 20 Pine St. Iron said we must find 20 Pine St. That's my property. The first thing Iron noticed was how well most of the blacks were dressed. The people didn't look like the people she left in South Carolina. Northerners were not starving because of the war. They walked around for hours until a black man stopped them. He knew exactly what they were. They looked it. Road weary ex-slaves. Iron had a slight limp, but she healed up nicely. The man knew the Freeman's. Said he was a dear friend of Gravy's. They were at the door in no time.

When she walked up those steps and Mama Pearl opened the door, it was as if time stopped. Nothing before mattered. Iron thought she would die in Mama Pearl's arms, her hug was that intense. Plus Mama Pearl seemed to have put on at least 50 pounds. She was a big woman. Gravy was not home. Working. Working. Mama Pearl said he was always working. To Iron's surprise, Mama Pearl had four young men living with her. Said she adopted them, all boys. She said boys don't break your heart. Chloe wasn't there. Mama Pearl said Gravy done tripled the money she had put up. He was working in lumber and had a shop selling shoes, plus owned three more apartment buildings. She said people gave Gravy money every month to live there. Chloe wasn't there. Said she was doing work in an orphanage. Chloe wasn't there. She hadn't cleaned up after other folks for years. Chloe wasn't there. Ruth said Iron was probably the richest slave that was left in the South. Chloe wasn't there. Than proceeded to tell Mama Pearl what the Southern way of life had been reduced to. Chloe wasn't there.

Iron could not stop staring at the door. Was Chloe about to walk in? Any moment Chloe would walk through the door. Ruth and Mama Pearl were making their acquaintances. Mama Pearl never heard of Chloe but she be welcomed there anytime. Then there were offerings of food. She was hungry, but Chloe should be walking through the door. No. They were walking to the kitchen. Lord, she thought about her medicine. She made it. She was in Philadelphia. She was free and in Philadelphia. In a house she partially owned. She made it from lying on the floor, chained like an animal; so much medicine in her, she couldn't think, couldn't walk, couldn't stand up, and couldn't eat. Crawling. Crawling into bed. Preferring death to sleep. She couldn't believe the things she had done. She could not believe the time she had lost. Why was it calling her now? How was she supposed to fight it without Chloe?

"Iron, Iron. Lord, you haven't heard a word I say. Girl, you sure you don't want to sleep first? You look some tired."

"Yes, Aunty Iron. Miss Pearl, and me we prepare the food. We'll wake you when it's ready."

"Girl, you can call me Mama Pearl; everyone does. We gwan make a feast! Lord, my baby's back. Praise the Lord he brought my baby back! Come on girl, I show you your room upstairs. Got it all ready. Call it Iron's room. First I was not gwan let anyone sleep in it, then we had so many slaves coming in. House get so full, so had to use it."

"You had runaways?"

"We help em get start up, once they made it here. Do a lot of work with the church. Don't spect another scared hungry slave coming through here. Didn't think I live to see it. Spend a lot of time thinking on those who didn't. Then I go to work with the children. Look in their little faces. Thank the Lord they won't feel what we felt. Thank the Lord they will have the chance. To do or be anything they want to be. I don't like seeing lazy living. That's why I work with the children. You got to teach them young. They got to appreciate the chance their Mama's and Daddies, and Grand mama's, and Daddies didn't have. Who knows how long we been in chains?"

"Oh, I think they will appreciate it Mama Pearl."

"They call this the master bedroom. So I wasn't comfortable in it. You don't mind, do you?"

"No."

"Well it's good cuz it's the only bedroom with a washing room right next to it. So you can freshen yourself up before you sleep. I'll get some clean clothes for ya when you wake up. Lord, Ise gawn call Miss Clara. She be happy to see you."

"Miss Clara here?"

"Yeah. She here visiting; been here about two weeks now. Lord, she be some happy to see you. I gawn have a party. We got to have a big celebration!"

"Now Mama, you don't got to go through all that."

"What? Now I know you're tired! Girl, you used to love a celebration. I have remembrance of Bad Bell. Girl, you was all about food and music."

"I changed."

"Child, we all changed. Don't mean we can't celebrate when there are things to celebrate. Now you rest up. When you wake up, friends will surround you. Lord, be nice if Shelly were here. My two girls. You know where's Shelly?"

"Sold."

"Dear Lord, I hope she make it."

"You know Shelly, I'm sure she make it."

"Alright, I let you alone."

Mama Pearl leaves Iron alone. Thinking of Shelly, Iron receives a strong desire for a taste. Shelly sure did love a good time. Iron smiles to herself thinking of her days with Shelly and Peaches; and her nights with Chloe. She could hear Mama Pearl laughing downstairs. Ruth must be saying something funny. That girl could always make you laugh. The funny thing was, she never tried to. It was just her way of looking at things. Iron heard Mama Pearl yell, "You ain't working in my kitchen like that! Now wash up and put this on. I be ready for you by the time you finished." Iron heard a distant "alright Mama." The two women seemed to take to each other instantly. Well there was something about Ruth's face that made you instantly love her, or fear her. She was strong, loud, tough, and beautiful. And Mama Pearl, well, she loved everybody.

There was something in her that couldn't stop giving. Maybe that was where Iron got it. Iron washes up and settles into bed. She hadn't been in a real bed in months. The comfort was luxurious but she didn't think she would be able to sleep. She had Chloe on her mind. Why wasn't she here? Lord, could she be toiling in some field? No, not this time of year. Or breeding? Could she be breeding? No. Chloe must have heard the news that Lincoln done freed everybody. Well, everybody that was left. Even if most Massa's down South didn't recognize Lincoln's laws. She was sure Chloe would.

For a quick instant Iron thought maybe Chloe was dead. She quickly shook these thoughts from her head. Chloe could not be dead. She didn't feel it. Iron could feel her presence no matter how far apart they were. Just like the way she knew what was going on in Chloe's head only by looking her in the face. Or she would know in the morning what Chloe felt like for dinner. Or she would know if Chloe felt like having Shelly and Peaches over, or if she would want them to talk quietly alone. These things she knew, these things she felt in her stomach. If Chloe were dead, she surely would feel emptiness inside, like a woman who bore a dead baby.

Iron rubs her stomach. No more dead babies. No more babies. Chloe's baby. Chloe's baby is downstairs. She can hear the laughter. Ruth seems to be taking the void of Chloe rather well. Ruth must feel it too. That she is on her way. God, she needs a taste. She is quite certain there is none in the house. She sure it would help her sleep. Maybe when she wakes up Chloe would be there. Iron closes her eyes and drifts off.

Iron awakens to the laughter of many people. She could not distinguish the voices but she was certain Miss Clara's was one of them. The sound of merriment got her out of bed and dressed her. Iron thought this would probably be the only party in the entire America with no taste to loosen ya. Iron looked at the clothes Mama Pearl laid out, trousers and a man's dress shirt. She smiled that Mama Pearl respected her love for trousers. All her life she had heard comments about a woman not wearing a dress. Mama Pearl remembered. Iron figured she might leave her a dress to wear, since she wore a dress in. But Mama Pearl knew her, knew how to make her comfortable. Iron hurried downstairs.

"Iron, Iron!"

Miss Clara jumped up and ran half way up the stairs to greet Iron. She grabs her and hugs her intensely. Iron also missed the woman and was extremely delighted to see her again, but she did not expect quite

Then, There Was Iron

a reaction. Adele also gave her a big hug and a broad smile, and a quiet "we missed you Iron." Iron thought she didn't know anyone who spoke like Adele, only when absolutely necessary, and she only said things that needed to be said.

"Miss Clara, I'm so happy to see you!"

"As I. You were the last of my stationmasters to make it out."

"The last?"

"Beautiful woman, you did not think that you were the only one?"

"Well, yes I did."

"Come down. Everyone is here. Now Iron this is Rowena."

"Rowena. Well I seen you years, years ago. Way back when Bad Bell used to call shuckings."

"Lord, them were days for sweet music. I can still hear that woman's voice in my head. Seem like Bad Bell headed off to England, didn't see you at no more shuckings."

"They wasn't the same. How long you been here?"

"I been here about eight years. Caught my own train."

"You were working for Miss Clara?"

"They were working for freedom. Now Iron, this is Mattie."

"Lord, I know you too. Weren't you on the Yarborough place, two days walk from Cummings?"

"Yes I was. I left soon as I heard about the shots on Sumter. I didn't know you had a station too. Lord the healing woman on your place. Whenever she came to fix up somebody, she be talking about you. What was her name?"

"Chloe. That girl there is her daughter."

"Well, yeah. I knew something about that girl looked familiar to me. Got her mothers smooth mannerism."

"Iron, Iron, girl you finally home!"

Miss Clara's introductions were put on hold as Gravy ran into the room.

"Girl, I'm so happy to see you. What took you so long? Lord, you must have been the last slave in captivity!"

Iron laughs and so do a few others.

"Come Iron in my study. I have some business to discuss with you."

"Now Gravy, ain't no time for business talk. This here's a party, and for Iron."

"That's alright Mama Pearl. I'm sure he won't keep me too long."

"That's right. Won't be long at all."

Gravy whisks Iron to a room in the back. He has a magnificent desk, and shelves full of books.

"You read all these books?"

"Yes. I have a lot of catching up to do."

"You got books by former slaves?"

"A few. I don't read much about slavery. Got enough memories to last a lifetime. I called you in here cuz I got some fine French cognac. I save it for my associates. You an associate."

"You a drinking man now Gravy? I never seen you touch no liquor."

"Well, once in a while when I'm discussing business. You sure look like you needed a taste and believe me, I know Pearl's parties. Coffee and juice from fruits flow all night and that's all you be getting. I seen enough slaves walk that road to know when they reach the end, whiskey soothes you more than juice from fruits."

"I thought you said it was cognac."

"It is. But I don't give that to everybody. I told myself when I see freedom, I'm getting a little more happiness out of life, and I work less. Even got drunk once. Only once."

"How you like it?"

"Well I never did it again. But when I do a successful deal when I have a particularly exceptional day, I like to come in here, light a cigar, put my feet on the desk, and have a taste of cognac. At first I felt like one of those big Massa's with hundreds of slaves. Man of importance. Thought I felt like a white man. Thought I knew what it was to have the power of a white man. Hell, I got people working for me. One time I had a hundred and fifty in the lumber yard."

"You still feel like a white man Gravy?"

"Hell no. I feel like a man, white or black. I'm a man that can feed his family and put his children through school. Got four boys now you know."

"I heard. I seen two."

"You meet the other two soon enough, they almost men. Now come here, this is what I want to show you."

Gravy motions her into the closet. On the floor sits a medium sized chest.

"What is it?"

"Open it up. No wait let me pour the cognac."

Then, There Was Iron

Gravy pours what Iron considers a very tiny amount in the nicest glasses she had ever seen.

"What do you want to drink to Iron?"

"Safe returns."

"Alright, here's to safe returns."

At that very instant cognac became Iron's drink.

"Lord Gravy, this stuff must laugh at our old whiskey. My Shelly would have loved this."

"Nothing but the best for us now. I deal with nothing but the best, for me, my woman, my children, all my family. That includes you."

"Thank you Gravy."

"Alright, now open the chest."

Iron gasps when she sees the chest stuffed with money, greenbacks at that.

"Gravy, where you get that? That's the most money I ever seen!"

"That's yours."

"What?"

"It's all yours."

"The little money I gave you, turned into this?"

"I been using your money wisely girl. I had it all in the bank. But when the war started, Pearl got a little funny. Didn't trust no bank. Had to take it all out and bury it in the yard. Ole slave women bury everything valuable."

"This here really all mine?"

"Girl, you got more than that. I buried the money once the war started. The money you made since is still in the bank."

"I got more than this?"

"Lots more. Girl, you got a stake in my lumberyard. Plus I got us other properties. People pay you every month to live there."

"Dear Lord, thank you Gravy. Thank you, thank you!"

"Don't give me too much thanks, it's mostly Miss Clara. She put up about 80% of our first investment. Then she let me buy her out. Believe me, she took a lot less than what it was worth."

"You making money in these war times?"

"Girl, the North is strong. It's always flourishing no matter what times there is."

"What you two doing in there?"

"Come in Clara."

Clara enters with Adele behind her.

"Now it's just bad manners to keep the guest of honor locked up to yourself during a party."

"Now Clara. You know that ain't no party. My wife is wonderful at almost everything but her parties leave something to be desired."

"Adele, you ever have any fine French cognac?"

"Gravy, can't say I has."

"Well, would you like to try it this evening?"

"I've never been a drinking woman Gravy, you know that."

"Come now Adele. This is a glorious occasion."

That was when Iron seen it, the look that passed between Miss Clara and Adele. A look that could have been easily passed between her and Chloe. A look that explained why Miss Clara never married. A look that explained why of the few blacks that lived with Miss Clara only one slept in the house, the one that was still with her. A look that explained the twinkle in Adele's eye when she said "Clara and me been together bout 40 years." Iron filled with pride.

Was Miss Clara like her? Miss Clara. Iron stared at the woman with admiration. This woman was responsible for saving thousands from slavery. Iron could only guess how many came through her station. Now to find out that Miss Clara managed other stations as well. All the new lives that will be created because of one woman. One woman that did not desire recognition, one woman that would live proudly with the secret of her glorious deeds. Iron hoped she was right. Hoped Miss Clara knew love with Adele. She deserved it. Iron continued to stare at the two women as they quickly made another toast. One that Iron did not even hear clearly. She just kept watching, noting their differences. Adele was and probably always will be the biggest black woman Iron had ever known, but she always had the sweetest little girl face, even in what could probably be her 60th year. She had the eyes of a mischievous 3 year old, and the smile to match. Miss Clara with her quite gray flaming red hair was tall for a woman, with very delicate features. Iron smiled and poured more in everybody's glass.

CHAPTER 31

That was five months ago. Chloe had not arrived as yet. Iron had decided to go mad. But it just wasn't taking properly. She had seen all there was to see and do in Philadelphia. She had gotten involved with the church. She had worked a few weeks at the orphanage, but didn't have the heart for it in the end. She now tutored for free, blacks that needed to improve their reading. She didn't work with those that couldn't read at all, she didn't have the patience for it. The more she drank, the more her tolerance diminished, tolerance for anything.

Iron drank heavily at night and moderately through the day. She even began silencing the voice that screamed don't look for medicines, which she now called something. She heard this word from a girl that was working for Ruth. The way she heard it was "you got something, he got something, don't worry, I got something." What you didn't want to hear was "he got nothing, he's here but he got nothing, and if nobody got nothing." You might as well leave cause the mood was not the same.

Iron was quite certain Ruth was running a brothel. She started with three girls, two white, and one black. She asked Gravy for two rooms in one of his buildings. He obliged not knowing her intentions. In a manner of a week, the two rooms were probably the most famous in all of Philadelphia. Gravy quickly asked his tenant to change her form of business, or move on. She did. Rented a house of her own and now had a dozen girls, nine white, and three black. Iron wanted to talk to her about it, but Ruth seemed so good at it. She had hired a piano player and had a big friendly buck working the door. In her heart Iron thought maybe one of the reasons she doesn't talk with Ruth is because most of the girls were always on something. More importantly they knew where to get something. Today was a particularly rough day. She was out shopping this morning and she seen a woman that looked like Chloe. Closer inspection of the woman verified it wasn't, but for a few minutes Iron felt her heart beating stronger and faster than it ever had before. She was now sitting in her windowsill drinking Gravy's fine cognac straight from the bottle. She decides that it. She was going to Ruth's. She needed it. She needed something. She gets up to put on her coat. Pearl and Gravy's oldest boy comes in.

Ellen Barton

"Iron, there's some strange people at the door asking for you."
"What's so strange about them?"
"White man, black woman, and little brown boy. White man look just like you."

THE END

About The Author

Ellen Barton was born in Montreal, Quebec and now resides with her partner in Ontario.
This is her first novel.

Printed in the United States
22521LVS00005B/208-213